The Kedera

By Kenneth Paul Jones

I dedicate this book to all those with courage enough to overcome. Along with all the mothers of the world for their tenacity is undeniable. Especially, my own mother for having put up with me. Given the fact, I likely have far more in common with my main character than I'd care to admit. Lastly, I dedicate this book to the Canadian Blood Services Pairs Program, and my sister-in-law's generosity, which together awarded *my Petra* yet another chance at a full life. Without whom not even Haeryn might fathom how truly lost I'd be. Oh, and trees because without their wonderful shade– 'nuff said.

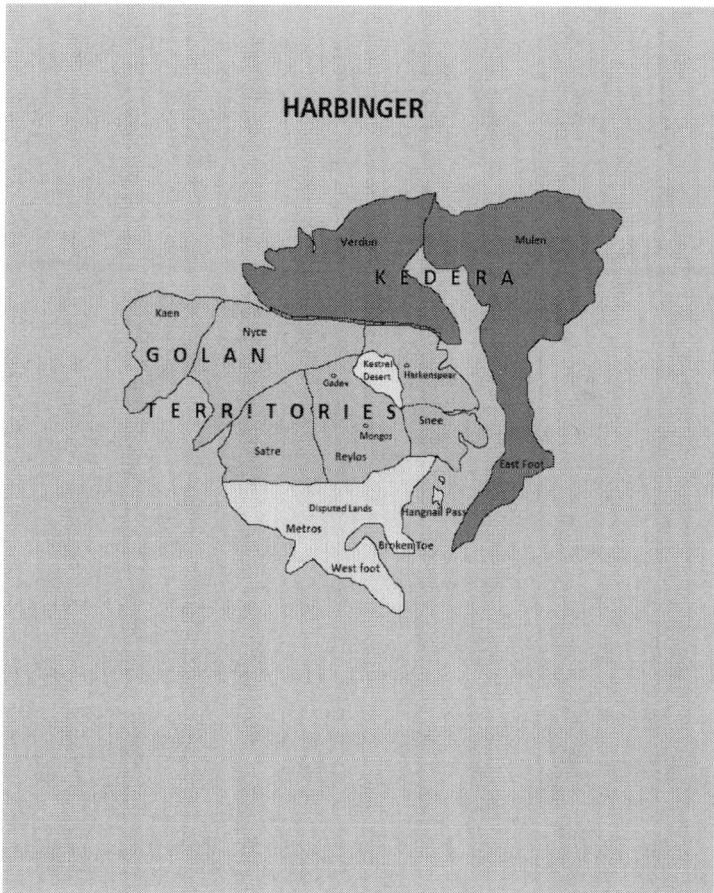

HARBINGER

Verdun   Mulen

KÉDERA

Kaen
Nyce
GOLAN
Kestrel
Desert Harkenspear
Gadev
TERRITORIES
Snee
Mongor
Satre   Reylos
East Foot
Disputed Lands Hangnail Pass
Metros
Broken Toe
West foot

Foreword

In a lot of ways, books are akin to the desert. Each wave of page not unlike a dune ascended in hope of envisioning not something different but something never presumed. For it isn't the unknown that compels us forward. It is having the courage to believe the best is yet to come. Therefore, pastures ahead always appear greener. Wherefore, the sky can't always be blue.

Though but a character waiting impatiently upon the crest of an unfound page, I do not sit idly. I deliberate; and occasionally I dare to dream. Which brings me to my obsession: deciphering the differences between you and me. After all, it isn't the page we find ourselves upon that matters more so than those that loom.

I am the stain marring the canvas. Having, most literally, been absorbed by pages transcribed by another the entirety of my existence is etched in ink. And that's when I realized my oversight. While pages ahead might hold every imaginable possibility, that wasn't where I stood. They might be magical or surreal; but that proposed them dreamlike; supposing them *unreal*. Consequently, I developed an appreciation for everyday irritants. A newfound gratitude for sand snuggled betwixt toes. It's the smallest of things that, oft times, remind us that we're alive. Why? Because it is only this precise moment that ever truly empowers us. You, rather.

Where we came from, or where we might end up, is irrelevant in comparison to ink freshly spilled. Drought has no silhouette for the shape of thirst is undefinable. Without you there can be no me. Devoid of discovery, I cease to exist. It is said that within a book every possibility lies. If so, then there's no place better than a desert to cultivate desire. For without darkness what need is there for light? Without pages pressed together what need would there be to pull them apart? Point being, unlike yourself, there is nowhere else I might go. All characters linger beneath the surface like seeds not yet sprouted. Devoid of illumination, they cannot grow. As pages turn our roots intertwine forcing shadows to form some semblance of shape. Which is to say, come *find me*.

Yours Sincerely,

Nitesh Alde Baran

There were painfully few reasons to ever attempt crossing the Kestrel Desert. To attempt the crossing on foot one had to be either exceedingly dumb or incalculably desperate. Each foot withdrawn from the sinking sand made me pray it was the latter. I wasn't fooling myself, though I kept up the charade all the same. Outside of shuffling onward, there was naught else to do but try to convince myself that I'd miraculously survive. It was possible. I had done it once before— *alone*.

I was far from alone this time. Petra was with me— *and our infant baby*. I know what you're thinking but you'd be wrong. We are not insane. At least, *not yet*. Petra was my commanding officer's wife. Yes, I did just admit the child was mine. No, he doesn't know that. And no; I have no intention of telling him. Let sleeping dogs lie as they say. I was rather adept at lying by every definition. *Haeryn help us!*

Understand, to be born of Harbinger was to be bred of Haeryn. Man, or myth— regardless of blood, whether it be Golan or Kedera— he was everything to us. The problem was that centuries of over-zealous worship had caused the legacy of Haeryn to flourish so perversely that all actualities about him had been swallowed up and lost— solely due to our fanatical obsession.

As much as we knew it to be true, no one ever spoke about that. He was our greatest hero and primary prophet. He was not merely the founder of Harbinger, for good or for evil, he was its fortune master. Our grandest achievements were nearly always named in his honor. *Haeryn's Wall. Haeryn's Halls. Haeryn's Hills.* Oddly, all meaningful profanities were jointly endorsed by his namesake for we credited him for our calamities and catastrophes no less. *Haeryn Owed! Haeryn Haggard! Haeryn Help Us!* All alliteration aside; good, bad, or indifferent; it was all *Haeryn's will.*

As expected, the relationship between Petra and I was arduous, and our surrounding world, no less complicated. I'd been transferred to the North 4th, Major Bryn's Company, barely six months ago. I met Petra eighteen months ago. Not counting our present journey, I'd known her for all of one glorious night.

In truth, the only memory I had of her was that she smelled pleasant. She didn't smell that great now— in fairness, nor did I. For that matter, even the new baby smell had proved itself over-rated. It'd been three full days since we had the luxury of a wash up. Chance of precipitation? Zero. A decent scrub was another three days away at the very least— *if ever.*

Contrary to my youth, hygiene had become an obsession with me of late. Blood, unlike sand, made one's body feel not just dirty but violated and corrupt. Regardless of how hard you scrubbed; it stained you for life. Like a leech shriveling interminably upon your skin; it was a scab that never healed for having never belonged to you in the first place. You didn't ask. You just took it. Like crusted paint, it marked you as immoral, shamelessly proclaiming your more recent sins.

The weight of it is inexpressible. I swear, even the smallest splatter can sometimes drench you to the bone. I couldn't wait to be purged of it. To fool myself into believing I'd been cleansed. To pretend I was something other than the vulture I'd become. Then again, lying to myself had become a favorite pastime. I was good at it– *or so I thought.*

To the north, the Kedera resided upon the opposing side of *Haeryn's Wall.* It should be noted, all those claiming noble lineage boasted some manner of wall. Point being, if you didn't have a wall named in your honor you were without question: *one of the masses.* Which is to say, like myself; yet another pawn without a pot to piss in. Haeryn's Wall was different. Haeryn's Wall divided stability from absurdity. We, the people of the Golan Territories, had been at war with the Kedera Rebels for more than a decade.

There had been five years of relative peace; and before that, yet another decade of war. Prior to that, before my time, we were one people. We were all Harbinger and governed by a single Rah. But when the Kedera murdered him the First Great War erupted. The three Rahs, with blood-stained hands, shared rule over Kedera; while eight Khalifah– *the Eight that Speak as One*– presided over the subsequent regions of Golan. Only there weren't eight of them any longer. That said, there were loads of things that *weren't any longer.*

The Khalifah were essentially appointed stewards intended to rule until a suitable successor to the One Rah might be established. The Second Great War marked the death of three Khalifah; making the concept of a single monarch increasingly less likely. Of the original eight, Golan held but five territories now; only three of which remained wholly uncontested. In retrospect, being that there were only five of them now; perhaps the *Eight that Speak as One Minus Three* might have been more fitting. Or the *Five that Spoke of the Missing Three?* No disrespect intended but it was a tad confusing.

Not helping matters in any way, twelve years ago the Kedera dogs crossed Hangnail Pass from East Foot to invade Broken Toe led by a self-appointed *Fourth Rah*. Yes— yet another bloody Rah. And yes, every Rah and Khalifah boasted at least one army. To keep the tale marching boldly onward— this new Rah claimed West Foot and Metros soon after having stubbed Broken Toe.

We'd been taken wholly by surprise; the main strength of our armies had been stationed in Snee and Nyce. Thus, having been sorely unprepared at our southern extremities; we'd not only paid a high price in casualties but lost most of our merchant ships and trading posts— not to mention a large smattering of smaller walls, though noble barriers all the same. The lost regions quickly became known as *The Disputed Lands*— to us Golanites. Though we'd generally abandoned the ideals of a united Harbinger; we would never concede the south. This was why we were fighting. We wanted to reclaim all that was rightfully ours *to begin with*. That and to eradicate them once and for all but that went without saying.

It had been a long and bloody affair thus far. I was granted one day's leave for every ten days of service. I'd been fighting nearly the entire duration of the Second Great War. What significance were my days off, you might very well ask? Well, since becoming reacquainted with Petra, I wondered if miniature armies routinely sprouted behind front lines. Question being: does mass killing perpetuate reproduction? Light and the dark. Fire and water. Do opposing forces somehow promote greater stability?

The things you don't consider. Sand. Sand. And more sand. The strangest thing about it being, it was reminiscent of new fallen snow. Pristine and perfect yet deeply foreboding. While they both absorbed your footsteps without hesitation, one bestowed a feeling of unwelcomeness far more so than the other. Did I mention how much I loathe it? *Don't get me started...*

Though typically not known as a thinker, I found myself with little other to do. Let's face it, I had ample time. I had purchased— *borrowed rather*—a small pyrament for the excursion. A pyrament was a triangular-shaped tent, uniquely camouflaged to blend with the desert. I nicknamed it the pyro-vent as the daylight hours were so unbearably hot, I felt certain it would ignite. We sat within it, either dozing or trying not to stare at one another for what seemed an excruciating duration. The baby cried far more than it slept. Petra cried too for which I scolded her. In the Kestrel, wasting any form of moisture could only be considered a sin.

Obviously, there was no choice other than to travel at night. Thankfully, during the nighttime hours, the skies were clear. We trundled in the general direction of Harkenspear. More truthfully, toward a constellation known, most commonly, as *Harmony's Mantle*. Depending on where you were raised, there were other names associated with that particular bright pattern of stars– *Khalifah's Gate, Kestrel Dawn*– along with more historical titles such as *Haeryn's Gospels* and *The Eight Great Chords–of Haeryn,* of course.

Petra carried the baby, swaddled within her windswept shawl. I carried everything else– a four, *hopefully five*, day ration of dried bread, fruit, and meat; three large water slings: two full, one half-empty– ahem, *half-full* rather; a small dagger; a fork; a spyglass; and my jingling pouch of silver. Outside of that, there was naught but the clothes clinging to my skin. The moment the sun began to set, I folded our belongings into the pyrament, tying its long sleeves about my torso, to continue our foolhardy excursion.

What you never expect, and can never prepare for, is the sudden onslaught of frigid air. Not unlike the rain clouds that appear each morning only to disappear at the preordained juncture; the nighttime cold is as sadistic as it is drastic. The moment it soothes your parched skin you immediately praise the Gods for having sent it; and then *it slaps you*. Like an open palm across the face, the chill invades your body to take up residence in your spine. It's not long after that your fingers and nose feel wooden and numb.

But a few hours ago, you would have paid any price to end the onslaught of insufferable heat; and now you find yourself shivering; likely due more to the radical change than actual cold. The only thing saving you is the urgency of movement. Should you not keep moving, you will most certainly die. That is a given; the *one truth* never necessary to explain. Everyone gets that. One only has so much endurance. The clock is always ticking; that tiny voice in the back of your head repeating the same words endlessly. *Get out or be swallowed.* It's only then that you truly understand the absurdity of questioning whether your flask might be half-full or half-empty. If it is *half-empty,* you're as good as dead already.

How ever did we end up here? Precisely who was to blame?

I thought about that a lot– most of the time in fact. Pondering my sanity, over and over, throughout the night. After a deep and prolonged deliberation, I concluded myself to be innocent– for once. The cruelty of it being it no longer mattered. Regardless of whether I'd made a rationale decision or doomed us irreversibly, that ship sailed in the instant of my choice. We were entirely committed. There'd be no back-tracking. No plan B. No, '*if at first you don't succeed; try, try again*'. We'd either survive or we wouldn't. Besides, it was *their* fault.

Way back, before the war had even started; we blamed the Kedera religiously for anything and everything that went wrong. It may not have been true, but it was bloody convenient. Key word being *bloody*. It didn't matter what might have happened, it was undeniably *their fault*. In times of pestilence, *they* were the afflicted and *they* were the blight. In times of drought, *they* were the obstruction that had triggered the dam. In times of prosperity, *they* had to be bitter and therefore the threat.

Strangely, after years and years of constant fighting, our need for condemnation stopped. It was as though the tide of hatred we'd created between us couldn't rise any higher and the more we reinforced it the more it lost meaning. As canine as they were, it was inane to ceaselessly point fingers at the Kedera. It was what it was. That being: we hated them, and they hated us. Reiterating the fact perpetually served little purpose other than to remind us of our mutually miserable existence. We needed no reminder. Tragedies of war had become the norm. It made us apathetic and grim as a people. It was sad, and it was cruel. But it was life. Our life. The ways things were– so to speak.

All that said, if blame for the ruinous path ahead demanded ownership, I'd lay it squarely on the shoulders of my commanding officer. This brought no form of comfort. The man did not back pedal or second guess. He offered neither condolences nor apologies. He wasn't prone to blinking *ever*. Still, although it most certainly had not been his intention, he had doomed us to our present course all the same.

Having been alerted that Kedera assassins would soon be sent to kill his wife and baby; while knowing I was familiar with the terrain; Major Bryn had dispatched me to accompany them to safety. Targeting family members was nothing new though most times they were ransomed– prior to being butchered. It'd been a short conversation as I recall. No surprise there. I'd never been much of a talker. As the joke went, if I grunted or shook a fist it should be considered small talk. I was praised for being a fearful warrior; not anyone's friend or confidant.

Let's face it, I'd turned down every promotion offered, and there'd been several. But for good reason. I did not fight alongside my comrades. I fought as though they never existed. It wasn't that I did not trust them. I just didn't trust them with my life. I learned at an early age, when push came to shove, there was only one person that ever truly gave a damn about my wellbeing. *Me.*

The rest of them would sooner trample you than yank you back up onto your feet. There are many forms of bravery, all of which will put you in the grave. I was not brave. I was fearless. There's a significant difference. Perhaps with some it is the same thing, but with me it was not. My so-called swagger wasn't due to courage, daring, valor, or any other quality dubbed falsely as *heroic.* It was just blind fury. *Hate,* I expect, to be perfectly clear.

Some fools misconstrued my indifferent disposition as an adulterated form of ruthlessness. Others saw it as being somehow chivalrous– largely because I never partook in terminating any of the wounded insurgents. Trust me, this wasn't due to being merciful, nor even the smallest measure of benevolence. It was the aftereffects of mindlessness– *bloodlust* some labeled it. Not to mention the wild crickets that rang incessantly betwixt my ears long afterward. How could I ever lead a troop of soldiers? I didn't even know where I was when my wits found shape again. When the fighting began, though physically I charged toward it, at the same time I ran away– at least in my thoughts. For all I knew that branded me a coward– though the expressions on the faces of my surrounding comrades spoke elsewise. As did the blood. *The blood.* Did it tell fables or truths far less palatable?

These were dunes not possible to ascend. These were thoughts I yearned to keep buried. But there was no escaping them now. A sea of sand had risen against me. The desert was the ally of no living thing. It had no needs, no requirements, and no forgiveness. It reaped but it did not sow. It had grown weary of burying the skeletons of foreign souls long ago– leaving my past demons nowhere to flee. I heard their voices, their cries of terror. I saw their faces dissolve in the swirling wind; only to reappear upon the ensuing ridge. Their crow eyes looked right through me scanning the desolate landscape apathetically. Occasionally, a slight smile formed on their boney faces. I told myself they didn't exist though all the while I wondered if it were the opposite. I was dead. I just didn't know it yet.

"Yester, the Kedera cracked the southern line in Reylos. They slew our sentinels at Standstill Pass, stormed Mongos and executed the resident Khalifah."

"Khalifah Morose?"

"Khalifah Morose," he confirmed gravely. Though I doubt anyone else would have taken notice, the Major appeared out-of-sorts.

His agitation and distractedness being reminiscent of others I'd known who'd received grave news. Such as a family member having gone missing or died.

"Soon they will be in Gadev where," pausing for breath, "my wife and son live." *Ah, so that explained it.* Having spewed the words through clenched teeth, his anguish was plainly evident. Though I can't say I'd ever seen him like that before, the major was not himself. He cleared his throat and spat before continuing.

"It won't be long before some weak-kneed traitor sells them out. You must hasten to Gadev and see them safely to Harkenspear."

"But *the Eight* said Standstill Pass was impregnable. Are you saying they were wrong?"

"The Eight are no more! And *the Four That Speak as One* are never wrong. We are soldiers. It is not for us to question such things— no more so than our given orders." He added more softly. "The One Rah *was* immortal; until he wasn't. Standstill Pass *was* impregnable. Now it isn't. Things aren't always as they seem, Radesh." He sighed.

"But the *Book of a Thousand Names*–"

"Had but one title, no doubt originally, even though we may not be privy to it." He finished. I frowned, nodding.

"But why me? And why Harkenspear?" I grimaced, downcast to learn yet another Khalifah had perished. I'd fought alongside Khalifah Morose. He was different from the others. Well, the two other Khalifah I'd met. He didn't cower and he wasn't swayed by greed.

"You know the region better than anyone. After all, your father was a local legend; the most trusted messenger of Diwan Ogi." He saw me cringe, quickly continuing with his persuasive rhetoric.

"Not surprising, you've proven yourself my best tracker and scout. Harkenspear remains our lone haven. It is beyond the reach of the Kedera. Nor would they ever dare to invade Snee. It is too well fortified. I need to know my family is safe. I hope to meet you in Harkenspear once my mission here is achieved. Speak of this to no one and leave at once." Sitting down at his desk he began writing feverishly.

"By all the hounds of Haeryn, I know no one in Gadev. How ever shall I find them?" I asked, trying to paint myself an entirely inept candidate for the job. Had I one sliver less of honor, I would have plunged my dagger into my leg to be free of the bidden task.

Long dead now and prior to the reign of the Khalifah, Diwan

Ogi had been second in command to the One Rah. As I couldn't recall ever mentioning my father, I expect the information must have been extracted upon my recruitment. It wasn't a soldier's place to question orders. But I was familiar with the surrounding terrain, not the people, nor the community. It wasn't the same. They were two different oxen entirely.

I was born and raised, if you can call it that, in an unnamed village two leagues north of Gadev. It was unusual for a village to remain nameless as, sooner or later, they were typically christened after someone's bloody spear– or severed body part. Admittedly, the naming of villages after detached body parts was a lot more common in foreign lands. If only I had a copper for every ransacked Kedera settlement renamed after so and so's salty old ball sack. Roasted nuts aside, being a direct descendant of *nowhere,* I was hoping the Major would realize just how inappropriate I was for the given task. He'd made a poor choice. I was a killer, not an escort; that much I knew for certain.

"You will find them at Studayo House my– *her father's*, that being *my father-in-law's* trading post. Follow the southern road to its conclusion. It is the only one."

Putting down his quill, he wound the parchment into a tight roll, sealing it with a globule of candle wax. He stared at me quizzically while blowing gently on the wax. At the time, I thought it was due to surprise more than anything; for having heard multiple sentences flow from my bread hole. Little did I know, there was far more to it. *Family secrets* had been set afloat. Secrets that involved me.

"Why should she believe me? Who am I to her for Haeryn's sake?" I asked, equally amazed by my increasing insolence as his newfound tolerance.

The irony hidden within my queries was entirely wasted on me. That would soon change. *Was that sweat on his brow?* He looked increasingly agitated, which was highly unusual. After slipping a second parchment into his desk drawer, he rose abruptly.

"Give her this." After pushing his ring into the wax seal, he handed me the scroll.

"And this is for you." He continued, tossing me a small, but surprisingly hefty, leather pouch.

"Take this silver purse for expenses and, should all unfold accordingly, I will award you one brimming with gold upon their safe return." He added soberly, and his tone became grave.

"Radesh, promise me– you will keep the *Red Rage* at bay. You must. You can't allow it to consume you– not while my family is in your care!"

He framed the words so oddly; a chill ran through me. He continued staring at me while I said nothing. I'd never heard him call me by first name before. *Twice even!* I didn't even know he knew it. But that wasn't what troubled me. No one understood. No one could.

The Red Rage wasn't something I spoke of. It was a force of its own. When it took hold– I didn't own it; *it owned me*. It wasn't a creature one could tame. It was a curse. It was a disorder; a disorder that devoured me utterly. I had no control over it. *There was no me!* As vicious as it was volatile, the nature of the beast was wholly and completely beast.

Realizing he was not going to receive the intended response, or any response for that matter, his demeanor quickly changed.

"Enough talk save *Haeryn hold you*, there's nothing more to say. Travel light, travel fast; stay to the shadows. Kill all who oppose you. May your days be long."

Embracing me, Major Bryn then whispered the word, *Seratego* in my ear. That threw me off! I was greatly taken aback. Having said, *may your days be long*; one of us was supposed to follow with, *and your nights full of cheer*.

Instead, we crossed right and left forearms and closed our fists tight. Though once commonplace, it had become somewhat of a forgotten tradition. As for myself, I had not seen the formality performed since the most infantile stages of the war. *Sera* was a proclamation of endearment; while *tego* denoted not only gratitude, but dedication– more precisely, a sincere commitment toward another.

A decade of war had served to undermine the custom's efficacy. War will do that. As a people, we'd become callous, caring little for outdated formalities that stank of self-importance. Pomp as such served no purpose, not on the battlefield. I'd been fighting since my youth. I'd been weaned on bereavement. I'd see far too many atrocities too often enacted by us– more so than those we fought. It was unheard of for a superior officer and subordinate to partake in such a ritual for it proposed us *equals*. Which we were not. Nor could we be. He was the hand that pointed. I was the knife that did the cutting. Either something was afoot; or something was amiss.

Completely dumbfounded, I was unable to think of a suitable reply. Wherefore, I simply saluted. *The hand* pointed resolutely toward the door and, as usual, *the knife* was all too eager to comply. More truthfully, feeling more than a little awkward, I was keen to remove myself from the premises without further ado. I had no friends and neither did I want any– and, most certainly, not my commanding officer. Any form of favoritism was a death sentence; a punishment I'd doled out myself on occasion. Forcing the unsolicited affair from my mind, I hastily saddled two well-rested horses and soon after departed.

Though the first two days were mercifully uneventful, the following night made up for it. It'd begun well enough, for I caught three small brook trout which I roasted over a fire with some briskly boiled wild cabbage. You must always tread carefully with wild cabbage. The timing is crucial. *Cabbage pottage boiled too long conjures evil bursts of song.* It's quite well known if you get my meaning.

I then made tea from the fish bones, so I might have something to sip in the dark. I'd decided to let my fire dwindle for being so close to my destination. I dared not risk being disturbed in the wee hours of the night by Kedera assassins. Though they likely wouldn't wake you, it'd be a lengthy sleep for certain.

As usual my dreams were fraught with bloody memories, most of which originated from the horrid war. Then, I heard something which awoke me– in a panic. As I was prone to do. Though cold out, I was saturated with sweat. It took a few moments to convince myself that it wasn't blood. I heard rummaging followed by several low growls. It was a large woolly-looking animal; a bear to be precise. It looked weirdly ghost-like in the soft moonlight.

I watched its silhouette ramble slowly forward. It sniffed the ground repeatedly while waddling ever closer. Fortunately, the breeze was with me rather than away. Reaching for my horseman's pick, only for it having been closest; I waited silently. *In through my nose, out through my mouth*, I repeated to myself to help curb my thrashing heart.

Despite recognizing that hollering would undoubtedly be my wisest course of action, I could not bring myself to utter a sound. In retrospect, I surmise my extensive training in the art of stealth simply did not allow for it. Bellowing aside, I knew I'd need to injure the beast quite severely if I was to avoid a mortal attack. It had been my experience that while an injured beast will fight most prefer to flee if given the opportunity. Especially when startled.

It was so close I could smell it. Steeped with fetid odors; the creature's bristly fur smelled like *rancid meat*. Twisting about and rising to my haunches; I lifted my weapon with the hammer side facing down. I couldn't risk the pick getting stuck. *One more step, one more dawdling step*. Having finally caught wind of me, unless it was the cabbages– as briskly boiled as they'd been– the beast froze.

Withholding nothing, I pounded the blunt end of the hammer severely upon its unwitting front paw. The crunching sound of breaking bones was unmistakable; though nothing in comparison to the mournful wail emitted by the bear– *as it fled,* thankfully.

I slept quite peacefully after that, knowing it was only the smallest of creatures that would remain within my vicinity following that raucous outburst. Upon the dawn, I noticed the whitish-grey fur. White bears were rare. Though I'd heard tell of them, I'd never crossed paths with one prior. Ghost bears were said to bring good fortune. Though I very much doubted that still rang true having hobbled the beast so harshly. Thus, I left the horseman's pick where it lay; imbedded in the ground, encircled by a paw print– minus two claws. Or would that be plus two claws? Either way, there were two missing claws. Missing from the bear that is. What I mean to say is there were two claws lying next to the hammer on the ground.

I expect it was the bones leftover from my tea that had attracted the animal. In hindsight, I should have been wiser. Only Haeryn knows had I allowed myself a fire perhaps the coming days might have been different. But I hadn't; and so, they weren't.

Later, that very same morning, upon the brook's grassy bank I observed three dead crows. There was a gaggle of wild geese nearby that looked rather suspect. Being quite certain they'd been corrupted by *mob mentality;* I kept my distance. Even so, they waddled about purposely, slowly trying to encircle me. And that was it. My hackles could not rise any higher.

Mounting my steed, while holding the reins of both horses, I hastened to a gallop. I stopped at the crest of the nearest hill to ensure they weren't pursuing me. A rogue bear was one thing; whereas a throng of geese intent on ill-will purely for the sake of it was completely another. As much as I enjoy roasted goose, these blood-thirsty ganders were positively begging me to have a go at them. Having been raised by chickens for a time, I knew they were not to be trifled with. It was best to avoid the confrontation all together. Thus, spurring my horse onward, I fled the scene of the crime.

There was an old saying–
One dead crow choked upon a crumb.
Two dead crows mark the death of a loved one.

Three dead crows foretell ominous days to come.
A fourth dead crow and you'd best be full of rum.

All scheming geese aside, the three dead crows were yet
another ill omen. I only wished there'd been a fourth. I would have
appreciated a swig or two of rum. As noted earlier, it was cold.

Continuing our pace at a mild canter, I tried to push my mind
toward brighter thoughts. It didn't appear to be working. A *gaggle of
geese*, I fumed. Don't get me started on that. *Too late.* The collective
names denoted to creatures seemed more than a bit odd. Take a
murder of crows for example. What was the point there? Why not an
assembly? You must admit, it did sound less bloodcurdling. And what
about the three dead crows? Though substantially short of a flock, had
they not been murdered? Not that the *waggle gaggle* were about to
confess to anything anytime soon.

A group of men was called a clan; a group of clans soon
formed an army. Returning to the crows– a lone dead man was oft
times referred to as *a murder*. Being that crows were rarely amongst
the accused– *why?* A dead clan was called a *slaughter* whereas a dead
army was said to have been a *massacre*. I'd seen a few of those. Being
that the deaths did occur on mass, that did make sense unfortunately.

There were so many odd communal titles. A *swarm of bees*
was entirely rational– but a *bask of crocodiles*? Hint, they're not really
basking. They're the same as the bloody geese. What they are doing is
attempting to blend in with their surroundings– all the while plotting
your demise.

Other designations grew increasingly complicated. I once heard
someone call a gathering of giraffes, a *geography* – or something
similar. I did ask him to repeat it. Not that it helped. Why not
something simpler, like a *colony*? Because the bloody bats took that
one. I'm thinking they'd claimed a few heads along the way as well. It
should be noted, rats also lived in colonies. What– did they cut a deal?
You take the floor. We'll take the ceiling!

Now a *mule pack* was sensible. At least initially. Because you
could pack loads of things onto their backs. Except of course when
they refused to move for being the stubborn asses they were. Why
were they so obstinate? I'm guessing it was due to the fact they were
adamantly opposed to packing things. I know I would be if that were
my sole lot in life. I mean put yourself in their shiny shoes for a
moment. You might get your ears scratched for pulling more than your
fair share or going the extra mile but other than that the reward is

being able to do it again tomorrow and every day after that.

There were also special names for the little critters. Consider a *litter* of pups– which grew into a *pack* of dogs. Why? What were they packing? And fleas don't count. A *kindle* of kittens turned into *a glaring.* Why were they glaring? I'll tell you why. Because had they been lions, their pride would have ruled. My point being, why not just be done with it and call everything a cluster or jumble? Why did it have to be so complex? I never had any proper schooling, so it was only natural to scurry about with a lot of unanswered questions.

I cantered on unable to understand how my head had festered itself into such a cluster. And then a shiver ran down my spine upon remembering the malicious gang of ruthless geese. It was them. They started it. I didn't like geese any more than I liked my thoughts jumbled with nonsensical stuff. I preferred empty. Empty was easy. Empty was effortless.

It was on the afternoon of that same day that I arrived in Gadev. The Major had not been ill-informed for I noticed several Kedera spies trade glances of suspicion the moment I trotted in. Had they glared at me any harder I would have thought them feline. At least there were no rebel forces present, for which I was exceedingly relieved. The people were understandably distressed. Not surprisingly, I had passed several residents herding livestock or steering over-burdened wagons northward in recognizable haste.

Though I nodded to each of them kindly in turn, nearly all of them frowned at me and spat. It didn't surprise me. Our people were as accustomed to fleeing as they were prone to spit. It was nothing new. Our customary wood-framed housing had largely become a forgotten trend. Tents and makeshift pavilions were prevalent now. Any damn hut really– providing it could be relocated as quick as the changing winds.

Being the dogs they were, the Kedera Doctrines demanded that all seized territories be immediately cleansed by fire. Seemingly, nothing was immune to flame. That being their undying inferno of hate. Fire was their poster boy. The sum of all their callousness. Try as you might, you can't argue with fire. All you can do is try to outrun it. Thus, a proper head start was key.

The village was larger than I remembered. Then again, I'd only ever visited after dusk. I recalled two establishments, one being its dingy watering hole. That was the actual name of the place. *The Watering Hole.* You could rent a room there for a silver. Two silvers, depending on who was working, could get you a room at the whorehouse at the opposite end of the road. Just how I came upon such knowledge I honestly couldn't say. My days off always began with a few stiff drinks. Anything that might have occurred afterward remained a blur– *as per usual.*

I followed the cobble stone path southward until it receded into a dusty road mired by deep ruts. I passed an old bald man with a swaddled infant. Though I nodded to him politely, he returned a stern look of distrust. At least he hadn't spat. Dare I say it? Things were looking up.

Further along, I came upon two men, traveling in the same direction, struggling to carry an over-sized chest across a narrow bridge. Their attire resembled that of merchants from more foreign lands. I couldn't swear to it for I knew little of the seas and far less of those lands distant to our own. Anything beyond the continent of Harbinger was of no consequence to me. The only thing recognizable in respect to their apparel was their footwear. It seemed strangely improper for both pairs of them having been leather boots more commonly worn by denizen soldiers.

Bypassing the busy little bridge, I trotted across the shallow stream. As neither of the merchants paid any attention to me, I quickly became distracted by drunken recollections of the whorehouse variety. First and foremost a soldier, if I wasn't attacking a town, there were only two other reasons to account for my presence; both of which *whetted my whistle.*

Unfortunately, I would have to forgo such cravings this time as I had a duty to perform. *I reminded myself.* Not to mention, the chance of stuffing a few gold coins in my pocket when it was concluded. I'd only rarely held a gold coin. I could barely conceive of a pouch full to the brim! After the war, *if I survived,* I could buy my very own horse. Never having had any real coinage to speak of, I had little experience in respect to commerce. Perhaps, I could buy an entire stable of horses. Which broached the concept of buying a house. Yet another thing I'd never considered before– and not one you could pack up in the blink of an eye. A real house with a solid foundation made of mud and straw. *Bricks,* I believe is the proper term.

For some inexplicable reason, the notion of buying a home felt oddly immoral. I wasn't sure why; and then it dawned on me. I'd never had a home– not really, so I couldn't relate to it. My mother died when I was very young and, being that he blamed himself– which made perfect sense, *being that he'd stomped her to death–* my father left in the wagon and never returned.

Though he'd looked plenty aggrieved, the bastard didn't shed a tear. Recalling the terrifying look in his dark eyes, as though it was but yesterday, I couldn't help but shiver. Uttering nary a word, he removed a large green shield that had been mounted on the wall, laid her in it, and placed her in the wagon. Strangely, I'd never paid any attention to the shield on the wall before. Though it had always been there, inexplicably, it had become indiscernible. After covering her with a red cape, outside of an old rucksack that had already been in the wagon; the only thing he took with him was her broken body.

I watched the red cape bounce in time to the ruts in the road as the old nag dragged the wagon away. I recalled pondering whatever might have been in the old rucksack anyway; and why was it always there? Just prior to deciding I'd never know; the answer suddenly dawned on me. It was akin to my mother and, at the same time, not unlike that shield on the wall. Yet another thing I'd taken for granted– *until it was too late.* Until they were gone.

I cried the entire day and throughout the ensuing night. Come morning I'd somehow convinced myself that my mother was not in fact dead. No. It had all been a bad dream. I even made up a story to tell myself. My mother had merely been ill; and my father had taken her to see a miracle healer. Having nothing else to do and no one to oversee me, I divided my time between tidying the house and looking after our livestock– feeding the chickens and collecting their eggs; milking the goats. And all the while blubbering. We never fed the goats. They fared well enough on their own.

On the morning of the fifth day, as it became clear to me that neither my father nor mother would be returning home anytime soon, I finally stopped crying. There were simply no tears left in me. I was broken– empty inside. Outside of the horrific event, the most unsettling thing was– I felt of less value than a musty old rucksack.

I reckon I was about seven or eight years old at the time. It was summer thankfully so there was plenty to eat. Oddly, what worried me most was our worldly possessions. Not that we had a lot. Still, I feared it would not be long before the neighboring *big folks* figured out that I'd been abandoned. That scared me. What if my father did eventually return only to find that all our belongings had been pilfered?

It was then that I decided to dig a big hole in the backyard and bury the lot of it– like a bloody pirate. It made sense. Not to mention my mother oft times called me a pirate. How did she put it? *If grime bred a tyrant, you'd rise a mighty pirate.* Digging was a lot harder than expected and, after several failed attempts, I decided to plant my shovel in the vegetable garden. The tilled ground gave way willingly and, by late afternoon of the same day, with the notable exception of two especially heavy paintings, I'd loaded the entire works into a wooden crate and buried it. Not to mention I uncovered enough potatoes and carrots for a hefty stew.

I kept the important stuff of course – bowl, mug, knife, spoon, axe, shovel (because I still had need of it), and a few tarnished coins. They were so grimy I could not tell for the life of me whether they were silver or copper. I hid the paintings in the chicken coop; and the rest, as I said, went into the ground. The paintings were so heavy I had to drag them, one at a time, behind a goat. Ever try to hitch a goat to anything other than a post? *Don't.*

As noted, there wasn't much in the way of genuine treasure. More spoons, bowls and mugs. A pair of leather gloves. A string of bear claws. Some large teeth– the bear's perhaps. There was a silver cross I happened across tucked beneath some clothes in a drawer. It took some stern talking to convince myself to part ways with it. In hindsight, I might have stood a better chance had I not lost the prior dispute involving the tarnished coins. But there it was– *that being gone.* Like the pains in my wee heart, buried deep. Well, barely beneath the surface in truth.

The cross inspired me to fashion my own out of some twigs. I placed it atop the heaped soil to make it look like a grave. That part was pure genius. Perhaps the only clever thing I'd done up to that point in time. Though I didn't realize it then, it was first and foremost a grave. It had nothing to do with what lay hidden beneath the dirt; but more so about the hurt lingering within me. It was part of my healing process. My memories afforded me a small measure of closure. Although unaware of it at the time, I was burying a portion of my past which, eventually, allowed me to move on. It was then I came to appreciate that I hadn't lost everything. Not unlike my mother, it was just out of sight. Some things were temporary. Other things weren't.

Coincidentally, the following day, that being the day after burying the crate– my father's brother moved his family into our dumpy hovel– promptly tossing my wee ass out. *I will not suffer a thief under my roof!* He'd cited at the time, shaking his wooden pipe at me sternly. I'd never seen anyone smoke as much as him. Not even the farmers at the local market and they smoked a lot.

I slept with the chickens after that. Fighting for scraps tossed to us by my *generous* uncle. The goats won most of them. To this day, I haven't much use for goats. That isn't to imply I'd pass up a plate of goat stew or a bowl of goat's head soup. What I'm simply inferring is– they're *bah-ah-ad* mannered creatures at the best of times. I much prefer them cooked as opposed to still bleating.

Then came the second worst day in my life– *night rather*. And that's saying something for the winter I spent in the chicken coop having been deathly cold at the best of times. It was early the following spring, but late during the night, that I awoke to the most horrible screaming. Bone-chilling screams. The kind heard after someone's fingers get flattened by a millstone. Or when a heavy plow snaps a farmer's shin. Or an arrow claims a hunting companion's eye. You know the sort.

The house had mysteriously caught fire. The flames were monstrous. So big, I feared my cozy chicken coop might be set ablaze. There was nothing for it– but to watch it burn. Our water well was right next to the house. I managed to save the bucket. Not counting the repulsive smell, not being able to help in any way was the worst part. I couldn't get near the place for having felt my skin might melt away. Retrieving the bucket by itself had made me physically ill.

Not one of the neighbors came to help though they must have seen the flames. You couldn't miss it. The sky was positively molten with sparks and shooting embers. Eventually, I just buried my head and hid. I laid like that, hands over ears, until the worst was over. The worst of the screaming, that is.

It reminded me of that dog we ran over with our wagon. Though a mangy-looking thing for certain, it deserved better than we gave it. A great spray of blood followed by gut-wrenching howls– the difference being as soon as our wagon disappeared over the next hill the howling died off. *Died off.* Just the thought of it gave me cause to shiver. It made no sense. Then again, catastrophes rarely did; if ever. Not exactly sure how it fits together but, *like a catapult in a monastery full of witches* was how my mother assessed misfortune. Nope. I don't know what that means either.

It was heart-rending. Not one of my uncle's family survived. Before the sun had chance enough to rise, the house had been burnt to the ground. Once the last smoldering embers had been doused, I searched the rubble for their remains. The bones weren't hard to find. Three of them were huddled together. I collected and divided them according to size.

While delving into the ruins, I caught a glint of something else beneath some broken charred floorboards. Believe it or not, it turned out to be a fancy gold-handled dagger. Next, I found two gold rings, followed by a pendant with matching earrings and some gold coins. At least I thought them to be earrings. The jewelry had been secured in an iron ring. I'd never seen anything so glittery. I counted eleven gold coins. Eleven– *more than a dog has teats* as they say.

Knowing full well there was no way I could sell any of them, without risking life and limb; I decided to add them to my trove of buried treasure. I sorely wanted to keep the dagger. The handle had dancing white horses on it. It was a fine blade indeed for I skinned an apple in one long peel. Though short-lived, it was a proud moment– right up until the goat stole it. To date, the dagger was still the most beautiful thing I'd ever seen. But I wasn't a fool. At least not entirely. Plainly, if anyone laid eyes upon the gold it would be lost. I was just a skinny young lad after all.

I held the earrings near my face admiring them in the blade of the dagger. Let it be known they were clearly made for a woman and never did I ever have even the slightest intention of wearing them. They did have bendable clasps– though I'd have to put a wee hole in my ear first. And that quickly put an end to it. Not to mention a thief might cut my ears off in my sleep. Which made me ponder what that might sound like. I mean, could you even hear it at all for no longer having ears? And what about the screams? Where did they go, I wondered.

I buried my uncle, his wife, and two young boys, *younger even than me I reckoned*, in four separate graves alongside that same *re-buried* treasure. As the weeping marrow smelled something fierce, I stacked rocks atop each of them for having feared wild dogs or jackals might come. I also stacked rocks atop my hidden bounty. Finally, I fashioned twig crosses for the real graves, ensuring each marker was akin to the rest. It was only proper to take some care.

By the time I'd finished there wasn't a lot of vacancy remaining in my garden cemetery. There was only one untouched spot left which I hoped might be set aside for me. It was my graveyard; I started it after all. It seemed only right that I be laid to rest there one day. It was a morbid thought for one as young as myself; but still, I'd had it all the same. Notwithstanding, dying wasn't unusual in my little village. You couldn't go anywhere without seeing something dead hanging proudly on display.

Though a lot of the townsfolk showed up to glare at me, not one of them offered to help. I don't mean digging the graves because that was done. I meant like asking if I might need something. Nothing too fancy. Just food, or a blanket– something other than a chicken coop to sleep in. I expect they were checking to see if there was anything worth salvaging. A couple of them did take the time to suggest that it was me who'd lit the fire in the first place. Which I hadn't. Their spitefulness made me snarl and I shook my shovel at them menacingly. I wasn't a killer– *yet*.

In retrospect, I suppose they had no way of knowing that. My uncle's reputation was not carved of righteousness. He'd found renown as a liar and a cheat and lost both his thumbs because of it. I only met him once before when he showed up at our door begging for coin. I was very young and vaguely recall my mother threatening him with an axe. Which is to infer, though the loss of his wife and sons was tragic; I doubted anyone would mourn his own passing. I didn't, and nor have I ever cried since my mother's passing. As I said, I had no tears left. Not unlike my once cheeky grin, they'd completely dried up.

A brief time later, a forlorn looking stranger arrived. He wore a heavy grey smock and carried nothing other than a sword in a well-worn scabbard slung over his shoulder. His long black hair flowed wildly in the morning breeze. I saw him searching through the ruins with a stick which perturbed me and, sword or no sword, I did not mince words in telling him so. He walked with a distinct limp, which had emboldened me. That is, until he turned to look at me. He was blind in his right eye– left eye rather, though it was on my right. The pupil bulged outward like a hard-boiled egg. A squashed hard-boiled egg to be clear. An unhealed gash ran through it from forehead to chin.

"How'd you lose your eye?" I called out brazenly.

"A stranger put it out with a hot poker when I was a lad," he replied casually, raising his stick.

"Why'd he do that?" I asked.

"To teach me to mind my own business," he answered, waving the smoldering stick through the air. He then pretended to jab it at me which made me jump near out of my skin. After planning a potential escape route, I stuck my tongue out at him.

"How did you really lose it?" I pressed him.

"Hunting unicorns in the Land of the Giants– not that it's any of your business." He chuckled.

I'd never seen a giant or a unicorn. Still haven't as a matter of fact. He then informed me that he'd known my uncle. It wasn't wasted on me that he did not claim to be his friend. He asked me about the fire; and who exactly had died. I told him the truth– that every one of them had perished in the unholy blaze. That's what he called it, an unholy blaze, which made me wonder whether there were holy blazes.

So, I asked him exactly that.

"Are you Kedera born, boy?"

"No," I spat. It was only proper given the rude query.

"Only the Kedera baptize with fire," he spat back. If it was to be a spitting contest, I was ready. In fact, my mouth began salivating purely from the thought. Haeryn knows, I could spit with the best of them. I'd learned that from my mother. As soon as my father left on one of his trips, she always took to spitting.

He then asked if, by every one of them, I intended Jacob Too Quick, also known as Four Fingers Jake, originating from Hawthorn Ridge; his wife Claris; their two boys; and their cousin, that being my uncle's nephew who'd been given the name Radesh– *that being me.*

I am proud to say, I did not wince once. Nor even when he pointed to each grave in turn, counting purposely aloud from one to five; before maintaining there were but four members in my uncle's household. His constant kicking of charred floorboards made my level of trust sink lower and lower for having concluded he must surely have come for, what was now, my buried treasure. It was as though he knew precisely where the dagger, jewelry, and coins had been hidden.

Withholding my qualms, I told him he had a shrewd *eye* indeed, *as in singular*, for having been positively correct in his assumptions. I then pointed to each grave in turn, as he'd done– but, whereas he had counted numerically, I cited their names instead; falsely including my own as I motioned at the mound layering my family's heirlooms he wanted so badly to steal.

The would-be crook then had nerve enough to ask who I might be; what I was doing there; and how well I'd known them. I gave him the name of another kid I'd happened to meet at a market once. I then obliged him by lying that my father had sent me to collect the eggs. Which prompted him to inquire why I just didn't take the chickens and be done with it? I informed him that my father said taking the chickens would be nothing short of stealing, whereas collecting the eggs was only prudent. I mean how could it be considered a theft if they weren't there yesterday?

He appeared satisfied with my response. He then asked if anyone else had been by. I told him it was likely that lots of folks had been by though I'd only just arrived myself. *They didn't bury themselves*, I added drolly. He sneered at that, shrugged his shoulders, and left shortly thereafter. I never heard tell of the man again; for which I was glad. That eye of his gave me nightmares. For a fortnight I dreamt I was being attacked by one-eyed chickens while riding a great white unicorn in the Land of the Giants. None of which was in any way comforting.

My hens not only adored me; every one of them had two respectable eyes. I was proud of that for I cared for them well. For the next three long years, I nested with the chickens. During colder months, we cuddled. I reckon I've eaten more eggs than any other man alive. Or dead for that matter– *raw eggs for certain*.

Long after I'd been forced to fly the coop for having grown too big; I still smelled foul– *as in fowl*. The townsfolk referred to me as *Rooster*. They kept me alive. Not because they were vaguely kind; but more so for being *unintentionally generous*. Translation: I stole a lot. And, for that one lone fact, they hated me.

Being an apprenticing bandit, I did not disguise my thievery well. Thus, I soon became renowned as the village's sole pest. One particularly chilly morning found me stealing root vegetables from a not-too-distant neighbor's garden. I could not plant our own garden of course– because of the bones. Though the potatoes were worm-riddled, the carrots and beets were as thick as my wrists. A couple of jackals were having a tug-of-war with a small carcass in the middle of the yard. I couldn't tell what it was– perhaps a small dog or hare. Whatever the case, it looked more gristle than meat. Their snarls awoke the owner who, upon noticing me, started throwing stones– at me! Which is to say, even the neighboring jackals were held in higher esteem.

Though my father had once been the pride of the town, no one took pity on me. Not even me. Adversity ruled. It wasn't up for debate. Life was no less hard than cruel. No one received preferential treatment. Only the strong survived. End of story. No not this one. We're just getting started. It was a dog-eat-dog world after all; *jackal eat dog rather*. The thing was the village folk would sooner stone you than offer a helping hand– which is what they wanted to do to me. Stoning was by far the most popular form of punishment in the district.

All things being equal, without question they'd prefer a good burning at the stake. *Who wouldn't?* Unfortunately, our surrounding woodlands had been soundly plundered long before I hatched. Rumor has it the trees didn't put up much of a fight. In my day, fetching firewood was a two-day excursion– if it went well.

To this day, a vein of man-eating Harbinger cats resides in the nearest forest. So, wiser folks travel to the subsequent one, a full day and a half further. Which is the long way of saying: the odds of me being burnt at the stake were slim. Side note: in case you were wondering, a family of Harbinger cats is called a vein; kind of like a pride of lions but with more attitude– a lot more attitude.

Being that all forms of weakness were religiously abhorred by my countrymen, there was no greater transgression than fragility. Lucky for me, no one could catch me. Notwithstanding, the more they tried, the craftier I got. This was only partly for being a proficient sprinter. I was also wiry and agile. *Slippery* was how the town's folk described me. *Greasy* would be more accurate. The fact I hadn't bathed since my mother's death undoubtedly accounted for at least a portion of my elusiveness.

Dirt, sweat, grease and grime never washed their hands of any crime was one of the very few sayings I recall from my mother. After which she'd heave me into the watering trough; clothed or not. Being that my survival was wholly dependent upon thievery, bathing didn't make much sense back then. If I've ever loved anyone in my life, I expect it'd be her. I can't say for certain. To refer to her as a stern woman would be doing her an injustice. Though she hadn't been raised in our village, even so, all forms of compassion were foreign to her. She did put food in my belly on a consistent basis; but no one ever accused her of being kind. There are two things that I'll never forget about her, quite likely due to the scars. She didn't like to say anything twice; and she was adept at throwing things– *very adept.* Unlike the other villagers, she only required one rock to stone someone.

Returning to my fondness for pilfering– trying to orchestrate my capture quickly became the favorite pastime for lads twice my age– *and size.* Almost daily, once their chores were done, they'd pursue me in packs. I feared for my life. Their parents encouraged them, oft times beating them for their repetitive failures. I was left with little alternative but to become faster and faster, and with that more brazen.

After a while, my trepidation began to wane. It became as much of a game to me as it was to them. My body matured very fast, upon the fruits of *their labor.* It wasn't long before they gave up all notions of ever catching me. There was no point. This is not to suggest life became easier for me. It didn't. Instead, they resorted to throwing stones and calling me Rooster. You can outrun a stone– if you see it coming. Note: my ensuing nicknames, allotted by the army, were far less kind. As cruel as I'd become in fact.

One day, while picking mushrooms in a field, three older boys felt obliged to confront me. It may have been because I'd stolen their bounty of mushrooms the day earlier. Which was how I'd learned the mushrooms were there. Having grabbed large handfuls of stones, they began hurling them at me, one by one, in turn.

"What came first… the rooster or the egg?" One of them taunted. That gave me pause for being a sound inquiry. I was about to suggest it must have been a chicken when the other two hollered: *thieving roosters!* I considered pointing out the obvious hurdle to their conclusion but decided it best to simply ignore them. So, I kept picking my fat, juicy mushrooms– until a rock hit me, opening a nasty gash on my forehead.

The blood trickled into my eyes. I saw red. That was the first time the *Red Rage* fell upon me. Typical to this day, I don't recall much of what ensued. That was the first time I heard the wild crickets for my ears ringing perversely as I sought to rediscover my wits. I beat them bloody. That much was obvious. Outside of my bathing, with hopes of hiding the evidence, things got a tad scary after that. Fortunately for me, it didn't last long.

Steadfast on teaching me a lesson I'd not soon forget; the three boys' fathers took to hunting me each day at sunset. One night, they cornered me in an old barn I'd holed up in. They took to beating me with some fence posts conveniently stacked nearby. Thankfully, there were no stones lying about. The wood had dry-rot, or I likely would have died. The last thing I remembered was a thick post breaking apart as it struck my jaw. Anything that might have followed afterward was a complete blur.

I awoke the next morning with a dreadful throb in my head. My ears rang terribly; the wild crickets were back. I recalled being struck and assumed I'd blacked out. My father had knocked me senseless once during dinner. Not unlike my mother, he did not appreciate having to repeat himself either. The two of them had so much in common. A beautiful loving relationship if ever there was– until of course he stomped her.

Anyhow, there was blood all over the barn, but none of it was mine. I hadn't blacked out. The Red Rage had consumed me– *again*. Village life for me was quite different after that. They still called me Rooster. But no one chased me and no longer did they throw any stones. I'd been upgraded from village pest to perilous outcast. It wasn't anything to be proud of, but it did make life in general a lot more tolerable.

Upon seeing the small trading post a short distance ahead, my mind instantly cleared. It wasn't much to look at but, then again, neither was the town of Gadev. I found out later that, in a previous life of a foregone era, the establishment had been the entrance way to an enormous concert hall. Yes, a concert hall of all things. The foyer, that being Studayo House, was all that remained of its original construction. A portion of its shake-roof had blown away and been patched with mud. You could tell, when the rain came, there'd be an over-abundance of mud. If gold was mud, I expect Gadev would have been amongst the wealthiest villages in Harbinger. Only it wasn't gold. It was mud. And mud wasn't worth a brick of shit.

A worn canvas hid the establishment's oversized banner. It must have been covered over only recently as the nail heads still twinkled with youth in the sunlight. I tied my mount to the railing after ensuring it was stout enough to hold. The second horse remained tethered behind it. The farthest end of the porch was missing a board or two having been redeployed to replace some broken steps. Apparently, Gadev was short on wood as well.

I must say the place looked as unwelcoming as it did rickety. The initial step creaked with displeasure as stridden upon. The second and third stairs proved themselves no sturdier. Then again, by all accounts, I was a big man. A sloppily handwritten sign, slung over the doorknob, stated the establishment, Studayo House, to be *CLOSED*. I knocked forcefully, signifying my urgency.

Annnnd you can well imagine the look on my face when *she* opened the door. Which quickly explained the odd sensations of *déjà vu* I'd been experiencing. We recognized one another at once.

As beautiful as she was, *and she was,* she did not look at all happy to see me. Her fiery green eyes matched her shimmering housecoat which, with the summer heat, clung to her body leaving little to the imagination– *not mine anyhow.*

There was something about her unlike any other woman I'd ever encountered. I could not help but admire her; all the while wondering why she'd ever slept with me? *Yeah, that level of awkwardness.* Having looked her up and down, her long dark hair was pinned at the top of her head in a tidy bun, while her bare feet took turns shifting below legs tanned and lithe. Her lips were full and red and, surprisingly, she looked as if about to spit. *Annnnd then she did.*

"Butcher!" She hollered, repeating it even louder as though I was deaf. "Butcher!!"

Sighing, I wiped my face with my sleeve. It'd been a long time since anyone had uttered one of my many nicknames– *to my face that is.* Not to mention having been spit upon. Though an unwritten rule, it was far wiser to utter slurs and such behind my back. Oddly, I felt less offended by the spittle.

All things being equal, I suppose it wasn't undeserved. Not unlike my father, I had left without as much as a *good-bye*. That said, it wasn't as if I'd stomped her to death. I expect I would have felt more besmirched were it not for the shock of seeing her. Strange. I remembered her, yet, at the same time, did not recall her being so profoundly striking. I must have been sadly inebriated to forget such a thing. It barely seemed possible. It was precisely then I recalled her being the Major's wife. *Haeryn help me!*

"Y-you!" I stammered in disbelief, intensely grieved by my grave misfortune. "You of all people in this God-forsaken land. Why you?" I pleaded to the heavens.

"My name is Petra," she chided. "And– *you* have no business here! Butcher! Your name is liar!"

Though I did lie with her I did not recall telling her an untruth. Thus, by my recollection, they were two different things.

"I despise you! Leave at once or I'll have my manservant put the dogs on you– every one of them! Butcher!"

She made a cross with her fingers which did little to dissolve my resolve. What choice did I have? I'd been tasked with bringing her to Harkenspear. So, bring her to Harkenspear I would. Even if it spelled my doom. Which very likely it would, considering how she was rattling on.

"Don't call me that. My name is Radesh if you recall– kinda like the vegetable but more peppery." I paused, forcing my face into what I imagined to be a smile. It was a pathetic attempt, fooling neither of us.

"Manu! Fetch the dogs!" she barked.

"The dogs again?" I continued. "Really? That's just plain hurtful." I was trying to pacify her with my incredible wit. It did not appear to be working very well thus far.

"The Golan Butcher." She purred. "Rrr-red Rrr-radesh! Everyone knows who you are! I thought I did but I was wrong."

Her 'R' rolling was nothing short of spectacular; making my comedic efforts appear juvenile in comparison. *Not too bloody annoying.* Worse still, her seething made me temporarily forget about the Major's note. *I should just kill her.* I mused lightheartedly while attempting to smile solely by dropping my lower jaw.

"Not everyone, thankfully," I sighed, pushing my way inside and closing the door. She tried to scream but I stifled it by stuffing my palm firmly over her gaping mouth. That was a mistake for she did not hesitate to bite. An odd combination, it seemed to me. How might such a perfectly formed mouth become such a menace?

Enraged, I shook my stinging fingers before swatting her indelicately to the floor. Assessing her teeth marks, I mocked kicking her and she curled into a tight ball– *not unlike a snake*. At least I didn't see any dogs charging toward me– *yet*. She then began to sob. I bent down tugging her housecoat over her bareness– *bare ass* to be clear. I saw no choice but to be chivalrous given the circumstances. Okay, so perhaps I shouldn't have brushed her aside quite so forcefully.

"Don't! Stop!" she yelled. I scratched my chin stubble, muddled by the double negative. Did she want me to cover her up or not? Strictly for the record, I wouldn't have been any less unhappy had I not let it be. See what I mean– *a trifle confusing, no?*

"Stay away from me! Don't touch me!" She bawled.

Ah, clarity.

She brushed my hand off her thigh angrily; before ensuring her hairpin still secured its tightly braided bun. It's all about priorities. Nothing odd about that. Thank Haeryn for all Harbinger, the hair bun was still shipshape. I took a backward step in gratitude while ogling her nonchalantly. Well, from my point of view.

"I'm sorry. I didn't mean to hurt you!" I sputtered, searching for words I knew would elude me, largely because I hadn't completely ruled out killing her yet. *Purely jesting, of course*! Though it would make meeting up with the Major far less uncomfortable.

As much as it pains me to say it aloud, the assassins got to her first– her perfect body being no less than cold upon my arrival. Though I pressed my lips to hers repeatedly, trying to breathe life into her ample bosom, it was of little use in the end. Haeryn had claimed her. She was gone.

A bit too much? It did seem preferable to her hollering to the Major that I'd forced myself upon her. Not that I had. At least I didn't think so. Although it would explain why she'd slept with me– that being her not having had a choice and all. *Hmmm?*

I was about to explain that I'd come solely to save her smug little ass when we were startled by several loud raps reverberating through the door. She looked like she was about to yell for help, but I smothered her cries by wrapping my arm quickly about her mouth. I then pinched her throat meaningfully to ensure she wouldn't sink her spiteful fangs into me again. Peculiarly, yet again, she seemed more concerned with the neatness of her hair than my strong-arm tactics.

"Don't bite– and *please* don't spit," I whispered. "I know it's hard to believe but you are in grave danger. The devil is at your doorstep." I shook her, urging her to believe me. It did make sense. After all, my mother used to shake me a lot when I was hesitant to do something she wanted me to.

"If you want to survive you must act as though everything is in perfect order– and stay well behind me." *Knock. Knock. Knock.*

"If you wish to live another day you must trust me," I cautioned her again. She didn't seem to be getting the full measure of the situation that was about to unfold. Then again, my arm was covering her mouth quite tightly so I couldn't be entirely certain.

Major Bryn's note!

I handed it to her. She tore it open and read it so quickly it was almost as though she knew what it said ahead of time. She stopped messing with her hairpin finally. Relocating her fingers to her mouth, they danced thoughtfully upon her lower lip. Her tongue moistened top and bottom as she folded the note neatly in half. Her provocative lips glistened in the soft light. Pursed, but slightly pouty, though not so much to make her look– my apologies, I digress. *Now, continuing with the tale…*

Knock. Knock. KNOCK. I swear the last one was more boot than knuckles.

"I am coming. I'm coming." I grumbled aloud. Letting go of her neck, I pulled her to her feet while giving her a stern look of reproach.

"Hide the letter," I whispered. Folding it twice more, she tucked it into her glistening cleavage. *Like no one would ever look there.* The mixed smell of fear and sweat upon her was intoxicating. As she stared into my eyes, I felt myself mysteriously drawn toward her. I had to shake my head to clear it of such wanton thoughts.

"Don't move. Don't speak," I shushed. I was about to press my finger to her lips but thought better of it– touching my finger to my own lips instead. *Wisdom, who knew?*

Opening the door ever so slowly, I was unsurprised to see the two men I'd witnessed passing over the bridge but a brief time ago. Their weighty chest was situated to block the entire doorway. No doubt to better *capture their audience.* They smiled broadly. Dropping my lower jaw instinctively, I grinned right back at them. At least I thought I did. Undeniably, I was greatly distracted by four rows of crooked teeth vying for my attention. The taller of the two had a long-hooked nose. Perfectly matching his twisted grin. He was sweating profusely. The shorter man was beady-eyed and broad shouldered. I decided he best be dispatched first.

Beaming foolishly, like foxes in a hen house, they introduced themselves as door-to-door merchants. *Only I knew better*. I felt Petra behind me press closer. *Foolish girl*. I hauled her back nonchalantly, pretending to tuck a loose hair strand behind her ear, when in fact I was tugging it quite firmly. If only I had more time, I would have knotted it around that tidy hair bun of hers. I'd barely turned about when I heard her voice cooing softly. It was a bit maddening. She hadn't used that tone with me.

"What are you peddling?" Turning around in a full circle, I was startled to see her breasts outlined perfectly through her gown in the sunlight. Tugging her housecoat securely about her, I exhibited a look of proper annoyance– prior to repeating her query *word for word*. It did seem appropriate.

"Clothes, tapestries, candles, and some of the most marvelous children's toys you've ever laid eyes upon," the sweaty man crooned, straining to see past me. *The vulgar swine!*

"Right, show us what you got then," I urged, feigning proper interest by jingling my pouch of silver. The broad-shouldered man bent down hurriedly to open the ornately decorated chest. Not prone to hesitation, as soon as his hands slid inside the chest, I dropped my full weight upon it with both knees. The sound of breaking bone was obvious even amidst his shrieks and the whinnying of the startled horses.

One down. Keep the Rage at bay! Keep the Rage at bay. I repeated to myself silently. I'd become numb to death and violence. It was all too easy to hide behind my disorder; plead temporary insanity. But this time was different. I had to keep my wits about me. I mustn't lose control. It was high time I held myself accountable for my many transgressions. Not to mention, I couldn't risk hurting those I'd sworn to protect.

Pulling my dagger, I lunged at the taller man who leapt backwards astutely. I saw panic in his eyes as I swiped at his face and throat. He seemed in no hurry to die. I, however, *was* in a hurry. For him to die, not me– just to be clear. I desperately needed to end him before the Red Rage fell upon me. It was paramount.

Feigning a sweeping strike towards his head, I tried kicking his feet out from under him. Once again, he proved more agile than he looked for he jumped backward, avoiding my frantic attack by a blade's width. The force of his landing proved too much for the rickety porch, and his left boot broke through a rotten board. He lurched, momentarily off balance, trying to free his stuck foot. I plunged my stout blade between his ribs and into his deceitful heart which spurted with contempt the second I retrieved it.

"Somebody really ought to fix that porch," I winked.

His shrieking gasps dwindled. A spittle of blood dribbled from his mouth as he stared at me incredulously. Dripping from his torso, a murky pool formed at his feet, while the front of his robes became darker in color. I closed his eyelids while forcing my dagger upwards beneath his chin. Reclaiming my dagger, I wiped both sides on his trousers before sheathing it. Flinging his carcass aside, a loud crack was heard. His shin bone had snapped. His boot was still beneath the floorboards. His body bounced once and lay still.

Hearing a loud scream, I turned and froze.

Petra sat hunched upon the chest, stabbing the heavy-set man in the throat, over and over and over. *With her hairpin I noticed finally!* Blood flew like scattered raindrops. It was all I could do to keep the Rage from erupting. Though dead for certain, he couldn't fall backward for his broken fingers having been pinned within the chest she was crouched upon. A gruesome scene, one of her dainty hands had knotted itself within the man's greasy hair while the other shot back and forth like a sewing needle. Neck, cheek, eye, ear, it made little difference. She just kept stabbing him. The flood of blood stirred the Rage so strongly I was forced to look away. I took a long deep breath.

"Petra!" I hollered as I regained my wits. I could hear her long braid slapping softly in time against her curved back.

"Petra!" I tried again in vain. Grabbing her thrashing arm, I unclenched her fingers to pry the hairpin free.

"Stop Petra! You've killed him! He's bloody dead already." I said, shaking her gently.

"And *bloody* for certain" I mumbled.

She looked at me in shock. The pain in her eyes pierced my very soul. Her face was covered with freckles—red splatters of blood. Her gown was stuck to her. She was soaked to the skin. Her face became blank. Then a look of terror returned. I think she'd forgotten who I was. Why I'd come.

Though disarmed, she began to strike out again. Only at me, this time. I can't say I wasn't startled. Leaping backward instinctively she was forced to revert her attention to the dead man which she did with renewed vigor. Her clenched fists pounded his bloodied face making his lifeless head rock this way and that like a foraging chicken.

I was stunned– utterly confounded. It was eerily akin to the Red Rage. Apparently, I wasn't the only one *so cursed*. She was at its mercy. She was fully under its spell. Reduced to her animal form, she was a most inelegant beast if ever there was.

Though crazed, I found her beauty no less terrifying than her madness. Clutching both her arms and pulling them tightly across her body, I rocked her back and forth for a time. *Why?* I haven't a clue; other than I knew naught else to do. Strangely, even covered in blood, she smelled good. Too good; that being, a very depraved form of good. Which could never truly be considered *good*.

At last, her thoughts began to clear, and I felt her struggling against me. Releasing her, I could tell she recognized me. Admittedly, I was relieved to know her hairpin had been tucked safely away in my waistband. I will mention, I did not return it to her for quite some time. Days in fact, for sleep did not come easy within her company at first. *Go figure.*

"Twas my father's chest!" she cried aloud, having rediscovered her wits.

"I don't understand," I said for not knowing what she meant. In hindsight, I expect I need not have explained that last bit but there it is all the same.

"He and my mother left a fortnight ago. They should have been back long ago!" She began panting for breath. Her slumped body began shaking slightly. Having diluted the freshly dried blood, her tears sent ginger streams down her flushed cheeks. Her breaths came in short, frantic bursts. The lines running down her face made her look– I don't know how to say it– from another world entirely.

"I killed him! I killed him! Didn't I?" She bawled, staring at the dead body only inches away as if seeing it for the first time. The pain in her voice was clearly palpable.

"It may have been the relentless stabbing. But not to fret; he did have it coming." I shrugged. What else was there to say? The man was dead. Pulling her up, after ensuring she was able to stand on her own, I lifted the lid of the chest allowing the corpse to slide free. Thumping loudly upon the deck, blood still trickled from his many wounds.

"Why did they have my father's chest? Why haven't he and my mother returned?" She wailed.

"That's your father's chest?" I asked with amazement.

"Have you not been listening at all? I can still hear them shrieking in my head!" She wailed, covering her ears with her hands.

"Who? Your parents?"

"No– the salesmen! Why would my parents shriek? What are you implying?"

"Nothing," I stammered. "There were no intended implications. I was not implying anything."

"It won't stop! My head– it echoes with the sound– the sounds of the salesmen screaming!" She blurted.

"Salesmen? Hardly! I can assure you they weren't salesmen. And nor were they trained assassins. Mercenaries, I expect. Come on now, let's get you inside."

In trying to walk she collapsed into my arms. I shook her gently, but she refused to wake. Carrying her inside, I placed her in a ridiculously large wooden chair. My arms were covered in blood. I hated that feeling– weirdly warm and sticky to the touch. She was about to slip out of the chair, but I pushed her back with my boot. I didn't want any more blood on me. Though glad it was not my own I hated it all the same. I had to slide her bottom lower to keep her from falling forward. As I did so, more and more of her tanned thighs became bared until– I found myself mesmerized for not knowing what to do or where to look. Only briefly, mind you. To be clear, I was not staring.

Spying a basin of water sitting atop a bucket, I hastened to fetch it– before she could fall out. Admittedly, the same moment I lay the basin in her lap was the same moment I hated it. Not as much as the blood though. Why I did what I did I cannot say for my own actions came as a surprise to me. Let's face it, I was no knight– not that they existed any longer. I was a scoundrel in my own right and not chivalrous in any way. I quickly scrubbed my own arms before splashing water on her face, rinsing most of her blood streaks away. Once again, I found myself flustered. Her face was flawless– or at least when her lips weren't moving.

She began to stir. As I went to refresh the bowl, naturally, she slid free of the chair and slunk to the floor. Her gown was slightly above her waist now. What I mean to say is, her body took to quivering again. As did my own– purely from distraction. Propping her against the chair, I pushed the basin between her legs again. Completely lost as to what I should do, I resorted to reasoning with her. *Yeah, reasoning. Me.* Some things should not be mentioned in the same breath. Let alone the fact she remained *lifeless*.

"Talk to me, Petra." I repeated, pinching her cheeks lightly. I strongly considered slapping her but thought better of it. No doubt there'd be ample provocation for that once she started speaking again.

"Where are your parents? Where did they go?" I echoed redundantly. The exercise felt pointless. I was wasting my time while acting like a dull-witted parrot.

"Mongos!" She blurted to my surprise. "They were traveling to Mongos! But they should have returned by now!"

She looked remarkably coherent– prior to looking about to vomit. *Annnnd then she did.* I couldn't help but frown for my boots having been lightly splattered. Had she no shame at all? As soon as she was done heaving, she began coughing. After which she cleared her throat and spat several times on the floor. Finding my throat to be a tad thick, I took the liberty of spitting as well. She stopped, staring at me coldly. To be fair, I took the basin away when she spewed in it so I expect she might have used that to spit in had it remained available.

"To each their own. I'm not one to judge. Your house, your rules," I blathered naïvely. After tugging her gown about her legs, she cast me an evil glare. Returning to her the emptied basin, I waited impatiently for her to finish retching before further daring to speak. Noticing a bowl of red apples on a table, I snuck one and took a large bite. Naturally, it was that exact moment that her composure returned. Given the look on her face you'd think I'd been caught grazing on her favorite horse's hind leg. I very nearly spat the thing out save for the taste being so savory. Never had I felt more discomfort trying to chew, let alone swallow the seedy bits. I did take a hefty bite mind you for my throat feeling parched.

"A Khalifah was executed in Mongos not five days ago," I informed her. "The Kedera have taken Mongos. They are on their way here as we speak. Gadev is no longer safe. And especially not for you."

"Another Khalifah?! Noooo!" she wailed. "My parents were there." She paused. "But they couldn't have breached Standstill Pass. That cannot be true."

"It's true, I'm afraid," I exhaled sympathetically. "But that doesn't necessarily mean your parents are dead." I reassured her– though the voice in my head said otherwise. *They were, without question, undoubtedly dead.*

"You don't know that for certain! And if not, how did *they* get the chest? How?" She implored.

"I imagine your parents abandoned it. Your father was, *is rather,* undeniably a wise man. His reputation is no less renown through the land than Studayo House itself." I added, swallowing the last of the apple.

"Did you just eat the core?" Posing the query as though it was somehow wrong to do so.

In truth, I'd never heard tell of her father. Notwithstanding, the core being the best part of the blameless fruit brought needlessly before her inquisition. Though I knew the name Studayo and been to Gadev many times, I would not have known the trading post even existed had the Major not mentioned it. Then again, the Army saw to all my needs. Which were few.

Allowing more time for my fabricated words of encouragement to sink in, while not knowing what next to say anyway, I peered about the small warehouse uneasily. Its construction was peculiar, preposterous if I might be so bold. The size of the timber employed was staggering; far larger than could ever rightfully be justified. Even after so long, I found the smell of Ponderosa pine unmistakable.

"The wood. It's enormous."

"Cried the empress from her bed chamber." She cut in absently with what appeared to be an instinctive response given many times prior. Having no idea what she intended, I ignored the outburst.

"It makes no sense; the size of it staggers the mind."

"Oh, you mean this. This is all that remains. This was once the entrance to a magnificent theatre from days long gone."

"Three udders? I had a goat with three udders. A bit peculiar though I'd hardly call it magnificent."

"No. Theatre— for plays and concerts and such."

"You mean jugglers, minstrels, fire-eaters and the like?"

"Yes— along with mimes, wrestlers, acrobats, dancers, actors, and storytellers."

"Acrobats? The night fliers with the pointy wings?"

"Don't." She held up a palm, shaking her head rudely.

"At her prime, Studayo Hall sat more than three thousand patrons. A true spectacle if ever there was. People came from everywhere if for no other reason than to claim they'd be there— *here*. Though barely out of infancy, even still do I remember it. It was stunning and massive. Adorned in accents of gold, ivory, and jade, it could only be described as glorious. This is all that remains following the great fire." She gestured in a broad circle with her hand.

"The Kedera?" I asked. Not to mention, it only made sense there'd be bats present within such a grand-sized structure so I'd no idea why she'd reacted so haughtily.

"The Kedera," she nodded, pointing upward. "Follow the

beams to their charred ends." She huffed glumly. It was only too obvious that her mind was currently absorbed by weightier contemplations.

I turned about slowly to better appreciate my surroundings. *Well, that certainly does explain the oversized chair,* I thought to myself. The startling architecture aside, there was quite a lot of merchandise lying about considering the establishment was *supposedly* closed. There were dry goods including salted meat, pickled vegetables, and sugared fruit. Several sacks of flour and wheat, one more of oats, and plenty of barley. There were farming tools such as pitch forks, hoes, and shovels. Alongside the hammers and nails were a decent selection of horseshoes which was a rare encounter devoid of a smithy. They had makeshift pavilions: tents and tarps. Being all too familiar with the smell of moldy canvas, I recognized more than a few of them being past their prime. Such was our lot for, soon enough, the cursed damp ruined everything.

Not far from me was a writing desk with many books piled atop it, beyond which I noted seed and grain sacks piled chest high– peas, lentils, onions, rye, flax, beetroot, cabbage, and poppy seed. Though I was not foolish enough to say anything aloud, I did question their potency for the bottoms of many were badly stained as if from a flood. The place even housed writing tools and books; notwithstanding other paper products, such as writing scrolls, made mainly of rice. A large counter stood cluttered with fancier wares: knives, scissors, and an over-abundance of cooking utensils. *How many bloody spoons does a man need? One methinks.* Picking up a strange contraption, I held it up to the window light. Yes, the place had windows. And not that colored glass for the panes were very near clear.

"And what in blazes is this?" I asked.

"A fork," Petra answered.

"A fork?"

Yes. It's called a fork," Petra insisted.

"But you didn't even turn to look." I acknowledged.

"There was no need. Everyone standing where you are standing asks the same thing." Being an odd-looking contraption, it was justifiable.

"Is it a toy?" She shook her head negatively. It looked like a tiny trident. Unquestionably, I would have enjoyed playing with it had I been a lad.

"Does it not look rather sharp?" She returned, shaking her head forlornly.

"Yes, it does." I grinned. "But what has that to do with anything?" I shrugged.

"Never mind, we'll soon all be blind," she huffed.

"But what's it do?" I inquired impatiently. While awaiting her answer I used it to scratch the back of my head. Perhaps that was its intention.

"*It*– doesn't do anything. You do it with it." Turning her green eyes to me she sighed aloud. "What do you think it does, yah great fool? You poke things with it. In fact, given your reputation, I think I best take that from you before you fork yourself with it."

Walking briskly toward me, she snatched it from my fingers. Holding the item in her teeth, she curled up her braid, before securing it in place with the item in question.

"Ah," I scoffed. "I should have known it was for women. Small wonder I never heard tell of it."

"I wouldn't rule it out quite yet," she said walking away. "There's still ample time for the two of you to get better acquainted." I couldn't conjure what she intended. I began to wonder if she wasn't having a go at me– which she was kind enough to clarify.

"If it was sticking out of your eye, do you think, maybe then, you'd see the point?"

Well, that gave me pause to think. It was a fair question– not unlike whether you could hear one's ears being swiped which I was still yet to fully sort out. Just what fueled her passion for sticking folks with pointy things, I'll never know. Given the state of the dead mercenary, I wasn't sure which might have been worse, the hairpin or *the fork*. Either way, I found her tone offensive which at least confirmed her to be her old self once again. That said, her foul mood only proved to make the choice before me more difficult. *Ignore her or kill her*. I must say, at that time and place, I could have gladly gone either way.

Truth be told, though having held it only for the briefest of moments, I'd taken a shine to that *fork thing*. In the very least I wanted a second look at it. But she'd taken it upon herself to stifle that opportunity without the slightest hesitation. An unprovoked action– as blatantly cruel as it was unfair. After all, the benefits associated with poking things through trial and error were, in my humble opinion, quite possibly boundless. Think about it. It'd be easier to count what you couldn't poke than what you could. Regrets cast aside, days later, when I finally conceded her hairpin to her, I wisely traded it for *the fork*. I was no fool. There was nothing quite like a *good fork* and I knew it.

Directly behind the counter was an unfinished area akin to an over-sized closet– which, apparently, it was at one time. Within it were rolls of wire, ceramic pottery, clay shingles, and livestock feed. A ridiculously wide stairway led to the second floor where the living quarters must certainly be. The upper floor appeared to be an open area, not unlike a loft. It was obvious that the stairway had been modified for had it continued upon its original incline it would have proceeded up and out of the ceiling's current limitations.

This brought me about full turn; that being, back to Petra who now stood as still as a stature, observing me severely. Her face was ashen, and her eyes ripe with gloom. Despair did not suit her. Not that it does anyone. Being so grievously attractive only furthered the awkwardness of the situation. Understandably, I found I could not bear to look upon her dour face any longer. Not to mention, she'd snatched *the fork* from me but a short time ago though I still had need of it. For what I don't know but that wasn't the point. The point was, she was being childish, and I wanted it back.

Fortunately for us both, the wall behind her posed a suitable distraction for boasting a remarkable tapestry above which hung the words: *Studayo Wall.* Woven upon the lavish textile were our most celebrated proverbs penned by the Khalifah of Old. Being that I couldn't think of anything more useful to say myself, I recited its topmost line. Albeit slowly, for having found the first word a bit difficult. Strangely, I didn't know what it meant at first until I said it aloud. At which point, to my surprise, I found I did.

"Opulence doesn't distract the dead. *Diwan Atari.*"

"Perhaps a good fork in the throat might make *the living* rethink a thing or two." She seethed.

See– what did I say? I knew it was a good fork! But what was she on about now? She couldn't still have a mad on for me having shown up uninvited– could she? Then again, she was still going on about that fire and Haeryn only knows how long ago that had been. Whatever the case, being that I had arrived just in time to save her from certain death, I wasn't about to indulge her. What was it about people and their pasts that caused them to cling to it so desperately? I mean which of us ever had a pleasant upbringing? I for one never looked backwards. Unless of course I was recalling earlier recollections while traveling and such when you had naught other to do but think. But that was different. Entirely different.

Defeatism was a plague I'd witnessed far too often. *Despair is like salt,* my mother used to say, *a touch upon the tongue flavors all to come.* Not a Diwan proverb but something she said whenever she caught me sulking. Wise words all the same though I never fully understood them as a boy. Haeryn knows to this day, I still cart about an unhealthy craving for salt. And Haeryn knows despair has followed me everywhere. So, there you have it. Truth.

"Why are the words of the prophets written on Studayo Wall?" I asked. It was very unusual. I was not even sure if it was officially permissible. Typically, only the Kedera indulged in such extravagances. I was told Harkenspear castle boasted a lot of art– whatever that might include. But the magistrates there were powerful and considerably wealthy. I did not sense a lot of riches anywhere close to where we stood; nor any leverage when it came to our imposed wartime regulations.

"It was a gift given to my father."

"Were it left up to me, I would hide it away. I would not flaunt such overindulgences." I frowned openly.

"Oh, and precisely what would you do with it? Cram it all into a large chest and bury it deep in the ground, I suppose?"

"It'd be safer." I replied, squinting my eyes to show just how confident I was. I'd seen many a general do it, after all. You could not argue with a good squint. Unless you were a woman it seemed....

"Until the cursed damp got at it, followed by the worms." She shook her head sorrowfully. "Are you really questioning my father's judgment– now– at a time like this– when he's missing– rendering his honor indefensible?"

"I'm merely hoping his décor choices don't reflect his sensibilities during a crisis." It was my intention to defer some of her sullenness– trick her into believing he might possibly still be alive. Which he most definitely was not.

"You don't know him. You never even met the man." She spewed angrily. Apparently, though I'd chosen my words carefully, while squinting, I somehow said something that offended her.

"No. I did not have the pleasure of knowing your father, but I knew of him," I lied. 'One does not manage a trading post such as this without being recognized for their shrewdness. Especially not here, in Gadev of all places, for as long as he did– *has rather.* Mark my words, a fool wouldn't last a day."

"'Tis my mother. She is the clever one. That's why she so often accompanies him." She sniffed. "And you're right," she continued unmercifully. "You didn't last a day, did you? You just up and left. I awoke and you were gone! I might have been murdered in my sleep for all you knew– or cared" She glared accusingly.

And so, it begins.

She was still on about that– after all this time had passed. I felt half-tempted to remind her about the great fire. Surely, we could relive that atrocity yet another time. No doubt, decades from now, I would remain the lone villain during her campfire tales– the great fire having finally been forgotten even whilst dancing flames twinkled in her eyes. Was I not the horrid Golan Butcher but a short time ago? Though a few definite distinctions came to mind in respect to running a store and sowing my wild oats, I sensibly chose to disregard her latter comments. I did loose a long-winded fart to better establish the full extent of my withheld disgruntlement. One can't withhold everything after all. Well, not all at once.

"So, your mother's the wittier one? Well, kindle the sun and color me startled," I muttered sarcastically.

Though I expect I need not mention it at this point, she hadn't stopped glaring at me. Thank Haeryn, I washed away most of the blood splatters. Up until then I'd only rarely witnessed such acts of unbridled violence for having been blinded by the Rage. Let me assure you; it was more than a tad unnerving. To be clear, she was unnerving. Her! The one with *the fork* protruding from her skull.

"Enough chatter! Where is the child? We need to get the two of you away from here. We must hurry. Take only what you cannot do without. We must travel light." I urged, releasing another long fart, though this time less expected.

"Must you fart?"

"Yes, I must," I confessed. "Twas the wild cabbages. They are to blame."

"Aye, there's a trick to it. You must briskly boil them first." She sighed.

"I know there's a trick to it! Do you take me for a fool? I know they must briskly boiled! And they were. I can attest to that– only a bit too briskly. I under-cooked them, I expect. Though there's naught that can be done about it now. I was afraid of spoiling them."

"Spoiling what– your linen or the cabbages?" She glared.

"The cabbages thus far," I huffed. It was then I recalled the Major was her husband and I suddenly felt sorry for him. Though but a maiden, there was no winning with the woman at all.

"Renan is with our manservant. Manu takes him for a stroll on sunny afternoons so I can catch up on my chores. He shan't be long.

Dinner approaches and Manu does the cooking." She attested.

Dinner approaches and Manu does the cooking. What a surprise. *Shall I fill a tub with warm water while you wait? Perhaps I could wash your hair and massage your feet— unless of course you'd prefer to be fed.* Just the way she said it gave me cause to cringe. Well, I for one had had my fill of it.

"I'm afraid Manu will be dining alone tonight. Go wash your face; your cheeks are still flushed with blood. We can ill afford to solicit unwanted attention. Hurry now, be quick! I want to be ready so we might depart in the very instance of their return."

"I'm not leaving! I'd sooner be impaled by a pitchfork then go anywhere with you— Butcher!"

"Pitchfork! That's it! That's what that thing in your hair looks like— a miniature pitchfork!" I beamed though the moment proved somewhat fleeting as she crossed her arms defiantly.

"You must leave!" I urged her.

"How could I possibly leave without knowing what's happened to my parents?"

"But what need would there be for a miniature pitchfork?" I wondered aloud. Admittedly, the apparatus still had me distracted.

"For Haeryn's sake! Would you shut up about the fork!" She scolded rudely. "This is their home." She stomped, gesturing widely with her arms. "This is everything they have in the entire world! If ever they needed me to stay— now is the time."

"No, they don't." I avowed. "The last thing they would want is for you to stay— and be killed *needlessly*. Mark my words. They will cut you. They will bind you. And they will rape you. After which, the Kedera will burn you at the stake. They will secure you to this very banister while the building dissolves into a sea of molten ash around you."

"My house, my rules! Mark my words— Butcher! If I concede to go anywhere with you, it shall only be to look for my parents!"

Why did she always have to pause prior to shouting Butcher? It was precisely then I knew I should have let *the salesmen* have their way with her. She was far too clever for my liking. And I had little love for clever folk. They caused all manners of trouble. They were the ones that handed you the rusty axe before sending you to war— to fight their battles for them. As noted, no one would be the wiser. I'd simply arrived— *too late*. Notwithstanding her rudeness in respect to the fork. That thing was a real *tourney changer*. We soldiers ate with our hands for the most part. I'd always be at the front of the chow line had I one or two of those in my hands. To be clear, I was quite mad by this point.

"Not anymore. Not for another moment! Your house, my bloody rules!" I hollered.

"Ah, there he is! There's our infamous Butcher! I was wondering how long it'd take for your true self to appear! Well, you don't disappoint. What a surprise."

"You are but a silly girl– and sorely mistaken." I seethed. To her detriment, my anger had been fully kindled. I had to take a deep breath to compose myself. Though nothing akin to the Red Rage, make no mistake, the bear had been poked; the beast within had been successfully stirred.

"If you have no concern for your own well-being, think of the child. As per the Major's directive, that being *your husband* to whom you're sworn to abide; you have no other path other than to accompany me." Softening my tone, I managed to unclench my fists.

"Take heart, we will dispatch your manservant to search for your parents. Have faith, I will tell him what to say should he be questioned. Furthermore, will I advise him how he might send word to you later in respect to their safety. *Now please*, go ready yourself. We need to make haste. Not to forget, we'll have a little one in tow."

"Baby," she retorted.

"Baby?" I repeated incredulously. "You mean a baby *baby?*"

"No, a normal baby."

"Yet still of a diminutive size as in one of those tiny, ever-crying infants?" Bending forward, I gestured below my knee trying to get a sense of just how small the little one might be. It was only prudent. It was important to know how much weight he may *or may not* be able to carry.

Offering no reply, she rose and stomped away like the spoiled child she was. Apparently, I'd somehow irked her unintentionally again. She was clearly in the most petulant of moods. Well, I for one pitied the child for having to be raised by one so easily riled.

"Idiot!" She chimed out impolitely while continuing to stamp her way up the stairs. Honestly, you'd think a parade of elephants had been following every footstep.

Instinctively, my eyes reverted to a hatchet I'd spied earlier on. Though in full stride, I could still knock her off if I hurried. Choosing the higher road, having forced myself to shrug off her taunt instead, I looked about the warehouse in search of items that might prove vital to our cause. I didn't think I should have to barter for them. I had been tasked with being their savior after all. Not to mention, the establishment was clearly closed. Thus, what sense would there be in letting it go to waste? It'd be akin to paying for a drink after burying the barkeep. In the end, I took some dried goods and a new kind of tent I'd only recently heard of. Though by no means as intriguing as *the fork*, it did offer…...

Great horns of Haeryn! The dead bodies! Having completely forgotten them, I'd left them lying on the porch for anyone to see!

Kicking the door ajar, I dragged both bodies and the blood-splattered chest inside. I then barred the door with a chair. Being that its hinge was broken. Being that I kicked it so hard. I then noticed long blood streaks had mysteriously followed both bodies inside. Though they most certainly had not been expecting me, the witless fools were still causing trouble. Which led me to ponder how long-ago Petra might have been *expecting–* prompting me to perform some feverish calculations in my head. *Something seemed amiss.* I began to fret. She did say *baby*, and babies were quite new to the world– were they not?

"My apologies for earlier but just how old is the wee one?" I called out nervously. Her face appeared above the banister. She was wiping the blood from her face with her gown. Though I could only see the tops of her shoulders, she did not appear to be wearing anything which did little to ease my discomfort. *The Major's wife. The Major's wife. The Major's wife.* I reminded myself.

"That is no business of yours!" She scolded. "He's not yours if that's what you're trying to imply!" Her green eyes were misted with distress and arrogant indignation.

"Mine? Of course, he's not mine! How could he be mine?" I squawked timidly.

"I cannot believe he sent you! You!" Then her voice drifted down softer which put me slightly more at ease– momentarily.

"The gods are cruel indeed. How is it possible?" She pleaded, before burying her face in her gown. I ignored the question. I was just as stymied; if not more. Just how much more, I did not discover until much, much later. But don't get me started on that for now is not the time– though I will confess there to be more than a fair measure of deceit involved.

"We need to hide these bodies somewhere. Should they find them hacked up like this, they'll dispatch an entire garrison after us."

I dutifully checked the dead men's pockets, relieving them of their coins: coppers and silvers, but no gold sadly. What need had they for them now? They may have had more hidden treasure, but I became preoccupied by Petra tugging a tight-fitting tunic over her head. *Careful− don't let her catch you looking!* Averting my eyes, I opened the chest. Rummaging beneath some silk garments, I retrieved a long-curved saber which I examined closer in the soft light.

"See! It is all as I declared. They were sent to kill you! They know you are the Major's wife. They want you and your child dead." I said matter-of-factly.

Ruining my twinkling of triumph, she looked about to cry again. Most gratefully she did not. Instead, her eyes stared at me imploringly which I found a little less unsettling. I felt at a loss not knowing what to do or say. *Massive surprise there.* Gathering my wits, I quickly determined her to be proceeding far too slowly. We should have been long gone by now. To be clear, having found out just how small the young one was, I felt far less keen to bring it with us. Though no doubt she'd cry for a day or two, I felt quite certain the Major would understand. Point being, if her man servant was accustomed to looking after it on sunny afternoons, while not rainy ones too. Why not a month or two for that matter? I mean how hard could it be? The thing cries you give it fair warning. It cries again you give it a smack. At least, though admittedly quite some time ago, that's how I remember it. But there she was, on the floor above me, begging for sympathy.

"Look, I am sorry; and I don't want to seem indifferent, but we simply don't have time for *all of this*," I said, gesturing widely with my arms as she'd done earlier.

"All of this?" she queried so tenderly I couldn't help but cringe. Her voice sounded so sweet, I felt adamant it could not be a good sign.

"Oh, you mean; *this* all of this… as in barging through my door mere months after stealing my virginity and leaving me to the wolves. You refer to the executed Fifth Khalifah and my missing parents who I have not heard from for a fortnight. You mean your likely intention of kidnapping my baby, so I have little choice but to follow you to Haeryn's knows where. You mean the assassins. Oh, I'm sorry− mercenaries! Those two dead bodies lying there before you on the floor− hacked up *like this*!" She made a series of stabbing motions with her hand causing the wee hairs on the back of my neck to rise.

You had to give her credit. Her theatrical talents could not be overstated. The more I thought about it, it was a shame about the great fire and all for she truly missed her calling. Obviously, she recalled her own role in things− such as the two dead bodies− more clearly now.

Not that I saw her helping to clean up the mess. It did attest to her not having been under the spell of the Red Rage though. Which was good for I wouldn't wish its curse upon anyone. Even so, she wasn't quite done mocking me.

"Please, forgive my insolence. The last thing I want to do is to *ruin your day*. I could not live with myself should I tread even slightly upon your well-proposed plans. I'm so sorry. I didn't mean to be so− so bloody heartless!" She scowled down at me. I frowned back, shaking the sword tip at her.

"Look, I didn't ask *for this* either," I stammered. "Not that that changes anything. What matters is− we're both still standing. We're both still alive and well. But we need to be gone. *And soon!!* When they− those two dead ones lying there− don't return, others− far worse− will be sent!" I pointed at the dead men stacked atop one another with the sword which had now become a thankful distraction.

Swish! Swish! Swish! The weapon was of superior quality. Well-balanced for its size; but that was the problem. It was too obvious; too fancy. Not unlike the fancy gold dagger I'd found as a lad, there'd be no way of concealing it without attracting unwanted attention. Thus, albeit grudgingly, I laid it on a nearby table placing it next to a telescoping spyglass− which I quickly pocketed. Having forgotten about Petra, I looked up to see her shaking her head with disdain. She was far too quick to judge!

"What? 'Tis a fair trade. Immoderate of me, in truth. The blade's superiority is tenfold at least!"

Her look said it all. That being the blade was never mine in the first place. My face reddened with anger. The nerve of her. I wasn't a thief− *anymore*. Frustrating me so was not an easy thing to achieve, yet she done it all the same. She'd reached the very pinnacle of my indignation. Nothing she might say could affect me more. Except of course, yet again, *I was wrong*.

"It's yours! Okay? It's yours! It's yours!" Petra blurted.

"No, no, no, no. Wait now. Hold steady. Don't say that. It's not! Okay? Look here, y-y-you can have it back." I stammered, pulling the spyglass from my pocket. "I don't need it. Never wanted it really."

"It's yours!" She sobbed with mounting despair.

"Okay, no harm done. I can keep it if that's what you truly intend." As soon as I'd deposited the spyglass into a pocket, my hands reformed in a prayer-like fashion beneath my stubbly chin. *Uh-oh...here it comes* every muddled thought mumbled within my head. I had a very bad feeling about this.

"He's *your* baby!" She sobbed.

Once again, I'd become the knife; only this time it was my own throat being threatened. Well, I for one wasn't about to spill my guts.

"Shush! Do you want to get us *both killed*?" I asked coldly. "Never speak of that again! Listen to me very carefully. Prior to today– *we never met*. Truthfully Petra, I never even knew your name."

"Nevertheless, he's still yours!" she wailed.

Haeryn's hells! What part of *never speak of that again* did she not understand? I'd reached my wits end. I thought I had before; but no, *this was it*. Not only was she intolerable; my entire world suddenly resembled an overturned apple cart. Only worse. Much worse. I mean the Major would not be pleased. And he wasn't pleasant at the best of times. My mind began to swirl with terrible thoughts. I mean, they were all evidence now, weren't they?

"Noooo!!!" I hollered. Grabbing the blade, I wedged it deep into the thick wooden table. I felt it vibrating while I closed my eyes; curtailing my emotions to ensure I kept *the Rage* at bay. Sometime later, though just how long I could never say for certain; I opened my eyes and turned to face Petra. To my surprise, she'd stopped crying. She looked markedly fearful, which I found distinctly preferable to her tearfulness. I was done. Oddly, I felt the same as I did as a lad watching my father take my dead mother away. Empty and alone.

"Enough! The time for talk has ended. Gather your essentials! Gather what you need to care for the child. I did not come here to negotiate a compromise. There'll be no concessions forthcoming. The Kedera grow stronger by the day. We must act purposefully. To dither is to die."

She stared at me with a worried look before finally disappearing behind the banister. What now? I was beyond frustrated. With a loud sigh, I sat down at a large writing desk beneath the building's lone window. I began picking through some books piled atop it. Books always intrigued me. I don't know why; perhaps due to my reading ability being so poor. Because that makes sense. Thankfully, I'd developed my own system when it came to reading books. I sounded out their titles; read their final line; then set them aside. I'd read a great many books in such fashion. Near every book I'd ever encountered in fact. It had become habitual. Looking back, I expect I thought it made me look less uneducated.

Having never had a teacher, other than my mother whose methods were rather painful given the severity of her impatience, my chief struggle was the order of letters within the individual words. That said, I'd managed to develop a respectable vocabulary solely for being an astute listener. I learned early on that listening was of dire import when it came to warfare, ambushes, rabble-rousing, and such. Most soldiers simply followed the bloke in front of them whereas I appreciated knowing everything I might just in case I got separated. Which the Rage tended to do to me a lot. Haeryn knows I'd sat through enough war councils. Which furthered my point. Reading took time– *a lot of time*. It would have taken me an entire year, or more, to read even the lightest book from cover to cover. Not that there were any thinner-looking books for it seemed anyone harboring a quill never found themselves short on things in need of conveyance. Advancing directly to the book's conclusion sped up the entire reading process immeasurably. I mean what other choice was there? It's not like I was going to drag a bunch of books behind me on my shield everywhere I went. *Chop, chop, slice, slice– now which page was I on? Oh yeah, the one with all the blood splattered across it.*

A shelf directly below the windowsill held the largest collection of the *Books of a Thousand Names* I'd ever seen. I recognized them immediately for their differing moon phase symbols. The original manuscript, written anonymously, was entitled *Corpora*. Which of course, was credited to Haeryn. *Who else could have written it?* Every successive work was given a new title with each being said to have been fashioned upon all of those that came before. Admittedly, I did harbor a few doubts about that. If for no other reason than how could there be anything left to say after reading that many books?

I'd never seen more than two or three of them at one time previously. It was said there were hundreds, though perhaps *not a thousand*, of them in total. I wasn't fully convinced what a thousand of anything looked like. I'd been in battles with thousands of participants– so I was told. But, from where I stood at least, it felt more akin to a sea. Not that I'd ever seen the sea. It's just how I imagined it from stories I'd been told. Wave upon wave crashing down upon one another without end. That was war. That was what we did– until *the Rage* set in– and everything turned black. Red rather– as in *Red Radesh*.

Additionally, though not confusing in any way, was the fact that many of the volumes had been allotted multiple titles. Written by the prophets of old, following a long succession of Khalifah, Diwans, and Rahs; they alone held the strict dogmas of Harbinger for Kedera and Golan alike. They were books I'd always avoided; not that I could have read the endings of them anyway even had I wanted to. Most were composed in *Scriptio Continua*; an ancient cursive employing continuous text with no punctuation which conflicted greatly with my reading technique. I mean how might I read the final sentence when the entire text is essentially one preposterously long compound word? At the same time, it did add credibility to my proposed reading technique.

I counted ten of the *Moon Books* in total. The first being a copy of *Corpora*. *Copy* being the key word there. It was well-known that there was only one original– which was no doubt guarded both night and day somewhere. Likely, locked tight in a shrine someplace. I recognized *In€qualia*; sometimes referred to as the *Imminent Script*. *The Concord Dance* sat next to it; followed by *Diserati*; *Prosody*; *The Passage*; *Consciousness*; *Wit*; *The Semantics*; and lastly, *Modern Militia*.

The Major contended that *Modern Militia* had been composed prior to the Stone Age. Which is to say before swords and axes and such. Which is to say a long, long, time ago. Even before Haeryn which seemed in direct conflict to our beliefs. Which is to say I'm not sure what the Major intended by that. Perhaps he was joking; though it did give me cause to think at the time. Thus, I briefly considered pulling it from the shelf to see if it might be full of crude drawings and such. In the end, though I appreciate a good petroglyph as much as the next man; I thought better of it. I mean once you know something you can't unknow it. As a lad, I once saw a woman through the trees bathing in a stream. Having ventured forth for a closer view, I stepped on a twig, and she turned about quickly. Never had I seen an older-looking crone. Never had I ever run so fast. To this day, I admit to regretting that decision. Not the running part. I meant the part about not peeking at the book.

My life was far from *an open book*. I didn't require a narrative to convince me of the horrible person I'd become. Like the Major, I made no apologies. I merely did whatever I must– to survive. Call me immoral but, thus far, I'd never found much reason for prayer. Tie me to a stake and light a fire beneath me and I'd likely find cause quick enough. Though until such a time, pious ignorance remains my sole comfort. I once heard an old farmer say, *"Wonder is the cost and cause of knowing"*. Which made me wonder just how many bathing crones he'd seen in his time.

The final version written was composed by Lauryn Bryn Mogashu, *the One Rah* himself. Never having been fully completed; it was rumored to have been destroyed during his assassination. Insisting it survived, while attesting that his final words lived no less than all those that came before, the Eight That Spoke as One named it *The Book of a Thousand Names*. The Kedera punishment for simply speaking of it is death by fire. Providing there's ample wood about, I reckon.

Of the lesser books, three were most notable for having already read their final lines. All historical narratives: *The Rise and Fall of Metros; The Forging of the Spears;* and *The Druid Influence upon Satre*. It was then that another book caught my eye, entitled *The Kedera*. Throughout the Golan Territories any literature involving the Kedera was rigorously banned with any such flagrant indiscretions being punishable by death. Know that my reading method was rationalized by a single assertion. That being that the final sentence must surely summarize all that preceded it. Also know that now, I fully recognized my allegation to be profoundly absurd.

Unable to curtail myself, I slid the forbidden book from the shelf. Opening its rear cover, I retreated one page. Far from what I'd expected, the words summed up my pitiful existence to perfection. Scratching my throat like splintered wood, I could not help but gasp and neither will I share the words for they've haunted me ever afterward. It was how I felt upon waking from the Red Rage. But it was more than that. It was how I felt upon waking every day of my life since my mother's passing. Slamming the book back into the shelf, I seized another from atop the desk to clear my thoughts. Flipping quickly through its pages, I read its closing sentence aloud. *May your days be long and your knights never-ending.* It was utterly absurd. It wasn't even the proper adage. Notwithstanding, the knights of old had long been forgotten. Having heard my feeble reading efforts, Petra called down from above.

"I haven't finished that yet. Please don't ruin it for me."

"If you haven't finished it, how do you know which book it was?" It was a fair question.

"I peeked ahead. I can't help myself. *That* is a love story."

"A love story?" I squawked, snapping the book shut as a shiver ran down my spine.

Though I can't say what prompted it; I shook the book physically for feeling utterly confounded. I'd no gumption that there could be books written about love. Then again, I once feigned to read a book ending with the words: *and they lived happily ever after.* Try stabbing a fork in that and see if it sticks. Which is to say, I suppose anything is possible in this so-called *modern world* of ours. If a book needs to be written about love, then I propose with the utmost sincerity that it be comprised of nothing more than a description of the supposed affectation itself.

"Love? In this place? Notwithstanding how might that be bound within a book?" I queried, shaking my head for no other reason than fear of the forthcoming answer. Love? As if such a notion even existed.

"Never mind," I hollered, having decided it best I not know. Far better to wonder than pay that weighty toll.

"'Tis a senseless book with an ill-advised ending." I chastised. "Not to mention being a book banned by the Five; *the Four* rather. You do realize it's forbidden by the Khalifah Decree? That tapestry is bad enough, but this book will see you stoned. You should really burn it lest it gets you killed."

"Eight, seven, six, five that spoke equals four that no longer do so. Leaving four which, by the way, live legions apart yet somehow still speak as one. Tell me, do they fire their ravens from giant bows or does the wind carry their voices upon the seeds of twirling dandelions? Honestly, I can't keep up. I will tell you this though— books don't kill; *men kill*."

"I'm pretty sure this one would," I winked, brandishing one of the larger volumes. "Depending how hard I hit you with it. Do you not realize, talk like that will see you beheaded, hanged, and stoned?" She laughed at that which irritated me. I hadn't intended it to be humorous. It'd been a stern warning. A prudent observation in the very least.

"In that exact order," she asked. More cheek. More insolence. More of her insufferable insubordination to be precise.

Gratefully, it was then that her manservant, Manu, arrived. More precisely, it was then that I removed the chair blocking the door allowing her manservant to enter the establishment— along with the *tiny ever-crying infant*. I was right about that. It did cry a lot. Thus, I had to do my utmost to avoid peeking at the *small bundle of joy* hollering incessantly while cradled so dutifully in his arms.

The way Manu stared at me made me quite uncomfortable. It was reminiscent of the way a man looks at you with disbelief as you collect his soul. There were no blood splatters on his face. Perhaps an inkling of drool upon his chin, but no blood whatsoever; and yet still he had nerve enough to stare. To be fair, undoubtedly, the two dead bodies did add a measure of tension to the room. As did the swaying sword sticking out of the table. Still, staring was impolite. Thus, I did not find him blameless.

If I was being honest– which I wasn't– for all I knew I might have fathered other children in countless other villages as well. What difference did it make? They'd all end up in the war one way or another. If what Petra said was true. And why would she lie? The important thing was to keep details as such strictly between the pair of us. After all, it was nobody's business and, if the Major thought himself to be the father, all the better I say. It was best not to question such things. It was best not to wonder about it at all. What I mean is, I'd met plenty of women with plenty of children and not once did I stop to inquire who anyone's father might be. I just hoped to hell the bandy-legged little thing didn't look anything like me. Should he be a handsome lad: well, problem solved. My looks weren't something you'd ever refer to as *appealing*. My face, arms, and torso were littered with scars. What prompted my dismay was that I had dark hair while the Major was fair-haired. Then again, Petra had dark hair. I did take comfort in that.

Manu turned out to be an unexpected welcome. He may have been old and bent but his wits were as sharp as his spirit was willing. Manu was a man of action– and we quickly threw the bodies to the household pigs. *Apparently, there were no dogs.* Manu scrubbed the blood smears off the storeroom floor while I attended to the porch. While he cleansed it using soap and water, I threw dried mud over the besmirched areas, sweeping the stickier remnants through the cracks. *Done.* There were so many interpretations of *clean* after all. Blood upon my skin always necessitated soap and water. Blood on other things, yeah, *not so much.*

I told Petra to give Manu the Major's letter, so he'd know where to send word later. He agreed to my plan without urging. I must say I did like him. He even argued with Petra when she tried to convince us otherwise. He'd fought the Kedera in the First Great War. He had no love for them and knew well how merciless they could be. Petra still protested, in vain, that we were simply sending Manu to an early grave. I was quick to point out that Manu was far too old for someone ever to infer that he'd somehow passed away *ahead of his time.* Which turned out to be no help at all. Ignoring my poignant observation, Manu ardently professed he'd spent near his entire life avoiding the Kedera and wasn't about to let them catch him now, which did gain some ground with Petra. I did more listening and a lot less talking after that. *Wisdom.* Twice in one day even.

Petra at last conceded and we fled soon after– with the crying baby– being that the two of them protested strongly when I suggested leaving it behind. I did not see what all the fuss was about myself. I was quite certain they would thank me later though, as it happened, some folks were simply unable to envision the future as clearly as myself. *Here, I have a letter for you stating both your parents are dead. Oh, and this crying baby so you might find some comfort in your time of loss.* Prior to departing, I advised Manu to block the door with the chair the instant we left. Manu said it was the lone door, in or out; inquiring how he'd ever leave should he block it with a chair. Petra laughed and hugged him whereas I began to have second thoughts, fearing for his safety. In the end I bid him farewell in our customary fashion. *May your days be long*, to which he rightfully answered, *and your nights full of cheer.*

He'd need all the help he could get. Which is to suggest, perhaps he wasn't as clever as I first thought. It'd been my wish to travel southward but word came that the Kedera had overtaken every village immediate to our path. Were it not for the child, *baby rather*, I could have picked a way through. But not with *the baby*. Besides making us appear blatantly obvious; it did not take to the road well at all. It cried constantly. Petra said it cried for being tired— or too hot— or too cold— or hungry. Which is to say for no reason at all for which of us wasn't always one of those things at any given moment whether it be day or night? Most regrettably, the only other option was to proceed east. *Yeah, east.* That meant crossing the Kestrel. *The Desert of Deserts.* Home to no man and barely a living thing.

This is where we found ourselves at precisely this point in time— trudging slowly forward in the middle of precisely nowhere. Forcing myself from my plodding stupor, I stopped to see how far Petra might be lagging this time. It was night two of our torment. The wind had picked up and, though but a slight breeze, it made it much harder for me to discern where she was immediately.

In fact, after staring into the grey for quite some time I still could not envision her. A sick feeling began to fester in the pit of my stomach. And that's all it took. A hot flash flared deep within my innards. I began to feel dizzy. Dropping the pyrament, I dug a quick hole in the sand with my forearms, hiked up my djellaba and squatted. It spurted from me like water. Shivering uncontrollably, I rid the over-spray by rubbing my calves with warm sand. Unraveling my headscarf, I cut a small piece from it to mop myself.

My headscarf was shrinking rapidly. It was my third bout of *the flux* that day alone— night rather. As it turned out, Petra's comments in respect to the cabbages I'd devoured a day earlier proved prophetic for my linen shorts had found themselves forfeited quite some time ago. Rising to my feet I felt so unsteady I very nearly buckled over. I took several deep breaths, supporting myself with hands on knees while staring at the vulgar patch of sand. The scarab beetles had nothing on me. While it might eventually gather some moss, this muck wasn't rolling anywhere. Then again, perhaps the scavengers would find it. The stench was so foul it made me gag.

It was too dark to tell if there was any blood. I was in a sad state and feeling extremely irritable if only for my flourishing self-pity. I forced myself up, denying a small measure of shame by dragging heaps of virgin sand over the hole with a sandaled foot. Mercifully, I did not vomit. Should that happen, I was done for. Yet another never to be found casualty of the Kestrel.

Thankfully, I could now see Petra's outline laboring against the stiffening breeze. She was tough. I give her that. Without question she had to be no less miserable and distressed than I. She'd barely complained at all thus far. If it weren't for her obstinate pride, one might have assumed she'd been raised in my village. We might be tough and exceedingly stubborn, but we had no pride. That had been stripped from us long ago. Namely, the moment my father disappeared. An old neighbor once requested the village be named in his honor. I wish it had. At least then I might have known his proper name– minus the *spear* suffix of course. Yes, I do know what a suffix is. It is distantly akin to the closing sentence of a book after all.

Pressing the water sling tightly to my lips, I forced myself to swallow a large swig of water. Gratuitously, it did not pass straight through me as per my fears. Even so, I found my buttocks tightly clenched depicting a desperate form of prayer. The water tasted strangely foreign as it slugged its way down my parched throat. I'd only allowed myself a few small sips since commencing the desert portion of our trek. Petra needed it far more than I. She had two mouths to feed. Not to mention, I was rarely able to retain any of it. As much as I detested having brought him, I worried about the little one. Thus, I knew for certain *she had to be*. We were both overwhelmingly disheartened. To her credit, yet again she did not show it. I routinely cursed myself aloud for being such a fool. From the onset this gamble of ours had been slim at best. But the onslaught of dehydration decreased our chances tenfold. I shook the sling gently listening to the water slosh back and forth while judging its weight– only four decent swallows remained, perhaps five.

Distancing myself from the soiled ground, I waited for Petra. It took my utmost control to quash the tides of anger I felt rising within me. We were progressing far too slowly. It was painfully obvious. There was no way we were going to complete the crossing at our present pace. As I watched, I found myself grimacing in time to every clumsy step she took. I soon came to the realization that she was simply unable to move any quicker. Thus, any chance of making up lost time was but the dream of a fool. There remained but one lone option. That being, alter our present course and head for Hell's Well.

Hell's Well! Indisputably, it was but another hotheaded delusion. But what choice did we have? None. It was clear to me now. We had absolutely none. Sadly, clarity was quickly becoming an unforeseen nemesis. It was as if the entire desert had been consumed by the Red Rage. If we did not attempt some new course of action— as in, try something drastic, we were doomed. Hell's Well, if it even existed, lay somewhere in the middle of the Kestrel. Yeah, *somewhere…*

I vividly recall my father mentioning it after returning from his second to last desert crossing. Having been long overdue, my mother thought him surely dead for she said so often and, consistent with her adoring nature, with nary a hint of sorrow. He'd been sent to deliver an urgent message to an eastern outpost far south of Harkenspear. Just for the record, not unlike my father, the outpost no longer exists. Strangely, the more my mother insisted he was gone for good, the more I pined for his return. But a wee lad at the time, I cried silent tears each mournful night.

Though he'd always been distant, rarely even acknowledging my presence, in those days I worshipped him. He represented something unfathomable to me. I didn't know how to describe it back then, but I do now. *Notoriety.* But he'd vanished, causing our entire village to bristle with unease.

To be unknown is to exist without purpose— declaring one a pretender. I once heard him say to my mother; after which he took an extravagant bow. And then, to make a long absence shorter, one bright sunny day, there he was strolling down our path as though nothing had happened. It was obvious something had happened. He was all smiles, which was uncanny by itself. Gritted teeth aside, the rest of his face was a sea of blisters. The back of his neck was bright red and ripe with bubbly pustules. A long time later, when it eventually healed over, the skin was thickly calloused and riddled with blotchy-looking scars. As looks went, it didn't make as much of an impression as you might think. We were used to it. There were scads of ugly people in our little village.

In respect to his other features, it was his hands that struck me most. *Pun intended.* As though but yesterday, I remember him grabbing hold of my shoulders and shaking me harshly. Though solely out of fondness for once. Huge and haggard, his hands felt like sandstone. You don't forget things like that. Mother knew it all too well for she scolded him for it. *Keep your granite paws to yourself!* She often referred to him as a hapless gargoyle. I think it was her way of expressing fondness. Though not expressly obvious, she was grateful he'd survived. Perhaps it was covert village-speak for: I missed you. *Nah.*

While mother tended to his wounds, he explained that a sandstorm had swept away all his belongings. He insisted he wasn't lost even while admitting he could not envision his hands in front of his face. *Humph.* That was crucial. My father would never admit to ever having been lost. *Not* ever. He was more than proud. He was Nitesh Alde Baran− a title bestowed upon him by Diwan Ogi himself. It meant *Follower of the Brightest Star.* As implied, I never knew his real name. To be fair, he did not speak to me often. We had an understanding. He pointed, I leapt. End of story. Well, that bit of it anyway.

More objectively, (though my father never would have admitted it) the title was purely narcissistic for the Diwan having made it clear on many occasions that he considered *himself* the brightest star. As for myself, on that day, I knew unquestionably that the brightest star was the sun. And all I wanted was for my father to stop following it before he was withered to the bone. All things considered, perhaps it remains an inherited family disorder. That was then, however. And they say time heals all wounds. That's plain gut muck! It doesn't.

Returning to the tale at hand, my father claimed he'd wandered a full day and a half before envisioning a massive-looking tree in the distance. *Yeah, a tree.* I know what you're thinking for he reckoned the same. He figured he'd gone mad, figured the sun had scorched his brain to the roots. Though convinced his mind was playing tricks on him, even so, no matter how hard he tried, he could not rid the deception from his thoughts. *But what was it? What did you see?* I recall blurting aloud. It was then my father said something odd.

When you're half-dead and lay eyes upon something other-worldly in the middle of nowhere you don't call it anything. It calls you.

Half-dead? In retrospect, I take issue with that portrayal. Being akin to that half-full cup thing; if you considered yourself more dead than alive, you won't survive. Full stop. End of story. Again.

He described how, despite his efforts to avoid what he envisioned to be a cruel delusion, it persisted in drawing him to it. He said it was inevitable. There was no escaping. Regardless of which way he turned, or which direction he strode, it wanted him. Being the lone landmark in a sea of endless sand once he laid eyes upon it, he simply could not look away.

There was no alternative other than to surrender to its pull. Oddly, once its shadow lay claim to him, he felt strangely rooted to the land— as though he somehow belonged in that forsaken place of the Gods. The tree's absurd height and girth grew upon every new step taken until it towered above him like a mountainous shrine. *This is madness*, he told himself. And it was madness for the closer he came, the darker his surroundings appeared. The giant tree was so immense it was more akin to a grove as opposed to one lone tree. Step by stumbling step, the landscape became murkier and murkier. Yet, in all other directions, the rest of the world appeared intensely bright; save for the path that loomed.

Half-crazed from dehydration, he staggered blindly toward the great tree— so blindly that he nearly tumbled into a hidden fissure ahead of it. He glared downward, unsure of what he beheld for the roots of the massive tree hid the hole perfectly. As his eyes slowly adjusted, its gnarled roots became visible careening down either side of the dank pit which appeared to be bottomless from where he stood.

It would be prudent to note here that the whole time he spoke mother did naught but sop up pus. She never looked up, not even once; while to the contrary I found myself utterly riveted to the tale. He then conveyed, with genuine eagerness, how quickly he'd perceived the prominent feeling of dampness in the air. It was overwhelming. There was water at the bottom of the hole. He was sure of it; and I needed no convincing for I couldn't have felt it plainer had I been tossed into our smelly outside trough.

Without the slightest reservation, he grasped one the roots and began lowering himself into the unknown darkness below. He felt quite certain he'd lost his mind, if for no other reason than his giddiness alone. He cared not. Continuing downward with renewed haste, the pit was far deeper than he ever could have imagined. Which is saying something being that he thought it to be bottomless initially. Outside of the iridescent glints of moss, he couldn't see much of anything. Thus, he began clambering down shorter distances prior to reaching out with a searching foot. Time and time again he did this, though never was there anything of substance to be found other than the roots he clung to.

Expressing how he very nearly lost his grip made my fingers latch upon his forearm. The tree's roots he explained, while my own fretful talons burrowed into his arm, were not only twisted but slick with moss making them exceedingly slippery. Upon those words, my fingernails dug in so hard he gave me a sharp prod in the middle of my forehead to set himself free.

Once he'd descended to what he calculated to be at least six body lengths from the top, he felt his toes splash upon the still surface of the water. Though he kicked it repeatedly, even so a part of him refused to believe it. I believed it wholeheartedly for feeling a warm trickle run down my forearm clear to my elbow. There was no mistaking it. Save for when I looked and found it to be a long drizzle of yellow pus. Shivering with disgust, I glared at my mother suspiciously. Though perhaps coincidental, I will never know for certain. That said, it would not have been beneath her to do such a thing.

Father attested to submerging his whole body while lapping up water for all he was worth. After which he began to cry *tears of joy*— a preposterous insinuation I rigidly oppose. To this day, I still don't understand what's meant by it. Tears of joy? Could there really be such a thing? Sounds like ant grub to me. All crying aside, father remained within the haven of the giant tree for three days stating that it took him that long just to recover his wits. It was during that time that he came up with the name *Hell's Well*. You couldn't argue with that. It did seem fitting. He said he could not have departed any earlier had he wanted to for it wasn't until the final night that the stars reappeared. It was only then that he finally knew where he was. That being, from my point of view, *no longer lost.* That being, from his viewpoint beneath the stars, somewhere in the heart of the Kestrel. So… *still lost* if you ask me.

He then spoke fondly of how the giant tree had not merely saved his life with the gift of water but with food as well for having been ripe with fruit. Fruit. If you can believe such a thing! Upon climbing it, he discovered several large nests woven within. The eggs of which he consumed eagerly; eleven in total. The only other thing I recall is him having stated that the tree was empty inside which, being a wee lad, reminded me of the time I asked mother why father wasn't more cordial. She told me, having suffered more than any man should, a certain *emptiness* resided within him. Which explained why I never asked father what he'd meant by the tree being empty inside; and neither did he ever elaborate.

Recognize, while awaiting Petra's arrival, those memories were as vivid as if they'd happened only yesterday. What bothered me now, and what I don't recall him describing, is *precisely* where that monstrous tree was. At its trimmest waistline, the Kestrel desert was five long nights of desperately hard walking. No one ever tried to cross it anymore. Perhaps a select few might cut across its outermost strands on rare occasions but not the heart of it. What I mean to imply is, it'd be easier to catch fish in a corn field than ascertain where in Haeryn's Hells the bellybutton of a desert might be.

Outside of my father and myself, I'd never heard of anyone who'd ever successfully completed the deeper crossing. Moreover, my father was infamous for having done so several times. Then again, he was empty inside so I'm not certain that even counts the more I ponder it. Sure, there was propaganda fueled by the Kedera proposing whole armies to have crossed but they were falsehoods; the sole intention of which was to incite panic. There were plenty of disastrous accounts; including one report of actual soldiers who'd retreated into the Kestrel only to be consumed without a trace. So, what led me to attempt my earlier crossing you might very well ask. I had no choice. I felt compelled to do so. It was a line in the sand that I simply had to cross. As it was, news had come from abroad that my father— sometime after stomping my mother to death and leaving me to fend for myself— never survived his next crossing attempt.

In my mind, it stands the lone instance proving the Gods aren't exclusively cruel. The Kestrel had not only caught the sick bastard but swallowed him whole. I do hope it was painful. To be clear, I hope it withered him like a fallen leaf. I hope it beat him to a pulp before crumpling him to dust. I hope it crippled him. I hope it blinded him. I hope it shook him like slow churned butter until naught was left but a sizzling smear. I hope it was as agonizingly slow as it was deliberate. Did I mention how much I loathed him? I suppose I should have long before now. Please recognize that the pompous ass never taught me anything— not even how to survive on raw eggs. I taught myself that tasty tidbit which saved my life. In a single day, one single act of unbridled cruelty, he took everything from me. And I hated him for it.

But don't misinterpret. I mourn his loss daily. I curse his hollow bones with every new breath taken for having denied me the opportunity to dig my fingernails into his throat and— oh, so gradually— choke the sweet life from his weather-beaten skin. Thus, the older I got the more I felt an overwhelming urge to cross the Kestrel. Most folk use the phrase *attempt* the crossing. That's ludicrous. That's why Petra and I were failing right now. Our will had been reduced to *trying* to cross it. That was not the required mindset. You had to believe emerging on the other side was a certainty, or it was over from the start. The only reason I made it previously was strictly due to my obsession to prove myself the better man. Yeah, better than Nitesh Alde Baran— some dead Diwan's witless errand boy.

At least that's what I told myself. More truthfully, I expect I had precious little to live for. The day he left was the day he stole my world from me. He took far more than just my mother. He took my home— and with it my sense of worth. He stole our village pride; what little we had left of it at the time. I had no one— save for two handfuls of blisters (from all the digging) and a gut full of sorrow devouring me from the inside out. As I matured, the sorrow soon turned to wrath.

And they whisper behind my back that I have anger issues. They propose I'm ill-natured; going so far as to suggest I don't get along well with others. In my own defense— not that I've ever found myself in need of any defending, because I'm quite adept at defending myself, and oft times without warning— it's not like I ever encountered any deeds of kindness in my early days. Far from it.

Not that I'm complaining. Because we don't do that where I come from. I'm just pointing out the facts. Do not misconstrue my temperament. I'm not bitter. I'm just a touch reclusive. Distrustful might be more apt. Did I mention I don't often sleep well? I hear their screams. I see their eyes grow wide as the tip of my blade splits their ribs. I am haunted by the countless faces of strangers I've killed. But that is not my worst nightmare. Far from it. My worst nightmare was one of inconceivable veracity for knowing the only person I ever truly hated is the same person I once cherished the most. He was my hero— my lone champion. And then he loaded my universe into a wagon and rode out of sight. He never even looked back. Not once. *Okay, so I was bitter*. Point taken.

Regardless, that was precisely how I found myself now— ripe with anger, rotting guts— with little, if anything, to look forward to. There was one consolation. I no longer felt I had anything to prove. Or apologize for. I was who I was, and I had every right to cross the Kestrel. I had every right to live rather— as much right as anyone. If you could refer to my present existence as living that is. It mattered little. Nothing mattered. I had a task to complete. *Tasks* to be clear; as in the plural. See, I'm not entirely illiterate. There were two of them. I had to save Petra and her baby. *Our baby.* Our little bundle of incessant wailing. He was a boy and, as much as I tried to force it from my mind, there was pride in that.

I also had a hefty bag of gold to collect. I reminded myself with a heavy sigh. What was that proverb again? Oh yeah, *opulence doesn't distract the dead.* I'll have to get back to you on that one. As if you couldn't already tell, I was feeling a tad distracted. Still, before I could account for any of my bidden obligations, I needed to find Hell's Well. If it truly existed that is.

Please acknowledge, in respect to my current plight; it wasn't that I thought my father had been deceitful in any way. But let's face it; the well was in the center of the Kestrel. So, its chances of having dried up were— well, let's just say better than any chance of discovery and leave it at that. Then again, what difference do the odds make when you find yourself blind-folded with a noose about your neck? It's that half full cup thing again. Only this time its contents had been absorbed by coarse sand— which I hated. There was only one path ahead that might change that. *Find the well.*

Petra arrived, looking nearly as bad as I felt. I could not hear the baby and supposed it to be asleep. I hoped it wasn't dead. No doubt that would beget a different sort of crying and there'd been hardly a hint of peace between us. Sloshing the water sling, I held it out for her. Though it hadn't been a question, naturally, she refused to take it.

"Drink," I ordered.

"I can't. I have the sin shits! There's no point. It will pass right through me." I knew the feeling all too well. Even so, it was the wrong answer. Especially for her. Especially for the wee one.

"All the more reason. Look, we're both parched. We must replenish our fluids." I sloshed the sling resolutely. "Here, take it. You must."

After watching her begrudgingly shuffle the baby to a single arm, I passed her the water sling. She took a small swig and tried to give it back. Refusing to accept it, I gestured that she need drink again. She did so reluctantly. I gestured yet again but she just stared at me blankly until, at last, I conceded the fight.

"You must force yourself, Petra." I scolded her. "As the grim parch takes hold, you know full well it will be your milk that dries up first. What then?" I asked soberly.

Yanking the sling from my hand, she drank until the water was very nearly gone. Shaking the sling venomously, she then threw it back at me. Wiping her tattered lips with her sleeve, she eyed me spitefully.

"And when it's all gone– what then, fool?" I did not accommodate her further. There was no need. The query was plainly rhetorical. We both knew very well what came next. We'd wither like fallen leaves; two sizzling smears on an endless canvas landscape.

"How is it?" I asked, expressing genuine concern. "Is it sick?"

"HE is fine." She glowered back at me. "At least so far as I can tell. He's been quiet. But we have bigger problems. We're being followed," she added with admirable composure.

"Followed? How can you be certain? It's dark and the sand is swept with shadows that feign to dance beneath the stars. The mind plays tricks on you in times like these. It is well known." It was my turn to stare.

"True, but I know a torch when I see one. Still, it makes no sense. Why light a torch? There's no need with this night sky and bright moon."

It was a sensible deliberation and, while I pondered whether to answer her truthfully, my eyes scanned the distant dunes for any small flickers of light. I could not see anything and returned to study her face. I could tell it wasn't a hunch. She was fully confident of her valuation. I decided to go with the truth.

"Because they want us to know they are coming. They're hoping we will panic and do something rash."

"You mean like attempt to cross the Kestrel?"

"Don't say *attempt*," I sighed. "Notwithstanding, what harm is there in knowing? There's nowhere we might run or hide." I continued ignoring the obvious dig.

"So, you do believe me," she said, widening her green eyes absurdly.

"Yes. I was hopeful they couldn't imagine us ever trying to cross–"

"Trying?" She wished to clarify– rub in my face rather. Once again, choosing the higher road, I ignored her. To be clear, I was speaking from *their point of view*, not my own.

"Or, if they did, choose not to follow us. Unfortunately, there is only one reason they'd pursue us through hell– death by decree."

"Death by decree?" Though I wanted to answer– *yes, not unlike possessing forbidden books and tapestries*– yet again, I held my tongue.

"*Decreto mortis* they call it. They won't stop. Not ever. Not till we're dead."

Or, in the very least, *you and yours*, I mused silently. It seemed very unlikely that they would chase the Golan Butcher into the great unknown. Not with a thousand bloated camels. Not even if thunderclouds were at their beck and call. Nor even if they rode the wingless wind itself. I was clearly losing my mind.

"Then we shall have to move all the faster." She blurted unexpectedly. "Fools!" She cried aloud. "The element of surprise is lost!"

That shook me from my stupor. So much so, it caused me to chuckle— a weird feeling given the circumstances. I couldn't recall the last time I'd laughed aloud. Petra grinned back and then she also began to laugh. Having reached our boiling point, our stress erupted from us in waves. We laughed long and feverishly. It was ludicrous. Tears began streaming down Petra's cheeks. She was bawling at the same time. Embarrassed, she took to snorting like a crazed lunatic— causing me to me lark even more. We were plainly going mad. Between gasping breaths, we took to hollering *Fool,* and other obscenities, loudly into the night. Until the baby awoke and started crying of course. I expect it awoke upon the onset of our name calling theatrics. We just couldn't hear it for our growing debauchery.

"Stop! Or I swear— I'll explode from the nether end too!" She confessed giggling, while jostling the baby up and down on her hip.

"How many do you think?" She asked after we'd managed to regain our composure.

"Hard to say. One lone assassin," I shrugged, "being that you saw a single torch. If there were more, and the goal was to panic us, surely, they'd all have carried one."

"We best get going lest they have the final laugh," she smiled feebly.

"True, but our plans have changed. We must alter our course. We're progressing far too slowly. I calculate us being barely a quarter of the way. We're not going to make it. We won't survive."

"Please don't say that. Change course? You mean go back?"

"No. We can't go back. I can kill the assassin, but I can't protect you and your baby from an entire garrison. That's just not possible." I then told Petra about Hell's Well— purposely omitting the part about me not knowing where it was. Nor the part about whether it still existed— *if ever it had*. Though she looked dismayed, she did not argue— *for once*— which conjured some favor with me.

"Even so, we need to find a way to hasten our steps. It's paramount. Hell's Well is a stopgap not a solution. It's akin to bandaging a wound that won't stop bleeding. You might slow it down but you're still gonna die."

"Well, that's a cheery thought," scowled Petra. "You do realize, I am going as fast as I possibly can. Not to mention, it's very hard to— to deal with certain rising unenviable needs— needs that cannot be repressed, if you know what I mean— while trudging through the desert with a baby in your arms."

"Quite right, I hadn't considered that, and I know you are doing your utmost." Though I'd graciously conceded her the point, she wasn't done yet.

"The sand, the wind, the heat, and the cold push against me without end. I'm exhausted. My arms are dead tired. I can't ever put them down— not ever! Admittedly, the journey has weakened me. But I am still trying! I haven't stopped. Not even once. Save for the flux which can't be helped any more than it can be avoided!"

Her eyes were brimming with tears. And there it was— a condition entirely foreign to me commonly referred to as… *complaining*. Thank Haeryn none of my fellow villagers were around to witness it. Though, no doubt the sand would have swallowed them long ago. Not that they would have openly bemoaned it. No, they would have held their tongues— in their hands, if need be— being that they would have fallen free of their mouths for being so dreadfully parched. Which confirms my assumption that they all would have died— though silently, rest assured, and without the slightest protest.

"Wait! I have an idea." I urged, stretching my jaw ridiculously wide and baring my lower teeth. Though disappointed, I was not wholly unsympathetic. One's values are their own after all. Therefore, you cannot expect the neighboring folk to uphold those same lofty standards. Emptying my makeshift backpack, I spread the pyrament on the sand prior to folding it into a large rectangle. Petra sat upon its center holding the baby, while I piled our belongings between her legs. Folding back the corners, I twisted them about until it held the pair of them snuggly with the resultant runner being just long enough to yank over my shoulder. Although a bit wobbly initially, I was able to pull it— with substantial effort— for my sandals being forced deep into the sand. It was the tent pole that afforded me the necessary stability. I used it much like a walking stick. *Clever me.*

"A dog sled!" She purported crudely.

"Sand sled," I corrected. "No Kedera dogs involved."

"Dog sled," she insisted. "What a marvelous idea," she crowed. "Now, get a move. Go on! Git!"

"I hope the little one shits on you." I scoffed, limping my way through the bottomless sand.

In truth, I prayed dearly that he did not. I had to sleep in that thing later and it smelled foul enough due to the sweat pouring off us throughout the day. Though I appreciated her *encouragement*, she was heavier than expected− a lot heavier. I had to stop often to drink, forcing down small bites of *dry food* down my *dry throat* afterward. I couldn't help but rehydrate more often. Still, it worked out well being that Petra had to relieve herself on the slip side of every fourth hill. Or so it seemed. In her defense, riding a camel would have been akin to a skiff on a calm lake in comparison. Fortunately, my own nausea had subsided, or my sled heroics never would have worked. Being woefully dehydrated, I barely broke a sweat even with the added exertion. On the bright side, I did feel warmer when the cooler winds began to gnaw. I expect we both did.

Prior to the dawn, we arrived at the crest of a monstrous sand dune. Finally, that is for there'd been a few moments where I questioned ever making it to the top. I needed to stop. My heels were burning from the relentless pushing− pulling rather. As badly blistered as they were, any excuse to stop would have sufficed by that point sadly. Gazing about, I noticed our bland terrain had changed. The waves of sand were strewn with tumbleweed. I couldn't tell what they were at first for they were hard to discern given the darker shadows cast by the mountainous dune.

This was it. The place I'd been looking for. No, not the well; but a different place for a different purpose. Walking back a few paces, I drew a protracted line perpendicular to the way we'd traveled with a sandaled foot. For the record, I did have boots upon our departure, but they'd been tragically reduced. When you can clearly see your toes bleeding out the ends, you can hardly call them boots. Though the makeshift sled had erased my footprints, still, the path we'd taken was unmistakable. It reminded me of the entrance to a den of river otters I'd once found; save for our current path being vastly longer and completely devoid of moisture, not to mention the nearest river likely being a hundred leagues away or more. Okay, so it was nothing like it at all as it turns out.

"Why did you do that?" Petra inquired upon my return.

"It's a message," I shrugged. "We'll make camp at the bottom of this dune. Keep your eye out for scorpions; they thrive amongst this type of vegetation."

"Oh, then we should most definitely camp here. Good thinking."

"Don't fret. They may scurry under the tent seeking moisture but it's doubtful that they'll enter it. Just don't step on one. It makes them grumpy." I warned her.

Having our camp set between the windward and slip faces of the broad sand dune, we immediately felt warmer if for no other reason than having ducked the brunt of the wind. I held the pyrament door slightly ajar to keep a wary eye out for scorpions. Not to mention, our advancing aggressor. The opportunity to rest raised my spirits and I felt a bit better. Petra was still quite weak in spite of not having had to exert herself. It was obvious her back was nagging her. I expect having to sit up straight for so long was the main culprit. I noticed she rubbed it often while fretting about the baby.

"Feel his brow," she insisted finally, opening her shawl slightly. "Does it feel hot to you?"

Averting my eyes, I reached a hand within gingerly. It was very warm indeed. His skin felt amazingly soft– supple yet firm at the same time. Rummaging about his soft round forehead, my fingers came across what I believed to be his nose. It wasn't.

"Are you quite done?" Petra asked. "The other side, fool!" She scolded. My face turned crimson. I slid my hand to the opposite flank briskly assessing his trifling brow. It felt very different– hairier for certain. His brow was warm but not hot; slightly moist but not clammy.

"Feels fine," I replied sheepishly.

"Which? Renan's brow or the other handful?" Her eyes locked on mine in that way she had that made me feel instantly uncomfortable.

"Renan's brow. Both– 'twas an honest mishap." I cringed awkwardly.

"But one more honest mishap and you'll be looking back at me from a lone eye! Both." She huffed, re-pinning her hair bun purposely. "You keep that filthy wandering paw to yourself."

I shook my head with a mournful frown but saw little point in arguing. 'Twas a welcome handful I noted once I'd found nerve enough to consider it more honestly. Petra was elegant, educated, and attractive. I, on the other hand, was but a clumsy-fingered buffoon. From that moment on, I felt increasingly agitated. We'd been cooped up together for what felt like forever. All the while, the same burning question came to mind, over and over and over.

Why? Why? Why? Why? Why? I stared at her blankly searching for any clue that might help solve the biggest conundrum of my life. Why ever had she slept *with me?* Dawn arrived in a blink and, while I didn't think my world could get any smaller; the pyro-vent felt as if it were shrinking for my increasingly chaotic thoughts as much as the severity of the sunlight.

"Quit staring at me," Petra chided, rubbing her back with her left hand. She lay the baby down beside her; yawned and stretched. The gods were feeling amiable for it slumbered peacefully.

"I'm not staring. You are." I mumbled, studying her every movement while struggling to chew a particularly tough piece of dried meat.

"I most certainly am not. But you, on the other hand, are glaring like a wolf. Like a penned bull. Like a cat in a cage." Which, oddly, were all animals the meat may have consisted of.

"Close your eyes, for Haeryn sake, if I upset you so greatly! Leave me to my own thoughts and get some sleep." I exhaled through rattling lips denoting the full extent of my frustration.

"You need sleep. All I did was sit. You were the dog. You must be knackered."

"Knackered?"

"Tired, worn-out, drained, which is to imply: exhausted," she generously explained.

"Ah, I see. Where I come from it means to put something out of its misery. In the army, any injured livestock we come across are knackered and boiled for stew."

"Good to know, I'll keep that in mind. I'm quite fond of stew. Would thick-headed dogs be considered injured? I bet that water sling would boil soon enough if we left it in the sun." Touching my forearm with a finger she then pressed it to her tongue.

"What did you do that for?"

"Just trying to figure how much salt might be needed. Never mind, off to sleep you go then."

"Humph. Well, aren't you riddled with mirth. If you must know, and I know you must, I must keep watch. My thoughts are bent on feeding that assassin to the sand grubs."

"Ah, now I understand– your little line in the sand earlier. A tad theatrical, don't you think? I thought you soldiers were all about *the element of surprise.* Oh, you're trying to get in his head. Aren't you? Not to shatter your tankard, but the winds likely covered it over by now."

"Which is precisely why I put it on the downward slope. And it's not complicated. 'Tis a warning. Should he cross that line he shan't cross another save for the one dividing this world from eternal darkness. I can promise you that much."

"Well, you won't see him anytime soon. It's positively sweltering. Think about it." She winked, tapping her temple with a finger. "No one could withstand that heat."

"Agreed." I sighed. "And that's twice your finger has offended me; a third time and you might find it considerably shorter." I cautioned her. "There have been strange reports of late. Tales of Kedera scouts appearing at desert fringes from out of nowhere. No doubt it's just gossip, or propaganda intended to conjure distress. There's no chance they've discovered a reliable route across this desert. Even so, I've found there's typically a bit of truth to most rumors."

I had to stop talking to pry a morsel of meat from my front teeth. My tattered nails proved utterly useless causing me to eye that finger of hers with newfound envy. It looked plenty sharp and very suitable for the task. Not to mention, I doubted the Major would have complained too fervently had she shown up short a finger or two. Fortunately for her, I managed to spit it loose in the end.

"Well, at least you're not farting for once."

"I don't dare risk it," I confessed with a chuckle. "When dusk arrives, you shall continue alone while I wait here," I continued soberly. "The assassin will show soon enough. He has nowhere else to go. At which point, I will make an end of him."

"We shall go on alone— the baby and his defenseless mother. Of course, once again that makes *perfect* sense. After all, I don't even know where I'm going." She huffed.

"I told you. Follow the dim light between two bright stars, southeast of Harmony's Mantle."

"The dim light? And what pray tell, have I been following till now? But don't sell yourself short. You're more than dim if you think for a moment, I'm trekking anywhere in this desert alone."

"No, you will go. Have no fear, I will point the way."

"Point the way? And just *what way* looks any different from the next?" She glared expectantly.

I ignored her. *It felt good.* Rather marvelous in fact, as I sucked the final remnants from a strip of tasty gristle. She needed to learn her place and I found myself with all the time in the world to teach it to her. The Major would thank me for it; likely toss a few extra gold coins my way to show his sincere appreciation. I could picture the moment clearly in my mind. *So, to be clear, she does what she's told.* He'd say with astonishment. *She does.* I'd answer bowing proudly. *And all for the cost of a single finger?* He wished to clarify. *So far.* I nodded. *Though the night is still young.* And clanking our tankards together we'd roar with good cheer while she scurried to refill them without ever being summoned.

"You will have to carry a water sling, but I will catch up with you soon enough. Alone, I can travel fast. Besides, the assassin was sent for you, *not me.* This gives us control, *not him.*" I must confess I felt rather clever while stating that last bit. Being that she still appeared to be less enthused with my proposal– direction rather– I felt obliged to explain things in greater detail.

"My surprise attack will be a lot less demanding if I don't have to worry about protecting the pair of you all the while."

"Surprise attack? You drew a line in the bloody sand. I don't think you grasp the true meaning of surprise. *Surprise* is awaking to find my hairpin protruding from your eye. *Surprise* is awaking to find yourself knackered and boiled as stew. *Surprise* is when you hear a knock at your door and your entire world is turned upside down." Haeryn help us and she had the nerve to call my line in the sand *theatrical.*

"Believe me, he'll boast a look of surprise when my dagger finds his heart. They all do."

"And what if he has a bow? What then my grand strategist? Ergo whilst you stumble uphill through the sand like a one-legged mutt, he will pound arrow after arrow into that dim-witted skull of yours." She sniffed indifferently. Chuckling aloud, I removed my dagger, spinning it about in my hand with stunning expertise. If I do say so myself. Which I just did.

"And if my head is half as thick as you profess, I shall be none the worse for it."

"I'm being serious. He may very well have a bow for all you *think* you know."

"Nah. Kedera assassins prefer the knife. It is well known. It's a religious thing. When he comes, *and he will come*; I will hobble the hound to ensure he suffers a slow painful death. Though no doubt you will shed many a worrisome tear, you need not fuss about my well-being. I will dispatch him and catch up with you before the morrow light takes flight."

"Unless he dispatches you with a single well-placed arrow! At which point he shall come for us!"

"Either way, we'll know soon enough," I grunted. "I must confess I find your lack of faith disheartening. Perhaps, I'll try to get some sleep after all. You are right about one thing. No one could possibly survive out there with this heat." Returning my dagger to its sheath, I mopped the sweat from my brow, flinging it outside to hear it sizzle.

"You risk far too much on blind hunches. Not to mention, the assassins pretending to be salesmen brought a sword not a knife." She reminded me.

"They were mercenaries. And, for the last time, it was a saber."

"Okay, so hired killers with a curved sword. It changes nothing. If you hadn't noticed, it was still considerably longer than your quaint little dagger." So much for having all the time in the world to curb her unruly disposition. So much for fetching a few extra gold coins from the Major. She was nothing short of infuriating.

"You are a woman. You know nothing. Tend to the child and leave the weightier matters to me."

"No, nothing at all," she confessed, feigning to pull her hairpin and stab me with it. At least she could be entertaining now and again.

"Okay, so there was that. Even so, you still know nothing. Less than nothing in fact about the art of conclusion."

"Enlighten me." Realizing she would not let up; I gave in with a heavy sigh.

"Foremost, Kedera assassins come at night. They always wear black. It would be nothing less than immoral for them to wear a disguise. It would be sacrilege, a degrading insult to their most valued principles."

"A degrading insult as opposed to one bristling with adulation. If only I had my quill." Having no idea what she intended, yet again, I ignored her.

"As I said, the two at your door were mercenaries not assassins. There's a substantial difference. Though similarly ruthless, mercenaries are strictly in it for the coin. They have no code of conduct. Kedera assassins belong to a covert cult known as the BroZil. Highly trained in the darker arts, they are as cunning as they are callous."

"The BroZil? Why have I not heard of them before?"

"Why have I not heard of them before?" I repeated in as high a voice as I could muster. It was my turn to mock and, wanting to make the most of the opportunity, I was far from done.

"So, you didn't receive an invite to one their more festive gatherings?" I queried aghast. "How odd. No doubt the omission was deemed a colossal oversight if ever there was." I huffed, rolling my eyes in the same fashion she employed all too often. "They're not a traveling theatre troupe or carnival circus. I did mention they were assassins belonging to a covert cult did I not?" I further disparaged her.

"No! I mean, yes!"

"I see," I fibbed, tugging at my ear lobe while nodding agreeably.

"It's just that I've read a lot about the Kedera and never heard mention of the BroZil." She blushed, making me feel awkward. I loathed the way she was able to twist things about making me feel as though I'd somehow besmirched her. I did not do that to her when she threw sand at me. Then again, I wasn't that clever.

"There are few who have— who still draw breath," I confessed with a purposeful wink. "The Khalifah forbid mention of the Brotherhood of Zil."

"Of course, they do. It makes perfect sense. Above all, the identity of assassins must be protected at all costs."

"Naming one's fear—"

"Only gives it wings. Khalifah Duren the Kind", she finished astutely. As for the author, I had to take her word for it. Why I even bothered to try matching wits with her was beyond reckoning. She was without question far more learned. Notwithstanding, I'd heard it from the Major and, being that she was his consort, it only made sense she'd be aware of it too. Even so, I decided to press my luck further.

"It is said that the Brotherhood follow the depraved teachings of Surat Muneakisa. They consider him a prophet. Rumor has it; he began as an executioner. Obsessed with killing while fanatical about his occupation, he scripted many of his more devious exploits." Having slouched increasingly lower unconsciously, my head was near ground level now. It felt so heavy I couldn't help but let it fall. It's important to note, due to the inordinate amount of space she awarded the infant, only one of us could lie flat at a time.

"I'm going to close my eyes now. Please don't kill me in my sleep." I whispered.

"I can't make any promises. I suggest you not fart, or I'll roast you on my pointy little skewer."

I dreamt I stood within an immense green pasture brimming

with golden rod, lavender, and lilac. Oh, and mushrooms; fat juicy mushrooms near as big as my sweaty palms. The aroma of the lavender alone was intoxicating. A meandering stream, boasting long rows of wild cabbages on either side of it, separated the meadow into two perfect halves. It was positively rippling with brook trout. There were deer, wild boar, and turkeys galore. Which is to depict, there were far more turkeys trotting about than deer or wild boar. Not that there weren't plenty of those about too. There were just more turkeys— a lot more— in comparison to the other two animal species mentioned. Namely, the deer and wild boar of which there were considerably less though not drastically. Did I mention how tired I was? I think so but, in the off chance I did not, I was exceedingly tired. As in, not thinking straight for being so terribly weary. Knackered, I think some call it. Though not all being that for many others, myself inclusive, it has a different meaning entirely.

And not a single goose; thank Haeryn! Not one. Though I had to look closely for turkeys can look quite similar at times especially when approached from the rear. Thickets, ripe with berries, rose upon the grassland's outer margin eventually giving way to extensive tree groves riddled with apples, tangerines, and pears. Scattered throughout the massive orchard were other broad leaf trees boasting gems such as olives, cherries, figs, and pecans. I ate so much I thought my stomach would burst. I'd never tasted tangerines before; nor even seen one, so you can imagine my disappointment upon waking later only to reaffirm that I still hadn't. Tasted a tangerine, that is, just to be clear.

Returning from the bountiful orchard, I cooled my tired feet by chasing trout and crayfish up and down the stream before dozing off on a warm, grassy bank. Which begs the question if you dream you are sleeping are you truly still dreaming? In the end I suppose it doesn't matter because I awoke to find myself cooking trout over a preposterously large bonfire— something I refused to ponder further even in my groggy state for fear of losing my sanity. It was so hot I decided to devour the crayfish raw. I heard buzzing sounds. A most irritating bee insisted on trying to land on my face. I was so bloody tired. At least the faces of the dead had left me alone for once. Still, all I wanted to do was sleep, but the infuriating bee refused to stop pestering me. It was then that I truly did awake with a loud anxious gasp.

"Cease and desist woman!! What are you doing? Quit poking me with that thing! And were you making buzzing sounds just now?" I inquired with great annoyance. Wrapping up her long braid, Petra curled it into an orderly bun securing it with the hairpin– being that she'd finished torturing me with it.

"And for Haeryn's sake leave it there! It's not as though I poked you with my dagger." I grumbled.

"If only that were true." She smirked.

I glared at her wondering whether she meant what I thought she meant. Why must she insist on speaking in riddles? Why couldn't she for once just convey what she intended? Then again, perhaps she had but I'd wisely chose to hear it not.

"I told you not to fart." She insisted sternly.

Ah, so that was it. How could it be helped while dreaming contently? It felt weird to be awoken from a dream not feeling as though I was covered in blood. Though my foul stench attested me to be in desperate need of a good scrubbing, on this occasion at least, it wasn't due to any cruelties I'd done.

"It was the brook trout and cabbages," I explained. "I was dreaming most peacefully."

"I could tell. But misery loves company and you've slept long enough. I need to lie down; my back is stiffer than a–"

"Frisky bull's bludgeon." I finished for her.

"I was going to say a scrub board. Either way, dusk will be here far before we're ready."

I sat up slowly, rubbing my stinging eyes. Everything was so frightfully bright. Petra slid her long legs alongside mine and closed her eyes. She folded her hands across her chest as if she were dead. *She'll steal ugliness from death one day*, I mused senselessly. Though a morbid thought, it did seem true. Her skin was flawless, like that of an angel. Not that I'd ever seen one. And then her green eyes opened and the devil within her awoke and spoke.

"I can't sleep if you're going to keep staring at me," she said. "Seriously, stop it! Or is there something you wish to say?"

Had I not been half asleep I would have wisely held my tongue. *But I didn't.*

"Why?" I asked. "I don't understand." She glared back at me for a long while before answering.

She was supposed to ask, *why what.* Or– *you don't understand what exactly?* And that would have provided me with the exit I so badly required– allowing me to preserve a small measure of dignity. *But she didn't.* She just answered my question as though she'd smelt it festering within me all the while. As if the wisps of smoke burning a hole through my gut were evident ever since she'd opened that door.

She might merely have fanned the flames– or, Haeryn forbid, doused them entirely. But, of course, *she didn't*. She told me the truth and, though I knew it was the truth, I had a tough time accepting it as such.

"That night," she began, and I couldn't help but cringe as a feeling of dread inhabited my spine.

"That night, so many months ago, while my parents were away–"

I should have known she would start there. The forlorn damsel all alone. I could feel my palms begin to sweat and she hadn't even begun yet.

"I should have been home long before dusk, but I'd run into some ill luck. Truth be told, I wasn't supposed to leave so I was hurrying to get back to Studayo house. But it got dark much faster than I thought it would. Then two rogues started following me. They intended me harm. I feared they would rape me. I was sure of it. I'd never been with a man before. I was scared to death. Not that I wouldn't have been scared to death even if I had been with a man prior. Not that it's any of *your* business." She clarified.

Because that was important. I could feel sweat trickling down both sides of my face now. My forehead was so hot I could have browned an egg on it. So, I supposed it hadn't been entirely unimportant at the same time. Elsewise, why would it have transfixed me so? Still, I reckon there were plenty of things I was yet to experience but you didn't hear me boasting about never having done them.

"Fearing for my life, I hid under a small bridge till they passed before fleeing back to the village. The only other way home was the trail through the woods which I wouldn't dare risk. At the time, I was hoping I might find someone I knew back in the village. Not that any of them, in hindsight, would have raised a finger to protect me." She sighed sadly.

"But the men were not fooled. They must have known that I'd return for they arrived soon afterward. I caught glints of their eyes in the moonlight, they were riveted upon me. Though they weren't quite running, they'd quickened their pace. Not knowing what else to do, I ducked into The Watering Hole. I begged the barkeep for lodging, but he said there were no rooms available. So, I sat in the farthest corner cowering in the shadows where the pipe smoke seemed thickest.

"Entering the establishment, the two villains sat down at the table nearest the door. There was no way out other than to try and run past the pair of them. I could see their crow eyes scouring the room for

me. It was then that I saw you sitting all alone. I knew who you were–
everyone knew who you were. I saw the empty chair at your table and
immediately felt certain they would not dare confront me. Not if I was
sitting with *you*.

"I was right about that. The two men got up and left no sooner
than I'd sat down. They left with such haste they didn't even bother to
finish their drinks. But I was wrong about you. More precisely, it
seemed to me that *everyone else* had been wrong about you. You were
a different story. Not at all like the ones I'd heard told on so many
occasions. You weren't what I had expected. You were generous and
kind, some might even say respectful considering you didn't know me.
I'll give you that.

"But I was a different person back then. I was foolish. I was a
simple girl who knew nothing of the world– other than what I'd read
in books. Though it seems to me but a charade now, you seemed
genuinely interested in all I had to say. That was a first. Understand,
when I say I'd never been with a man– I'd barely shared words with
one prior to that day let alone a table. Though I can't rightfully say
what was in your mind, I don't know how you put up with me for I
was blathering on like a fool no less.

"You bought me dinner and ale; followed by a second pint–
none of which I asked for. I'm not sure if I've somehow blocked it
from memory but I don't remember much after that *either*. But that
doesn't make anything that happened afterward even vaguely
appropriate– the difference between us being, at least *I* had an excuse.
I'd never had ale before. I do recall crying and you comforting me. I
also clearly recall waking up alone.

"Oh, I'm sorry. I haven't answered your question, have I? Yet
again, I'm blathering on like a witless wench. How bloody thoughtless
of me. You want to know why I slept with you. Hmm, let me think."

No doubt more wisps of smoke arose as her green eyes begat
burning a hole through my own. My entire back was a sea of sweat
now. Never in my life had I felt so uncomfortable. But I had nothing to
say. Because there was nothing to say. Stab me with a rusty fork but I
simply didn't remember. But she did. Though a moment earlier she
claimed she couldn't recall anything afterward it all magically came
rushing back to her clear as a daylit stream.

"Now where was I? Oh, I remember, sitting across from you,
unable to curtail my wagging tongue. Beneath the table, my hands
were clasped tightly together on my lap– so you wouldn't see them
trembling. I was petrified. I didn't know what next to do. All I wanted

was to escape and go home; but I thought those two frightful men might be outside waiting for me. So, I chose the lesser of two evils. I chose you."

That explained it— *like a hairpin to the heart*. Stuck between a rock and a hard place, she'd opted to pet the mangy stray dog as opposed to playing *hide and seek* with the plunder twins. Petra kept looking at me, but I hadn't the faintest idea how to respond; or if I should risk speaking at all. I was stymied. The answer to my riddle was beyond anything I might have imagined. There was no refuting it. She'd slept with me purely out of angst. The more I thought about it, the more sense it made. What other reason might there be? She was no harlot. And what, for Haeryn's sake, had I expected her to say— that I was the trophy she'd always longed for? No, the best I could hope for was that she'd slept with me out of pity. Things being as they were, I could have lived with that. I wasn't sure what was worse, the truth or my ill-advised conjecture from the outset? Outside of the gruesome truth, what bothered me most was why I even felt the need to know? *Why did it matter?*

I hated not being able to recall anything about that night— other than her pretty face and how good she smelled. I felt sick to my stomach. Even more so than before. Though I'd hoped the answer might bring me some measure of closure, it'd done the exact opposite for being left with far harder questions now. Did she lay there quaking in fear while I ravaged her like a heartless beast? *Had I really fallen that low?* The Red Rage was one thing but plundering innocent maidens? What excuse had I for that?

And that wasn't even the worst part. The worst part, by far, was that she no longer seemed angry. I was just another thug— some dumb brute that meant absolutely nothing to her. I wasn't merely a reminder of yet another bad day. I was the worst night of her entire life. I was something she'd forced herself to stomach— an instinctive survival response to a grave predicament she'd found herself in.

It was over. It was done. She'd found a way to live with it. I could see it, plain as day, on her face. It wasn't a moment she ever wished to relive. She needed no reminder. It was a scar she'd nourish, and watch grow for the remainder of her days. Unless of course the war took him— or the desert. Which it probably would. She had no need of me. She had no expectations— other than for me to see the pair of them safely across these desolate lands. Yeah, that same desert I'd so recklessly led them into. Once that was accomplished, *if we survived rather*; she wouldn't care whether I lived or died. Nor should she. The traitorous bag still hung at my side. I'd already been paid in full; earned every tragic gasp without ever having taken the slightest notice. The truth of it was, I'd saved her from the devil's clutches simply by being myself. I didn't do anything special. I didn't change anything. All I had to do was be me— *the Monster I'd become.*

I was nobody's hero. I wasn't even a man. I was a beast— a brazen selfish beast at that. Never in my life had I felt so deeply ashamed. I avoided her eyes by scratching the back of my head while staring at my feet. How long could I continue the ruse, I wondered? But what was there to say? It was too late for apologies. Notwithstanding, there were no suitable words. There was no justification for my part. I was the mindless ogre favored over a pair of malicious imps. All that remained were the consequences. One of which began to cry.

"Take him," she said blearily.

Take him? Take who I thought, looking quickly toward the door. The last time I heard those words it was following a nod from the Major toward a napping Kedera guard the neck of which I promptly snapped. Oh, she meant… *it.* That being the original sin, the product of our initial acquaintance.

"I'm exhausted; I must sleep."

She held the baby out for me and, being the *lesser of the two evils* confronting me, I took him without hesitation. Lesser of two evils? Hardly. He was the outcome of my unprovoked corruption. He was her escape— her sole refuge from *that day* forth. Petra lay down and, before I would have thought it possible, she'd fallen fast asleep. I'd never held an infant before. He was a strange little thing, like a miniature person with an oversized head.

It was clear he took after his mother. He didn't have any of my scars; not one. He had dark hair, and straight like Petra's. Not curly at all. My own was curly. I gave him a little shake and the wee pup stopped crying. A couple more shakes had him squealing like a piglet. I kept up my shaking as it was better than the alternative. After a short while we both got bored of it and, curling up in one of my arms, he too fell quickly asleep— nearly as fast as Petra had.

He slept for quite a while; and then I smelled something as terrifying as it was foul. After which the pint-sized sapling awoke boasting an evil grin if ever there was. It was so horrid I reverted to holding him at arm's length again. *It* being the smell for his look of utter triumph quickly faded. In fact, he looked about to cry again. I was too scared to shake him lest some uncouth bits wriggle free from his hind cloth. I considered waking Petra; but then decided better of it. Which isn't to say the idea of holding him over her face didn't cross my mind. Once again, I'd been forced to choose between the lesser of two evils. *Just remember, I chose you*, I whispered. And, though I hoped for some form of appreciation in response, none was given as far as I was able to discern.

It, that which he conjured from his loins with needless resolve, was a lot messier and harder to clean up than I reckoned. I figured it'd be a small stain or at least somewhat firm. *But it wasn't*. It wasn't just smeared to his buttocks; it was performing a full retreat down his chubby hind legs. While recognizing he had but two of them, given the long trailing smudges, they did seem more akin to hind legs at that juncture in time. I'm not questioning his upbringing mind you but, let me tell you, the little monster showed little gratitude. In fact, before I'd finished wiping him, he bent his legs like a plucked chicken, took aim, and tried to piss on me. *A wee rooster* for certain, I clucked with pride as I directed the tiny steaming stream outdoors.

It was then I noticed I'd gotten some of his spoils on one of my hands. *He had rather*. I was innocent for once. Gagging aloud, whilst balancing him on a lone knee, I finally managed to get the nasty mess fully sorted. Placing his wee palm upon his chest, I made him vow never to mention the incident between us again. Though I had to speak for him of course, he did appear to nod so I found little alternative other than to award him the benefit of the doubt. Having completed the gruesome task, I spat on my hands to better cleanse them. At the risk of sounding overly attentive, I sacrificed a fair section of my head scarf swaddling him. Though I did briefly consider leaving him bare, that seemed akin to playing with a loaded crossbow. Given his stubborn nature and utter lack of remorse, it was only a matter of time before his wanton ways erupted again.

With the worst of it behind us, though easier said than done, the little peacock was all smiles again now. He seemed rather proud of himself. I wasn't sure I liked him anymore, mincing few words in telling him so. *Whispered rather*. Somehow, he found that amusing too. I felt certain the little man was toying with me. Which only furthered my annoyance. In that regard, he was just like his mother. I only wished Petra would wake so she could take him from me. But I was too unsettled to rouse her. I wasn't ready to look her in the eyes just yet. The way I was feeling I might never be able to look her in the eyes again.

I don't know why I cared. *But I did*. It was uncanny. The only emotion I recalled having before was anger– that being the Red Rage. Outside of that, I didn't feel much of anything. I wasn't ever happy or sad, just somewhere in the midst. I did feel hungry a lot. Not sure if that counts but it should. It's a feeling gnawing within you if ever there was.

Then it struck me. The answer was staring me right in the eyes– *bright blue eyes*. Which caused me to ponder the color of my own. I had no idea. It'd never come up before. Perching him on a knee again, I unsheathed my dagger, trying to discern my reflection on the blade's face. If anything, they seemed more grey than blue. Then again, the blade was tarnished. Inexplicably, I felt disappointed. I'm guessing the little fellow was too because he quickly took to crying. It was then that Petra chose to wake up. Now, there's timing.

"What are you doing with that knife you bloody baboon?!" She hollered crossly.

"Just giving his wee whiskers a trim." I said, secretly amazed I'd come up with such a fitting response on short notice.

"Are you entirely thick? Give him to me at once you dimwit! He's no doubt famished."

"Never mentioned it to me," I grumbled, handing her the infant. "If you feed him, he'll just mess himself again."

"Oh-oh-oh," She laughed. "Is that what I'm smelling? I thought it was you– farting again. Go bury those soiled rags outside; they're twisting my innards about." She looked Renan over thoroughly before tucking his rotund head within her shawl.

"Humph. I can hardly believe you mopped him up. You– the Golan Butcher. Rrr-red Rrr-radesh cleaned his poopy mess? In all my days never would I have imagined such a thing. And you did a fair job swaddling him," she nodded with approval.

A compliment? *What madness was this?* Notwithstanding, had I detected a hint of a smile? From *Her Royal Highness* no less! But a bit earlier, I'd been condemned as the vile creature that had stolen her innocence. It's plainly evident that I shall never understand this nonsensical world. Having enjoyed a chuckle at my expense, Petra was positively beaming now. Except there was more to it. There was a strange twinkle in her eye that made me feel uneasy. Undoubtedly the same look a cat has upon seeing a blind mouse stumbling its way. Though difficult, I quashed the urge to return her smile. To be certain, I was more adept at blathering profanities than subtleties of joy. I suppose what I really wanted was to put an end to it. Confess my guilt. Tell her just how sorry and ashamed I felt. And then what? Plead on bended knee to the heavens for forgiveness?

Fair maiden, having discovered that it was I who plundered your virginity; I beg thee pardon.

That wasn't about to happen. It wasn't that I wasn't worthy of absolution but more so the fact I couldn't even recollect the incident in question. No, there'd be no smile or apology forthcoming from my lips. I'd wronged her. Though wholeheartedly remorseful, I wasn't about to tell her that. What for? She'd proved herself no less repentant than she was unabashed on many an occasion thus far. It wasn't the first time she'd taken to spewing insults to my face. With no fear of consequence, I might add. Though far from smug, I did have a bit more pride than that. As much as I loathed admitting it, in more ways than one, I was my father's son. Through no fault of my own, it was his blood that coursed through my veins after all. That was what spun through my mind at the time. Until my mouth opened, that is. It was then I discovered I'd been lying to myself– again. *And why not?* Everyone else did.

"I'm sorry," I blurted. Recognize, I was speaking so quickly I could barely believe what I was hearing. I'd clearly gone insane from the heat and over-exertion, and it spewed from me no less than the little man's earlier equally sordid affair. The difference being, I was able to clean that mess up after which we'd agreed to speak no more of it. Whereas no doubt anything I might say from this moment onward would only add to our calamity. Even so, out from me and down my hind legs it continued to pour.

"Though hardly deserving of forgiveness, I am remorseful. I regret not being able to remember. It pains me greatly. Believe me when I say, there's a part or two I wouldn't be opposed to recalling."

I made sure to look at her legs to ensure she knew it was a tribute– which she immediately crossed and covered for the record. Fair is fair; she'd recognized my swaddling skills after all. Albeit baby dung and a woman's legs were two different things though she insisted on swaddling them all the same. Thus, I expect the flattering remark was wasted on her.

"I make no excuses. I'm sorry for being the shameless creature that I am."

While I poured out my soul, Petra's eyes remained fixed on her nursing baby. Her own face was expressionless. It was fine by me. Had we made eye contact my confession would have ended abruptly.

"I wish I was a better man. But I'm not." I blathered. "I am as cruel as I am merciless; as ignorant as willful. I do not deserve your pity any more than your company." I bemoaned.

Still, she did not look at me— gratuitously, so I told myself. I was not good at this apologizing thing. Then again, I'd never done it before. It wasn't that I didn't have cause for it because, undoubtedly, I did. There's just no point in apologizing to the dead— cause they're dead. Not that I bemoaned killing any of the Kedera dogs. It's just that occasionally there was one or two of our own lying about which I couldn't rule out having had something to do with. That said, shrugging is a whole lot easier than carrying around a wagon full of guilt that you can't say for certain belongs to you. Which is to say, I began to have second thoughts— while unsure how the first thoughts had found their way out of my head. Honestly, I wasn't convinced I'd even fully thought about them yet. Then again, perhaps my words weren't sticking because I wasn't pouring them on thick enough.

"Petra," I said solemnly. "If there was any way by which I might take back all that happened *that night*; believe me, I would. Even the naked bits being that I can't recall them anyway." I clarified prior to wondering if I might have wandered slightly astray of my original intentions.

"But, more especially, the part where I'd made you feel uncomfortable." I finished unable to think of a better word. Or, more truthfully, not wanting to employ one more pertinent to the crime. *Unjustly breached* had come to mind though it seemed overly frank to me— akin to using a mace to hammer a nail. Though it might suffice, it put one's fingers at risk without due cause.

At last, she looked up. She stared at me for a time and to my amazement I did not look away. For as much as I wanted to, I found that I could not turn my gaze elsewhere. And neither could I distinguish the look in her eyes. It was neither pity nor anger. If anything, I suppose she just looked sad— and sweaty— and tired— and rather dirty to be completely truthful. Finally, she spoke, and her words pounded through me like a spike. As much as I'd tried to avoid it, I'd chosen the mace after all.

"I would not change a thing," she said quietly.

What game is afoot now, I wondered. It was hardly the expected reaction. Though I waited a fair measure of time, it seemed apparent that Petra felt no need to elaborate, which only added to my prolonged feelings of confusion.

"I don't understand," I blurted. "I wronged you. What do you mean you wouldn't change a thing?"

"Please, just shush," she replied curtly. "*You* said never to speak of it. *You* said it never happened. So, let it go."

"I wish I could; but I can't," I confessed. "I feel all torn up inside with guilt. You're supposed to say, *and rightfully so*. You're supposed to say, *you hate me*."

"You are thick, Radesh. As usual, the answer is right in front of you, but you refuse to see it for your own selfish presumptions. Everything is not always about you."

"Please!" I begged. "Help me understand and I'll gladly let it go."

Shaking her head with a heavy sigh, she pulled the baby's head out of her shawl and held the infant up in front of me. She kissed it on the forehead before returning her gaze to me.

Finally, I understood. Though I did not feel the least bit appeased. I just felt empty— emptier rather. As sad as she'd looked but a moment before. Twas a feeling I despised. Sadness was for the weak.

"I am thick," I sighed. "I've always been thick."

"No. You're just another victim blinded by war. Our world, *this world*, will swallow you, Radesh— if you let it. It will swallow the lot of us if things don't change. We can't see past our swords, flags, and creeds. Hatred breeds hatred. If only we could curtail our agendas for a short time, we'd discover the world to be a simpler place. It's us— *we* complicate everything. We declare the world black and white when it plainly isn't. The world is a living canvas. All we need do is look beyond ourselves to appreciate its beauty."

"The Kedera are the cause of all strife." I reminded her. "Even had they not murdered The One Rah, Harbinger would never have remained united. The Kedera are self-righteous, conspirators at heart. You can never trust any of them. They're all the same— liars, thieves, murderers."

"No. You are wrong. You are simply repeating all that you've been taught. What if you'd been born on the opposing side of Haeryn's Wall? Who would you fight for then? And more importantly, what makes you think you'd be any different?"

"Different in what way?"

"Different as in following a diverse path."

"Diverse?"

"Yes, diverse as in diversity pertaining to our differences and, know it for certain, had you been born in the far north you'd be fighting for them instead of Golan."

"Ant grub! Besides, Haeryn's Wall didn't exist back then. It was built when I was but a little less wobbly than Renan."

An awkward silence ensued. I'd purposely avoided saying his name until that moment. Had we somehow bonded— over *poop?* As much as it'd caused me to shiver; it was still a moment of shared intimacy, I supposed. When first recruited, I walked the wall— defecated off the top edge of it a time or two if you must know. But we don't talk about that. The first part to be clear; the part about ever having been posted there. It was a different time. There were so many sayings and songs— long forgotten now. It was claimed the wall had but one side back then. Now it has two— our side and theirs. It was said to be invincible in the earliest days of the First Great War. Now, as I said, we don't talk about it. Not ever.

"It changes nothing, Radesh. We are the same and equally to blame. We are peasants, for the most part, caught up in someone else's long-time feud. Regardless of where we were born, we want the same things. We want secure shelters. We want protection. We want to provide for our families. Forget the war, forget the assassination of the One Rah; and what have the Kedera ever really done to you— that being, *you* personally?"

"Forget the war! Forget the One Rah?" I fumed. "What is the meaning of anything if we forget all that forged us? What was the point of so many deaths? Are you suggesting, they died needlessly without reason or purpose?"

"No. They didn't die needlessly. Unless we fail to realize the error of our ways. Every one of them died, on both sides, praying their children wouldn't repeat the same mistakes— have the same atrocities thrust down upon them. While the wall steadily erodes, graveyards grow thick on either side of it. Though their buried bones may perish, their dreams live on in their children— each mound a grim reminder that there is a better way. Don't you see? They are all martyrs for a brighter day to come. If only there was someone of worth to follow— things might one day change. Then again, I am but a witless wench."

"The Kedera have naught but martyrdom to look forward to," I grumbled. "Nothing will change until they're annihilated."

"Then we agree to be at odds," replied Petra softly, "which, unlike all you've been taught, is not cause for war. Our eyes are blinded by supposition. We see only what we wish instead of what we need. Haeryn help us should we ever stop long enough to blink. Look outside right now, Radesh, and tell me what you see?"

"Dusk." I sighed.

"And with it the prospect of a brighter tomorrow." Petra contended naïvely.

A red and gold horizon spat oblong flames at the sinking sun while we sat watching it in silence. Though I recognized she might very well be right, it was all too obvious that the sun sided with me. It looked positively molten with anger. You couldn't fault it. She could be remarkably annoying at times.

I enjoyed watching the sun disappear. Though, it must be said, this one caused my skin to burn— quite literally. *A brighter tomorrow?* Brighter forearms perhaps, if not blistered. Of course, it would be bright! We were in a bloody desert after all. And hopefully somewhere near its fiery core— if we were to survive and all that. *What if I was born on the other side of the wall?* Haeryn help us. What if I had three horns and a pig tail? What if the sun ran away with the moon? And to be clear, I did not call her a witless wench. *She* did that— unto herself no less. I shook my head to clear such foolish thoughts.

"It is time," I said, looking at the overcast sky.

"The gods are scheming. It's going to be a dark night. We must pack our belongings and see you on your way. Have no fear, I will catch up with you before the morrow threatens any measure of *brightness*." See, it was possible. I could be clever on occasion.

"I suspect you will— providing you're *still alive*. But—"

There it was. I'd been waiting for that.

"I for one do not leave things to chance. Thus, I've formulated a plan of my own," stated Petra defiantly.

Of course, she had.

"I will depart alone, *as you insist*, on one condition."

Putting my hands on my brow, I rubbed my head feverishly before looking up at her. *Must everything forever be a contest?*

"This isn't a debate." I acknowledged. "You are in my charge. You must follow my orders as though I were your husband! Oh, and did I mention you talk too much? Because you talk too much."

"You talk as much as me!"

"Yes, but *before you* I never said naught."

"Just for the record, *never said naught* entails that you spoke all the time— as in talking without ever stopping." Tapping her fingers to her thumb repeatedly with her free hand, she stuck out her tongue.

Why must she be so infuriating? Being that I may as well have been speaking to the wind, I broke wind to better convey my burgeoning discontent. As ill-advised as it was malodorous; I discerned no trickles of moisture gratefully.

"Pass me your head scarf," she said, ignoring my clever retort.

"My head scarf? That's it?" On the verge of wrath, I took it off and threw it at her.

"Now, may we please get on with it?" I begged her. Regardless of whatever brighter morrows we were on the cusp of, I was not beyond begging by this point.

"Now, all we need do is fill it with scorpions– only after which, Renan and I shall depart."

"Scorpions! Are you completely mad?" I asked, feeling increasingly exasperated. Apparently, the pair of us had lost our wits. Though her, far more than me.

"Yes, scorpions. You did say there were scorpions here. We will wrap them up in your head scarf; tie it safely in a knot; and then Renan and I shall be on our merry way."

La de da; la de da, she might have added, for all the sense it made.

"I said, there *might* be scorpions and, *if there was*, to use extreme caution."

"That is not what you declared at all," Petra corrected. "You said, they thrived in this particular kind of vegetation and that you wouldn't be surprised to find some under our tent seeking moisture."

"Perhaps I did say something to that effect. What of it? I'd sooner stab myself with, with, with– a fork– than try to trap one! Besides, what probable reason could you possibly have for bringing them with you? You do realize they are apt to sting when threatened? The fat-tailed ones are particularly lethal."

"Then those are the ones we want. The fat-tailed ones! The more lethal, the better." She replied, looking bizarrely enthused.

"But why Petra? Why?" I pleaded. "Was the sun pounding upon your pretty head whilst you slept? This is absurd."

"For protection, of course! I shan't leave myself completely defenseless! What will happen to us if the assassin slays you? I'll tell you what– he'll murder us too! No, you get me those scorpions– or I'm not leaving! It's *your* choice. Take your time. Oh, and feel free to stab yourself for all I care. I expect a wounded body will only aid in attracting them."

"Fine! Makes perfect sense the more you think about it. I'll risk life and limb; bundle up some big fat scorpions for you; then watch you traipse off with them in one hand and your baby in the other– *cause that's not bloody crazy!* Unless, of course it is. Cause it is."

Snatching my head scarf from her outstretched hands, I stormed out of the tent, muttering obscenities all the while. But that wasn't the worst part; nor was it upon finding several specimens under the tent– notwithstanding a fat-tailed one! No, the worst part by far, as I suspected, was catching them. I was still shivering, in fact, long after she'd left. Thank Haeryn I had *that fork*, or I'd likely never have caught any of the horrid creatures. Having tied the fork to the tent pole, I expect it preserved my sanity.

Good riddance! I thought watching them waddle away. I was glad to be purged of her antics. She was crazed. The desert sun had clearly made her mad. There was a reason I avoided the more admirable harlots whilst on leave. Besides having to pay more for equivalent services, they always wanted some sort of courtesy extended afterward as if to imply the coin had somehow been insufficient.

I was right about one thing. The encroaching darkness swept away her footprints swiftly. The nighttime air was frightfully chill. Bundling the pyrament about me, I tried to retain some measure of warmth. In the off chance you were wondering, I only referred to it as the *pyro-vent* during my daytime prison term.

Amongst the darkest shadows, stiller than buried treasure, I sat in the warm sand awaiting my foe at the dune's lowest extremity, but a short distance away from my *line in the sand*. The wind had left our tracks untouched for the most part save for the crests where they'd vanished long ago. My advancing rival would receive little warning. I was fully prepared to live with that– providing he didn't. *Live*, that is.

Huddled with evil intent, I sat re-inventing my murderous plot recurrently in my head. I'd killed him at least a half-dozen times already. Though I'd killed so very many times before, oddly, this felt different. Case in point being, I'd almost always been under the influence of the Red Rage previously. This time, I was determined to keep it restrained. Which is why I'd been so adamant about Petra having to leave in the off chance I failed to subdue my primal state. Which was quite likely, being that I'd only managed to do so once before. Notwithstanding, the promise I'd made to the Major. At least I think I had. Being that it was quite some time ago, I couldn't precisely recall all that might or might not have been said. Unfortunately for me, I did recall the part about seeing her safely to Harkenspear– by which I expected he meant *alive*.

I thought about what Petra had said about the world being a living canvas. She was right about that for all that might come to pass did seem not unlike a blank page in an unwritten book. A feeling that only intensified each time I slew the assassin in my mind's eye. Though living, my adversary would soon stain my canvas of sand. Not sure if that's what she'd intended but such was life. The world as I knew it.

That led me to ponder her *being born on the other side of the wall* remark. Strange, I knew nothing about the assassin. I didn't know whether he had a wife; or whether he might have had children. He was a faceless character with no name− that I would soon kill. Every word longing to be written upon the blank page before me was devoid of description. The more I thought about it, the more it changed nothing. He had to die; and the less I knew about him the better. Being just another scorpion to me, the venomous fool was about to die. I shivered, though not from the cold.

I should never have compared him to a scorpion. I could still picture the fat-tailed one. It was almost as though I was still holding it. There's a trick to that. You need to grab them by their toxic tails; *fork them* should you find yourselves so blessed. It's best to sneak up on them from behind then stab their tail end. Which makes them rather angry. That way their mouths and pinchers can't clamp down on you; at which point their tail would sting you for certain. If I never saw another one, it would be too soon. After which, I'd squash it flat like a bug. Ever try to squash anything on a dune? I thought not. Believe me when I say, it doesn't work well.

And there he was! An elongated shadow sliding sprightly down the dune with dagger in hand. *What did I say?* The dagger appeared to be all he had with him which did not sit well with me. I loathed him at once if for no other reason than how gracefully he navigated the dune. He had no pack nor sled to pull. I arose ever so slowly. Inhaling deeply, I bit my lower lip so hard I tasted blood. He was as vague as I'd imagined him which gave me pause for being uncertain if I might not still be dreaming. But this was no fantasy. He was not fictional for the taste of blood lay heavy upon my tongue. I could smell *his*! The canvas awaited him. My dagger was the pen; his blood, the ink− and an abrupt ending was about to be written.

Unfortunately, it appeared he wished to have a say in that matter as well. Having seen me, he dropped to his haunches instinctively. For all my scheming, at no time had I envisioned that outcome. All those feelings within me I'd kept bottled for so long ignited. There was little point in hiding now. The moment had arrived. It was time he looked *Death* straight in the face. It was time for him to accept his fate. Thus, unsheathing my dagger, I strode purposely toward him.

As I drew close, he hunched even lower. No doubt he planned

to lunge at me. It mattered not. I was ready. But I was wrong for, as much as I anticipated it, he didn't move at all. At least not yet. Hastening my advance; my plan was to either step aside or use his own momentum against him. I was but a body length away now and still he didn't move. Unexpectedly, he opened his palm and let his dagger fall free. As it glimmered upon the sand, his other arm swung out and my eyes instantly stung. The pain was intense. Both of my eyes were riddled with sand. I couldn't see at all.

Retreating into a backward roll, I lashed out violently at imaginary shadows. Though I knew he held no bow, it took all my control not to cower and cover my head for which I held Petra to blame. *And what if he has a bow? He will pound arrow after arrow into that dim-witted skull of yours. Blah blah blah.*

Rolling further away in desperation, I tried to clear my eyes with my unarmed hand. I didn't dare let go of my dagger. Let me tell you, sand has a taste unlike no other– bland, yet terrible. Not as bad as decaying bone though still somehow death-like. *Don't ask.* It is the taste of infertility; horribly crunchy while offering but the merest hint of salt. Its grit ratcheted my entire throat causing me to hack and cough repeatedly. *Did I mention how much I loathe sand? I think so.*

My efforts to clear the sand from my eyes, nose, and throat did little good. Being the gritted teeth of desire, sand clings to whatever it encounters. Surviving utterly deprived, it yearns to be a part of anything within reach. Ground from the eternal bones of forgotten mountains, it craves all forms of flesh without mercy. It took all my resolve to quash the Rage surging within my hateful core. My world had turned fuzzy, watery looking and obscure. My eyes wept uncontrollably as I did my utmost to force them open. Nevertheless, I did not relent. I was determined not to let the monster roam free. Swiping madly with my dagger, I heard laughter in return.

"I was sent to kill the girl and her baby. *You* are but a boon I'll collect at my leisure. I know they can't be far."

As his blurry shadow danced nimbly up the leeward hill, my black heart froze. Petra had a decent head start but his undignified tactic had caught me wholly by surprise. Cursing my carelessness aloud, I stumbled blindly up the hill in chase. While sputtering grainy smudges from the corners of my sand-caked mouth, I kept trying to clear my seeping eyes by dragging them across the shoulders of my sweat-soaked djellaba.

As the rogue disappeared over the crest of the dune, I staggered onward in fretful haste, tripping constantly until I finally reached the top. No sooner had my head prevailed above the dune when his boot caught me square in the temple. Having collapsed, he kicked me several more times in the face until I lay still. Dizziness took hold and, though I could no longer tell whether my eyes might be open or closed, my surroundings grew increasingly darker.

No! I mustn't! I can't! Though I'd fought so hard to curtail it, only the Rage could save me now. *Swallow me whole! Unleash the beast!*

But it was too late. Perhaps I was too far gone. Or perhaps it was simply that the beast felt unduly scorned. Whatever the reason, the monster refused to answer. For in my time of need, it chose to abandon me. Though I felt my world slipping away, it was solely my pigheadedness that refused to let it consume what precious few remnants remained of me. Dragging me backwards by one leg, he kicked heaps of sand into my face while laughing riotously at my misfortune. Fortunately, having anticipated as much, I'd closed my eyes tight; all the while tormented for knowing they might never open again. Venturing a peek, an opaque face bent low. His breath was vulgar, unbearable in truth, were it not for the other more pressing matters at hand.

"Watch," he whispered. "Watch them die. After which, I shall disembowel you— though ever so slowly."

It was only then, to my horror, that I discerned Petra's form ahead of us. *Why is she still here? Why had she not left?* And that was it. I felt the flame within me dwindling upon the verge of extinction. I was but an ember in a dying fire. Adding to my horror, I could see one thing very clearly now. I'd failed her. She sat crossed legged before us in the sand with her baby cradled in her arms.

She hadn't gone anywhere. *She'd given up entirely!* It was my fault. I was to blame. Whatever inkling of hope I had left was trampled. The assassin sauntered toward her with his dagger drawn. Neither did she rise, nor attempt to flee. She made no movement of any kind. She was resolved to her fate. Though I wanted to shout, I couldn't make a sound. It was anguish— akin to one of my horrifying dreams; save for it being anything but. Exhaling with despair, I had to force myself not to look away.

It was then that the most puzzling things occurred. The assassin inexplicably disappeared. I thought I was seeing things— but, having vanished, he was nowhere to be found. Laying her infant aside, Petra calmly arose as the assassin's head bobbed free of the sand in front of her. She waved my headscarf over him. His head quickly vanished again. I heard a horrendous scream, followed by more. Petra stood looking down where his head had appeared but a moment before. I could hear him hollering profanities at her. I saw his arms briefly thrashing about. Sliding across the sand on my belly, I dragged myself toward him with my hands. He'd fallen into a deep pit. Though he clawed at the sand feverishly, it only served to widen the hole. His legs kept buckling beneath him. He could no longer support himself. Lower and lower he sank. His obscenities grew increasingly slurred until they were but pure gibberish. His body became rather rigid and though not quite dead yet, I did recognize the words *venom* and *bitch*.

"I'm sorry," shouted Petra. Losing her composure, she soon started crying.

I wasn't sure if she was talking to me or the assassin initially— both of us perhaps. I kept rubbing my eyes— and not because of the sand for once. After what seemed an eternity, my wits finally returned, and I forced myself upright. My own legs were wobbly for I was scuttling through the sand like a three-legged camel. Bending down, I tugged the assassin's head backward by his hair and spat in his face. The veins in his neck were dark blue. His eyes still held a bit of life though his limbs had ceased functioning.

"Not this time, dog!" I scoffed. "You've been bested by a girl."

"Kill m-m-me," he pleaded in a hoarse whisper, discharging a large yellow drizzle of thick saliva. Where was all that bravado now, I wondered? One would think in your final moments you'd want to— well, I don't know but— do better. Certainly not spew slime from your cakehole like a squashed slug. Albeit you're dying but you can still show a wee bit of pride. I mean it's not like your guts are split open with your innards scattered all over the sand. The worst of it being, I still had need of him.

"Tell me where it is," I demanded. "Where is the well?" Being that he carried no water slings he had to know where it was. He must! There was no other explanation possible. It had to be close— a half-day at best.

"Tell me where the well is, and I'll grant you a quick end." I reiterated.

"The w-well," he grinned cruelly. He was toying with me. He wanted me to know he knew exactly where it was. Twisting his head back, I put my dagger to his throat.

"Yes, the well in the midst of the Kestrel." Though I strongly considered trimming an ear from him in the end I declined to do so.

"Hell's Well, they c-call it," he gurgled.

"Yes. Where it is? Tell me and I will end your suffering. On my living soul, I swear it." His eyes grew increasingly cloudy. I shook him hard, very nearly slipping into the pit myself. That would have been calamitous. He'd already outwitted once. I wanted to kill him before the poison robbed him of his wits. I wanted to watch the light within him grow dim by my doing. He owed me that much and more.

"F-fool," he sneered. "You can't miss it. W-w-watch out for the c-cat." Sheathing my dagger, I reached down with both hands and– *crack*! I snapped his neck. As his body slid into the pit, I turned quickly to Petra.

"What did I say? I told you I'd kill him," I winked. Exhausted, I fell backwards into a soft mound of sand. I was utterly spent. My head was ringing like a brass bell and my eyes felt as though they were aflame. It wasn't the wild crickets for once though. No doubt, they would come in full force later.

Petra was hugging her baby, rocking back and forth as she had after impaling the fat salesman– *mercenary rather*. I could not console her. I had nothing left. Rolling onto my side, my thoughts were completely garbled. Nothing made sense. Yet again, my entire world was completely mad.

Recovering from her stupor, Petra started spewing words so rapidly I could barely discern a word. Then it struck me. She was apologizing *to me*. After which she began asking if I was hurt. Hurt? My head was pounding like a bloody drum. Not to mention a worm had less sand up its nose. I was groggy. I was angry. I was tired– and the Red Rage had left me to the dogs– *dog rather*– as in singular, though no less conniving. It quickly became evident that the longer I remained silent the more perturbed *she* became. Deciding the apprehension might do her some good, I chose to remain mute. No one had ever accused me of being kind-hearted. Why start now?

Was I hurt? Yes– though mostly my pride. Though not prone to self-import, I found humiliation wasn't something easily swallowed. My dignity had been completely trampled– *by her*. She never listened– *not ever*. Worse, the truth glared back at me with lifeless eyes from the bottom of the pit. There was no refuting it. I owed her my life. *She'd* miraculously saved us all.

But I wasn't about to tell her that. Given a choice, which it appeared I may have, I was not opposed to her boasting feelings of regret. Besides, I favored feelings of vindication over forgiveness which, as I'd proved earlier, was no attribute of mine. It did seem fair. Though her act of contrition was by my own admission unwarranted, it remained *the lesser of the two evils* confronting me. Tit for tat.

"I know I should have listened. I never meant for you to get hurt! It wasn't part of my plan. But I knew you'd never go along with it. You would have dubbed it madness!" She blathered erratically. I closed my eyes, realizing it might further inspire her flourishing need for forgiveness. She was talking so fast my aching head could barely keep pace.

"I had to do something. I couldn't just leave! So, I dug a pit– just beyond the dune's crest where you couldn't see. I wanted to tell you so very badly, but I just couldn't risk it. I shook the scorpions into the pit; except for the fat one. Covering the pit with my shawl, I sprinkled sand delicately atop it. And then I sat down and waited. I was scared to death. I very nearly ran when he started kicking you."

She was beginning to irritate me. She was forgetting her place again. I did not want to relive getting kicked. That wasn't what I wanted to hear. I wanted her to apologize. I liked that part. The fact her plan had been so clever did not help matters. Yet another thing I'd never admit to.

"I'm not as strong and brave as you. I was so cold– and scared."

I believe they called it *Petrafied.* I mused silently. Ah, so I hadn't completely lost my wits. That was good news. I decided to save that one for later. Undoubtedly, it would come in handy. She wasn't done. Far from it. Hopefully, she'd pick up where she left off. Particularly, the part about me being brave and strong while being the only thing saving her from certain death.

"But, had I not departed, I would have been far more scared– not knowing what may have happened nor who might be chasing us! What if he'd killed you? I'd never survive without you, Radesh."

There it was. She needed me. In fact, it resonated so well that I decided to open my eyes. She was staring straight at me– and rather passionately, I might add.

"I can't believe it worked!" She smiled, shaking her long braids. "I shook the fat-tailed one straight into his face. It stung his neck. You can see the red welt. My hands are still shaking."

She was biting her lip hard. She desperately wanted me to speak. She was right about one thing. She'd never survive without me. That much I knew for certain– and that BroZil assassins carried daggers not bows– notwithstanding a lot of other things that I would have made mention of were it not for my pounding head. It was time to take charge– assume full command again if you will. Not that I hadn't been from the get-go. It is just that I, myself, prefer training and prudent planning over blind luck.

"No, you didn't listen but, when do you? It doesn't matter. It's over now," I added quietly.

"Are you hurt?" She seemed genuinely worried. "Did he injure you?"

"No!" I said curtly. "Just a bit of sand is all."

"I saw him kick you— more than once. Your cheek is quite swollen."

"Kick me? No. I got sand in my eyes. Twas the wind. I was just about to hobble him. But I couldn't see properly and slipped. You'd think sand would be softer. It isn't." I grumbled.

"Hobble him? Is that what you were doing with your head?"

"A lesser-known skill, admittedly." I assured her, nodding. "You should have left." I stated clearly. If only Renan could speak. No doubt he would have been similarly disappointed with her unadvised meddling. I did have the situation well in hand after all. Or, I would have soon enough. Who throws sand anyway? There's no honor in that. Had he not been burned at the stake, Surat Muneakisa would be rolling in his grave. I was sure of that much.

"Sorry," she whispered, "I was too scared to go alone. I was terrified— and what if you'd been badly injured?" *Wonderful!* She was crying now.

"I was pretending." I felt forced to clarify. "I needed to distract him, so he wouldn't notice your trap." I further embellished. "It seemed so obvious to me that I could ill-afford panicking him lest he catch wind of the ambush himself. Given the circumstances, I saw little alternative other than to feign injury to ensure he'd take the bait. You put me in a tight spot, Petra. It's not easy for a soldier of my stature to feign any form of vulnerability. You should have trusted me."

Okay, so I was lying but what was I to do? Besides, the more I thought about it the more I realized she was just as much to blame— if not more. Point being, had she not advised me about that *lesser of two evils thing* I wouldn't have had a leg to stand on. In which case, I suppose I would have thanked her and been done with it— eventually— once I'd recovered my pride— from beneath the assassin's body— where undoubtedly it had fallen.

"I said I was sorry." She blathered, making me feel even worse than I had a moment ago.

"Still, no harm done, I suppose. It ended well in the end." I sighed, widening my eyes which caused them to sting even more.

"I couldn't have done it without you!" She sniffed.

At last. Now, she was getting it. Now, we were getting somewhere. *I couldn't have done it without you!* I could live with that. That's all she needed to say in the first place. That's all she *ever* needed to say.

"I needed those scorpions." She added pointlessly. "I could never have caught them myself." Shrugging helplessly, I gave up. *Those scorpions—* as in *her* sunlit idea.

"You did well," I conceded and then quickly changed the subject. "But there is a problem I neglected to mention. I don't know precisely where the well is." I saw little point in dwelling on her lone achievement thus far and, seeing as we were being honest with one another for once, it felt like the right time to confide in her.

"You don't know where it is?"

"No, but the assassin confided that we can't miss it, so I expect we are on the proper course."

"Yes. That's good news, right? I did hear him say that as well."

"Then again, he was dying so he might very well have lied."

"He was trying to kill us." She sniffed worriedly. "That is until—"

"Unless it's dried up, I suppose."

"Dried up? What do you mean dried up?" She implored in vain. Though she might think it to be true, I wasn't talking to her. I was just thinking out loud.

"But that doesn't make sense either. He didn't have a water sling. Therefore, I see only two possibilities. He either has water stashed nearby; or he planned to visit the well."

"Perhaps, he planned to take our water after killing us." I hadn't thought of that. It seemed a definite possibility… momentarily.

"No, that is absurd. He would never chance it. Our slings might be empty for all he knew— which they very nearly are." I grimaced. Truth be told, had she not just saved our skins, I likely would have reacted differently. But I wasn't telling her that. We'd only just begun to make some small measure of progress after all.

"We must be close," I smiled, not wanting to alarm her further. "But we must be careful. I fear there's something afoot. Something we're not privy too."

"But what choice do we have?"

"None."

"But you said you knew where the well was." She doubled

down.

"Not exactly. It's a bit like catching scorpions." I winked.

"How so?" She asked.

"I feared you would never have gone along with my plan. You would have called it *madness*."

"Where have I heard that before?" She smirked.

"Consider us even." I replied, scrunching my face the same way she had. She stared at me blankly— then her face erupted into a broad grin.

"Even it is." She beamed. "Every step taken is madness. We will head for the well, wherever that may be, and do what we must when we get there. Shall we proceed or do you need more time to recover?" She did appear concerned.

"I'm not recovering. I told you— I was pretending."

"Well, I must say you did an admirable job of it. You certainly had me fooled— not to mention the assassin along with that cheekbone of yours. It looks about to burst through the skin. Notwithstanding your eyes are as red as an evening sun."

My mother had warned me about people like her. Folks who wanted nothing other than to *get your goat* even if you didn't own one. I didn't understand back then— largely because we had plenty of goats and nary a one that I would have missed had it vanished mysteriously. Which is the long way of saying, she could walk the rest of the way. Haeryn knows she refused when I told to do so earlier. I wasn't about to drag her wagging tongue a single mad step further. Not that I could have because... I hadn't fully recovered yet.

"We'll proceed onward; slowly and cautiously. Though the well can't be far, we can't risk being surprised by whatever awaits us. First things first though, I'm going to search this rogue then take his garments."

"Take his garments? Whatever for?"

"*Whatever for?*" I mocked. "To wipe my bloody arse if naught else!" I scolded. "Must I explain every decision I make or simply seek your approval prior?" I glared.

Still seething, I hauled the assassin's body from the pit, carefully flicking off scorpions with my dagger as I went being that the fork was wrapped inside the pyrament with the rest of our belongings. After removing his robes and retrieving Petra's shawl, I tossed his naked body back to the scorpions. They did seem hungry. I then commenced burying him scorpions and all.

"The winds will take care of that," Petra advised. "I thought we were in need of some haste."

"Have you no shame woman?" I scolded. "Avert your eyes–
look away!"

I wasn't about to have her peering at him all bug-eyed. I'd left
the rogue naked. The least I could do was heap sand over his failings
before the gods dragged his soul to their flame scorched cauldrons. As
he was clearly beyond our touch now, I saw little sense in degrading
him further. I'd not only stripped him of his clothes but his life as well.
To be clear, it was I that had killed him. Not Petra, as much as his
chances for a full recovery did seem highly unlikely at the time. Still,
it was I who'd administered the final blow. Then again, I did stop far
short of filling in the hole completely. After all, the winds would take
care of that soon enough by themselves.

With that out of the way, I took to searching the pockets of his
garments. Besides the dagger he'd dropped, he carried but a single
possession– a message with a broken wax seal adorned with the *Circle
of BroZil*. I'd never witnessed their seal before though I had heard
tales depicting its symbol. Coincidentally, from a certain angle, it
looked strangely akin to a naked assassin hunched in a pit– from the
rear, that is. To be clear, the name was either poorly conceived or the
Brotherhood were not adept circle drawers for had I etched it in the
sand it would have looked something like this.

Upon opening the message, I read it aloud.

Kill Petra Bryn and child.

You'll find them at Studayo House in Gadev.

——Rah Delevan

"It is as we feared," I said, handing the message to Petra. "Take
pride you've been condemned to die by the Fourth Rah himself."

She grimaced and returned it to me. After pocketing the death decree, I fetched the assassin's dagger. Upon closer examination, I immediately flung my own into the sand with disgust. The steel was far superior in comparison. But that was nothing. The instrument was nothing short of miraculous— like nothing I'd ever seen previously— until I saw its hilt— and my jaw dropped wide with disbelief.

"What is it?" Petra inquired.

"Nothing." I lied. "Just another ghost from my past."

"You've seen it before," she persisted. It wasn't a question.

"I have." I admitted with a sigh. "But it's not possible. I buried it as a lad."

"The same one? I don't understand."

"Nor do I." I grimaced scratching my chin with mounting uncertainty.

"I expect if you buried it, and it somehow found its way back to you it was meant to be yours."

"That is a fact. Although—"

I was unable to speak my thoughts were so jumbled. How could it be so? But the evidence was before me; I held it in my hands. There was no mistaking it. Twas the same one I'd found in the ruins following the fire— the worst time of my life. Emblazoned with gold, it boasted two ivory horses on either side. It was perfectly balanced— made for throwing. Not that I could envision myself doing so. I would never risk tarnishing it. It was that stunning. Even more so than Petra— being that it could not speak. But I'd buried it in a backyard grave so how could it arise from the bowels of the dead. Though it plagued my mind greatly, the assassin had no further need of it. He was dead. It was mine now. It felt peculiarly warm in my hands. I had to alter my sheath, cut free a bit of stitching, to accommodate its broader girth.

Forcing the incident from my mind, after sacrificing some precious water to purge my eyes; we gathered our belongings and departed. Though I'd made no suggestion of dragging Petra with the tent, apparently, she'd anticipated as much for she'd already started walking ahead of me. Which is to say, she did know the way. I was hurting and, though she knew as much, she was wise enough to know she'd best not mention it again. Humph. So, it was possible. She could be as silent as an assassin's blade— on rare occasions.

Our progress was quicker than I would have guessed. I surmised this was due to our adrenalin having been peaked. Kindly, it no longer seemed quite as chilly for the wind had subsided, which no doubt also aided our progression. We passed a few large cactuses, which were rare. The tallest one sported several dead kestrels skewed upon its spines. How they ended up as such only Haeryn knows. The desert's name was derived from the abundant kestrel carcasses oft times found at its southern and northernmost fringes. Why? I had no idea. Though Petra did, of course. Okay, so not solely Haeryn.

"They migrate every spring." She announced proudly as though the dead birds themselves might be keenly interested.

"My great what... every spring?"

"Migrate. It's when herds of animals or flocks of birds move to other realms purposely."

Petra explained that kestrel hawks migrated each spring, flying from the Isles of Eyre in Hangnail Pass to cross the Kestrel Desert with hopes of arriving at the northern coast of Verdun; prior to venturing back again in late autumn.

"That's more than a hundred leagues." I calculated, utterly astounded.

"A lot more," she agreed.

"What could prompt such an arduous task repeatedly?"

"Procreation, I expect."

"Poor crow nation?" I stopped to ask. "What have crows to do with anything? We were speaking of kestrels, not crows. Not to mention, you'll find no crows here." I assured her.

"No! Procreation as in breeding: building nests, laying eggs, and such." she clarified.

"Ah, to make babies. But why leave only to return? Why go so far?"

"Not babies; we have babies. They have chicks and hatchlings–fledglings they're called once they flee the nest. It is said that they follow a food source; and when it dries up, they return south again."

"But why cross the kestrel? Why not go around instead?"

"Who can say?" she shrugged. "Why do we encircle the sun? I suppose it's simply the shortest route. You're right though, even with wings and their incredible speed the journey is oft times catastrophic. It's a morbid endeavor at best."

"Morbid? There's the truth. It's not rash, it's a tragic mistake." I corrected her. So, she was one of those fool hearted believers. I should have known. As obvious as it was to me, I learned long ago trying to convince *them* that the sun fell from the edge of the world was pointless– even though it happened right before our very eyes but yesterday. Petra then recited a poem. No doubt from one of her many books, I mused.

Kestrel, kestrel; dawn ends night.
What lure doth dangle haughty height?
Kestrel, kestrel; sharp eyes impaled-
Upon sights so bright yet nimbly veiled.

"Like a skewered boar— impaled for certain. That's more than a mind full. Who penned that lofty thought?" I queried.

"I wish I knew, but I don't," she acknowledged. "If only my mother was here. She could tell you; save that she's most likely dead." She added sadly.

"I wish I knew one way or another; but I don't." I said, echoing her weighty sigh. It was good she was finally beginning to see reason. Like a spike-breasted kestrel the woman was, undoubtedly, dead.

We said nothing to one another after that. Instead, we shuffled along in glorious silence; stopping only to share an occasional sip from what we hoped wouldn't prove our final swallow. For some unknown reason, I began to feel increasingly uneasy. Our surroundings seemed to be growing progressively darker though it should have been the other way around. They should have been turning brighter. Traipsing slowly up and down each dune we continued along until, just prior to the oddly stifled dawn, we finally saw it. It was so breathtaking we hugged one another, which frankly felt awkward.

There it was just as my father had described it— *the mighty tree.* It was massive— colossal if ever a thing was. That explained why everything seemed to be getting darker. We'd infringed upon its shadowy domain. It looked to be so close though we knew in truth it was still quite distant. But there was more to it; something I never would have anticipated. Dropping my possessions, I fumbled blindly for the spyglass for finding myself unable to avert my eyes. *No, it couldn't be!* While still rubbing my eyes, I raised the spyglass feeling certain the mirage would abruptly dissolve. *It didn't.* It was preposterous. It was outlandish; and yet, there it was all the same. *So that was it!* The thing the assassin knew that we did not. Until now.

A large pavilion arose just ahead of the massive tree. It was copper-colored; oblong in shape and made of enormous wooden beams. A waist-high white stone wall encircled what *I assumed* could only be the well. Above it stood an arbor with mud-thatched roof below which a large pottery vessel dangled from a rope. Which is what led me to believe it had to be the well. It was a shrewd deduction.

I saw movement— *two guards!* Dropping to my knees, Petra

mimicked my actions instantaneously.

"What is it?" Petra whispered. *Silly girl*, I thought to myself. There was no need to whisper. They were far too distant to overhear us speaking to one another.

"Two guards." I whispered back. "Kedera guards by the looks of it. Of all Haeryn's bloody luck." I don't know why we persisted in whispering. It must have been instinctive for I found I couldn't help it.

"But *what* is it?" She repeated.

"It looks to be a pavilion with guards stationed nearest the well."

"The well? You can see it?"

"The thing with the white wall and roof. They couldn't possibly see us from there. Even so, we should stay low." Admittedly, their startling presence promoted great anxiety within me.

"The pavilion looks enormous."

"Yes, it's ridiculous; unfathomable by any stretch of the imagination. How can the Kedera have troops posted *here?*"

"Troops? You think there's more of them?"

"As they appear to be guarding the well, there must be more of them. I swear, had the assassin declared it so I never would have believed him. It would explain their mysterious appearances. But how did they accomplish it? They could not bring that across the desert. It'd be madness; it's just not possible."

"Evidently, it is possible– or it wouldn't be staring us in the eyes." Petra stated the obvious which made me chuckle. Which I immediately felt guilty for. Not that I was laughing at her but rather for us being in such desperate need of water. We were so close. It was right in front of us for Haeryn's sake! But how to get to it? Now that was a dilemma.

"Perhaps by horse."

Whatever was she on about now? Perhaps by horse. We had no horse and, even if we did, how might a horse fetch water from a well?

"Perhaps they pulled wagons and carriages a short distance each night." Oh, she was still talking about the pavilion. Not that *that* made any more sense.

"Wagons and carriages across this sand? No." I shook my head. "The place is akin to a small fortress. I can't tell where the building ends and the great tree begins– not even with the spyglass. Besides, those beams are too long for any carriage. It would take years; the death toll would be steep."

"Camels?" Petra mused.

"Camels?" I smirked. "Camels are sturdy pack animals, but they don't take to a yoke or harness. At least not those that I've come across. Not to mention, they're unruly beasts at the best of times."

"Well, how did they do it then?"

"Though beyond my reckoning, it matters not," I said, shaking my head. "It changes nothing. We need to reach that well. We must replenish our water slings. There's barely a drop between us— let alone any to spare for a horse."

"What?"

"Nothing. Forget I said anything."

"Then what shall we do? What mad plan will you conjure to save us?" I couldn't help but smile. She could be funny at the darndest of times.

"I don't know. I need time to think. Inspired madness takes time."

"But time is the one thing we're short of— outside of water, that is." Petra frowned.

"Haeryn knows that's the truth. First things first, we'll set camp at the base of this dune and formulate a plan." Petra started to rise but I pulled her down.

"No, stay low! There may more guards posted in the bloody tree for all we know."

"Well, you might have mentioned that a tad sooner," she sneered.

"I only just thought of it now. Though it seems unlikely, we'd best not chance it."

"And what if *they* have a spyglass— one they traded for fair and square as opposed to a stolen one just to be clear?" I stuck my parched tongue out at her. It was so hot already, I felt exhausted. Then again, it was more than likely that she was the one exhausting me so.

"Wait, they're leaving," I proclaimed with a grateful sigh. "Aah— no, they're not. They've fetched something— a cage. Now they're leaving— very hastily. Oh-no!" I huffed placing both hands on my head.

"What is it? What do you see?" Petra implored impatiently.

"A Harbinger cat— and a full-grown one at that. There's no mistaking, I can see its stripes plainly." I grimaced. Our predicament had just gotten worse— a lot worse. Monumentally worse, that is.

"A Harbinger cat— creatures known for devouring the hearts of their prey and leaving the rest?"

"The same."

"Clever," Petra observed with a frown.

"Clever? Are you mad? Whose side of the wall are you on anyway?"

"Whichever crumbles soonest. It's brilliant considering they're known to survive in the harshest of climates. And it can't run away. It can't risk leaving the shade of the giant tree— not in the daylight. But what I don't understand is, why guard it at all? What do they fear? What threat could there possibly be during the heat of the day?"

"Don't look at me. I've no clue."

"Us?" She blurted fearfully. "Do you think they might somehow be *expecting us?*"

"No!" I shook my head. "As I think more on it, they can't risk leaving the well unguarded. It's all they have. It's everything to them. Without it, they're lost."

"But it's not as if anyone can take it from them." Petra stated.

"True but should anything foul the water their geese would be cooked as they say. My father proclaimed the tree to support all manner of small creatures. Should a desert rat drown in the well the water might become contaminated— making a quick end of those within."

"A quick end?" She wished to clarify.

"No, slow and painful. I just didn't want you to fret being that it might very well be us should our luck not change soon."

"How thoughtful." Her expression suddenly changed.

"I know what it is." She beamed proudly.

"Know what *what* is?" Admittedly, the query was poorly phrased. That said, in my defense, I didn't have much to work with.

"It's a baobab tree. I've read about them."

"Um, that last bit goes without saying. Of course, you read about it. What haven't you read about?" I guffawed, rolling my eyes.

"You can eat both their leaves and fruit. Studayo House once sold cooking oil harvested from their seeds— which is what piqued my interest to learn more about them."

"It's only natural. How could it not?" I scoffed unfairly. "I for one don't know what to do with myself if not sufficiently piqued."

"I'd heard they can grow to ridiculous proportions, though I had no idea any tree could grow *that large.*"

"Right you are. It's so large you can't even discern its peak— though I'm sure it's up there somewhere— *peeking* back at us." As clever as it seemed to me, she ignored the pun.

"I think it may be a grove as opposed to a single tree. I recall reading that their roots produce offshoots that–." She stopped, staring at me while biting her lip. To be clear, she stopped talking, not staring. *Did I mention how mesmerizing her green eyes could be?* They were.

"What is it?" I asked. "Do tell– what else did you read?"

"Only that their trunks occasionally fuse together in large clusters forming circular rings oft times rendering them *hollow* within."

"Hollow?" Admittedly, I was finding it hard to keep pace with her.

"Your father called the tree *empty inside*."

"He did. So, you're suggesting…" I was unable to complete my sentence because my tongue had leapt ahead of my thoughts. It did catch up eventually. Though, in the meantime, Petra kindly took over.

"What if the pavilion is not unlike Studayo House of old?"

"You've lost me again."

"But a foyer to something far grander?"

"Like a theatre? That's ludicrous. I'd no idea you were this far gone. Speak no more of it, you've clearly lost your wits, girl."

"What if the monster tree… is hollow? What if the Kedera… shelter within it?"

"'Tis my brain that's in need of sheltering. But yes, I see what you're implying. As implausible as it sounds, at the same time, it does make sense. Either that or we've both gone mad."

"Think. They'd not only have water but possibly food stores– perhaps an armory even."

"You assume much. Though, I suppose, it isn't not possible."

"Impossible. You don't say: is not *not* possible. You say: is not impossible– or simply *possible*."

"Thank you for the grammar lesson but I did not say: *not not*, I said: *isn't not*– 'tis entirely different."

"Entirely different? 'Tis not. 'Tis the same."

"But… 'tis not what I said 'tisn't it?" Haeryn help me, what did I just say? It was her who was exhausting me. I'd nothing left. She'd broken my spirit and not for the first time.

"I surrender." I glared hopelessly. "I concede already. Still, 'tis best we get out of this heat before my skull shrivels. In all earnestness, I swear you threaten what precious little remains within."

Twas my head that was throbbing– thanks to her. Unless that's supposed to read *no thanks to her*. I couldn't tell, I'd completely given up she had me so bloody baffled.

Slithering backward through the sand, until we felt certain

we'd be safe from prying eyes, we set up camp. As the tree's shadow retreated in long strides, we took refuge within the pyro-vent just prior to the sun's rays becoming unbearable. While nursing Renan, Petra's eyes suddenly locked on my own. It was disconcerting. I knew what she wanted but I had no answer to give. Running my fingers through my damp hair, I cursed aloud in frustration. I was completely dejected. My mind was a blank; even blanker than usual. I had to think of something. I must. But there seemed but one lone option; and it wasn't good.

"I envision but one alternative," I admitted miserably. "Advance, kill the cat; refill our slings."

"One, two, three; just like that," she snapped her fingers.

"I must go. It is the only way."

"The only way?" Petra objected.

"They don't post guards during the day, not even in the tree. It's far too hot. Besides, the Harbinger cat would make short work of them if they did. Those beasts kill purely for pleasure."

"Rendering your proposal senseless!" Petra chided. "You're not leaving us! Not again."

"I swear, you pout near as much as Renan," I laughed loudly solely to make light of my foolhardy scheme. There was nothing vaguely amusing about it. What I needed was a bow though I had none. Why must I always be right? *Why must it always be a dagger? Just for once, why couldn't the assassin have carried a bow?* I could have shot the cat from a distance with a bow.

"I do no such thing," she sulked, tugging Renan's head free of her shawl.

"Do you have a better idea?" I asked, with brows raised.

"Because feeding oneself to a cat is somehow a *good idea.*" She shook her head sadly. "I'm still thinking…"

"That's it then, I'm going and that's all there is to it."

"No, that is not all there is to it." Petra insisted.

"What– are you going to dig a hole and push me in it? I'm not some witless assassin. Oft times the hardest path is the only way forward. Either we act now or die in the sand. It is that simple."

"The difference between simple and simpleton is what's simplest. The well is still half a league away. The sun will fry what little's left of your brain before you get halfway. As long as a few meager swallows of water remain we still have a half a chance. So, the answer is: no. You will remain here with us. I was right about the assassin and I'm right about this."

The answer is: no. As if every decision hinged upon her approval. Yes, my lady. No, my lady. Will that be all, my lady? You do realize all I'm trying to do is fetch some water for you, my lady— so you need not perish, my lady? That is, unless you prefer needn't not perish, my lady— though, either way, you're still going to perish. If for no other reason than I can't take much more of your ceaseless gibberish.

"I've half a mind to trade you for a sling of water. I could likely get two if you could learn to keep your mouth shut." That brought the hairpin out. She was positively fuming. I couldn't blame her. I'd spoken unfairly. If not for that hole of hers, only Haeryn knows where we'd be now. And I didn't mean her cakehole for once. I was referring to the grave she'd dug for the assassin. I only wished that it was me lying in it as opposed to him. Let me assure you, by that point, I would have traded all my worldly possessions, *fork and spyglass included,* for some uninterrupted sleep.

"Forgive me; I spoke recklessly. It's the heat. Not to mention, I'm tired and my head's still pounding. That said, if you'd just agree with me once in while it'd be easily avoided." I added drolly.

"I'd sooner bury you than forgive you. Know that whatever *we* decide *we* must do *together.* You brought us here, so you don't get to leave without us!"

With the hairpin tucked away, I felt relaxed enough to think again. The more I thought about it, and as much as I loathed admitting it, she was right. If we were to split ways, one of us would surely perish. Both likely— me first, followed soon after by them. I needed a better plan. *But what?* If ever there was a time for shrewdness, it was now. Our situation was beyond dire. Speaking metaphorically, because she'd confused me to such an extent, we were stuck between a rock and something intent on churning that same rock, along with ourselves, into a sea of endless sand. Which is to say a hard place; a very hard place indeed— and not solely because I hated sand. Still, it was the well or nothing. We had to go for broke.

It was then I got the single worst idea of my entire life. Yeah, even worse than trying to cross this miserable desert— a second time— with a baby no less. It was so horrendous, as the thought struck me, I felt physically ill. In hindsight, it was so absurd it made the kestrel migration seem akin to an evening stroll. Petra took notice at once. It was as if she could read my thoughts. Save for this time, there was no horse involved. Thank Haeryn.

"Well, spit it out man! How bad is it?" She always had a way of making me laugh at the worst of times. It really was uncanny. Have I mentioned how encouraging she can be? *No?* That's strange.

"As the Harbinger cat is withdrawn at dusk, we will approach the well." I started with a brave face. That was the easy part. What came next, not so much.

"We?" She asked.

"We." I confirmed.

"Brilliant." She replied politely. "Although, it's not as though *we* have much of a choice." She added waiting patiently for me to continue.

"But… there is more to it, right?" *Impatiently,* rather. It must be said that I had little choice other than to pause at the juncture upon discovering the appropriate wording wasn't about to depart my mouth. Hardly fair and never would I have rushed her in such fashion. *Spew it if you must.* I bade myself finally.

"And then?" She further encouraged, her emerald eyes locking on mine— which I found greatly distracting. So much so, I decided to insist we stand back-to-back next time, Haeryn forbid, should I ever find myself in need of imparting something of dire import again.

"And then… being that the Kedera will undoubtedly await our arrival, I will tell them that I am the assassin and that you are my prisoner."

"Prisoners," she corrected.

"Yes, quite right— *prisoners* rather."

Note that that was all I'd come up with thus far. From that point on I was thinking as I spoke— hardly my strong suit. Especially while facing one another in such close quarters, I should add.

"I will claim to have orders stating I must bring you *safely* to Rah Delevan for… questioning. Yes, for questioning. We will destroy the death decree. With no evidence to the contrary, they will have little choice other than to take our word for it; *my word* for it to be clear." Removing the unsealed message from my pocket, I tossed it outside.

"Bet you a silver, it's aflame within a wink."

"That's it? That's your plan?"

"Yes, and why not? Why couldn't it be true?" Fetching the assassin's robes, I held them over top of my own.

"I think they'll fit well enough," I grinned, commencing to disrobe.

"Wait," said Petra.

"I'm not going to undress outside if that's what you're proposing. The sun would scorch my humble ass. Cover your eyes should it make you feel uncomfortable. I care not." I shrugged.

"No! I mean, yes." Her face flushed awkwardly as she shook her head to clear her thoughts. At least, I'd managed to fluster her. It did seem fair.

"I've a better idea." *No, you don't,* I thought silently.

"Of course, you do," I muttered instead.

"What if we change the note?" She suggested eagerly. "What if we make it say something else entirely?" I didn't understand. Horse or no horse, she was talking nonsense again.

"And what if we sprout wings and fly to Harkenspear? I think the wind favors us," I said, licking a finger and holding it aloft.

"I think we can do it," she insisted. *Madness!* And to think I thought she was over it.

"No," I assured her. "We can't fly. It's the heat talking."

"Radesh! I think it is possible. I think it can be done!" She smiled, biting down upon her lower lip. Though a provocative smile to be certain, it did not win me over.

"No, it can't!" I protested. "I read the Decreto Mortis aloud! It says what it says– *already.*" I objected. "This isn't a faery tale where everyone lives happily ever after. You don't get to rewrite the ending. It is but a forgone conclusion, not some bloody debate."

"Yes, but it was sealed with wax. Only the sender and recipient were privy to what was written. No one else. Fetch the note! Please, let me see it again!" She spoke urgently.

Retrieving the note reluctantly, while quashing an inclination to crumple it, I handed it to her. So, it hadn't caught fire as quickly as I'd imagined it would. Lucky for her. After reading it, she immediately removed her hairpin. Her dark braid tumbled down her shoulder making her look far younger. *Patience,* I reminded myself with a lengthy sigh. *She is but a girl.*

"I can fix this! I can change this! know I can." She insisted. As for myself, let's just say I felt somewhat less confident and leave it at that. Which I didn't, of course.

"This is absurd. Allow me to explain things once more. The note in your hand is a death decree. Death decrees are final; written in blood as a matter of fact."

"Written in blood? That's perfect!" Apparently, she wasn't listening– as usual, so I spoke more purposely this time. Though I'd shown remarkable patience thus far, I wasn't about to coddle her.

"The message within is irrevocable. I don't know how to say it any plainer. Regardless of one's obstinance, some things can't be changed." I jeered.

"But what in Haeryn's hells have we got to lose?!" She huffed, glaring back no less sternly than I had at her.

"Humor me, Radesh! Allow me this one small courtesy and I shall never ask naught of you again."

"But did you not say some time ago that never naught means *always*?" She was trying to trick me again and I for one was having none of it.

"You remembered. So, you do listen. Please Radesh, let me at least try and, should you not be pleased with the results, we will let the damn thing burn. Same as before. Nothing changes."

"Fine." I conceded. "Do as you will but then it is done with."

"Agreed. Now, all I need is some blood. Give me your finger." She demanded hotly, shaking her trusty hairpin as though it needed to be fed. She'd clearly gone mad and, as much as I wanted to blame the heat, I couldn't help thinking a major part of it was her– the way she was so to speak. There was no changing it now. She'd been poorly raised– too many books. She'd been mollycoddled, to be frank.

"You're not poking me with that thing. Haeryn only knows how many poor knaves it's killed! Use your own dainty finger! Notwithstanding, you'd need a lance to breach these cal:louses."

Closing her eyes, she stuck out a finger. Immediately she began wincing and she hadn't even poked it yet. It was amusing until she found courage enough to stab at it. Seriously, she very likely would have impaled her wrist had I not grabbed her arm.

"Wait. Fine. But this better be worth it. But you need not thrust as though trying to pierce bone. On second thought, I'll do it myself."

Unsheathing my glorious new dagger, I cut a small slit into my left palm, which bled like a stuck pig. Likely due to the insufferable heat, I expect– not that she hadn't brought my blood to a boil.

"For Haeryn's sake, Radesh, you'd think I was about to compose a book of a thousand names as opposed to a few small edits."

"A few small what?"

Ignoring my query, she laid Renan on his back prior to flattening the note across her lap. She studied it *judiciously* for a few moments. And no, I didn't know that word prior and still don't in fact. It's just what *she said* she was doing when I asked what she was up to.

"Take your time, "I quipped. "There's easily enough here to write a bloody love story."

"Bloody for certain, and don't you dare drip on it." She replied without looking up. Instead, she just shushed me with a quick wave of her hand. She really did know how to get under my skin. *Literally*. She was concentrating so hard I could envision tiny windlasses spinning about in her pretty-little head.

She made a few imaginary attempts in the air; small sweeps and flourishes to replicate the writing style. She then dipped the point of her hairpin into the blood pooling in my hand, and began to scrawl, slowly and carefully. Initially, I could not see what she was doing— no doubt due to that pretty-little head of hers already beginning to swell. Which is to say; her luscious locks were blocking my view. Finally, she dropped her hairpin and leaned back to better admire her handiwork.

"There!" She declared proudly, blowing softly upon the paper with badly chapped lips. Even so, it must be said, they puckered rather nicely. She held it up for me to see but I was still staring at her luscious-looking lips.

"Look! Hello! Eyes over here." She clarified indignantly. Dutifully doing as told the following is what I saw:

> *Don't Kill Petra Bryn and child.*
> *Bring them to me unharmed.*
> *You'll find them at Studayo House in Gadev.*
>
> *—Rah Delevan*

I read it over and over, sounding out each syllable silently in my head. Though it took quite some time initially, it did get quicker as I went.

"It's only four lines. Surely, you must be done by now. So? What do you think?"

For the record, had I not been embarrassed to sound the words out aloud I would have been done long ago. As for her revisions, they were bloody amazing. It looked perfect. It could not have looked any more authentic had it been written by the Fourth Rah himself. Never had I wanted to hug her more. But we'd done that upon witnessing the giant tree which had proved uncomfortable for both of us. Still, I wasn't about to admit how proud I was of her. Regardless of beauty, swollen heads were dangerous things. One wrong glance, a suspect shiver, the smallest hint of treachery; and we'd be dead.

"Y-you," I stammered, trying to find the right words. It wasn't a good start. I didn't want to hurt her feelings. She'd done well and, the truth of it was, I was more than just proud of her. I was astonished by her supreme cunning. It wasn't a feeling common to me. Truth was, there weren't many flattering moments during battle. Tripping hazards, yes. Feelings of fulfillment, not so much.

"You," I tried again, "will never cease to amaze me!" I blabbed, adding to my incredulity. "It's positively brilliant! You're so bloody clever. It's perfect." I beamed joyously.

"Do you really think so? I was so fearful I'd make a mess of it."

"It's staggering– beyond anything I might have imagined. Not that I thought for a moment that you didn't have it in you."

Her green eyes glazed over like dew on grass. I felt good for having confided my true frame of mind. It wasn't until her gaze dropped that I recognized I was only half-dressed. Trying my utmost not to appear flustered in any way, I stepped casually out of my robes prior to assessing the assassin's black attire. I ignored her– her snickering, that is.

Though I recalled little trouble removing the robes from the assassin's dead body, they were entirely dissimilar to my own djellaba. The problem being that they, or it, *was* essentially one large hole. I was unsure whether to step into the garment feet first or simply try pulling it over my head. Deciding upon the latter technique proved to be a mistake for my chest having been wider than my waist. Thus, for several frantic moments, I was unable to free my arms. Petra began laughing aloud which didn't help matters, causing me to thrash even more. Having managed to free my arms, followed by a crimson face– if the burning sensation on my cheeks was any indication– it was then that I realized an unfortunate lack of under garments. I'd been forced to sacrifice them as *the flux* first took hold. The whole ordeal proved immensely trying. Which is to imply that I'd brought new meaning to the phrase *growing incompetence.*

Furthering Petra's hilarity, I was forced to swaddle myself with what little remained of my head scarf. The same one that had the scorpions in it but a short time ago. Being that the material wasn't large enough to girdle my waist I found little alternative other than to *bundle and tuck.* Try doing that openly and preserve a measure of dignity. I'll save you the time– *never not impossible.* Having at long last deciphered the assassin's peculiar garb, I dusted myself off and sat down as though the preceding affair had gone entirely to plan. All the while disregarding Petra's giggles, which strongly testified to the contrary. Having unwittingly made myself the tent's main attraction, I diffused my inelegance with humor.

"It would seem that some assassins aren't so *well-armed*." I quipped.

"Bring them to me unarmed." Petra guffawed aloud.

An awkward silence ensued for neither of us knowing what to say after that. I could tell my face was flushed again. And then we both started laughing, thankfully. Though a much-needed distraction, it proved itself short-lived. What distressed us both need not be said aloud. We could see it plain as day in one another's face. Fact being facts, the charade we were about to enact had a far greater chance of calamity than any inkling of success. There were too many *what if's* than we might possibly devise strategies for— likely even the least of which would pronounce us dead. Still, being that we had some time on our side, it was only prudent to fortify our plans as best as we were able.

"I know little about the Brotherhood of Zil," I confessed. "They might have a clandestine codeword, branding, or greeting for all I know which could end our sham promptly."

"Perhaps," said Petra. "But they're a covert guild. That favors us. Be covert— say as little as possible. Don't offer them anything they might use against us. Stick to your mandate. The contract is solely between you and the Rah."

"And no one else," I agreed.

"And be bold," she continued. "You are not under their command. You are your own chieftain. Assassins don't waver; they attack. Ensuring our safe passage is your assigned task. It has nothing to do with them. Should they interrogate you, which they will, become irate. Remember, they're not merely questioning your honor; they're undermining the authority of the Forth Rah himself."

"Undermining?" I grimaced. "So, you think they've a tunnel. You think that's how they brought that pavilion here. Nah, you can't tunnel in sand." How she could be so clever yet daft at the same time was beyond reckoning.

"No." Petra put her head in her lap momentarily. "I swear, your head's as thick a post. Why must it be so hard?" She lamented, looking skyward.

I didn't know what she was on about. Being largely comprised of bone, my head was no harder than anyone else's. Pushing her senseless tunneling notions aside, the rest of what she'd said wasn't just sound, it was exactly what I needed to hear, and I knew it. Though I'd heard tell of traveling troupes putting on performances, I'd witnessed very few bards in person myself. The whole concept seemed ludicrous to me. In my thinking, the world was hard enough to decipher without a plague of wandering minstrels purposely pretending to be something they were not.

Though admittedly a bit different, I did see a juggler once. It did not go well for him. After applauding his talent for tossing seven knives at once magically through the air he had the nerve to insult me for not tossing him a coin. Haeryn knows just because he was tossing things didn't oblige me to pay him for it. What sense is there in that? Not to mention the unexpected delay he'd imposed upon me for had he not been so distracting I would have been much farther along in my journey. To be clear, it was strictly due to his rudeness that I broke both his thumbs. Though he appeared somewhat disinclined to appreciate the lesson at the time, I do hope he realized it eventually. Regardless of expertise, one's expectations should remain modest. What I'm inferring is, hearing music by happenstance is not cause enough to pay the piper.

Even more outlandish, in faraway lands, I was told there are thespians whose sole purpose is to make fools of themselves in exchange for coin. Yeah, coin! Try that in Harbinger, I dare you. These *so-called jesters* could stitch a thousand jingly bells onto their hats for all the good it would do them here. Point being, we were far more inclined to hang people for their improprieties than compensate them. Unless there was ample wood about. In which case we'd burn them. I only hoped Petra and I weren't wandering a similar path for sticking our own necks out recklessly. Not to mention that great tree entailed there being plenty of wood about. But that was far from the only thing worrying me presently.

"Words don't come easy to me," I conceded. "I've never pretended to be someone else. To be honest, that's what scares me most— and certainly not those Kedera dogs! I'm afraid I'll blunder my role and get the lot of us killed."

"No, you won't. Don't you see? The role is tailor-made for you! All you need to do is be yourself. Don't try to be someone else; *that will* get us killed. The only difference between you and the assassin is the commander giving the orders. I hold every faith you can do this!"

I bit my lip angrily, condemning her in my head silently. It took her a moment to interpret my resentment.

"Of course, it's not the *only* difference. There are many differences. You are a fearless warrior. Assassins, on the other hand, are clearly dishonorable rogues. What I mean to say is…"

"I get it." I huffed. "I know what you intend. You infer that neither of us is innocent. We both have blood-stained hands. I thought we'd agreed to disagree on that. Still, I do understand. Be myself. Envision the Fourth Rah as though he were Major Bryn."

"That's what I was trying to say." She exhaled. "Only you said it better."

Strange, though I recognized she was placating me, I was not disenchanted by it. My abrupt flash of bitterness dissolved. Apparently, I was more prone to flattery than I'd previously thought. *Humph*.

"Which brings us to the Kedera dogs," I winked, clearing my throat.

"What about them?"

"That's just it. I don't know a lot about them— other than they squeal like piglets when skewered."

"You might want to keep that nugget to yourself." She winked, feigning a look of mock disillusionment.

"I'm sure you know more than you think. It wasn't all that long ago that we were all one people."

"That was before my time; and yours," I reminded her.

"Yes but, outside of regularly trying to stick one another with sharp, pointy things, we haven't really changed that much. We hunt, fish, and farm to support our families; *as do they*. We trade with foreign lands; *as do they*. We speak the Harbinger tongue; *as do they*. We just live on opposite sides of a largely invisible wall and abide by different leaders and ideals."

"Haeryn's Wall isn't invisible," I retorted. "I've stood atop it more than once."

"I said *largely* invisible. I was speaking metaphorically."

"Who'd you meet what for?"

"No, *met-a-phor*." She pronounced each syllable deliberately.

"Like a centaur?" I queried, mildly intrigued. I'd heard tell of these metaphors once before— hairy beasts, twofold in temperament if I recalled correctly.

"Forget it." She sighed. "You do know the names of all four Rahs and their territories— yes?"

"Yes, any fool knows that much." I responded pretentiously. I very nearly tugged my headscarf out from between my legs to ensure she hadn't sewn a bell onto it. *Ding! Was she having a go at me?* I was nobody's fool. I was the farthest thing from a jester if ever there was.

"What else do you want to know then?" I liked the way the

corners of her mouth scrunched upon posing the question. She often twisted her face when she spoke. Which made me wonder if I did that too. *What else do you want to know?* It was not lost on me that she'd phrased it as though she knew everything there was to know. Then again, I wouldn't put it past her. She quite likely did. Those damned books of hers. They'd be the death of her one day. I was certain of that.

"Okay, I'll play. Why am I bringing you to the Rah for starters?" I asked, flaring my nostrils in hopes of heightening the question's severity. Though intended to be a face scrunch I don't think it came off as such. Either way, it was acting, embracing the role to the fullest. Or at least I thought so.

"I don't know," she answered thoughtfully. "Good question. I expect it's because I'm somehow of value—"

"You?" I sniggered, expelling air through my lips to mimic a quieter farting sound.

"Yes, me— perhaps to the war effort. Or my brother being—" Then she paused, biting down hard on her plump lower lip again.

"It doesn't matter," she smiled suddenly with a shake of her head. "Because it's none of their business." Her green eyes sparkled.

"None of their damn business," I concurred smiling. "You were saying something about your brother. I didn't know you had one."

"I don't— not now anyway. Not anymore." For a moment she looked as if about to cry but quickly got over it. *Thank Haeryn,* I thought. After which I immediately felt bad. The war had taken so many of our brothers— and sisters. I had no family. All the same, as grim as we'd become, the pain endured.

"What else do you want to know?" She asked.

"The lay of the land, I suppose." I said, cocking an eyebrow. By which I meant: where things were in respect to where other things were located. I'd heard the Major say it that way once and, if you took time enough to ponder it, it did just lay there after all. The land that is.

"Is there something in your eye?" she asked genuinely.

"No." I sneered, scrunching my nose at her. I was a bit perturbed initially prior to realizing the best acting talents were likely those that went unnoticed— prior to recognizing that she *had noticed*, making me feel rather perturbed again.

"What are their major ports?" I clarified, resting my chin upon my interwoven fingers with my elbows on my knees. A very uncomfortable position I might add as dignified as I pretended it to be.

"I know most of their main travel routes but only the names of a few villages." I added, pursing my lips tightly together to better convey my frustration. My new facial antics did not appear to be having much of an effect. Though undeniably a form of *acting*, they felt rather contrived. Thus, I decided to put an end to my middling theatrics. Notwithstanding, it was then I remembered she'd said not to do it. Just be yourself, she'd said. A thing that, curiously, was suddenly proving near impossible to accomplish.

"I'll tell you the names of villages and ports I recall and roughly where they are. You need not remember it all anyway. You're an assassin after all, not a geographer."

"A geographer? What have they to do with anything?"

"Nothing. It was a poor jest. The lone similarity being they help shape the land."

"With their long necks?" I queried. It did make sense. They were tall creatures after all, less hairy than metaphors though surprisingly nimble for their size. Which led me to ponder, if a gang of giraffes was dubbed a geographer; was a metaphor a single beast or a herd? As charmed as I was, I decided it was best not to ask. Haeryn only knows to what foul depths that might have taken us. Besides, when planning and scheming it's of dire import to stay focused.

I will, however, admit that I was trying to convey to her the true worth of firsthand experience. Books were hardly equal to viewing something with your own eyes. Reading about a geographer in a story, *not that I ever had*; would never be comparable to witnessing them picking leaves from the tops of trees in the wild, *which I had*. She continued to stare at me with that look of hers— the scrunchy one. It wasn't as though I hadn't learned a thing or two marching across the open plains for years on end. I was hoping she'd see that finally— develop a greater appreciation for the vast fields I'd traversed. Still, she acted as though we were speaking different languages at times. I was more than just a soldier. I too was knowingly enabled. Knowledgeable, I later discovered, is how it is said.

"Never mind," she sniffed. "But you should know at least one Kedera location well. You had to have been raised somewhere after all."

"In a nameless village. In a chicken coop, if you must know."

"In a what?" It was obvious, I'd flustered her. "No, I meant in your assassin's role; not your real life." She was plainly stressed. "But a chicken coop? Really?" She felt obliged to reiterate.

"Never mind," I grumbled. "That won't be a problem. South

Verdun is the obvious choice. I did most of my fighting along that border. I know the names of lots of villages– we sacked and burned."

"Probably best to omit that last bit."

"Omit?" I queried for being unfamiliar with the word.

"Don't mention it."

"You're welcome." I nodded back proudly. Like a wagon pulled free of thick mud, finally, we were getting somewhere. Or so I thought at the time.

"Just remember you don't have to answer all their queries. Should they question your orders, tell them to mind their own business. Just—"

"Be my highly approachable self," I interrupted. "You can stop jawing on about that. If I wanted a parrot, it'd be on my shoulder. I get it. I get it. I get it." I replied mockingly.

"No, I can see it won't," she laughed. Her mirth warmed my starving innards. I too had spoken in jest– partaken in playful banter of equal joy and wit. Though unsure why, it was rare for someone to recognize my humor– devoid of a few broken bones being somehow involved. Evidently, my sly endeavors weren't overly subtle for her deft wit. Who knew? Not to mention, parrots tended to repeat themselves which is why I said *I get it* more times than once– on the off chance that wasn't apparent.

Though having been proven *the fool* on numerous occasions, I doubt I would have garnered many coins had I lived in more distant lands. Which is to imply, for some inexplicable reason, at that moment, I felt oddly glib. *Dong!* Without question, the insufferable heat had taken a toll. I gave my head a quick shake only to cringe for feeling sand flee my ears. *Hmmm?* That gave me cause to pause. No, it was undoubtedly the heat. Elsewise, my head would have felt heavier. Sandbags are heavy things; whereas my head was just tired; and understandably so. I'd likely spoken more on this one afternoon than I had my entire life.

While such prominent thoughts rattled through my mind, all the while, Petra rattled off the names of numerous Kedera settlements many of which I already knew. Which was fortunate, being that I was only half-listening. That surprised me. Not the ones we'd crumbled, and not the part about only half-listening; the other settlements– the ones we hadn't despoiled. Though I'd peered over plenty of smelly old maps while planning attacks, they had always intimidated me for some unknown reason. Thus, I rarely looked beyond areas of immediate conflict or consequence.

To me the world was so big it could not help but boggle the mind; not to mention reportedly being *round* suddenly. If you believed that sort of nonsensical logic. Not me; I had enough trouble finding my way from one watering hole to the next; not to mention back again to wherever that might be. *A round world— like a man's head? I think not!* Had they never paid attention to the rain? Ahoy— it fell downward not sideways. Not to mention, at certain times of the year, if you held up a coin, which everyone knows is flat, you could block out the whole sun. Because they were the same. Elsewise, how might it be possible? In my mind, all sailors were fools. It was only a matter of time before they plummeted off the edge. Knowing the gods to be as cruel as they were, why tempt fate? Not me, not ever.

As it turned out, to the surprise of no one ever, Petra knew a great deal about the Kedera and their customs. She didn't know as much as I did about their roadways. Should you require greater clarity, please refer to my earlier notations regarding the benefits of having *firsthand experience.* That said, she did know a lot about their crops, livestock, and textiles. Textiles refer to outfits, garments, fabrics, and such. I knew that— never once implying they were distantly akin to snake-like creatures with legs. She didn't need to explain it to me. Even though she did, of course. Main difference being, we soldiers wore chain maille— which was far too heavy to ever be considered stylish. In the heat of the day, it was positively stifling. I despised it so ferociously I rarely wore anything other than a simple breast plate. I mean how are you supposed to fight if you're too tired to swing your arms about?

She also shared stories concerning Kedera heroes; both real and fictional. Fictional means legendary; like Haeryn; having nothing whatsoever to do with fish if that's what you were thinking. Only Haeryn was real— no matter what *she* purported. She described our religious differences at great length prior to droning on about their flourishing love for the arts. She called it flourishing. *Flourishing.* A word that rolled off your tongue like spoiled spittle. *Flourishing.*

Though you'd expect it might warrant a worm and a hook, it didn't. *Just heading to the lake to do a little flourishing.* Once that bit was settled, I knew precisely what it meant. We called it extravagant, excessive, utterly shameless. Continuing, she advised me that immodest wall-size paintings and life-size naked statues had become their newest craze. Craze means stupid— though Petra, being as naïve as she was, professed it had something to do with passion. In my mind, wanton starkness exhibits a fair bit more lust than passion. Not to mention frustration. It'd just so happened that we'd come across a statue of similar repute once in the center of a village we'd just finished ransacking. Major Bryn had it smashed to pieces in the end. I'd never seen so many open-jawed, drooling men— and they called themselves soldiers. Admittedly, it was a tad distracting— what with her being bent over and all— struck solid in the act of fetching water from the well. I told Petra the story to which she replied that such forms of art were an *acquired taste*. Acquired taste? Talk about selective listening— did she not hear the part about the drooling?

Nakedness aside, she knew plenty about their clothing fashions, which bored me. Until I realized she might have provided some pointers regarding the assassin's garb; but had chosen not to. I didn't know what to make of that. It seemed akin to *not telling* someone there was a horsefly poised upon their cheek. You could hardly describe it as *polite*.

"How did you learn so much?" I felt obliged to ask while secretly dreading the answer I knew to be forthcoming. *Why did I even ask?*

"Books," she shrugged. "I've never been anywhere before this. They were the only way I might catch glimpses of the outside world. Emphasis on *catch glimpses*."

"Emphasis?"

"Stressing the importance of something in particular."

"Oh, like that Kedera love story?" I joked. "I'm so grateful for having been able to present you with this wonderful glimpse of the *outside world*. We call it sand in truth." I winked.

"Yes, it's been a real eye-opener so far. As I said before, I hadn't finished reading that story yet. I was enjoying it. The author's a definite romantic."

I thought the way she pronounced romantic was nothing short of adorable as I mopped the sweat pouring from my brow. *Adorable?* Without doubt, the extreme heat had me worn thin.

"Be advised, should I ever meet him, I'll be sure to collect his head."

"Now, why would you say that?" She scolded. "You don't know anything about him. Just because he wrote a love story is no reason to slay the poor fellow. I think you're taking your new assassin role far too seriously."

"I didn't like the ending," I said, fighting to keep a straight face. Admittedly, sometimes I enjoyed upsetting her. Okay, that was a lie. I enjoyed doing so every time.

"But neither did you read the beginning nor anything in between," she huffed. "And I suppose you have a better ending?"

"As a matter of fact, I do."

"Well, all right. Let's hear it then," she insisted.

"And reaching for my sword, I severed the author's swollen head. The. Bloody. End– emphasis on *bloody*." She threw an empty water sling at me while larking aloud.

Two for two, I chuckled silently, happy to have offset the dread hovering about us if only for a moment.

"I'll tell you what was funny," she chortled. "Watching you put on those garments was the most absurd thing I've ever seen. You looked like you were trying to re-enact your birth!"

"I told you I can't act to save my life."

"You did. You're no bard, that's for certain." She laughed, reciting my precise thought. Renan yawned, and her face turned grave. A tear fell, melting all semblances of jest. Removing her hairpin, she dusted his wee face with the bushy end of her braid.

"It's a good plan," I said reassuringly. Knowing truthfully, it was anything but. "We will survive this; you'll see." I exhaled.

"It's not that," she sniffed. "Well, it is but it isn't." Her fingers rubbed her temples feverishly.

"I lied to you," she whispered hurriedly. *Not this again.*

"Lied to me?" I repeated. "It doesn't matter. The whole world's been lying to me since birth." She stared at me quizzically.

"Expunge it from your thoughts. It's the heat. Get some rest. You're just tired. We're all tired." Yes, I said expunge. It was but a fortnight ago that I watched a healer expunge an arrow from a soldier's chest... for all the good it did him. Either of them.

"No. I must tell you the truth. In case tomorrow ends other than we hope." I waited in silence, watching her clutched hands twisting her braid with unease.

"I lied to you about *that night*."

Ding! My ears perked up.

"What I told you was not quite what happened. Some of it was. But things didn't unfold quite the way I said they did." She stared at me, her eyes welling with tears.

"You lied? About that?"

It was inconceivable; her story had made perfect sense. Not only could I not imagine any other viable alternative, but I'd also been utterly convinced of her genuineness. Nothing else made sense. How could it? I was a vile rogue through and through.

"I don't believe you," I said. "It's the heat; this insufferable heat! And don't you dare cry!" *Too late.*

"It's not the heat!" She sobbed. "I just couldn't bring myself to tell you the truth. How could I? I was young and defenseless while at your mercy. I have my baby to think about. Notwithstanding, I went roaming abroad with *you* of all people!"

"Ouch," I said, jokingly. Okay, *half-jokingly.* At least we knew which of us was the better actor. Not that it helped matters.

"Think about it. You showed up and, bare moments later, two men were dead. I killed one of them! *Me!* I thought you were taking us someplace safe, but we ended up here— in the middle of a desert. *The desert of deserts* in fact. I didn't know if you were going to rape me; kill me; or roast my baby on a spit!"

"Roast Renan? Really? You though that— about me?" Those words hurt. I was positively seething inwardly. Though famished, I wouldn't eat a Kedera dog let alone a child. And what would I use for a spit— our lone tent pole? I think not.

"Well, what was I to think? I was scared out of my wits; yet even more scared lest I show it! I'm still scared. I don't want to die. But I believe you now. You'd never hurt me or Renan."

"I'd die for you, if it came to that," I avowed. "My orders are to see you safely to Harkenspear and that is what I intend to do. That is what I have always intended. Nothing more; nothing less."

She could see it plain as gravy on my chin. She'd done more than wound me; she'd reopened a gash that swiftly began to fester.

"Yes, I know that *now!*" She pleaded. "But you must understand; it is not my fault! After that night, after our first encounter you— just left. You never said a word. I fell asleep and then you were gone. Months went by. I'd heard the odd tale. But that was nothing new, there were always stories about you. For nine long agonizing months I carried your seed within me while the rumors spread. Harlot they called me— in front of my parents no less! I gave birth to your baby boy— *alone.* There was no midwife. Only my mother whose shame was written all over her face. It soon became clear to me. *That night* meant nothing to you. *I meant nothing to you.*

"Then *you showed up* never knowing it was my door you'd knocked upon. You showed up for no other reason than having been ordered to do so. Next, you confide that you could not recall a single thing about *that night.* Though it was painfully obvious that you recognized me straight away."

That night. Why did she persist in referring to it as such? She made it sound akin to a bloody plague. Oh, you mean, *that night*... when the heavens rained fire and the peasants scurried about ablaze. Oh, you mean *that night*... when the outside world ceased to exist for our thoughts being consumed by something other than tragedy for once.

"The truth is the truth. I can't make it be something other than what it is." I implored.

"That isn't the point."

"Then what may I ask is the point?" I demanded with growing aggravation.

"The point is I couldn't take the risk, *could I?* Though I might have been privy to things you were not; I saw little choice but to tell you a lie."

"What could you possibly have known?" I asked skeptically.

"I knew you were coming for starters," she divulged.

"That's impossible! I didn't even know I was coming. I mean, I knew I was coming but I had no idea you'd be standing there. It's inconceivable that you could have known!"

"But you must appreciate, it wasn't until I lied that I realized you'd been telling me the truth all along."

Admittedly, it took me a moment or two to untangle that bit. Not that she waited.

"You accepted every falsehood I told you without the slightest reluctance. That threw me for a millwheel, and I didn't know what to do. Recognize, the pit I'd dug was getting deeper by the day. But it wasn't as though I wasn't hurting too."

I stared at her dumbfounded. Was it that she wasn't making sense or wasn't it rather that she was. Either way, I wasn't ready to hear it. Things were getting increasingly complex. Every word she uttered only made me increasingly fatigued.

"Can you imagine how I felt? Have you ever even tried?" She paused for a breath slighter than a hummingbird's wing beat.

"It feels akin to being stomped on and left for dead."

I had to ponder those words too for having little clue what she intended. I'd stomped on plenty of Kedera soldiers before. Was she proposing that they might not have been dead? The brains on my boots spoke otherwise. I could not help but begin to harbor doubts in respect to her argument. Still, I decided it wasn't worth pursuing in the end. Notwithstanding, she had more to say.

"But what was I to do? I'd made my own bed, hadn't I? And now there was naught to do but lie in it."

It then became clear to me that she was having more than a few lapses in respect to her memories. First and foremost, I doubt she made up the bed as the innkeepers took care of that sort of thing. Second, unless I'm entirely daft, I suspect it was lying in bed that created the predicament we presently found ourselves in. She was speaking in circles and riddles at the same time. It was time to be direct; and I was.

"Ah, and there's the difference; I haven't been lying anywhere I never confessed to be in the first place. I've told you nothing but the truth."

"That's unfair!" She bawled. "Some truths are easier than others, aren't they? You couldn't find more comfortable amor! *I don't remember. I don't even recall your name.* Some words are all too easily worn!"

More bloody riddles.

"I don't understand," I admitted. "I've never worn words. I utter them. This is utter foolishness. I still blame the heat."

I'll have you know that gave her cause to pause. She had to put her head in her lap and rethink things for quite some time. Then again, it wasn't like reckoning the arc of a catapult's volley. Why complicate simplistic things? Think before you speak, or don't speak at all. As her pretty lips parted, I prayed she understood my meaning.

"What I'm trying to say is, I've relived every moment of that night a thousand times over. What would you have done differently had you been me? What if *you* were but a fledgling girl confronted by the *Golan Butcher*– while knowing him to be the father of your child?"

Ouch! That made me wince.

"What would I have done? Kept my distance, I suppose. Reminds me of the proverb: *you can't whine about the meat for having slept with the butcher.*"

"Pig!" She blurted. "And that's not a proverb; it's a slur."

Plainly, I'd angered her. It wasn't my intention. I may have reacted spitefully, but there was some truth to it. Besides, it was quite a popular saying within my circles. I was tempted to say, *if the sandal fits you may as well wear it*– but thought better of it. Fact was, I still had no idea what she was blabbering on about– or why.

"I'm sorry, that was unfair. I only meant to imply that you knew who I was." I asserted earnestly.

"But that's just it; isn't it? I didn't know who you were."

"Yes. You did. You said so yourself."

"No. I didn't. I thought I did but you weren't at all like the rogue in the stories. You were nothing like what I'd expected." She sniveled.

"Rogue! Me?" *Guilty as charged* but I still didn't get it. Besides, she'd already made that point many times. It felt as old as the sun to be frank.

"What you said was needlessly callous. I did not deserve that."

"No, you didn't But, that doesn't change the fact that I said it. After which, I did admit to being remorseful. What more do you want?" I was so tired. It was so bloody hot. I had more than enough to chew on without her bombardment of insights and insults.

"You really don't care, do you? Is that the truth of it?" Tears began to pool in her eyes.

"Answer one thing," I sighed. "And you can keep the rest of your secrets to yourself. Why hang the dirty linen now? You had me paddling along in blissful ignorance. Why confide in me now?"

"Because we may very well die tomorrow. Because you deserve to know the truth. No, that's not true either…"

"Ah, more lies; do go on."

"Shut up!" She snapped crossly. "When will you realize this isn't about you? That ship sailed when you walked out *that door*!"

Haeryn help us! There'd be no way of ever escaping *that night* now that she'd created *that door*. Would there ever be an end to it or would I forever be confronted with that ever-glistening knob— a lever she could wrench whenever she felt a need *to twist something*.

"You don't *deserve* to know. You have no right to ask anything of me! Nothing."

I opened my mouth in protest, but she stopped me with a raised palm. I thought that'd be the end of it. Unbeknownst to me, her sails had only just begun to fill.

Admittedly, the preceding sentence was added purely to convey the fact that I did eventually discover what a *metaphor* was. It is akin to pinning imaginary wings on a cloud. As much as they might not belong, they helped fly one's thoughts toward other places. Perhaps not heaven, but someplace else.

"It's my turn to speak." She grumbled. *For Haeryn's sake! And just what did she think she'd been doing up to now*, I wondered.

"You're just following orders after all. Were it not for your *precious orders*, Renan and I would already be dead."

She stared at me sadly. I could not argue it. Her claim was accurate. But was that not a good thing? The mercenaries would have undoubtedly murdered them— or worse. There were far worse things than dying in this so-called *cultured* world of ours. That much I knew for certain.

"Why am I telling you this now, you might very well ask?" Just for the record, *I hadn't−* not that it mattered and nor would it ever.

"Well, don't flatter yourself. I'm not doing it for you. I'm doing it for me− to preserve my dignity, my self-respect. It's become clear to me now that I had every right to lie. It wasn't shameful; but shrewd of me in fact. It's what any good mother would do. And it wasn't a mistake. Because I am going to tell you exactly what happened *that night* before and after you walked out *that door* and you're going to shut up and listen to every word of it."

Told you. If only she'd acted like this on *that night.* I would have thrown her to the wolves and none of *this* would be happening. She took a deep breath. I held my tongue. I'd been told to shut up enough times already. Whereas contrary to that, I only recall saying it once to her. Not that I was counting.

"You can say whatever you like afterward," she sniffed. "You can call me a harlot. You can call me vain; foolish; simple; senseless! I don't care. You can call me anything; except a liar for I refuse to take this to the grave. I am not a person of bad character. You should treat me better. I deserve better."

A slap in the face for certain though neither undeserved. Without question, she was right. She was a good person, kind at heart and fair of mind− a far better character than me. No one would dispute that. But she still hadn't told me anything I didn't already know− yet. It was as though she was waiting for something. At the risk of being told to shut it yet again, I obliged her with an apology− of sorts.

"I'm sorry," I began, watching her nibble her lower lip.

"You're right. I'm a mindless ogre; a hapless baboon on my best day. I didn't consider things from your standpoint. It is all as you said. I was simply following orders− *blindly.* It's what I do. I am a soldier after all. It's what *we do.* I'm sorry that I don't remember… *that night.*"

How bloody wonderful. Now, she had me doing it. Without doubt there was sand in my head for I found had to shake it more than once just to get the words out.

"I don't know why I don't recall anything, but I don't. I suspect it was the drink. I don't mean it as an excuse, but they don't let me out often. For good reason, I suppose. While recognizing it speaks poorly of me, I was content being the lesser of two evils. It made sense. I am a simple man with simple pleasures after all. And I like things that make sense. Which is to imply, you're far too beautiful to share a table with the likes of me– let alone a bed.

"I expect, it's the truth of things that frightens me most. I am a coward when it comes to truths. I don't like them. Like copper pot wine, they rot my innards. I suppose what I fear most is that I did something terrible– something unspeakable to you. I'm tired of being the monster. I've wished I was dead more times than toes. For all it's worth, I am ashamed. You deserve better– better than I could give you."

"But that's just it, Radesh. You're anything but a monster!" She blurted while I stared at her with mounting uncertainty. *Was I going mad? Had she not called me the Golan Butcher barely a moment ago?*

"A monster had been what I expected– and for that it is I who is sorry. The first part, what I told you about the two men following me, was entirely true. I was frightened out of my wits. And you're right; I did choose what *I thought to be* the lesser of two evils when I sat down at your table. There were no gallant knights present. You did seem my one lone hope."

"I feel so much better," I quipped. I shouldn't have.

"Shush! Allow me to finish lest my piss and vinegar dissolves unto tears."

I held my tongue while gesturing that she held the floor. That said my attention had not waned since *you're anything but a monster*. To say my interest was aroused would have been a lavish miscarriage of the truth. And we had enough of that to sort out already– if only I'd let her finish.

"When I ran to your table, you greeted me warmly. You asked what troubled me, and I confessed my fears. You wanted to confront the two ne'er-do-wells, but they'd already bolted. You were about to give chase, but I asked you to stay with me instead. I did not want to be alone. You made me feel safe. I needed that more than anything at that moment.

"You ordered food– and ale– followed by more ale. We talked until it was late. You drank more than I ever thought possible. But you were always kind. I'd never drank ale prior. You offered to walk me home but nearly toppled over. You told me to take your room, offering to sleep in the stable instead. I confessed to being too scared to stay there alone so you offered to keep vigil at the doorstep."

Being that her green eyes were rivetted to mine, I knew every word of it was true.

"After procuring a bottle of wine and an extra blanket, we laughed every step of the way to your room. I perched myself on the mattress and you sat on the floor leaning against the door. We talked until the bottle ran dry. You were thoughtful and witty, telling tales of your youth though more about the war. You spoke of the Red Rage and how it terrified you. Then we both fell asleep."

I shifted nervously as she continued her tale. Petra no longer made eye contact; furthering my feelings of unrest while her long legs shuffled back and forth beside her uncomfortably.

"I awoke with a frightful start. You were having a bad dream. I woke you. You were confused while breathing very heavily. You couldn't remember who I was nor where you were. I told you to lie down on the bed. You fell asleep again. At least, I thought you were asleep for your breaths being so regular. I was cold. You looked so peaceful– a gentle giant, my protector. So, I climbed in too. To this day, I don't know why I did it, but I did."

She looked up to study my face. I could tell she was unsure of what to say next. I thought she'd cry but she didn't.

"We snuggled. I felt safe in your arms– as though no one could ever hurt me again. I'd never been with a man. What happened next was never my intention. I did know that everyone was wrong about you. The stories weren't true. I liked the way you smelled, like ale and fresh baked bread at once. Except when you farted– and you farted a lot. You were forthright and unapologetic, and I felt immeasurably grateful. You were considerate, but more than that, you listened to all I had to say.

"To me– you were like a book I couldn't put down. I was afraid it would end before it ever started and, admittedly, I wanted more. There was so much more to know. I could see it written in every crooked line etched upon your face. I didn't see scars. I saw tales and stories of heroic adventures. I saw hidden truths; secret chapters likely never told to anyone other than myself. You've been to so many places; done so many things. Whereas I'd only rarely left my village prior."

She looked about to burst into tears. I squeezed her hand. I wasn't about to speak. I couldn't believe what I was hearing. It was like– well, I don't know what it was akin to though I imagine a love story would not be so far amiss. It all seemed so mythical somehow.

"Feeling emboldened, I kissed you. It wasn't something I thought about. It just happened. I was as surprised as you were. You kissed me back. I rolled on top of you and– well, I think you can guess what happened next. I felt delirious. I was crying while– while– while staring into your face. I didn't know what I was doing– what we were doing. We kept it up for quite some time and then I fell asleep."

Her choice of words made her blush. I couldn't help but smile. As it turned out, I wasn't a complete ogre *that night.*

"When I awoke, I was alone. I felt unwanted and ashamed. I waited a long while, but you never returned. Having cried all the way home, eventually, I convinced myself it never happened. As much as I wanted to deny it, it soon became obvious that it did happen. Recognize, none of it was your fault. It was my doing. You did nothing wrong. You saved me– and then you left. Though you may not remember, you are blameless in this. The shame is mine alone though that doesn't make it hurt any less." she sobbed.

"I'm far from blameless." I blurted aloud. Though a moment earlier I'd felt somewhat vindicated near to the point of feeling triumphant, suddenly, if truth need be told, I felt so horrid I thought I might vomit.

"It takes two if I recall correctly. Admittedly, the temptation of you would prove too much for most men– let alone in a drunken state. I do apologize but I am the man that I am. Though relieved not to have proved myself a monster, I had no business sharing company with the likes of you."

Sighing, I lay down. My head was all fuzzy. There was far more to think about than my mind was able to assess. I felt exhausted– and I was already exhausted before any of this had started if you care to recall. Notwithstanding, I'd gone from being her champion to a cowardly deserter in less than a heartbeat.

"We should get some sleep. You can squeeze in beside me if you like. I promise to behave." I said, exhaling my anxiety.

"I am tired. I'm so glad I told you. You deserve to know the truth."

Cradling Renan in her arms; she laid back and put her head very near to my chest. I could feel my heart pounding. The scent of her was wholly intoxicating. Never more so had I wanted a woman. But that was my penance, wasn't it? The punishment for reaching for things that could never belong to me.

"There's more," she continued. "I have one last confession."

"Not now. It can wait. I swear my head will burst. Let us sleep if we can find it. We'll need all our wits come morning– should I have any remaining."

"It's important," she whispered. "I must say it."

"It'll keep. We will talk again. You have my word. I promise you that."

She was pouting. I didn't have to look. I could tell. The slender curve of her body felt strangely foreign. She was warm and alluring while I was a stone statue. I had to be. She was the Major's wife after all and I, but a foul tide staining pristine lands forbidden to speak of let alone touch. I stared blankly watching waves of heat drift upward from our tired bodies. The tent was ripe with the smell of perspiration. I liked it– especially those lingering beneath her dark braid of hair. I'd heard other soldiers speak in detail about their personal exploits. I never spoke of such things myself. It wasn't due to any form of chivalry. I just never remembered. Truth be told, though I didn't dare ask, I would have appreciated a few more specifics regarding *that night*. Upon closing my eyes, the darkness walloped me like an iron fist.

"Awake! Awake! To arms!" I hollered aloud, instinctively reverting to the soldier's alarm cry– completely terrifying Petra. Renan, naturally, began to bawl. Having had yet another bad dream, I felt quite disoriented. My hair and djellaba were soaked with sweat.

Petra cursed me for which I could have no complaint. It was obvious we'd both been torn from a particularly deep slumber. Though entirely unintentional, her moment of awakening had been admittedly harsher than my own. Not by much mind you.

"We've missed the dusk," I grumbled angrily. "Who knows how long we've slumbered unaware. Take Renan outside so I might pack our belongings swiftly," I ordered. "We shall leave at once!"

Still cursing, Petra arose; immediately handing the crying infant to me. I was about to object before realizing, as was usual when she awoke, she simply needed to relieve herself. I jostled the baby up and down impatiently awaiting her return. By the time she re-entered the tent, I had managed to compose myself somewhat. I smiled at her rather sheepishly before passing her a piece of dried fruit, followed by the water sling which was very nearly empty. I took a bite of what I thought to be fruit and grimaced. Petra laughed, nibbling at her own tidbit rather skeptically.

"Yam," she smiled. "It's not so bad– compared to nothing."

"Yum," I replied. "Sorry to wake you so cruelly. I startled myself half-to-death in truth."

"Try harder next time," she retorted. "I could not have been more asleep had I been dead. I'm soaked to the bone with sweat– more yours than mine, I think."

"Your robes will dry soon enough. We must make haste. We chase the dusk; by how much there is no way to tell."

"Not by much." Petra said, shaking her head. "Renan only ever sleeps a couple hours at a time. I recall only three times he awoke so I'm quite certain it's only just passed."

"Well, I never sleep well− yet oddly, I did. Though I expect you are right in your assumption." I sighed. "We can do this. I am the assassin and you, my prisoner."

"Prisoners!" She corrected. "So, essentially, nothing has changed."

"No, nothing. Be at ease, I will treat you as cruel as ever." I winked. "I only hope I'm not forced to beat you."

Pressuring her outside the tent, I packed our belongings before setting a hasty pace toward Hell's Well. All the while I called out final preparations as they arose amongst my jumbled thoughts.

"Remember Petra, above all else, you must not call me by my given name. I've killed many men in battle and, though most men know me as the Golan Butcher, there may be some who've heard of the name Radesh." It felt strange to say my alias aloud; for only rarely having spoken it before.

"What should I call you then?"

"I don't know. I'm told the Brotherhood forsake their given names along with their possessions. Still, it would only make sense that you refer to me by some moniker."

"How about Turnip? Or Rutabaga? Or is that too similar?" I stared at her bewildered.

"To Radesh." She finished, making me guffaw.

"It seems your wit never slumbers."

"How about Zil?" Petra grinned. "Is that more palatable?"

"Zil, as in BroZil. Yes, I think that should suffice."

"Onward Zil− lead the way. Herd your captives forward; drag us if you must!" She commanded me.

"Oh, there'll be no sled today. I'm so tired I can barely drag myself."

"Knackered?"

"Utterly knackered." I confirmed, chuckling aloud.

The moon was bright white. Though waning, you could still envision its entire circumference. Had it been closer to dusk, it would have appeared more aflame. *A peach slice on a grey plate* was how Petra described it the evening prior. This night was windy and chilly.

Our damp attire only furthered our discomfort. Gazing upward, I prayed secretly that radish wasn't about to be added to the Kedera's menu.

About that tree. Admittedly, the pavilion had initially distracted us, but now that we'd come to terms with that, the tree gravitated over us without contest. The sheer grandeur of it was preposterous. Not merely for its size but more so its placement. It simply did not belong. Yet there it was. I'd seen castles and fortresses, many of which were undeniably larger, though the tree somehow appeared more grandiose. Though it hurt the mind just to look at it, it couldn't be helped, however. The massive tree rose from the sand like a mammoth rood-tree— a crucifix upon which there was no telling how many lifeless forms had hung. Kestrels mostly, I expect. I could only hope we'd prove ourselves more fortunate.

After countless leagues of walking, we'd seen four, maybe five haggard cacti— and then this monstrosity rises from the depths of hell without warning— and ripe with leaves, no less. It was unbelievable. A tale no one could swallow without witnessing it in person. Only Haeryn knows how it ended up in such a place. Then again, perhaps he planted it. It would make sense. It was the very thing fables and myths were bred of. A seed found only in dreams until it stood before you. Though neither of us said as much, we couldn't help but feel in the presence of the Gods. A behemoth if ever there was, it couldn't possibly be real. Except it was— watching every step we took. It didn't lurk in the shadows, it owned them.

It proved a far longer trek than it looked. It was an illusion of sorts. The tree was so massive it feigned to be but a short distance away. It wasn't. Not by a long shot. Becoming increasingly dark with every new step taken, it took us three times as long as I thought it would to come within shouting distance of the posted guards.

There was no need to shout. They saw us. By the time we reached them, there were far more than two. I could not discern a precise count however for their numbers being continually bolstered. It was obvious that our sudden appearance had caused quite a stir. They lit a small bonfire ahead of the well and waited. And, as we came within earshot, I called out to them.

"We come in peace! We seek only water and shelter for a night!"

Day rather, but I was certain they knew what I intended. It wasn't as though it was an Inn where we'd simply rent a room after a hearty meal while downing several pints. Or so I thought at the time.

It's uncanny how often one's thoughts revert to food and ale in the middle of a desert. More than leaves on that blessed tree, I expect.

There was no reply other than a tall man with a covered face beckoned us forward with a hand. It seemed obvious he was their leader. The closer we got, the more still they became. It was as though they were dissolving into the surrounding world of shadows. Though the others did not wear the hijab, still they seemed faceless for their expressions were drab and devoid of emotion. The only distinct feature being the firelight flickering in their eyes. Fixated entirely upon us; they were captivated yet utterly detached at the same time. Furthering our feelings of unease, beneath the looming shadow of the massive tree, it grew increasingly cold. The faces of the men were so grim a shiver ran down my spine the likes of which I'd never felt before. I'd faced battle-hardened men before, but this was different. If they chose to kill us— there was nothing we could do. Even if I managed to summon the Rage, there were far too many of them. Simply put, we would die.

Our vulnerability was palpable to the point of being overwhelming. They knew it. We knew it. Red Rage or no Red Rage, my resolve felt akin to the moon— swiftly waning. I felt so cold and helpless I thought for certain I'd piss myself. Stopping but a few yards short of them, I was fearful that I would not be able to stop my legs from trembling. I was right. I couldn't. They weren't trembling from fear but shivering from the cold just to be clear. Still, I did not soil myself so not all was lost.

"By order of the Forth Rah, I request water and shelter for me and my prisoners."

Being so inordinately dry, my voice sounded abnormally gruff— even by my standards. Petra kept her head— along with Renan— buried deep within her shawl. A long silence ensued. Dropping our belongings and turning to the tall man that had beckoned us forward, I engaged him more forcefully.

"Are you deaf? Are you mute? Do you not bow to the Four?" I implored loudly.

The man retracted the lower portion of his headscarf, dropping it about his shoulder. The skin all about his mouth was frightfully scarred, though evenly proportioned as though done deliberately. As he spoke, I found myself wholly transfixed by his eyes. I felt a powerful sense that I'd met him before. In battle I could only assume for seeing no other possibility.

"I am neither deaf, nor mute, nor senseless. You are a stranger to this place. Only a fool would heed the command of an outsider. We do not trust strangers. We add them to our wall." He said curtly, gesturing toward the waist-high white wall surrounding the well. Following his cue, which only seemed polite, it quickly became apparent that what I had originally thought to be stones were, in fact, human skulls. *Wonderful.* I decided to start over.

"Ah, I see you are a collector. How quaint." I noted.

Pretending to be unimpressed, while on the very brink of fouling myself, I walked slowly over to the skull wall and spat. Widening my stance, I leant back, hoisted the assassin's djellaba, and let loose. Closing my eyes, I uttered a grateful sigh of relief.

"I don't keep tally myself." I called out with my back still turned and bare ass exposed. Continuing my most urgent mission, I made sure to glisten as many skulls as possible with my urine. It was foul smelling. Dropping my robes and turning about, I noticed their leader's raised hand. Having waved it downward the man nearest to me sheathed his sword. It was obvious he'd wanted me to recognize just how close to death I'd come. Walking past his henchman, I winked, prior to standing directly in front of Petra again.

"At least someone with brains is in charge. What is your name?" I inquired.

"What is my name?" The tall man laughed. "He wants to know my name." He roared loudly. His men broke into pretentious laughter. Pushing past me, he grabbed Petra, tugging open her shawl.

"What have you hidden in there?" He scowled. Her eyes wide with fear, Petra immediately brandished her hairpin. *But of course, she did. What part of being a prisoner did she not understand?*

"Get away from me!" She quailed, shivering with as much fear as cold. She made several short jabbing motions at the man, but he was so shocked by what he saw he took no notice of her antics whatsoever. *Thankfully.*

"She's a bloody woman! Harboring an infant!!" He gasped with astonishment, echoed by shouts of disbelief from his kinsmen. Whirling about he soon found my dagger next to his throat.

"As I told you, they're my prisoners. My orders are to deliver them *unharmed* to Rah Delevan."

I did not like the man. Never in all my life had I wanted to slit a man's throat more. I pushed him back in the direction of his men, who'd begun encroaching on us, before hastily sheathing my gold-handled dagger.

"Ah, but there's no need for bloodshed." I smiled broadly

whilst praying it was true. "We seek only water and shelter. I merely requested your name. What harm can there be in that? It's only customary when two parties meet. Where I come it's considered proper conduct." I added quietly.

He glared at me until his indignation abated enough for him to speak. I'd seen his quick-tempered type all too often and they weren't to be trifled with. Had he been a soldier in my company, I would have beat him to a bloody pulp, so he learned his place. But he wasn't. Save for the jester standing before him, he held all the cards.

"You do realize you'd be dead already if not for me. You'd do well to recognize the only person keeping you, and your prisoners, alive— is me. Have no misconceptions— unsheathe your pretty dagger again and you will die where you stand."

"My apologies. I did not mean to startle you. Even so, did I not confide that I am following orders and under the protection of the Forth Rah?" I queried. "Did I not say, I am to deliver my prisoners to him unharmed?" Knowing how cold Renan and Petra had to be, I grabbed her forcibly by the arm and led her closer to the fire, talking calmly all the while.

"Our water ran dry shortly after dusk. You have water," I gestured, nodding toward the well. "Just because it's surrounded by the bones of your enemies is no reason not to share. I am not your enemy. We are thirsty. We are cold. We are tired; and we are hungry. Give us all that I ask, and I will gladly answer your questions— as best as I am able. But know this: the Rah's business is the business of Rahs."

"Yes, yes. Our business is their business; but their business is no business of ours." The man mocked. "You'll soon discover we do things a bit differently here." He concluded.

"And the more things differ, the more they stay the same." I countered. I'd heard someone or other say that once. Not that I fully understood what it meant.

"Ah, but it's only within our differences that our true strengths lie." He spat. "Look around you, my strength is readily apparent whereas yours… not so much."

"But are we not all the same blood? Do we not follow a like-minded agenda?" I asked. "Are we not all Kedera?"

"My patience grows thin. The crown of the Great Tree belongs to me. I rule these forsaken lands. I ask the questions here."

"These lands?" I sneered with a laugh. "Have them! We want no part of them. We're only passing through. Give us water for

Haeryn's sake— then ask what you will. Be at ease, I will answer all I can." I affirmed, slapping the empty water slings dangling slung about my neck.

"Though I really should kill you," he said, "admittedly, you've piqued my interest. Bring them water!" He commanded irritably.

His boisterous decree startled Renan who begat bawling. The guard nearest the well swiftly carried over a large vessel putting it down in front of us. He then passed me a long wooden ladle. I had to brush away several hairs on the bowl's edge— cat hair undoubtedly. I cared not. Well, in hindsight, I suppose I did— having taken the time to brush them away. Still, it was more water than we'd seen in days. It was cold and it was beautiful— glorious in truth.

Brimming the ladle, I held it to Petra's lips who drank without hesitation. Dipping the sleeve of her shawl, she then moistened Renan's lips. He immediately stopped crying. I filled her a second ladle before having a long drink myself. Reaching a hand into her shawl, Petra began to nurse Renan who now made suckling noises as opposed to his normal soft whimpers.

Never had I tasted water so sweet; it was positively delightful. I poured yet another ladle over my head. After scrubbing free the sand clinging to the back of my neck and ears, I rubbed my numb fingers quickly together. Holding them over the fire, I returned my attention to the tall man who seemed unable to peel his eyes from Petra. All the men were gaping at her which made me feel increasingly uneasy. This was not good. This was not good at all.

"You were about to tell me your name and how so many of you came to be in the middle of the Kestrel." I proclaimed hoping to quash their collective rudeness.

"If nothing else, you are persistent. I give you that." The tall man replied, reverting his gaze toward me finally. His voice was gravelly reminiscent of a soldier I once knew who'd miraculously survived an arrow that had whistled through both cheeks. But it was *those eyes* of his that held me spellbound. Surely, we'd met sometime prior. I was certain of it. If his face was any indication, I expect I'd wounded him badly— though mortally would have been by far my preference. I swore to myself right then and there, if given the chance, I would not make the same mistake twice. He was perilous.

"No, I wasn't." He corrected me flatly.

"Just when I thought we were making some progress," I sighed. "Thank you for the water." I wisely added.

"You are going—"

"You are welcome." I interrupted foolishly. He glared at me spitefully. "You are supposed to say, you are welcome following an expression of gratitude." What can I say? I despised all forms of rudeness.

"You are welcome– to answer my questions– to my complete satisfaction– or mark my words, Haeryn himself will turn his eyes away for the doom I will inflict upon you." He paused.

I held my tongue. It was obvious. His wrath had reached its breaking point. I must admit, I did take some pride in that initially. Key word being *initially*.

"No one knows of this place," he began, tapping his fingers against his lips thoughtfully. "And yet, here you are. Do you know how many men have crossed the Kestrel without aid of this place?"

Knowing it to be rhetorical, I made no reply. I know what you're thinking; and yes, I do know what that means. Speaking metaphorically, though not without a measure of irony, it was akin to asking a lion whether it's hungry. It need not be asked for it knows nothing other. Notwithstanding, it will eat you alive should the question be posed– though not out of spite nor any other form of indignation but rather, simply because that's what it was designed to do– gnaw flesh from bone.

"None, not even one." He continued. "Yet here you are with a woman and baby no less. First, you will tell me who you are. And, by that, I mean *all of you.* Second, you will inform me how it is that you've come upon this place– *this place,* which no one knows of, other than our own company."

I was about to answer him, but he held up a hand to stop me. Even by my fellow soldiers' low standards, I found his rudeness appalling. In fact, had we been somewhere else and the circumstances different I would have seen him demoted– a thumb or two.

"I am obliged to caution you. *Think!* Do not answer hastily; for should your answer disagree with me in any way it will precipitate your demise."

I took a short breath, never once taking my eyes from his own. I hated those eyes. Not to mention his raspy voice. As noted, it was as though he'd been strangled at some point. I knew the sound well for having throttled a neck or two in my time. A notion I did not find unappealing at the time. If for no other reason than him having used the word *precipitate*. Pompous ass. Who speaks as such? Having recognized the word *demise*, I did reckon his intent, however. Well, if it was to be a battle of wits, then reign over him I would.

"The truth hath no need of deliberation," I smiled, solely for having employed a word of comparable duration. "It does not ponder. It is what it is— simply the truth. Being of the Brotherhood, I forfeited my birth name long ago as is our custom. We are the Nameless. Should a name prove vital to your cause, you may call me Zil. As I declared openly upon our arrival, our paths have crossed strictly for my services having been commissioned by the Forth Rah. Who my prisoners are is the lone business of *that same Rah,* Rah Delevan— not mine; and certainly not yours." I paused.

"As for your second query, our presence here is strictly by chance. It was Haeryn's will. The will of the Gods. If that answer does not suffice, I can elaborate. I can tell you precisely how we ended up here, but not in this setting for not all I would share is intended for every ear. Rest assured; I can offer a better answer between us privately— whilst sharing some wine perhaps or something stronger still."

There was no harm in trying. Not to mention, the previous day's conversation had left me feeling rather desperate for a drink. Furthermore, its availability seeming highly likely given the presence of so many men.

"I will tell you," Petra blurted to my utter astonishment. "It was a bloody miracle! We'd be dead by now had we not seen that tree!" I raised my hand to slap her, but the tall man grabbed my arm. Know that I would not have struck her were it not fully warranted and integral to my role.

"Don't hit me, you coward!" She hollered. Understand, she'd taken me by surprise— prior to realizing she was only playing her part. Which is to imply, had I struck her it would have aligned with her own actions and, therefore, hardly improper given our charade in progress.

"We got here purely by blind luck! By all the Hounds of Haeryn, we were utterly lost! He had no clue where we were going! He's a filthy liar! He kidnapped me and my baby! He raped me! Kill him! Kill him now!"

As was typical with our ever-evolving relationship, but a moment earlier, I'd found myself admiring her creativity and cleverness— and then came that last bit. *Kill him? Kill him now?* She said that— no, really, she did— and with devout enthusiasm no less. I thought my acting had been convincing but, as it turned out, Petra was a natural as they say. Point being, she was so good at it I now had doubts as to whether she still had my best interests in mind. Worse, it seemed to me that most of those present preferred her version of the events over my own. I did notice several hands touch the hilts of their swords. Acting was one thing but… was she trying to get me killed? It was downright scary. Not to mention, I thought we'd ironed out our differences but a night earlier. Perhaps not. Perhaps she was still on about *that night*. But what about *this night*? This present night– the one that had dramatically taken a turn for the worse. Thanks to her meddling ways!

"Pay her no heed," I stated calmly. "She'd desecrate Haeryn's Holy Halls to save her skin. Take comfort, Rah Delevan will deal with her soon enough. Take heart, had he not requested she be delivered unharmed I'd be dragging her in a sack. Should any of you devise a way by which to prove her literate, I will gladly remove her tongue. I am rather famished." I smiled subtly.

Two could play this game. Admittedly, her antics had blindsided me initially, but I was ready now– *with bells on*. If it was a role-playing duel she wanted, she'd soon discover that she'd met her match. It seemed the fight had been drained from her however for she became much quieter. *Who's the better actor now,* I mused. Me.

"I've heard quite enough. You know where to take them. I will question them further as the sun rises." The tall man said. 'There is more to their tale for certain and I will wring every last damp bit of it from their tongues if need be if that's what it takes to hear it in full."

"What of the infant?" Asked a man stepping forward from the shadows. Having not noticed him previously, a chill stifled my bones for I recognized him instantly. He was none other than that same stranger I'd witnessed combing the ashes of our burnt home so very long ago. The same one I'd spoken to as a young lad when my uncle's family had perished in the fire. A long facial scar ran the length of his face through an eye– the useless one that wobbled about like a boiled egg. There was no mistaking that hideous face. It was him.

"Where is Myrna?" Asked the tall man, turning about.

"Painting," replied the straggly-haired, bulbous-eyed man.

"I did not ask *what* she was doing. Of course, she is painting! She's always painting. *Where* is she?" The tall man inquired with mounting agitation.

"Doesn't matter," he continued dismissively. "Find her and give her the infant. Tell her to put down her bloody paintbrushes and look after the wee one until I call for her." He frowned.

"As you say, it will be done." His sidekick cyclops nodded piously.

"Oh… and tell her if she paints but a toenail on the child all her privileges will be revoked."

"You're not taking Renan!" Shrieked Petra frightfully. "I would sooner die than let you touch him!"

"That can be arranged," smirked the leader. "Though all in good time, fair maiden."

"The prisoners are my responsibility," I attested, blocking the men from Petra. "They are to remain with me and under my watch at all times."

"Why Haeryn, why?" Sighed the tall man. "Why must it always be so hard?" He asked looking up at the night sky.

"This is the will of the Forth Rah; it is non-negotiable." I insisted, sticking my chin out defiantly.

"Of course, it is," he smirked. He then pointed a finger at the sky. Staring upward, besides the odd flicker of flame, I saw only darkness in the shadows above. *What is he on about now?* Unbeknownst to me, he'd also made a chopping motion with his hand. Whether I was looking upward or down I cannot say though, either way, I immediately saw stars.

* * * * *

I awoke. My head was aching. My eyes stung. They were unable to focus, everything looked watery and opaque. My heart was racing to find myself in a state of proper panic. I wanted to rub my eyes and throbbing head, but I was unable to raise my arms. I couldn't move them at all. I coughed violently while recognizing a repulsive sensation– *sand*. It was not just in my eyes. I could taste it in my mouth. That and a hefty lump of clotted blood which dribbled from my nose like a broken spigot. I hate sand. I really do. It's horrid– like a cloud of grit intent on devouring your soul. The soldier's cry rang out.

"Awake!" Shrieked Petra loudly. Though she sounded very close, strangely, I could not discern her shape at all. I adored the shape of her, the way her body moved in time to her ceaseless mood swings, not unlike the way the wind bent grass according to its own desires and temperament. To be clear, I was only half conscious with my thoughts still fighting to divide my dream world from reality.

"Awake! Ra… Zil! Are you alright! Answer me!" She hollered to my rising chagrin.

"I'm here. I'm here. But Haeryn have mercy, please stop yelling. My head is throbbing like a marching drum. Is it the drink?"

"No!"

"You're still yelling." I grimaced forlornly. "Either way, I've had more than my fill and need to leave. Besides, what vile tavern caters purely in sand?"

"It's a cavern not a tavern! Fool!"

"Where are my legs, let alone arms? What in Harbinger have they done to me?"

"To us! They've buried us alive, Ra… Zil! We're up to our necks in it! It's even in my hair! My braid is completely riddled with it."

"Your hair?" I stammered in utter disbelief. My head was in complete agony while her chief care was her sandy hair. *Truly?*

"Yes, but that's hardly the worst of it."

"Don't tell me your hairpin is gone."

"Yes, it is. But, more importantly, that one-eyed man…."

"One-eyed man? I dreamt of him. The one from the land of the unicorns and giants." But what, pray tell, could be more important than her hair, I wondered. Now, I was genuinely alarmed.

"What? No! Do you not remember anything— the desert, the pavilion, the great tree?"

"The great tree." I mumbled as my thoughts finally began to clear. "The one-eyed man. I've seen him before— long ago."

"Yes, him. He said we have until mid-day to speak the truth, or they'll let the sun bleach our skulls white and add them to that dreadful wall."

"Wonderful. I expect mine won't take very long. It feels half-baked already."

"Don't say that!"

"Then stop yelling. Please." I begged.

I could hear her voice to my left, but I could not see her for only being able to turn my head but slightly. I'm not sure I would have attempted to look at her anyway— being that it hurt so badly. As my watering eyes cleared, I spied a small bird perched within a cage that hung from the ceiling. It appeared to be a kestrel. Beneath it and straight ahead of me, I envisioned a large striped hulking shape padding back and forth within yet another, albeit much larger, wooden cage. Its low growls were quite unnerving.

"What's in Haeryn's Hells is that?" I asked, fearing the answer.

"You know very well what it is— the Harbinger cat."

"I was afraid you'd say that. Hopefully it's been well fed."

"At least it stopped trying to claw its way toward us. It was pulling its cage closer and closer but, when the cage rolled over, it appeared to give up. Thank Haeryn, or you'd have had a rude awakening for certain."

"How long was I out?"

"I don't know– a long time– felt like forever. I'm terrified, Rrr... Zil! They took Renan! Do you hear! They've taken Renan from me!"

Apparently, in her despair, she was finding it difficult not to refer to me as Radesh. At least she hadn't said it in its entirely for I had every confidence we were being closely watched.

"It is beyond my power now. I have failed Rah Delevan." I bemoaned loudly. "Is there no honor to be found in this place?" I lamented.

"Well, they've made their beds now, haven't they?" I added. "Mark my words, they'll get what's coming to them. They'll be made to answer soon enough. There's plenty of wood here. The Forth Rah will see they all burn, one by one, at the stake!"

"What are you on about? Did you not hear me? They've taken Renan! *You* must fix this! This is your mess, and it is you who must answer for it!"

"What lies have you been sowing, wench?"

"I've not told them anything– *yet*. But I will tell them everything and more if that is what it takes to get my son back! You do understand; Renan is *everything* to me– my entire world."

"You do understand the *entire world is listening*. Do not give up the fight now." I whispered.

"Your lies won't save you!" I added loudly. "When Rah Delevan discovers we are missing his anger will be kindled and he will come looking!"

"When faeries wear boots! Unless they've a caravan of flying camels, I very much doubt you'll see anyone anytime soon. Save for a pale horseman harvesting the dead– though he may choose to ride a Harbinger cat instead." She huffed.

"No, Rah Delevan will come." I insisted. "And, in the meantime, *the truth* remains our sole savior. All we can do is tell *the truth* and hope that *the truth* is enough." I pleaded.

Petra did not seem to be catching on. Ironically, being wholly reliant upon her astuteness and discretion, she appeared to have abandoned her wits entirely just when I needed her most.

"And you understand; I will do whatever it takes to get my son back."

"And precisely what might that entail?" A voice arose from somewhere behind us. Haeryn help us! If Petra didn't get with the plan soon, we were done for. In hindsight, I expect it was due to her never having been captured before. Had our present plight been captured within a book entitled *The Many Atrocities of Sand,* undoubtedly, she'd have known precisely what to do. But that was her, wasn't it? If it wasn't in a book she didn't know up from down. Then again, it wasn't that complicated. It wasn't slingshot sorcery. All she needed to do was to simply stay the course.

"There is naught to tell," I stated flatly. "Save for petty details about how we became lost and ended up in this dank hole of evil intent. For this you will be made to answer! I can assure you of that. The Forth Rah does not tolerate insubordination."

"I was not talking to you, assassin. Know that I will not suffer your insolence so charitably a second time."

"Charitably? You broke my nose. You buried us in sand. How might that be considered *charitable* in any way?"

"I gave you fair warning, which you did not heed. Now, we will do things *my way.* I am curious. You do recognize our country is at war? Surely, during such times, you can't expect us to accept the assertions of outsiders ahead of our own welfare."

"As I told you, I am of the Brotherhood. As I told you, I am following orders dispensed by the Forth Rah himself."

"So, you say. But you are lying. How is that you arrived here? Who told you about this place?"

"No one. As I told you before, we just got lucky."

"Lucky?" He laughed. "I think not. Luck is akin to catching a fish not a unicorn tusk on a mule. You arrived with four empty water slings dangling about your neck. How so? Unless you knew about the well. Unless you knew you could replenish them."

"You assume much." I spat angrily. "The only tusk we envisioned was the giant tree from afar. As unlikely as it seems, it became our sole grail. We needed a miracle and we found it. Why? Ask Haeryn for who might answer such things? And what would you have us do? Resign the fight? Give up and die? Devoid of hope, nothing remains. And so, we endured. And so, we were delivered."

"Liar! Your words are thick with thorns! You dare speak of hope. You know nothing of hope. Ask her, ask the mother separated from her son the true meaning of hope."

"But who is it that balances the scales of hope and hopelessness? He who is not buried in sand. He who is free to go but chooses rather to stay."

"You know as well as I, hope abandoned you the moment you

set foot within the Kestrel. But somehow, miraculously, you traveled to the only place that could save you. Know that my patience hangs upon the merest of threads. I ask you again, who told you about this place?"

"No one. I've told you the truth. Believe what you will."

"Lies, lies, and still more lies! I have half a mind to remove that deceitful tongue of yours. Tell me this, why did you not simply present your written orders to me upon arrival? Would it not have made things simpler?"

"The orders are mine." I seethed. "A contract solely between benefactor and beneficiary– Rah Delevan and me. Did I not inform you of my orders? Allow me to refresh your memory– I did– upon arrival. I did so in good faith which should have been enough."

"It wasn't. I have no faith… no more than you have hope. Especially, not in you. Why should I?"

"But how might I presume your state of mind?"

"My state of mind is strictly that– my own. Only fools presume. Only a fool would assume they'd be taken at their word. I do not abide fools. I bury them."

"What choice had I but to be wary?"

"Did you really expect us to welcome you with open arms? Could you really be that simple?"

"Simple? It is your stability that remains in question, not mine. The pact is in your possession. You know the entirety of things. Yet, still, I remain buried in sand. It seems the truth holds little weight."

"*Truth*. We did not find the contract within your belongings until *after* you were buried. *Truth*. It's wiser to substantiate your identity *prior* to being rendered unconscious. *Truth*. Acts of insubordination have consequences. *Truth*. I've had about all I can tolerate of you on this day."

"Release us at once and I shall see that no harm comes to you or your men."

"*Truth*. Shut your mouth or you will quickly find my boot in it. Now, allow me to talk to the girl *without interruption* or, so help me, I will kick your skull with such enthusiasm it will clang off the wall."

He did seem sincere. Thus, after careful consideration, coupled with the fact the mere suggestion of my head being struck yet again made it feel as though it might erupt, I bit my tongue.

"What is your name girl? Your full name as given to you at birth?"

"Petrella Ursula Bryn."

"And where are you from?"

"Gadev. My parents run the trading post there."

"Studayo House?"

"The same."

"Humph. I saw a concert there once— long, long ago."

I saw a concert there once—long, long ago. It was only by the barest of margins that I somehow managed to hold my tongue. Such nerve. I would enjoy killing him— *later*. Once I'd figured out how to free myself. And then, many long years afterward, as someone made mention of the Kestrel, I would reminisce about it fondly. *Humph. I killed a man there once— long, long ago.*

"Now tell me, I beg of you. What horrors have forced you to travel with such woeful company."

"*Woeful* and *forced* are the proper terminology for I had no choice in the matter."

"You're educated?" He sounded surprised.

"I can read. Studayo House has many books and I little other to do— until Renan that is."

"Ah— reading, one of my fondest pastimes. I have an extensive library. I do hope you're able to see it at which point we shall have a discussion at length about our shared passion. Providing our present circumstances change, that is."

Of course, he read. Of course, he had a library. They had so much in common after all. Why wouldn't they? One being buried up to her pretty neck; the other, likely leaning on a shovel. The only thing I wanted to have with him at length was taut a rope about his neck.

"How did he capture you? You said he raped you. Is that true?"

"No. He didn't."

"Why accuse him falsely then?"

"Because he kicked our door in and took us at knife point. I said it because I hate him. Who in my place wouldn't have said it?"

"Though you may be smart, it doesn't deem you trustworthy. Why even admit to lying?"

"Because I'm buried up to my neck in sand. Because you have my baby! Because the only chance I see of surviving is to tell the precious truth however bad it might appear." Petra sniffed.

"You're right about that. But your parents own Studayo House— surely there were some family members present or servants that might have protected you."

"The salesmen are dead," she wailed. "After killing them he fed them to the pigs!"

Admittedly, I did not like where this was headed. It seemed I didn't have a leg to stand on. Or did I? Being buried in sand was confusing that way. Regardless, she wasn't done— *as usual.*

"My parents are gone!" Petra sobbed. 'They disappeared near three weeks ago while traveling to Mongos. Understand, they played no part in the war. My parents are peaceful, law-abiding shopkeepers. Following their disappearance, he broke into our house and kidnapped us. *Please* return my son and let us go. We are innocent in this."

"Innocent? Humph. Let you go? And where would you go within this endless sea of sand? Left, right, forward march?"

"I don't know. You might provide us safe passage— provide us an escort. Just free us *please*. As I said, we are innocent!"

"There you go again. I learned long ago, no one is innocent. Of that I am certain. Tell me, why do you refer to this rogue as Ra-Zil?"

"I don't know. Why does it matter? *Please!* We aren't of any importance to anyone. I implore thee, just let us go." She whimpered.

"She is not what she feigns to be," I interrupted. "She knows things— *of import to the war.* It's true she's clever, but no less vindictive than cunning. She calls me *Rah Zil* purely out of spite. She mocks me having no fear of reprisal." I huffed. That part was true. Being that I was on a bit of a roll, I decided there'd be little harm in pressing my luck a wee bit further.

"Still, who she might be remains none of *your* business," I barked. "It is the business of—"

"I— end— mad— bulls." He said purposely.

"Wait! Wait!! Let's talk about this. Don't! Don't! Let's not—" Regretfully, it was precisely then that I discovered my captor was indeed a man of his word. Translation: I saw stars again.

* * * * *

All was dark. The wild crickets were back for my ears were ringing as never before. Something damp touched my face. Lashing out, I heard only hollers in return. My hands were soon tied and soon after my legs. Someone was forcing me to drink. As parched as I was, it felt like some new form of torture. My throat ached. It was so swollen I could not help but gag. Though wet, it didn't taste like water. Nor ale, not that I was expecting as much. Perhaps, they were poisoning me.

I tried to bite whatever came near. They were too quick. Or, more likely, I was too slow. My lips flapped like weathered rags being split and badly tattered. Each time I awoke they continued to pour while I continued to gag. Undoubtedly, it was the tall rogue with the thoughtless eyes. He was trying to drown me.

My eyes refused to open. They were bandaged. That explained it. I tried dragging my face against the cot to free the bandages, but it felt as though an eye might depart its socket the linen was so crusted with blood. I knew the feeling well– though only rarely from my own injuries. It was that final line in that damn book torturing me again– *when every wound crusts hard with salt*. I tried to tear the bandages away, but the weight of the world came crushing down upon me. Or, more accurately, my hands remained tied. Entirely helpless, I slipped back into the void. I did not see stars, only blackness. Greater blackness. If there was such a thing. Which there was.

I woke up sometime later. More darkness. Having been pried open with a wooden stick, my lips split apart again. They felt more akin to bark than skin. My throat was so dry it was indescribable. It felt inside out somehow as though it'd absorbed an entire sea of sand. Okay, so not indescribable but bleak all the same. I stopped fighting. There was no point. More truthfully, now that I ceased to resist, I realized the tacky liquid tasted quite good. Wonderful in fact, both sweet and sour at once. Not to mention, being cool and moist, it felt soothing. It did nothing for my current state of mind, however. My head was positively throbbing as though my haggard heart had been crammed between my temples.

I opened my eyes, but I could not see anything. Perhaps, I was dead. Perhaps, the evil swine had blinded me; snuffed my eyes with a molten rod. It was then that I remembered the bloody bandages. Though damp, they felt less crusted at least. I could move neither arms nor legs. My breath came in loud, short rasps. I may not be dead but, without doubt, I was dying. Dying for more of the sticky tasting stuff. Dying to see my surroundings. Dying to be free again. Dying to have my vengeance. Dying. Dying. Dying.

Strangely, I did not care. I was done. There was no fight left within me. The Red Rage lay but a distant memory. It wasn't real. It did not exist. What did exist, like a river rushing toward me, was the darkness. It was as if I'd been thrown into a cold black lake. I was drowning in gloom. Whatever the case; it was swallowing me whole. And I welcomed it. The spinning stars were brighter than anything else in my world. The pain of living was too much. I would not endure.

* * * * *

"Praise Haeryn! Thank the gods, you're awake!"

"Is that you, Petra?" I croaked. I didn't even recognize my own voice– what it had become. I felt a damp cloth pressed upon my forehead. The bandages covering my eyes had been removed. Forcing my stinging eyes open, I felt dizzy and sick to my stomach. Everything was but a broadening blur. All I wanted was to fall back asleep– return to whatever dark hole I'd crawled out of.

"Yes. You're alive though I'd thought certain we'd lost you."

"You can still be alive and feel like this?" I crowed. "No, I think not. I want a second opinion." I saw shapes bustling about. It was very unsettling. "Wait. Why are my hands tied? Where am I? Who are all these… women?" I wondered aloud.

"Manners, please. They've been tirelessly caring for you. If not for them, you'd be dead. You were unconscious for three full days and two long nights."

"Mightn't we have a bit of privacy?" I whispered. "And it's not as though I had called them wenches."

"Ladies," she said loudly, but politely. "Could you leave us alone for a time please? There's too many of us. He finds your presence disorientating." Which I definitely would have if only I'd known what the word meant at the time.

"Yes, of course, Petra." One of them answered.

"Did she just bow to you?" I asked in bewilderment. I remembered Petra but as for the rest I had no clue.

"Shush, now." Petra reprimanded me.

I watched them file out a flimsy-looking door from the viewpoint of my wooden bunk. Yes, that wooden bunk. The same one I was tied to. The women were dressed in bright robes of various colors whereas I did not feel the least bit cheery. Petra was wearing an emerald robe that matched her eyes to perfection. Not that I noticed. When the last of them had fled, I turned quickly back to Petra.

"Am I naked under here? Where are my clothes?" I whispered. "I can't feel anything other than this inordinately scratchy blanket."

"Are you referring to your stolen robes and that filthy headscarf? I don't know what happened to them. I would ask one of the women, but it seems they're no longer here. I suppose, you'll just have to make do with the scratchy blanket for now." Haeryn help me. Were empathy comprised of air I surely would have suffocated.

"Where are we?"

"How much do you recall?"

"About what? You? I remember you. And Renan. And…"

"The desert?" She queried hopefully.

"That." I stammered. It was coming back to me now– though slowly.

"Being buried in the sand and kicked in the face?"

"Him!" And that's all it took. I was seething with hatred.

"Does the great tree ring a bell by chance? For that is where we are– within the great tree itself."

"We're inside it?"

"Yes. The space is enormous. There are many floors."

"Is that a tub in the center of the room?"

"Yes. Term # 9 if I'm not mistaken."

"What?"

"Never mind, we'll get to that later. Now, open wide. I'm to make you eat this." A large spoon appeared in front of my face.

"Just untie me and be quick about it! I'm perfectly capable of feeding myself."

"Sorry, I can't. An agreement was made."

"An agreement? Without me? That's ridiculous. No one's here. Untie me this instant." I demanded. Ignoring me, she pushed the giant spoon between my torn lips.

"Ouch! A little slower please and do you not have a smaller tool? My mouth hurts to open that wide. What is that stuff? It tastes like a sour pear only sweeter."

"So, a sweet pear. You're most definitely back." She laughed.

"It's Baobab pulp." She continued. "Swallow it. I'm told it's quite good for you."

"Every part of my face feels broken."

"Though I can't speak for the rest, your left cheek and nose are broken. Greta reset your nose as best as she was able considering how many times it had been broken before– so she reckoned. She said your cheek will mend in time. The right side of your face looks more like an eggplant than any form of radish. Promise me you won't provoke him further, Radesh." She whispered.

"Oh, I promise. You have my word on that. I'm done being nice. I am going to murder the bastard first chance I get. And who in Haeryn's Hells is Greta?"

"One of his seven wives. He keeps a harem." She whispered.

"A harem– *seven* wagging tongues?" She ignored me again. As I recall, she'd become increasingly skilled at that. I felt immeasurably relieved. Haeryn forbid she'd kindled any form of meekness in my absence.

"Greta is a healer. Listen, I've straightened everything out,

Radesh. *Please* do not anger him again or all will be lost. I fear you will not survive next time. It is only by the barest of margins you survived this last venture."

"Shush. Don't call me by that name. Other than Zil, I have no name, remember? Or have you sold us out? Tell me, what have you told him? What does he know?"

"Nothing."

"Nothing?" I glared. I had my doubts about that. When had she ever said *nothing*? Hmmm, let me think... *not never.*

"Well, nothing that changes anything." And there it stood in all its glory– the inkling of truth ahead of tide. I'd witnessed it in motion so many times before. There was no escape– a flood was forthcoming.

"I only told him the truth... about you."

"The truth about me!" I blathered in disbelief.

"I mean the kind of man you are– not anything else. You are still the same assassin; and I, your prisoner– at least for now."

"What do you mean *at least for now* and precisely *what* did you tell him?"

"He was going to kill you... Zil! I had no choice in the matter. I shouted at him to stop but he simply inquired why he should. The man has no empathy. He has no heart."

"Tell that to my thirsty dagger."

"Cease!" She scolded. "It was as if he was kicking a sack of potatoes. I had to do something. So, I told him that I was a seer. I told him that being kicked to death while buried in sand was not how the Gods intended you to depart this world."

"You said that?" I chortled with amusement. It hurt to laugh.

"Yes." she said, biting down on her lower lip as she was so prone to do. "More than that, I told him if he altered the will of the Gods, they'd frown upon him forever."

"And he bought that?" I guffawed. *Ow,* my poor ugly face.

"Well, not the frowning part. He said the Gods are cruel regardless of our ways... though he did stop kicking you."

"The Gods are cruel. What was it that he said right before?"

"You mean before he started kicking you?"

"Started kicking me?"

"Did you think he kicked you just once? Truly– and did all that to your face? Hmmm, what was it? *I end mad bulls.*"

"He is a strange fellow; as perplexing as they come."

"Did you really just say perplexing?" She mocked.

"Yes, it means–"

"I know what it means."

"But of course, you do." I winked– which proved to be a mistake for my eyelid getting stuck momentarily.

"Initially, he did claim my assertion to be unfounded demanding I give him one good reason why he should not kill the man who'd kidnapped us and led us witlessly into the desert. He asked why he should not kill the man whom I hated enough to accuse him of raping me. He asked why he should not–"

"Enough said. I get it. I get it." I huffed.

"I explained about killing the salesmen and feeding them to the pigs. He believed that."

"For the love of Haeryn, they weren't salesman!"

"I did expound upon that too."

"Joy. Hurrah, hurrah two peg holes for me."

"A wee bit of gratitude would be nice. At least you're alive."

"Alive. You keep insisting I'm not dead, yet my head begs to differ. Whatever did you say next? It seems an impossible dilemma."

"I told him he could not kill you because I had foreseen you to be our savior. I told you were fated to do something of dire import that would save the lives of many. I reminded him you did not rape me after confessing that neither had you kidnapped me."

"I expect he'll be petitioning sainthood from the Four imposters any day now. And look at me, my face in tatters with no suitable attire at hand." I joked, being frightfully careful not to smile.

"And yet somehow I remain the assassin." I shrugged. My brave face aside, the account was proving too much to bear. Worse still, I feared it was highly likely that she had more to confide.

"Yes. You are still the assassin but, more so, *my escort*. I confessed that, *upon your instruction*, we'd expanded upon the truth to make our tale, account rather, appear more *convincing*."

"And he believed that?" I asked incredulously.

"Yes, because I insisted you were a man of great character; a man who revered honor and duty above all else. I attested that the wellbeing of me and my baby remained your predominant concern."

"I felt concern prior to dominating what?" I inquired sorely wishing I could scratch my head.

"No, predominate as in *what mattered most*, that being, *your chief priority*."

"Predominate," I huffed. "'Tis a stupid word." Apparently, her *predominant concern* lay in her lap for, upon looking down, she shook her head sadly prior to continuing. *Rrr-rude.*

"I told him that it was true that you were of the Brotherhood and therefore keenly wary of strangers. I told him that it was also true that you were taking me to the Forth Rah for he having formally requested my services— as a seer."

"You told him all that?" I laughed aloud. *Ouch,* my aching head. "Are you certain I was only gone three days and two nights for it would take me a fortnight to say all that." The sad part was, I could envision her doing it in one long sentence no less with no breaths between words.

"Yes, not to mention, I have reinforced my story with his wives upon every opportunity."

"I've said it before. No mistaking, you're a clever girl. How many wives did you say?"

"Seven." She confirmed. I knew the answer. I just needed to hear it one more time.

"I can't even take care of you let alone six other wives. It would appear I'm not much of an escort. No surprise to anyone. For the record, I did tell the Major as much."

"I'm no wife of yours," she scoffed with great offense.

"I wasn't suggesting—"

"You can hardly take care of yourself." She glared.

"I'll have you know I wash myself quite regularly whenever I'm able." Though very sincere, she found humor in that oddly.

"Still, you've done well for the most part— save for opening your mouth more times than wise. But we can't fault you for that in fairness. It's who you are. Though far from mad, you can be a definite bull at times." She somehow found time to confess— about me.

"Where have I heard that before?" I asked with a grin—quickly dissipated into a scowl for the pain.

Needing a break from her charms, I looked around the rustic-looking, candle-lit room. Its longest wall was curved whereas the adjoining ones were straighter and fastened together with nails. The floor was of the same type of wood as the tub in the center of the room. It did make sense. We were in a giant tree after all. I mean, of course we were. Given the fact we were in the middle of a desert, where else might we be?

Weirdly, I could not discern anything of the ceiling. It was but a continuous, ever-darkening blur. Across from where I lay was another small bunk. There were two tables in the room. The largest of which boasted a chair on either side. Outside of that, there was a clay bucket and, in the farthest corner, a large wooden bowl. The bowl looked to be full of blankets. The same prickly ones pestering me no doubt. I swear there was not one part of me that did not itch right down to my nose.

"Where exactly are we within that monstrous tree? And why are my hands and legs still tied?"

"Well, as it was put to me and these are his words, not mine; your bedside manners were found to be lacking. I suppose I can untie your legs however." Which she promptly did. It was a start.

"My bedside manners? I was barely alive for Haeryn's sake."

"You did try to throttle us upon the slightest touch. As for where we are, we've been graciously allotted the bath chamber." She bowed, gesturing broadly with an arm. "I've seen some of the other living quarters. Trust me, this is a step up. The largest rooms house two dozen men or more— with no tub, no tables. Not much of anything really— just swords and shields, and other senseless things like that."

"Swords! You must fetch one at once."

"Shush. I will do no such thing!" She scolded.

"So, we're really inside the massive tree." It all seemed so implausible— dream-like in truth.

"Of course, Zilly. I was right. It's a grove of trees that, over a lot of time, have grafted themselves to one another. I expect there was a mother tree at one time. Though now, it's as though her children all joined hands to form a protective ring about her. I don't pretend to understand it. It's positively enormous! There's even a common room for eating if you can believe it. It's twenty times the size of this if not a proper copper."

A peculiar saying admittedly though I've no clue as to what it means. How could a copper coin be made of anything other than copper? Notwithstanding, I'd visited uppity establishments that insisted they be allotted three of them for a single loaf of bread.

"*That* I will have to see for myself. And don't think for a moment that *Zilly* remark was wasted on me. Rude. Know that I would stick my tongue out at you if I did not fear it falling free."

"I was teasing," she pouted. For Haeryn's sake, you'd think I'd stabbed her. Where was all that ill-advised stubbornness now? No doubt, she'd left it *in the library*.

"Perhaps it wasn't entirely undeserved. But never repeat it, or I'll poke you with a sharp stick— providing my hands get untied. Would you mind? Please. I sorely need to scratch."

"I can't untie you yet, unfortunately."

"What do you mean you can't untie me? I demand that you do

so at once!"

"I can't– not until you've agreed to his terms."

"His terms?"

"Yes, his terms. I think you'll find them quite practical."

"I think you'll find them quite practical," I mocked. I was so mad I nearly spat. I was positively seething… again. Whose side was she on, anyway? I took a long slow breath to compose myself.

"Tell me his terms," I exhaled. "After which, untie me so I can use the ropes to strangle the haughty fool. My wrists are so chafed I can't tell them from the prickly blanket."

"That's one of his terms. The first one in fact."

"All prisoners must be tied with scratchy twine and covered with an itchy blanket?"

"No, prior to that bit."

"Oh, no strangling with ropes. Can I use my bare hands then? What about a dagger through the heart? Might that be apropos?"

"He's taken your dagger; took a right shine to it in truth."

"Of course, he did. Will you please just tell me his bloody terms? I sorely need to piss." I added with a whisper.

"*Relieve yourself* is the proper term."

"More bloody terms. Wonderful."

Petra picked up a scroll of parchment, identical in color to the walls– and everything else for that matter.

"Not surprising you need to pee. Greta managed to force a lot down your throat this morning. Which isn't easy to do."

"Just so you're aware, the constant reminders aren't helping. The terms, please." My knees were knocking against one another for having to– *relieve myself* so profoundly. I wasn't joking.

"Term # 1: No aggressive acts or malicious behavior will be tolerated. That, unless I'm sadly mistaken, which I am not, entails there to be *no strangling* allowed."

"And what if I do it quietly?" She wasn't impressed. "Got it. No strangling, punching, kicking, breaking, cutting, biting, clawing, chopping, cleaving, slicing, or dicing. Next!"

"Term # 2: You must always obey my commands. Recognize I'm reading precisely what it says– by my commands he means *his commands*. He said, normally that was Term # 1, but he'd made an exception in your case due to your unruly disposition. That means stubborn." She whispered behind her hand.

"I'll be sure to express my gratitude. Read quicker please, I really do need to *brim the bowl*."

"I can bring you the clay bucket if you roll onto your side."

"What? I'm not rolling onto my side. I'm not some lump you can do with as you please. I don't roll over for anyone! Wait. How long was I befogged?" My mouth gaped open in alarm for having forgotten entirely about *the other end*. It was different with soldiers. I mean some of them even took their dinner bowl with them when they *went for a stretch*. But alone in a room full of women— that did make me cringe.

"Let's just say that you've sullied more than your fair share of blankets and leave it at that. Far more than Renan at any rate." She added with more eagerness than warranted.

"What happened to *and leave it at that*?" I glared... but she just kept on chattering as per her *unruly disposition*.

"Never managed to hit the pail once, as I recall. Can't say we didn't try but, given your *stubbornness* and all, it was akin to juggling fish. At least, that's how Greta put it. Though the women wanted to draw straws, out of respect for you, I took the gruesome task upon myself in the end— *both ends* to be clear. I must say after *that night* I expected more from you. A great deal more if you know what I mean. But it is what it is, I suppose. In hindsight, for humility's sake, I really should have swaddled you."

"Humility's sake? Humility's sake!" I spat, losing a tooth in the process. "That's enough! Far too much in fact." My face was burning though not solely due to the pain for once.

"Whatever happened to *the truth hath no need of deliberation*." She smirked, mimicking my voice. "*It does not ponder. It is what it is*— though perhaps not as robust as it might be at times."

"Term # 3! Honestly, if it isn't a term then I don't what to hear it." In all seriousness, I could have kindled a fire with my cheeks had I been but a thumbnail nearer to the wall.

"Term # 3: Never go near the cat. It will eat you."

"So far so good. I have no problem with that. Quicker please."

"Stop talking then. Ahem, term # 4: We will resume our conversation the moment you are able."

"Wonderful, I can't wait. You know how much I adore the man— even more so once he ceases to breathe." I added through gritted teeth.

"Shall I continue," Petra chided, "or is there something more you'd like to say?"

"No, seriously, I can't wait!"

"Yes, cynicism; I'm quite familiar with it. You were my

traveling companion day after day after all."

"No! I can't wait as in *bring the bucket now!*"

"Oh, that." Petra smirked, before scampering to retrieve it. "I'll fetch one of the women."

"Haeryn no!" I shouted with escalating aggravation.

"One of the men then? Are you certain? We are quite capable."

"Shut up!" I hollered rudely. "We'll handle this. I don't require an audience simply to– *relieve myself.*"

"If you say so." frowned Petra reaching under the blanket with a searching hand. "I can do it easily enough… it's just a bit more awkward when your eyes are open."

"Stop! What are you doing? Keep your hands to yourself, woman! Untie me, I'll take care of the rest, thank you kindly."

"I can't. I swore a solemn vow, and you haven't agreed to everything yet."

"I agree. I agree already!"

"He insisted you hear them. Sorry, but I make neither the rules nor promises idly. Now, roll onto your side, take a deep breath, while I'll position the bucket."

"Take a deep breath. I'm having a go not hatching a newborn. Put the pail on the floor. No, nearer to the other way. Right there. Stop. Finally." I sighed.

"No offense, but I don't think it's–"

"Shush! But yeah, purely for the sake of safety and no one's pride, move it a wee bit closer. Now angle it. No, not that get your hands away– the pail! Now, hold it at an angle. That's it; full stop!

"Why are you looking at me like that?" She grimaced.

"I'm not looking at anything. I'm concentrating. Now, grab my shoulder. You need to pull me forward slightly."

"But what about the pail?"

"I don't know. For Haeryn's sake, put a foot under it."

"You're positive we don't need more help?"

"No, we're good. Okay, now look away and pull the blanket aside."

"With what? I've only so many hands." Petra wailed. "And you haven't the faintest how heavy you are."

"I could fill the bloody tub woman! That's how heavy I am!" Kicking my legs irritably, I freed the blanket myself. And not a moment too soon, thank Haeryn.

"You're splashing everywhere!"

"Potàtoes, potatoes; there's no curtailing it now. It hath no need of deliberation. It is what it is– forthcoming."

"Well, you're no archer," she huffed. "Renan has a better aim. And is *that face* necessary? The smell is foul enough, worse than asparagus. But that face; it gives me the shivers."

"You're ruining the moment."

"The moment?" Petra queried, stifling a laugh.

"Speaking of shivers; I'm done."

"Uh-oh!"

"Uh-oh? Hold on, am I not tied to the bed?"

"Not any longer. I couldn't roll you onto your side otherwise."

"Put your head against me. Push me back!"

"Stop leaning! You're too heavy. My foot is slipping!" And that was it. I was at the mercy of the gods and, Haeryn knows, the gods were cruel.

"Hold fast! Hold fast!' I cried in vain. Too late. Spilling from the bunk, I fell onto the floor with a loud crash–followed by a *splash*– followed by several well-justified profanities. Having been made of clay, the pail shattered beneath my weight. Of course, it did. What else could it have done? Bollocks to the wind, overturned and naked, my lower extremities were awash with urine. I felt the blanket thrown over me. Thank Haeryn for *that blanket.* Did I mention how much I adored that blanket?

"Sorry! I'll get help!" Petra yelped.

Abandoning me in my calamitous predicament, she fled the room before I might restrain her. For the life of me I could not find a way to right myself. I was lying face-down with both my hands tied at my sides. Had I been given the choice, I'd have opted to remain buried in sand. I heard footsteps. Straining my neck awkwardly, I saw a large woman staring back at me. Greta, I assumed.

"I am Greta," she smiled down at me. Finally, I'd got something right.

"How wonderful to meet you, Greta," I managed through tightly pressed lips. "How's the weather?"

"Hot." She replied, studying the landscape before her cautiously.

"It is a bloody desert," I sighed. Her expression changed to a frown as she placed her mammoth-sized hands firmly on her hips.

"To each their own but too soon for this it is," she scolded, thrusting her hips back and forth meaningfully. "Backwards are you doing it. Of that am I certain. It is known."

"It wasn't that!" blushed Petra. "We weren't doing that. He had to pee is all."

"Changes little, still doing it wrong are you." She replied skeptically. I think it may have been a question though I had no way of knowing for certain.

"Wet are you." She noted astutely. Question, not a question, who knew?

"Of course, I'm wet. I fell on the bloody piss bucket." I smiled courteously, straining my neck so I might better frown at her.

"Stop fretting, I will mop you up ahead of the floor."

"Mop me? What precisely do you mean by *mop me*?"

"May his hands I untie?" she asked, continuing to flourish an accent I'd never previously been acquainted with. Regardless, her suggestion did seem encouraging.

"Yes. Yes. Untie me at once."

"No." Petra butted in irrationally.

'No one asked you," I blurted. "This is strictly between me and Greta. Your own business must you mind."

"Not yet," insisted Petra. "He hasn't agreed *to the terms*." She added in a whisper.

"You think I can't hear you?" I asked, banging my head against the floor with mounting frustration.

"But to *the terms* must he agree," insisted Greta, nodding with approval. Disapproval, perhaps. "Difficult is as difficult does."

"Might the pair of you agree to help me up?" I sighed with unfathomable annoyance.

"But of course." Clucked the buxom woman prior to, lifting the blanket for a quick peek. "Like a basted turkey." She kindly observed.

"You can lower the blanket. That's not helping." I moaned.

"He basted my foot more so than the pail," snickered Petra. "Which is why I slipped."

"I see." said the big woman. "Difficult it is for one alone. For help you should have asked. Too heavy for you is he though pick him up can I with ease."

"Nope!" I hollered. "No. No. No."

"No, no, no with ease so can I." She insisted.

"He's a bit modest," whispered Petra. Though I couldn't see her, no doubt, she was beaming like a cat before a crippled mouse.

"Clenched buttocks conjure copper coins." Greta recited.

Yet again, with the copper coins. And was that really some form of proverb where she came from? Because, if so, I never want to go there– ever. Forcing one side of the blanket beneath me, Greta twisted it tight before hauling me, very roughly I might add, to a sitting position for having scraped both my knees in the process. *Yup, that's a splinter.* Must everything be so prickly– including Greta?

"You do realize you will have to untie me at some point. Please don't make me kill you," I vented huskily.

"Stubborn is the path of thorns which is why you sit there so."

"I did say please," I reminded the over-grown galoot.

The blanket was heavier than I recalled. Oh yeah, because it was saturated in urine. Lucky me. Still, I expressed a loud sigh of what could only be described as sincere gratitude. Being the lone kind thing in the room, it hugged me firmly, *adhered* might be more fitting. Never has a soiled blanket felt so virtuous. Okay, perhaps not virtuous though it was undeniably less scratchy now.

"I will read quickly," said Petra. I could tell she was grinning, which annoyed me to no end. If only I'd strangled her at Studayo House, I never would have been in this present predicament.

"Term # 5," she continued. "Leave is granted by permission only; that being, *my permission*. Term # 6: no excessive drinking– ale, water, or wine unless I say otherwise. That being–"

"Got it– him saying it, not you. Go on."

"Term # 7: Everyone must contribute to the greater good. Term # 8: Save for the *Black Pail*, to use a pail is to empty a pail." Petra paused. Knowing precisely what she was thinking, I beat her to it.

"I think we can cross that one off today's list. The pail has *most definitely* been emptied." I hissed. "Dare I ask what the black pail is?"

"Don't." Replied Petra and Greta in unison shaking their heads.

"Term # 9: Get in the tub and scrub. You stink. He circled that last bit." Petra declared proudly. "The *you stink* part to be clear."

"Over ripe." Chimed Greta needlessly.

"Ahem, term # 10: Your belongings will be returned at my discretion which may, or may not, include the dagger."

"He actually wrote that?" I asked in disbelief. It was my dagger after all. I'd seized it fair and square from a corpse.

"He did, followed by a final notation."

"Which is?"

"The punishment for not signing these terms is death by daylight. The punishment for breaking any of the terms is whatever I declare it to be. Expect neither trial nor mercy." She stopped reading to stare at me.

"Is that all?" I inquired, craning my neck to see. "Are you certain there isn't something on the other side? I'd hate to forgo anything?"

"No, I checked. The aft side is blank."

"The aft side is *blanketed*," corrected Greta, causing Petra to giggle aloud. Though I did not turn to look, I could feel her pointing.

"I don't know which is worse; being swaddled in a piss blanket or your sense of humor?"

"Forgive us." Petra obliged. "Admittedly, your current state is a bit distracting. That said, just affirm your agreement to *the terms* and we'll get you quickly sorted."

"Yes, I concur. It's not as though I have a choice in the matter." I grumbled.

"Will you assign your mark?"

"Yes− but, at the risk of sounding immodest, is it to be a quill up the arse or are you finally going to untie my hands? Take your time. I'm in no hurry. It's not like I need to pee."

"'Tis the pulp." stated the big woman matter-of-factly. I stared at her quizzically. Whatever was she on about now? I wondered.

"That conjures the smell," she added at long last. "Like sparrowgrass, both a blessing and a curse." She sighed despondently.

Having been humiliated quite enough, I chose to ignore her. Petra untied my hands prior to the pair of them assisting me back onto the bed. Feeling dizzy, I felt as though I might see stars again. Following several deep breaths, I felt steadier. Thank Haeryn.

"The bath we will fill for you now," said the *greta-big* woman.

"Thank you," I replied.

"For the stink." She added needlessly. "Then in it will I put you." *Joy!*

"Thanks… but manage it on my own I think I can." I felt Petra jab me in the ribs.

"For certain can you." She shrugged skeptically. As usual, I wasn't sure whether she was posing a query or not. Either way, upon standing, my legs did feel rather shaky.

"One step at a time is always the best approach," I said, pulling the scratchy blanket up to my chin and giving it a sniff.

"Fetch the water we will then," she nodded kindly. Having watched her pry her way through the narrow doorway, Petra turned to me and huffed.

"Must you always?"

"Always must I what?" I shrugged despairingly.

Thankfully, Greta returned sooner than I would have thought possible. And not alone either as behind her strode all the other brightly dressed women jostling large clay vessels in a variety of manners— one atop her head, two on their hips, with the rest hugging them tightly against their bosoms. I sighed wondrously upon witnessing the steam rising from the badly chipped pails. One of them mopped the floor where I'd fallen after picking up the sharp shards of broken clay. Quickly motioning the women out of the room, Greta turned to me and smiled.

"Put you in and scrub you up good, I will." She beamed. I could not help noticing, she still had all her teeth which wasn't common where I came from. It wasn't that I wasn't appreciative of her efforts. I was. Not to mention, a hot bath was not something I would have ever thought possible in a desert of all places. It was just that, well, to be frank, I felt her increasing kindness directly proportional to my growing unease.

"No, nope, no. I'm feeling better." As she didn't seem to be catching on, I tried again.

"Fine by ourselves will we be." I said, waving her away. Still, she appeared reluctant to take my hint. So, I decided to be more direct.

"No offense but, I am perfectly capable of washing myself. Thank you but you may depart now." I replied with a wobbly bow. It was Petra's turn to scowl. She was quite masterful at it.

"As you wish," Greta conceded finally.

Returning a curiously long bow; she then took leave of us. Something about her bow felt slightly insincere. Bending my head low, I tried to gauge whether she might have been trying to look beneath the blanket draped about my thighs. It clung tight to me however, due to it being so thoroughly drenched. Casting my seemingly unjustified fears aside, a rush of blood surged within my head for having bent so low. I then heard Petra laughing— which only worsened the sensation.

"Tis nothing she hasn't seen before," smirked Petra. "I think Greta's taken a shine to you. Are you still feeling modest? Your face looks a bit more purple— if that's even possible."

"Quiet." I admonished her. "Fortunately for me, she's spoken for. Tell me, of his seven wives, how many does she account for? Two at least, I should think."

"Back to your old self so quickly? You should be far kinder to her. I'll have you know you likely owe your life to that selfless woman. She barely left your side. If not for her you'd most surely have died."

"I'm still not entirely convinced I haven't," I said, fingering my cheekbone gingerly.

"Well, you could act a tad more grateful. I'll have you know the biggest thing about that woman is her heart." Petra chided.

"And I'll wager a proper copper that it's not." *Wonderful, now they had me doing it too.*

"You're being discourteous again."

"Forgive me for not knowing all those in need of thanks whilst I lay in a state of blind dormancy." I retorted. "I'll be sure to pay more attention next time." That made her frown.

"Listen," I continued. "While I do appreciate all that was done, you must recognize I am hardly myself. I feel like half a man. Thus, if I act slightly less courteous, you'll have to excuse me."

"I'm sorry, were you courteous at some point that I fail to recall? I'll excuse your condition, but never your ingratitude. I refuse to accept rudeness any more than crudeness."

"Yes, the pathways of the *high and mighty* are riddled with those never kicked in the face. I'm sorry, I made a jest in poor taste. Are there any other terms you'd like to add?" My patience was quickly growing thin.

"Only the same terms we agreed to in Gadev at your insistence. Oh, and forgive me for not recognizing the pathways of the *high and mighty* for all the damned sand!" She exclaimed.

"Can you not see? I am apologetic. I aggrieved you and had since repented. What more must I do to earn your forgiveness?"

"Listen. You must listen." Cupping my hands about both ears, I sat quietly. I wasn't trying to mock anyone. I was simply exhausted.

"Radesh…" I silenced her with a quick finger to my lips.

"Zil, there is nothing more you need do than listen. I am simply trying to explain how things are here. He is not the malevolent beast you think him to be— though as unforgiving as he is totalitarian there is more to him than that. Take his wives for example; they told me that he asks nothing of them other than that they do their fair share. He rescued six of them from the slave traders! He then offered to marry them solely because he saw it as the only way to ensure their safety here, in this place, amongst so many men."

"Or, more likely, it was part of *their terms* to promote such a tale."

"You're impossible. They told me that, not him. Put yourself in their place and speak of it to no one. They fear for their safety in respect to other, less moral, residents here. It's far from what I expected. If you think about it; it's his own men that he's protecting them from."

"Don't worry; I won't say a thing. I'd hate to start an uprising and risk something grievous happening to him. Haeryn forbid, he should ever be kicked in the face; or buried up to his neck in sand; or fed to his fancy-striped cat."

"Promise me you won't."

"Feed him to the cat?"

"Promise!" she demanded again.

"More terms. I should have expected as much." I sighed dejectedly for feeling beaten yet again.

"Do me a favor, *Your Highness*… the water grows colder with every new term I'm forced to oblige. Assist me to the tub if you would, please." I gave my head a good shake if for no other reason than to free the cobwebs that had accumulated during my long slumber– and immediately regretted doing so.

"Yes, of course. Put you in I will." Petra clowned.

"No, you won't." I corrected her.

After walking me to the tub, I did allow her to steady me as I slipped into the peculiar-looking basin. I'd seen plenty of wooded tubs; but never one shaped like a miniature ship. The water within was marvelous. Being wondrously warm, my pain melted away– *almost*. Though my aching face was undoubtedly terribly swollen, I was unable to catch my reflection in the water for the light being so dim. Even so, the water felt increasingly soothing. Until I felt a stiff scrub brush attacking me from behind, *scouring my behind*, more accurately.

"Scrub you up, I will." Petra chuckled. After swiftly disarming her, I splashed water at her until she backed far enough away that I felt my privacy no longer in jeopardy. I shook water from the scrub brush at her several times before sinking back into its soothing warmth. Ah, how I adore a good long bath. There's nothing quite like it.

"So, that was his harem that carried in the water?"

"Greta, Maya, Helga, Sully, Ora, and Anna. All but one. No doubt Myrna was painting. She's always painting, so I am told."

"Why?"

"Haeryn knows. Because she's a painter, I expect. They all have their talents. Greta's a healer. Maya's a cook. Helga ferments whatever she lays hands upon. Sully is an adept weaver. Ora makes candles and a variety of ointments; and Anna was a tailor by trade."

"And you are a seer." I chuckled, twisting about to gauge her reaction. It was preposterous.

"When it suits me." She stood on her tiptoes feigning to peek into the tub. She could be quite amusing. I flicked more water in her direction which made her laugh. It was good to see her laugh.

"Tell me, all cruelty of the gods aside; what use is a painter in a place like this?"

"Haeryn knows. They say art has been reborn. They claim it is good for morale."

"Morale?" I huffed.

"Yes, it means–"

"I know what morale means. But cheerfulness… here… in these god-forsaken lands?"

"And where else might it be more important? Regardless of the preposterous heat, the sun still rises with the dawn."

"I completely forgot… where is Renan?" I asked, worried. "How's the little man faring?"

"He's good; now that I have him back. He's sleeping," she smiled. "That him in the big bowl over there in the corner."

"All this time? Well, he's going to be in a right sour mood. The little man would have adored watching me fall– takes after his mother that way." I snickered. It was the truth. He did seem to delight in my many misadventures. As did she, save for when they involved her.

"He's a bit cranky in the heat of the day but which of us isn't? Fortunately, most of us sleep during the hottest hours."

"And what is that I smell?"

"Urine. It's in your hair I expect."

"Not that smell, the other one," I gasped after submerging my head to give it a good scrub– just in case she was right as she was, far too often, prone to be.

"Ah, that smell; fermenting wine and ale. They make loads of the stuff. I forgot about it. You stop smelling it after a day or two."

"Ale," I sighed, longingly. "They have ale here?"

"It's quite good, I'm told. Greta would have been only too glad to fetch one for you had you not banished her so abruptly."

"Would she have?"

"No, she wouldn't. No one drinks outside the common room to my knowledge. There are other rules at play."

"I'm sure there are. So, am I to believe you haven't tried it yourself?" I queried in disbelief.

"You know full well I never touch the stuff… outside of your company." She blushed.

Her words had taken me by surprise. Just the way she said it, being so matter of fact about it, made me feel awkward. I didn't know what to say or how to react. Though kind of her, at the same time, it seemed improper. She made it sound as though we were fast comrades, which was hardly the case. Or was it? Had shared misery somehow bonded us?

Honestly, until that moment, I wasn't sure we'd even formed a friendship. I'd always assumed she tolerated me purely out of necessity for having little other choice. But what if that wasn't the case? What if she, most inexplicably, had grown fond of me? And what about me? Why had her words caught me so off guard? I saw little alternative but to submerge my head again. It had clearly been damaged. Yet again, she managed to fluster me when I least expected it. I was not thinking straight. Rising from the deepest depths of thought, I noticed she hadn't stopped talking. At least some things never changed. If there was one thing in this world that I liked, it was consistency.

"As I said, the place is much larger than you could ever imagine. Boredom, if you can believe it, is their major foe. Everyone tries to keep busy but, in truth, there's not much to do. The massive tree is God-like to them— for good reason. Besides attracting birds and other small creatures, it also produces an over-abundance of fruit."

"And they make wine from it?"

"Yes, and ale. I expect it's more of a mead in truth though they refer to it as ale."

The combination of heat and thoughtfulness was making me feel light-headed again. Even so, I had little inclination to climb out. Had the gods been bred of kindness and given me the choice, I would have stayed in that tub till the end of my days. Though I did not recognize it at the time, in all my days, even as injured as I was, never had I felt more content.

"Can one sweat in water?" I asked. "If so, I fear certain the tub will soon overflow. Does it ever cool down, I wonder? Even so, I will advise them next time they needn't heat the water."

"At which point they'll tell you to fetch it yourself. Typically, they don't heat it, but Greta said the warmth would be healing so, take pride, the lot of us here suffer on your behalf."

"Surely, you jest. I very much doubt that," I guffawed.

"As the kestrel flies so it is the truth. *Heal he will with warm water better.*" She laughed. "It's simple, they just leave it outside."

"Well, as bad as it makes me feel, for the rest of you scoundrels, that is— I expect it's best I remain here as long as I can."

"You're such a bad liar. Warm water aside, the heat can be

quite insufferable during the day. Which is why everyone tries their best to sleep through it. As dusk arrives the temperature becomes more bearable; almost pleasant at times."

"And what do they eat?"

"Loads of things surprisingly; though for you– only baobab pulp for now. Greta's orders. Maya makes jams from the fruit and a crude form of dry bread from the leaves which are also edible. Being the *rough* part of roughage, they don't make for a good salad though."

"Salad? What strangeness is this?" She ignored me. I hadn't been joking. Only cows and sheep were meant to eat grass whereas goats would eat anything. Don't get me started on geese– evil creatures right to their hollow bones. I beg pardon, my thoughts wandered off on me again.

"Helga makes preserves when she isn't making ale or wine."

"Jam is good. I like jam." My mouth had begun watering.

"Then you're in luck. Be forewarned, it tastes strangely akin to the pulp mixture; only sweeter. A lot sweeter."

"Ah, like savory pears. I was hoping for plum."

"Sorry, no plums. They do have prunes however, along with other fruits. Currently, they have cherries, apples, and a few precious grapes– which they're turning into wine of course. As it turns out, Renan adores cherries. After I pit them, of course, even over the pulp."

"Cherries and grapes? How could they survive in this heat?"

"They don't. Which is why most end up as preserves or in a cup of some kind."

"So, either way they end with some form of toast." That made her smile. Then me, more so.

"Twice yearly, a small band of them travel to the markets for food and other supplies. Mostly honey and sugar, Greta says– for the ale and wine, of course."

"But of course, there's no wit without wisdom." I laughed. "How many men are there? How long have they been here? Do other Kedera stop here? Have there been any new arrivals?"

"Slow down, one question at a time," she smiled. "No. That's just it; it's not at all like we imagined. Sully told me they're outcasts. She said no one comes *ever*. She said no one knows of this place– which hopefully sounds familiar."

"Sully, the water-bearing weaver said that."

"Well done," she clapped. "You do listen at times." I twisted my head about to look at her. She really did have a beautiful smile– especially whilst belittling me.

"Though I don't know the whole story, I was told their leader did something to greatly offend the Four Rahs— well, I think there was only three of them at that time as I ponder it."

"Offend the Rahs? That's not good. I mean it is good though not for us so much. What did he do?"

"I don't know; there were several of them talking at once, it was confusing. Let me think— there were insults and accusations; a good deal of thievery; leading a revolt; attacking a palace; followed by burning a palace. What didn't he do would have proved easier to answer. Honestly, I couldn't keep track of it all."

"That would do it. Am I to understand he was never imprisoned for any of it?"

"He was— several times and sentenced to death. They say he was tortured for days on end," she whispered. "But he escaped— freed his men and *they all* escaped."

"Escaped? How might the Kedera escape the Kedera?" I asked though the only possible answer came to me in the same moment.

"By fleeing here, of course. Where else might they go?"

"Where else indeed. But that means they had to have known of this place beforehand. It's unconscionable to believe they somehow just *happened upon it*. Not with so many while your need is so great. As my face bears witness, there's more to the tale. It's not possible."

"And you wonder why he's so adamant on finding out how we came to be here?"

"Point taken." I nodded. "Undoubtedly, it would be highly disconcerting."

"Did you just say *disconcerting*? Have I truly influenced you that greatly?" She quipped.

I ignored her. In truth, I knew the word for the Major having confessed he found my behavior, that being the Red Rage, entirely disconcerting many times prior. As for the word *influenced*, sounding suspiciously akin to the flux; I thought it best to leave it untouched.

"But how did *he* know of it?" I pondered aloud. "Then again, the BroZil assassin had also known. He even knew about the Harbinger cat. We're missing some vital information for certain."

"All I know… is that an army was sent after them and they fled into the desert. As for how long they've been holed up here; I haven't the slightest. Those I've talked to seem to have completely lost track of the days. I agree, how they ended up here is rather puzzling. They did confess that many were lost in the endeavor. As for how many men reside here, I'd bet at least fifty if a not proper copper."

"And eight women," I added perplexed, if for no other reason than her having answered questions I'd long lost track of.

"And one sleeping baby boy," Petra smiled, nodding toward the large wooden bowl.

"Fifty hiding men. But where does that leave us?" I asked, turning myself about again so I might better look her in the eyes. Okay, I should not have done that. They were far too distracting.

"With you in the tub and me standing here, I suppose." I frowned at her. Though a fair observation the time for jesting had ended. This was serious. Notwithstanding, she'd reminded me I was naked just as my thoughts had begun wandering places they shouldn't. I had to force myself to look away just to regain my fragile composure.

"If they do not support the Kedera, where do their loyalties lie? I don't understand. If they think me to be the Rah's assassin, while they themselves are at odds with the Kedera; then why am I still alive? Why do I still draw breath?"

"I have no answer for that. What little I've learned has come from the women. I've avoided the men for obvious reasons."

"And rightfully so. But you said *he* was receptive whilst you were conversing."

"Yes, though he was far more direct than he was forthcoming. He is a good listener." *Here we go...blah, blah, blah. Lest we forget his grand library and profound adoration for books.*

"He appeared to accept all I had to say though he spoke mainly of his expectations and how things worked within his little community. Contrarily, he offered very little of himself; whilst sharing nothing of their on-going predicament."

"This is not good. I foresee no way of this ending well."

"Don't be so certain. Don't forget between the two of us here, I am the seer. Though I can't fully justify why, I am not without optimism while considering myself a fair judge of character."

"Point taken. You did sleep with *the Butcher* after all." I chortled absent-mindedly.

"Hush! Don't make this about something other than it is. I'm simply saying, the man thinks differently than anyone I've ever met. I'm not convinced he entertains any loyalties to anyone other than himself— *which could be played to our advantage.*"

"Because you're so experienced with this sort of thing; being a world traveler and all." I added sarcastically.

She looked about the table, but she couldn't find anything suitable to throw. In that moment, she oddly reminded me of my mother; difference being, my mother would have heaved the table.

"No, the man is cornered." I continued. "He has nowhere to go, making him no less dangerous than that damn cat in the cage. Tell me, do you really suppose he will allow us to leave after feigning to serve the very same faction that wants him dead?"

"Admittedly, it doesn't sound good when put in those terms." Petra confessed, making me want to turn about again for no other reason than to see what she looked like whilst feeling like-minded.

"Terms. I'm beginning to hate that word. What is this leader's name; the one who bade me surrender to *his terms*?"

"He cordially declined that query."

"Of course, he did." Never more had I wanted to wind a cord around a man's neck.

"He did say he'd have plenty more to say once you were feeling more inclined to listen."

"Not sure why but, I really don't like him. Oh, I know– because he tried to kick me to death while utterly defenseless. I'll show him the true hand of Haeryn once the tables are overturned."

"Don't do anything rash, Radesh! He holds all the cards here. Do not give him a reason. He's no fool; and, if you haven't noticed, his tolerance is less than a thimble wick."

"His tolerance? My tolerance is at an end; his end if I haven't yet made myself clear." I replied curtly; splashing water over my face while imagining all the ways I would seize my revenge. I was so wrought I forgot I was the center of attraction. Thus, I submerged beneath the water for a spell, so I might seethe in private.

"He has no honor," I said resurfacing to spit out a stream of water. "All my life have I been, or watched others close to me be, kicked in the face. While I for one tire of it. He's a desert rogue, nothing more."

"Undeniably, he is a rogue; a rogue with an iron fist."

"Iron boot, rather." I assured her, rubbing my jaw thoughtfully.

"Promise me Radesh, you will not do anything foolish. This is *his roost*. Do not test him. You will lose– again."

"Why, have you foreseen it? Or did Haeryn himself whisper it to you whilst you slumbered?" I mocked her. "I think not. You have no idea what I'm capable of. On a field, no man can best me."

"And precisely what part of this perpendicular tree do you feel to be level?" I hated it when she was right. *And she was*. Not that I had any clue what *perpendicular* meant. An extended form of *peculiar* perhaps though, if so, why not just say that. It was akin to calling a skunk an essence-peddler.

"I recognized his eyes from somewhere," I frowned. "I fear he remembers me as well. That would explain things. No doubt, I bested him and now he's intent on revenge."

"You met him before? Are you certain?" she asked with mixed alarm and doubt.

"I think so. I'm near certain. I don't know where; in battle I would imagine though quite some time ago. Given the aftereffects of the Red Rage, it would explain why I can't fully recall."

"The Red Rage," she mused. "You've never made mention of it save for *that night*. If you're right, I don't think he remembers. I would have known. He would have given something away."

"And the seer emerges!" I laughed. "All the better then– he won't see my attack coming." I turned and smiled. Petra returned a more stoic gaze.

"If you think you can draw one of your fancy lines in the sand and surprise him, you're wrong; dead wrong. He doesn't trust you."

"I don't need him to trust me. I simply need a chance."

"A chance? As in a sporting chance? Hardly. Enrage him again and you'll be staring outward from his wall of skulls. It doesn't take a seer to know that. Only a fool would think otherwise."

"Whose side are on you on anyways? What terms did you submit to, I wonder?"

"The terms of the living– those with intelligence enough to find a way to continue doing so. That's whose side I'm on. And no, I did not submit to anything profoundly different."

"And what may I ask has he demanded of you? Are you to join his harem? Has baby Renan found yet another father?"

"*By the hounds of Haeryn*, you always go too far, Radesh! Why would you say such a thing? I am no man's property."

"I'm sorry," I sighed, slicking my hair back. "I fear my pride has been dealt a death blow."

"Yes, exactly. It's all about your foolish pride– as always!"

"I did not mean to lash out. It's just that this latest development has me unsettled. Please forgive my impertinence. I spoke poorly; it was unjust."

"It was." Petra huffed. I'd hurt her– again. Which, to my chagrin, hurt worse than my aching face. And that, was saying something.

"I must think of something fast. There must be some new angle I can play."

"The Brotherhood!" Petra blurted.

"How so?" I asked.

"Your unwavering allegiance is the only angle required."

"How so?" I chimed again. I still didn't understand.

"Make it known that, though you were commissioned by the Forth Rah; your true loyalties lie with the Brotherhood— at the detriment of the Rahs if need be should you ever be forced to choose betwixt the two. Insist that nothing is more important to you than *duty and honor*."

"And what of my *duty* to the Forth Rah?" I asked. "Does that not warrant some measure of loyalty?"

"The task was assigned to you; not something you sought. Twas a burden thrust upon the Brotherhood. Being a man of your word, you will see it through to the end no matter the cost. But that doesn't proport you condone their corrupt agendas. Make it known that you have not sided with either party in this war. You're simply follow orders."

"I am following orders."

"I know. And he will respect that. Convince him you are a man of your word, and you will gain some respect from him."

"Humph. That does make sense. I knew there was a chink in his armor somewhere— and you've found it." I could only marvel at her shrewdness. She was clever; more so than anyone I'd ever met.

"Make it clear; the safe passage of your escorts is paramount to you solely because *you gave your word*."

"Yes, of course." I was on the same page now.

Not to be confusing but, in retrospect there weren't any pages back then being that I only wrote this just now. Which is to say, much later. Okay, so Petra wrote it; but I told her what to write. Admittedly, she did improvise gratuitously at times— which is why I implored her to add this vital clarification. Case in point being, I harbor doubts whether she will even include it. Why? It's Petra. Need I say more?

"What else might he do but praise such dedication?" I agreed with mounting enthusiasm. "After all, the man devoted himself to seven women solely to ensure their wellbeing. I change my mind; the man is a saint deserving of Knighthood at the very least." I added glibly, twisting myself about to display my pretentious smile. It did seem appropriate, notwithstanding the pain imposed to fashion such a face. I believe they call it single-mindedness. Though no doubt Petra penned the word *stubborn* instead for I would not put it past her.

"Knighthood? The legacy of the knights ended long ago. The

Rahs had them imprisoned if I recall correctly." Her face became scrunched with worry.

"Be careful, Rr—Zil. His sense of humor, or lack thereof, is an animal of itself. I would not jest with him and nor does it suit the character traits of an assassin."

"Have no fear," I reassured her, raising my arms, and stretching them wide. "I will be at my best behavior. I've a duty to perform after all. This isn't about my wounded pride. I've put that behind me."

"Have you now? Say it isn't so?" She tittered.

"Mark me, as soon as I'm well enough, we will leave this place. I will see you and Renan safely to Harkenspear as sworn. Suppress your fears, we will succeed, Petra. For, unlike the other inhabitants of these god-forsaken lands, I am a man of my word."

"I believe you, Zil," she replied sincerely, before pausing to smirk. Now why did she have to do that? I thought she'd captured it succinctly prior to that needless facial antic.

"Then again, I've no one else to turn to. Though, rest assured, you are not the lesser of two evils here. You remain my lone hope and savior. You see, I am a seer after all." She winked.

"I couldn't save an ash flea right now," I grimaced. "Damn, that man has a temper."

"And little patience. *But we know that now.* Yet another seam we might further unravel to our benefit. As I said, he's been relatively receptive when we've spoken. He may be a brute; but he's a forthright brute. He admires honesty; remember that." She paused in thought.

"What is it?" I queried.

"As you've noted on several occasions, I am largely inexperienced in the world of men. Still, I've never met anyone like him before— except that isn't quite true. Though I expect you haven't had time to notice, the two of you are strangely akin."

"Strangely akin? Ant grub! Have you lost your mind? I'm nothing like him at all."

"You are alike in more ways than one. You are both hard men. You are both demanding, forceful, intolerant, and unwavering— not to mention belligerent." She winked.

"You forgot charming."

"Did I?" She cooed, cocking her head quizzically.

"Belligerent?" I squawked, splashing water about angrily.

"Yes. It befuddles the mind to think the two of you haven't seen eye to eye thus far."

"And they call you a seer? Ha! As my soggy arse bears witness, you can't see past your nose at times."

"Such a charmer."

"The only person he sees eye to eye with is that one-eyed fat bastard— who I do recall seeing before. And I'm not belligerent," I wasn't entirely sure what it meant but it didn't sound good.

"You've seen him before? Where? Darian One-Eye they call him."

"When I was but a lad shortly after the death of my mother. He was searching the ashes of our home after it burnt to the ground. All within perished by flame— my uncle's whole family. Though but eight or nine years old at the time, I buried them all."

"He was there! Way back then! Are you sure it was him and do you not find that odd?"

"Odd? And pray tell, precisely what part of my life hasn't been odd? It was him alright. Though his injury was yet to fully heal, there's no mistaking that sorrowful eye of his. I swear, it causes me to shiver as much now as it did back then. I'd be tempted to give him my full pouch of coins if only he'd put a patch over it."

Renan began fussing and she hurried over to gather him up. I heard the familiar suckling noises as she began nursing him. I watched for a bit then decided to swing myself about for beginning to feel like an improper copper which is to say superfluous.

Note, though I very much doubt she will include this, the fore mentioned line is a perfect example of Petra's improvisation skills— but you likely already guessed that. Though perhaps I mentioned this before, yet another telltale sign is how often I refer to her "cleverness". Truth be told, I might have said it once; quite likely with dubiety— which is to imply, a measure of disparagement. That said, judging by the look on her face right now as I recite this, no doubt she'll scratch that last bit out too.

"Belligerent." I muttered, still bemoaning the unfair accusation.

"It means aggressive, stubborn, quarrelsome, and overly competitive. Pig-headed will likely ring a bell." She hooted.

And there she was defining the word *belligerent* as though I hadn't managed to guess as much already. What— did she think I deemed it some form of praise? Regardless of meaning, the mere suggestion that it proposed that the two of us held something in common made it wholly irrational. Rest assured, should there be an opposing side to belligerence it lay firmly beneath my feet; or it shan't be found lying anywhere at all. Debate ended. Argument closed.

"You may have had a point had I not vowed to behave." I reminded her. "Stubborn— me? Shush! I still find it hard to believe you convinced him you are a seer. Did he not put it to the test? I most certainly would have."

"He did. And there you have it, yet another thing the pair of you have in common." It took all my resolve to keep from spitting.

"And?" I encouraged her finally.

"He asked me how many men he'd killed."

"And what did you answer?" I inquired keenly. "How could you possibly know?"

"I couldn't. Hence, I answered that he'd killed *many men*."

"And he accepted that?" It seemed illogical.

"Hardly. I did say he was intolerant, did I not? Such being the case, though I'd deemed my reply as witty, it merely arose his anger."

"And then what?" I asked anxiously.

"I reminded him a seer was more adept at witnessing things yet to come as opposed to the past. Knowing I'd have to elaborate to have any chance of truly convincing him, I then asked for his hand. Closing my eyes, I ran a finger slowly across his palm. I saw my aunt do it once. She was a seer."

"Your aunt was a seer?" I asked incredulously.

"Yes— or so the stories went. That's what made me think of it in the first place."

"Then what?" I asked with heightening impatience. Having grown tired of straining my neck, I swung myself about just in time to see her eyes close.

"Then, I said in a calm voice… *so many deaths, so much pain, 'tis but misery that surrounds you now. What would you have me say for there is much I see? There are no walls between us. There is no place to hide— especially, not here. As the night sky cast stars, each grain of sand is doomed to remember. Unlike the multitudes above and below, a single sun spelt your undoing for this is what I see…*

Though not by your own hand, whilst traveling to this place, you claim responsibility for the death of seventy-two men. And for that are you awake as many hours as those you mourn for the departed were your own comrades. How many men you killed prior it is not possible for me to say for over the years have your hands grown callous and hard. I do know there is one you regret more than all others combined. You can never outrun it and you can never forget it for it plagues you as though it happened… but yesterday."

I was aghast. Having employed the same tone used while

reading his palm she'd rendered my own voice largely ineffectual. As far as role playing went, I could only bow down to her. To say she have a knack for the theatrical was akin to calling the desert hot. Though a moment ago I was sweating profusely, a shiver now tickled the full length of my spine.

"And what did he do then?" I croaked, pulling a hand free of my mouth.

"He retracted his hand as though it had been scalded. He sat there rubbing it while scowling silently at me. He then conceded I was indeed a seer; asserted we were done before departing in great haste."

"But how in Haeryn's hells did you know? Are you akin to your aunt? Do you truly have *the gift*? Did you somehow read his palm in fact?" Her eyes widened bizarrely as she bit her lip, staring at me with that devilish green-eyed grin of hers. Which is to say, I felt that same eerie shiver again.

"I think we're all seers of sorts providing we look in the right places. As alluded to earlier, not so very long ago, my mother used to tell me stories about my aunt while speaking in the same fashion. Being that those tales held me transfixed as a young girl, it only made sense to traverse a similar path. Though the truth of it is− I got lucky."

"You got lucky?" I larked. "No. You could never have guessed as much? Twas the most amazing account ever gracing my ears. Far better than any bard by a fully drawn bow. It was *fantastic* if ever the word found meaning. How did you manage it? Tell me!" I implored.

"Do you remember the wall of skulls ahead of the well?"

"Yes, of course. It's not something easily forgotten," I said. "I've seen plenty of heads mounted on pikes but never a wall of forgotten faces. But what has that to do with it?"

"But that's just it; they're far from forgotten. The moment I saw it− it seemed a memorial to me. A shrine of sorts, if you get my meaning. Though unintentional, I'd somehow counted them without ever thinking about it. Every row is the same; eighteen skulls and four rows high." I discerned a slight tremble in her voice as she continued.

"Had they been foes they would have been heaped in a pile and long forgotten. But this wall was built with great care and attention. Thus, I knew they could not have been their enemies. It wasn't a warning to outsiders but rather a reminder. It was built to ensure they'd never forget their fallen comrades."

Walking forth, she stopped to glare while Renan pointed a tiny finger at me. It was as though the wee man was accusing me of something− and then Petra opened her mouth to remove all doubt.

"And you have nerve enough to piss on it!" She scolded. 'You're lucky they didn't kill you then and there. Your lone savior being that the transgression was ruled to be of less import than how we came to be here. This is why you must be exceedingly cautious. You insulted them and they despise you for it. Don't make it easy for them. Don't give them a reason."

"Understood. But what about the one he'd killed earlier— the one he regretted more than all the others combined? How could you possibly have known that?"

"I could see it in his eyes. You can't hide that sort of pain. *If regret and death are intertwined, and murder lies the thread; then guilt has nowhere left to hide for the past can't entomb the dead.* I read that in a book once. Though I can't say why, I've never forgot it. What about you? Is there one you regret most?"

"One what?"

"Killing. Did you not hear a word I said?"

"Killing?" I was purposely procrastinating. It wasn't something I ever spoke about. I knew exactly why she'd never forgotten the wall of skulls. You could have heaped all the sand in the world over some of the things I'd done, but it wouldn't have made a brick of difference. Though what's done is done as they say, such atrocities find a way to resurface. They always do.

"Not one as in *one.*" I replied soberly. "Though many have I killed, precious few I remember. That alone conjures regret. Outside of that, should I not kill that pretentious fool, I expect Haeryn will haunt me the remainder of my days— and *that* I would regret."

"If you are truly to see us to Harkenspear, you must forgo such foolish thoughts." She sighed loudly. "There is still something I need confess to you. Promise me you will allow me to speak my peace before you say anything."

"But of course, being charming by nature I would not have it any other way."

Petra stuck her tongue out at me; followed by Renan. The mutiny had begun— until we heard a sharp rap upon the door. Though Greta's face appeared, my attention was still consumed by Petra. It was obvious, whatever she felt compelled to confess pained her greatly. I could also tell— that she could tell— that even though I knew not what it was, I had little wish to hear it. What? It makes perfect sense. *And yes, I did dictate that entirely unaided for the notion having proved too complex for Petra— as clever as she was.*

It was plain to me which of the two pained her more. In

hindsight, I hold the latter to blame for things finally coming to light in the untimely fashion in which they did. Which is to say, it was by large my fault. Nothing new there.

Understand, I no longer felt myself the same bold soldier that had ridden into Gadev but a few days before. The hardest part for me to stomach being, it wasn't the desert that had broken me; *she* had broken me. Without doubt, my broken face, and dehydrated physical state in general had taken no less of a toll. I suppose what I'm struggling to convey is, it was my own misgivings that troubled me most. A fire had been kindled. She'd ignited something that smoldered within me. She'd caused me to question all I'd ever stood for. Truth was, I didn't even feel as though I was acting anymore. My new role had completely consumed me. Like a giant python, it had swallowed me whole.

I'd inadvertently become *the assassin with no name* for no longer being able to recognize myself. Ironically, had I gazed into a mirror, I would have learned how precisely true that really was. I did look quite hideous. Was it a miraculous rebirth; or had the monster within finally chosen to reveal itself? Either way, the only thing I felt certain of was that I was tired of hiding– tired of lying to myself.

"Fresh linen and clean clothes have I brought." Greta announced, strolling in, and placing them on the nearest table. "Anything else might you be in need?"

"I thank you for your kindness," I replied blankly, "but we have all that we require." Having farted, a barrage of tickly bubbles rumbled to the water's surface. "Are you certain you won't join me?" I joked, winking at Petra who wisely ignored me.

"For you would I bring a bowl of hot soup." Greta acknowledged.

"You mean soup as in *very nearly food*? I'm afraid I may have spoken too hastily." I chortled. "I would be most grateful."

Once Greta departed, after motioning Petra to turn herself about, I climbed out of the tub and dressed hastily making no attempt to dry myself. The djellaba fit me well and it wasn't black which took me by surprise. It was beige colored. Anything other than blue, black, or red would have sufficed. There was a saying amongst soldiers regarding clothes that matched the sky. *Green, brown, or white is a comforting sight. Red, black, or blue and we'll run you through.* Or something similar. Albeit the rules weren't half as stringent as they once were.

The soup arrived! Twas a wonderful broth consisting of

something not unlike chicken. It wasn't chicken though. I could tell because chickens don't have horns. Though small, I could not understand how any self-respecting cook might have missed it. Leading me to conclude, it must have been added solely for flavor. Having suckled it for quite some time, it was rather salty. The soup was thickened with some form of cabbage, though sweeter in taste. I discovered another plant-like thing swimming about as well. Not being meat, while offended by the look of it; I set it cautiously aside. In the off chance you hadn't guessed, Petra's urgent revelation had been set aside as well.

It took an additional two days and nights of recuperation before I felt well enough to have a gander about the place. To my surprise, a steep ladder was the first thing to greet me on the opposing side of the door. I had no idea I'd been soaring so high above ground. *Snoring*, corrected Petra. Though it had been my intention to proceed down the narrow ladder first, Petra took offense to that. Thus, I explained to her that I was still feeling a tad wobbly and, Haeryn forbid, should I lose my balance and slip, I feared bringing Petra and Renan down with me. Petra would not have it however, suggesting it no more than a ruse to peer up her garments. Strangely, though the thought had never occurred to me, I suddenly found it hard to force it from my mind.

Thanks to her, I felt an escalating level of stress with each pending downward step. Trust me, it's not easy to keep one's djellaba tucked tightly between one's knees whilst clamoring down a ladder. That said, I felt confident she had more than enough to contend with for having to carry Renan who was tightly bundled within her shawl. It was precisely then that I conjured greater respect for Greta and the other women. Carrying a baby was problematic enough; transporting jostling vessels of hot water, or soup even, was another animal entirely. I expressed this to Petra who pointed out the rope and pulley system I was yet to notice.

"They've harnesses for carrying smaller items though they employ the rope and pulley for anything of consequence. How do you think they got *you* up there? What– did you really think Greta carried you in her arms?" She laughed from below.

I'd never met someone quite so aggravating. And I didn't mean Greta. *However indeed* I marveled. I could not imagine it; leading me to express my intense gratitude for not having been coherent at the time. Then again, when considering the extent of my injuries, perhaps they did drop me once or twice. It's not as though I'd know the difference.

It was quite a climb to the floor, having counted four other doorway tiers during our sluggish descent. Petra explained that this side, namely *West Branch*, had five upper levels from top to bottom. *The Crown*, where we were staying. *Harem's Hold* which speaks for itself. *The Burl*, which she said was a small work area; followed by *West Warren*. Most of the men lived in either of the two warrens. *Knot's Grove* was a larger work area. While *East Branch* housed but two upper levels: *Heartwood,* where our host resided and *East Warren.* There were three, in truth, if you counted *The Eye* though I was told it was essentially just a one-man lookout.

The main floor consisted of five separate areas: *The Rookery* being the largest and therefore the common room. *The Sand Coffin* conjured less favorable memories; not to mention being the place where the *housecat* was kept. *The Red Room* served as the library. Yes, that library– cause every tree needs a library. Petra insisted they had nearly five hundred books. Which prompted me to wonder if reading the last line of five hundred books was comparable to reading an entire volume by itself. Coincidentally, such food for thought led us straight to *The Galley* which was likewise the pantry.

Last but never used least, *The Black Pail,* also known as *the Tainted Pail* or the *Grim March* or *Mucky Bucket.* You get the idea. A place of deep contemplation no doubt; that being: the communal lavatory. As Petra so adeptly put it, the great tree needed some nourishing too. Petra attested that, in comparison, the climb to The Crown was well worth the extra effort for the stench alone, even if you did have to lower *the huck-it buckets* five floors down by rope.

Being that I was on my feet again, it was only a matter of time before the preceding information would prove vital. The smaller *alternative* buckets were emptied and swept away magically by the sands I might add– on the North side of *Grumble*, which was what they called the Great Tree. Petra had no idea when the Grim Pail was emptied last– if ever it was. As far as the naming of the tree went, it did seem appropriate given the constant chorus of grunts and groans emitted by the massive tree.

I awoke late afternoon the next day to find Petra and Renan still sleeping, Renan in his basket and Petra on her cot. Unexpectedly, I felt somewhat refreshed and oddly content. Petra, on the other hand, had a rather restless night. Giggling aloud during what I expected must have been early morning, she'd leapt suddenly from her bed and scurried across the room. She startled me so severely I'd tumbled from my cot. I assumed she was rushing toward Renan, but she did not, she just spun herself about several times.

"Where are you going?" I called out.

"I'm good. I'm good. I'm good." She returned gleefully. I, on the other hand, felt less confident for being scared she might venture out the door. Thankfully, she did not. She just kept twirling about. Finally, after circling the room three more times, she returned to her cot.

"Go to sleep," I huffed softly.

"I am asleep," she whispered back, followed by soft snoring sounds which brought me comfort. Perhaps I should latch the door from now on, I recall thinking. With her monkeyshines concluded; I slept quite well after that.

After discerning a way by which to latch the door, I could not help but notice the back of Petra's neck was badly scalded for a tender-looking red stripe ran downward from her shoulder. It made me feel insensitive− a feeling that was entirely new to me. The thought of parched skin being covered by such a bristly blanket seemed a travesty. I had no idea she'd been hurting for she'd given no such indication. It wasn't as though she'd ever had a chance as I considered things. It had been *all about me* since our unwelcome arrival. I then recalled what she said about Greta being a healer and had an idea.

Sneaking quietly out the door, I climbed down one level to Harem's Hold. Rapping softly upon the door, I waited patiently. Perhaps they had a cure for sleepwalkers as well. Which was undoubtedly a rope the more I thought about it. They had plenty of rope. I heard the latch slide on the opposing side, and a raven-haired woman appeared.

"Ah, you're alive," she smiled. "Wonderful. It's good to see you on your toes." She smiled, displaying a mouthful of very even teeth. Though I can't say why, first and foremost, I always seemed to notice people's teeth. More unnerving to me, she wore a plain gown made of the same material as the scratchy blankets. It looked very uncomfortable; notwithstanding her ample hips must surely rub upon every step taken.

"I was hoping to have a word with Greta," I smiled.

"Greta is in the galley." I frowned, knowing it'd be pointless to visit the galley for it being unlikely for her to have brought what I was hoping to procure. Another thought struck me.

"Is Ora within?" I asked.

"You've found her," she said with a slight bow. "I am Ora. How may I help?"

"I was wondering if you might have an ointment suitable for soothing abraded skin?" I asked.

Ora raised her index finger briefly before closing the door. It seemed a positive indication, coupled with the fact I did not hear her re-latch the door. A few moments later she reappeared to hand me a small jar.

"This is very good; soothing with healing powers, yet mild enough to rub all over." She ran her large fingers over her breasts, then down her hips and thighs, to ensure I understood. I did unfortunately; far more than I felt was warranted.

"Everywhere." She reaffirmed with a frightful wink.

After stifling a shiver, I thanked her. Retracing my steps quietly back to The Crown, I found Petra still sleeping. Easing her blanket back gently, I discovered her neck and shoulders were much worse than I'd thought. A blistered red swath ran from her left shoulder, across her back, disappearing beneath her right armpit. The skin was chafed and swollen. Dipping a finger in the ointment, I ran the flat of my finger softly along it and she cringed.

"What are you doing?" She yelped.

"I'm sorry." I empathized. "Try not to move. It's high time I tended to your needs for once. Your neck and back need some attention. It looks rather tender."

"It's nothing," she replied. "A bit of sun is all." She tried to cover herself, but I pushed her hands away.

"Lie still," I insisted. "I fetched an ointment from Ora. I had no idea you were hurt so. I hope it helps." She winced as I touched her. I could do nothing about it; my hands had never been anything other than rough. It was then that it occurred to me, of all the things he might have left me, I had my father's hands. Or so I'd thought at the time.

"It's better than before." She sighed, trying to relax her shoulders.

"Seems worse than what the sun might conjure. Has someone taken a strap to you? Speak their name and I'll stuff their fingers so far down their throat they'll shit knuckles for a fortnight." I blustered.

"Calm yourself." She blurted, half-laughing. "You'll wake Renan. No one laid a hand on me. 'Tis from carrying my son across a desert, day after day. You are far too quick to anger and quicker still in your errant assumptions."

"Sorry. As I said, I had no idea you were hurting. This should have been addressed much earlier. It's begun to fester."

"Thank you, 'tis very kind of you, thoughtful in truth. Who knew?"

"It's best to let it absorb into the skin before dressing." Though I wasn't certain that the last bit I'd said was true, the curve of her back agreed with me greatly. It'd be a shame to cover it too hastily.

"It does feel soothing. You can do the rest if you like."

Rolling flat, she raised her arms above her head. I needed no further urging. Her back was softer than anything I'd laid hands upon before. At least that I remembered.

Gingerly, and methodically, I rubbed the ointment over the remainder of her back. Each time I stopped, the farther the blanket fell away, which only emboldened me. She finally caught on and reached round to pull the blanket back up. In hindsight, it was a good thing she did, for I'd begun to question my true intentions. *Hindsight;* what a curious word. It seemed nothing short of glorious in truth.

"Thank you. That's the best I've felt since— since I don't remember when." She sighed softly.

"My pleasure," I replied, wiping my hands off on my djellaba. "Ora said it should be applied at least three times daily." I lied.

"Three times? Are you certain?"

"I don't see the harm either way. Providing we employ due diligence; it will get better."

"You are incorrigible."

"Guilty as charged," I replied feeling it could only be another way of saying knowledgeable.

We spent the early evening sharing idle chatter though I did send a message to our host informing him that I finally felt well enough to attend that night's communal dinner.

Later that evening, as we entered the Rookery, a pleasant woman, introduced to me as Sully, guided us to our host's table. I counted seven tables and estimated there to be close to forty men present. The women's bright colored robes contrasted starkly with the men's dark attire. It was all I could do to hide my delight upon finding myself seated next to the one-eyed man who was much larger than I recalled, which only served to double my overflowing glee.

More improvisation from Petra, if you hadn't guessed, being that I'd referred to him as elephantine. Which isn't true either, for my actual remark being far more inelegant. In fairness, what I whispered to her was: should elephant not be in season; he'll no doubt starve. After which, she'd kicked me in the shin with little warning— save perhaps that look of hers. But when didn't she have that look?

Unlike the others, likely due to fabric shortages, his worn robes were grey in color. A speckled chestnut-colored kestrel with a blue and yellow beak sat quietly on his shoulder; undoubtedly the same one I'd glimpsed whilst buried up to my neck in sand. The cyclops's long unruly hair had grown grey since our first acquaintance as a young boy when I spied him rummaging through the ruins of our burnt hovel. Even had I arrived on a mythical alicorn, I harbored little fear of him identifying me. Too much time had passed. I looked nothing like the village pest, dubbed Rooster, the other boys used to chase and throw stones at. No, I could slap him on the back sporting an expression of fond recognition and the pompous fool would be none the wiser. For Haeryn's sake, *I* didn't even remember what I looked like back then.

Petra, with Renan bundled beneath her shawl, was seated on my opposing side beside our *gracious host*. Sadistic scoundrel was how I appraised him, though I was adamant not to show it. Not that whispering as much didn't fetch me another sharp kick in the shins.

Honestly, betwixt the three of them I wasn't certain which of them was worse. All jesting aside, the mere sight of him made me cringe. Still, I could not risk offering him the slightest rationale to take offense. If that was even possible. The man had a temper akin to a crocodile's smile. Either way, time would tell, I feared inwardly. Unlike the other men, the hood of his dark pin-striped djellaba concealed most of his face much as before. All you could see were his piercing dark eyes. *Those bloody eyes. Like daggers were they.*

"Ah, so glad to see you could make it," he said with such joviality you'd think we'd grown up together. His facial garment twisted into a smile that seemed genuine despite the fact his face was covered, not to mention my growing apprehension at being forced to tolerate his mere presence.

Tapping his cup, he said aloud, "Gentlemen, our guests have arrived." The men ceased their chatter at once, turning their attention toward us.

"No, no, no," he declared. "I was simply being polite. As you were; as you were; I will speak privately with them for the time being. Announcements will follow once dinner is served." He motioned at one of the women pouring wine from a large pitcher.

"More wine if you would please, Anna. Thank you, thank you," he beamed as she topped his mug to the brink.

"Drink up everyone," he insisted, raising his cup high. "For I am in a festive mood tonight!" The men roared their approval, pounding their cups on the table in response.

"Steady now, no need to spill what you have already." He cautioned jokingly.

Judging by the spillage and overflow whilst pouring, there seemed to be no fear of ever running short of wine or ale. The ale tasted strangely akin to the wine, only bitterer with a slight hint of effervescence. Regardless, both were strong in alcohol and readily thirst quenching. Though I'd have liked nothing more than to get falling-down drunk; I decided it best not to over-indulge given my present condition and predicament.

"I am glad you're on the mend and regretful we got off to such a rough start," he confided softly. "Here's to new beginnings and new friendships," he continued, clanking his cup against my own.

"This is my good friend, Darian. He'll be keeping a close eye on you, just in case," he laughed. "But not to fret— the wandering orb is merely for show. It doesn't see a thing," he added in a whisper. "Still, I find it best to approach him from the left side— that being his right. It's safer that way."

"'Tis why he never sits next to me," asserted Darian. "I would gut him for his cheek were he but a trifle closer."

"Then I'm glad to be of service," I lied, feigning a smile. "I've always found blood and wine mix poorly." They found amusement in that for they both laughed aloud whilst pounding their cups. After which they both called out for more wine. Apparently, the rules about spillage did not apply to them.

"Well said," grinned our host. "Petra and Renan, we know already; but what shall we call you?" He asked. "A man needs a name for without one he ceases to exist. If no one remembers, the man is forgotten. He may as well be buried in sand." He sighed.

"I have no name," I contended. "Though Petra calls me Zil."

"Rah Zil, if I remember correctly." He nodded after a short sip of wine.

"No, I spoke in jest. Twas an unpleasant jest at best." Petra interrupted. "In poor taste to be truthful."

"Unlike the wine," winked Darian. "Not to be undone by a rhyme in good time." He winked again.

"Ah, so Darian One-Eye does indeed blink. Who knew?" Howled our host with overzealous merriment.

"Never in battle," retorted his friend, invoking more mirth between the two.

"And what shall I call you?" I inquired politely, looking straight into his dark sharp eyes.

"One thing at a time," he said curtly. "First, we must sort out your name; for I will not call you Zil. I do not favor the Brotherhood if you must know the truth, and you must; for the truth is all we have." He stared at me for a time.

"I have it!" He blurted finally. "I will call you Assad, the Assassin– for seeming but a *sad assassin* when you first arrived."

"Assad will suffice," I agreed. "My livelihood is something I rarely profess openly. Besides, on this occasion, I find myself reduced to an escort." I decided it best to let him have his little joke.

"Understood, understood," he said, lowering his voice. "I intended no ill will; notwithstanding everyone here is already aware being that you did profess it openly."

"Openly?" I contested.

"Perhaps not as openly as you might have; but let us not rehash the past. What's done is done."

"What's done is done," I granted him. I rubbed my jaw if for no other reason than to clarify which of the two of us it had been easier for.

"Allow me to speak plainly," he began. "I have staked my entire life, and the lives of all those under my command, upon being able to discern when someone is telling the truth; or not. Believe me I know; ask Darian, he will attest to it. I am never wrong."

"No, you are never wrong; except when you are wrong. Remember the day we left for this place? Remember the day we built the wall?" Darian smirked, eyeing his compatriot.

"Yes, yes, I remember. Twas a dark day indeed. I swear, make one mistake and they'll remind you of it forever. If not for me, how many of those sitting before us would still be alive today?" He asked pounding his fist upon the table.

"None save yourself no doubt." Darian shrugged. "I've seen him bludgeoned and I've watched him hang. I swear the man cannot be killed." Darian whispered to me. *We'll see about that soon enough*, I schemed silently.

"But that wasn't what I was referring to and you, of all people, should know it. I ask you, and be truthful, can I or can I not tell when someone is lying to me? Must I be forced to recite instances?"

"No, he can tell," Darian admitted grumpily, whilst bumping my forearm with an elbow. "He knows things; and what he doesn't know he'll attest was noted by Haeryn as unworthy of knowing." He guffawed loudly.

"This woman may be a seer, but *he* is a reader. Therefore, what he doesn't yet know he will stumble upon soon enough on some page amongst his great herd of precious books." Darian whispered yet again in my ear. I could only nod for finding no fault in what he'd said.

"This woman's name is Petra," admonished our host sternly.

"He's got bloody sharp ears too," he whispered quickly prior to continuing. In truth, he wasn't good at whispering. Though he did lower his voice, it was too deep not to be easily overheard. Objectively speaking, I don't expect any actions of his could ever be considered a form of stealth.

"Yes, Petra; my apologies my lady. No harm was intended." Darian avowed with genuine remorse.

"None taken," smiled Petra. "I must confess, I profess a profound love for books as well."

"The Khalifah and Rahs act as though reading was somehow perilous. Fools! Books are a most worthy source of knowledge," nodded our host. "Not wisdom, but knowledge; for never can the two be confidently entwined." Our host emphasized.

"Ah, but experience is the greatest teacher of all– there's nothing quite like falling. You remember, if for no other reason than having scraped knees. You don't forget those lessons." Darian countered. Though I agreed with him fully, having scraped more than a knee or two in my time, it was plain he relished a debate.

"Ah, but if you bind such lessons within a book, the reader might choose a wiser path. Therefore, you limp Darian whilst I do not."

"I limp for having followed you into a bloody desert. Harbor no misconceptions, that is why I limp." Darian grumbled.

"In a lot of ways, books are akin to the desert. Each wave of page not unlike a dune ascended in hope of envisioning, not merely something different but, something never presumed. For it isn't the unknown that compels us forward; it is having the courage to believe the best is yet to come. Therefore, pastures ahead of us always appear greener; wherefore the sky can't always be blue." Our host sighed.

"Returning to point," he continued, "which wasn't about what someone knows or does not; but rather whether I can discern when they know more than they admit. This I know."

"I know, you know and now we all know," summarized Darian before commanding more wine.

"More wine *please!*" corrected his colleague using the tone of a superior. I heard it many times before though never for improper manners. Oddly, had our roles been reversed, it's what I might have said which gave me cause to shiver.

"Yes, of course. *Please. Please. Please.* More wine please! Enough riddles! Let us stop talking in circles that not even Chitter could fathom without a stiffer drink first." He said, shaking his head and perching his falcon on the edge of his cup to better make his point.

"You said you wished to speak *plainly*, so allow me to say it for you." Darian turned to look me in the face. Which always felt awkward as, though I did resist, I felt increasingly drawn to his roving eye.

"It is simple," he smiled. "He knows there are things you are not telling him, and he will *not stop* until all your secrets have been revealed."

Returning to his *whisper*, "And, being that the cat is *always hungry*, I would strongly advise you to tell him all he wants to know." Exhaling a deep breath, he returned Chitter to his shoulder and sat back in his chair.

"There it is said. Was that so hard?" Darian queried, turning to his hooded comrade. "Please, please, please," he continued, prying the pitcher out of the server's hands instead of allowing her to refill his glass. "I'll have you know, unlike the rest of you, there's two of us sharing this bit." He declared nodding toward his wobbly little kestrel.

Following Petra's example, I placed my hand over my cup when he tried to replenish it; causing him to scowl at me with contempt. Thankfully, dinner arrived to distract his attention, sparing any need to explain my reluctance.

Dinner consisted of bread and a hearty bowl of stew. Though I could not name precisely what kind of stew it was, there were a few bones in it for which I was thankful. Which is to say, none of the salty little horns were present. Not that I would have complained in the slightest.

"May I speak plainly," I asked, causing Petra to grimace.

"Of course," asserted our host. "I insist on it as you will witness later as we finish our meals." Being that he'd removed the lower portion of his head scarf, I noticed his face was frightfully scarred which did little for my appetite. Not that I let it slow me down in any way for being completely famished. Not to mention, thus far the stew was quite delicious.

"Following the announcements, the men are allotted time to address any grievances they might have. They can speak openly without fear of consequence." Darian clarified. "So, speak your mind." He encouraged, waving me on with his spoon which startled his falcon. The kestrel circled the room several times before returning to perch on his shoulder. No one, not counting Petra and I, appeared to take notice.

"I only wish to inquire; who amongst us does not harbor some secret? It is the most difficult predicament that I find myself in. I've sworn many oaths never to divulge certain things. I will not forsake these oaths at any cost. I seek neither wealth nor power. Outside of duty and honor, my reputation is all that I have. This is not up for debate, and neither will I negotiate." I paused briefly to ensure my point had been made before continuing.

"You wish me to be truthful, yet there are many things you are withholding from me. You call me untruthful, yet I am at a distinct disadvantage for I do not even know where your true loyalties lie. You dress like the Kedera, yet you do not act like them. I consider myself an honest man; more honest than most; but I have a task to perform. Namely, to escort this woman and child safely to their destination. That is it and that is all." Our host was studying me closely.

"Beyond that, I care nothing about this war. I hold no stake in it. I do not have the luxury of choosing sides. That is not how the Brotherhood works. For countless years it remains the same. We are commissioned with tasks, and we see them done. We do not question our orders nor ponder their rationale. We complete them as bidden." After which our host began to clap very slowly and purposely.

"Did I not tell you he would profess to be a saint?" He said, smiling at Darian before returning his attention to myself.

"I'm no saint." I said hoarsely, before swallowing a mouthful of something quite likely never intended to be eaten. It felt like a small bird's egg still in the shell. Withdrawing the offending gruel from the corner of my mouth, I placed it on the edge of my bowl, feeling entirely validated. The small blob was indeed ripe with bits of shell. I was greatly fond of eggs– the inner parts only.

"Ah, and there it is… the look of the truth." Our host shook his head forlornly. It was his turn to shake his spoon in the air while contemplating his response.

"Don't get me wrong; I appreciate your candor, but you omit certain things at your convenience. We ask the questions because it was you who impeded upon our territory. We did not come knocking upon your door– and certainly not in the same fashion you employed with Petra." He admonished.

"Yes, she told me about that. You want to know where our allegiances lie though *you lied* to us from the onset. By your own admission, you boast no allegiance; other than the Brotherhood of which we have little choice but to take you at your word. Refresh my memory, just so we can all be clear. What story do you profess to be true at this juncture in time being that your first spoken words were a lie?" His tone rose impatiently not that my own anger had not been kindled.

"If it's honesty you want− know that I would have proclaimed Haeryn your long-lost son if I thought it would save us. I was desperate. We were dying. We'd been wandering aimlessly for days. Our water slings were dry. You resembled the Kedera. Therefore, I said what I thought prompted our greatest chance of survival. Admittedly, I lied. Admittedly, that was a mistake. I lied when I falsely stated Petra to be my prisoner. Why? The answer is simple. To protect her. I deemed it the best way to ensure her safety. It is my sole task, my only concern."

"And yet he insists he's not a saint," he said, raising his hands in surrender while looking at his compatriot for answers. "Perhaps you're right, Darian. Perhaps it's just me being over-protective," he smiled. "What do you think? Look into his eyes Darian and tell me if *you think* he's telling the truth. I know what I think." Sighed our host with frustration.

"What? Do I look like a seer to you?" roared Darian. Our nameless host glared at him until he finally conceded.

"Alright, alright; I will gaze into the depths of his very soul if that what it takes to appease you."

Turning his big face toward mine, he scowled whilst considering me closely. *That damn eye!* It was unnerving. Not unlike a full moon on a clear night, or that giant tree, there was a strange gravity to it− a pull you could not ignore. It was spellbinding. Not to mention, his little bird was eyeing me no less vehemently. So much so it crapped all over Darian's arm which caused me to chortle. If only Renan could see it. He would have been proud.

"Haeryn's hells! You little shitter, Chitter!" Darian shook the bird off him in disgust. Flying to an empty chair, it squawked at him sullenly.

"I don't know. I don't know. I don't know." He stammered uncomfortably. "I don't see anything. Just one more fool not unlike the rest obsessed by poop and blindness!"

"For the record, I have asked him to wear a patch," stated our host. "I even fashioned him one− which he wore for all of one glorious day. The truth is, he likes the effect his *poached egg* has on people. It's true, is it not Darian?" Darian glowered, silently pulling apart his bread and moping the sides of his nearly empty bowl with it. He stopped suddenly.

"I will tell you this. As much as he insists on not having a side in this war, within him does it fester to his core." He noted somberly. "His roots are entangled by its venomous web. I sense much discontent— a void— a disorder of some kind. That said, war breeds death and try as we might— even here— no one is immune." He added in a brighter tone before returning his attention to ensuring every morsel had been judiciously mopped from his bowl.

"You claim duty and honor to be all you have. Well, all I want is the truth. Something you're not giving to me. That much I'm sure of."

"I don't know what else I might say." I shrugged, deciding I may as well upend the metaphorical apple cart that separated us.

"And what about you?" I asked with eyebrows raised.

"You will not even tell me your name. Why is that I wonder? What secrets do you hide??" I felt Petra kick me beneath the table and knew she feared I was swiftly approaching dangerous ground if I hadn't already trodden past it.

Pushing his bowl away, our host glared at me indignantly. He then rose from his chair. Though knowing I'd raised his ire, I saw little to be gained by retreating now. It would only make me look weak and I could ill afford that. Perhaps, it was just my foolish pride. Haeryn knows, I felt weak enough as is.

"I know, let's all play a game," he announced loudly to the room.

"Dead Man Quaking?" Asked one of his men to the applause of those nearest him.

"Trust me, you do not want to play Dead Man Quaking with me right now. I fear my mood has soured somewhat. No, this is a different game. It's a new game. I call it *Honesty*. You will like it. I will explain the rules. Assad will…"

"The assassin?" someone queried.

"Quiet. Yes, but he doesn't appreciate that," he said, raising a finger. "It's supposed to be a secret," he feigned to whisper. "He does adore secrets." He winked whilst clearing his throat.

"The rules are as follows: Assad will ask any question he likes of any one present which you must answer as honestly as you can. That is an order! I will then ask a question of him which he must answer honestly. See, it really is quite simple. Ask and answer. Does everyone understand the rules?"

"Yes." His men answered so loud it made Petra bounce in her chair. Renan did not wake up, however. Which I found no less fortunate than surprising.

"I have a question," said the man who'd spoken earlier.

"Of course, you do Ruok. Could someone bring him more ale please?" The men laughed until their commander raised his hand.

"Not that it was your turn!" our host barked, eyeing him sternly.

"Assad, you may begin," he said at last. "Ask anything of anyone."

"Without consequence?" I felt a need to clarify.

"No, that's purely an after-dinner thing. Of course, there are consequences. What's life without consequence? Not worth living. Tell the truth or feed the cat." He illuminated.

"Feed or be fed to?" I attempted to clarify.

"Potàtoe, potato; tomàtoe, tomato," he huffed. "As I said, it's a simple game with nothing to lose— unless of course you lie."

Though I had little wish to partake in the game, I saw no way of declining which didn't lead directly back to the Sand Coffin. Did I mention how much I loathed sand? I positively hated it. Rising, I pointed at the man who'd last spoken for no other reason than it being the only other name I knew besides Darian and a few of the women who I had little inclination to involve.

"Ruok, what is your commander's name?"

"Truthfully, I don't know his rightful birth name if that's what you intend. I'm not even sure he does." The men chuckled at that. "He's been called many things. As for us, we call him Alde Baran; *bright star.*" He beamed proudly.

Falling back into my chair, I very nearly slumped to the floor. My heart froze when I heard that name. I could not believe my ears. I felt giddy and weak, as though I might crumple like a dried leaf upon the merest nudge. *It can't be! That's not possible!* My own father was once known as Nitesh Alde Baran. It was an impractical coincidence. But in the next moment, to my horror, I knew it to be true. *Those eyes! Those dark piercing eyes!* Forget the apple cart, my entire world had been turned upside down in an instant. I needed to leave. I needed to return to The Crown— and think.

"My turn," said Alde Baran. "Besides being her escort, by what other way do you know this woman?" he asked, pointing an outstretched finger rudely at Petra. My knees felt so weak. I had no stomach for games. Especially, not now. *How might it possibly be so?* And yet, there he stood. I could not have lied to him at that moment had I been daring enough to try.

"She is the mother of my child." I heard Petra utter a loud gasp. I did not dare look her in the eye. There was far too much on my mind already. Feeling tears welling in my eyes, I wiped them away swiftly. It was clear, I'd reached my wits end. How any of them didn't recognize the full extent of my distress I'll never know. Perhaps, it was due to my disheveled appearance for my face was still quite swollen.

"Ah, you see. I knew it. *Your turn.*" The wild crickets were back in full force. I could barely make out his words for the frightful ringing in my ears.

"My apologies but I'm feeling unwell. I have no more questions and no longer wish to play."

"But I do have questions. *Ask!*" He demanded hotly. Seeing no alternative, I turned to Ruok once more.

"Do your allegiances lie with the Kedera or Golan?" Not caring in the least what answer was returned.

"I cannot speak for every man. Each heart is its own. But, as soldiers, we recognize neither. Our sole allegiance is to the motherland, Harbinger. To be plain, Golan does not even know we exist. Whereas the Kedera want us dead. Either way, we are outcasts."

"You might have simply said *neither* and left it at that," jeered our host, *Alde Baran*. "That was akin to four or five answers in one. I must confess, I feel somewhat cheated." He shook his head spitefully.

"No more ale for him; it makes him too chatty." He added sourly, causing his men to roar with laughter.

"Where did you get this dagger?" Removing my gold-handled dagger from within his djellaba, he stabbed it forcefully into the tabletop. Its hilt sprang back and forth, making the ivory horse appear to gallop. To me at least given how unsteady I suddenly felt.

"From the Brotherhood." I replied distractedly.

"They gave it to you?"

"It was passed on to me by another of the same faction."

"He gave it to you willingly?"

"He had no *need* of it anymore."

"He was dying?"

"Yes."

"And what pray tell is this?" Darian interrupted, unveiling the fork I'd borrowed from Studayo House and stabbing it likewise into the table.

"It's called a fork. You poke things with it."

"What kind of things? Small creatures like mice?" he asked curiously.

"I expect so," I shrugged. "Scorpions are a bit trickier."

"It's for eating!" Petra blurted. "To hold your meat still while you cut it!"

A collective sigh swept the room as we all nodded in unison; before breaking into uneasy laughter. Truth being, not one of us was certain whether she'd been jesting or not. As distracting as it was, I could not turn my eyes away from... *him*. It was entirely unfathomable. After so many years, even still he found a way to kick me in the face without lifting a finger. Even so, I'd felt the sting of it far worse for my head was swimming with reckless thoughts all of which ended with carving out his heart.

"There, I think that makes us even; *your turn*." Baran acknowledged, intent on continuing his little game. Forcing my fingers from my mouth, I did my best to ignore multiple visions of my mother being kicked that danced like torrid flames within my thoughts as I stared at him.

"What other names does he go by?" I asked, unable to think of anything else for my mind had become completely consumed by his mere presence. Okay, that and the fact that Darian had stolen my fork. Not unlike my dispossessed dagger, it too was mine. The fork, that is. It belonged to me. It was all I could do to stop myself from grabbing it and plunging it into his eye. Just prior to killing my long-lost father that is. *Father?* He was no father of mine. That much I knew for certain. And yet.... at the same time, wasn't he just so?

"Though I am told he has many names, I only know what the Kedera call him."

"And what is that?" I snapped. The man refused to answer until his commander flung his cup of wine at him.

"Answer him! Tell him!" He hollered. "Say it together, everyone! What do they call me?" He raged. Apparently, there was yet another *woolly mammoth* lurking within the room that needed to be addressed.

"The Sun Rah!" They rumbled in unison.

"Yes. They call me the Sun Rah," he mused lugubriously as though having only just remembered himself. "The one that speaks as none." He recited slowly.

He sat down, and it quickly became apparent, the game had ended. For me however, it had only just begun. Could this eccentric raging lunatic truly my father? It made no sense. And yet, here we were within the giant tree he once spoke of. Understandably, I felt precisely as he'd first described it– *empty inside.*

I did take some comfort in the fact that my final question had distressed him. I found I could breathe again. I could feel my hands again. I no longer felt like chaff at the mercy of the wind. I stared at him; whilst trying to look as though I wasn't. His face remained shrouded, as always. I could only catch small glimpses of his eyes; and they haunted me.

I had so many doubts yet at the same time I felt entirely convinced of it. My father left so very long ago. I was not even sure of my age. He did seem old enough. I began rehearsing everything I recalled him ever saying. Like a grating mill stone, his words churned, over and over, in my thoughts. There had to be something. And then it struck me; that thing he'd said about the stars upon our arrival. More precisely, about *looking up but not seeing them for what they really were.* He'd said that to me as a child. *It was him. It had to be!* I was certain of it– near certain for certain. And should it prove to be true, nay, even if it somehow didn't, I was going to kill him. Not now, not in this instance, but sometime soon. Fate had brought us together for one reason and one reason only– so I might avenge my mother's death!

"What's past is past," said Darian eerily and for the merest of moments I thought he was speaking to me. "Let it go. It does no good to brood upon things we cannot change." But Darian was wrong– dead wrong. The past wasn't gone. It was sitting but two chair lengths away.

"But it is not past," said Alde Baran. "We are still here; are we not? Because of our failure is Harbinger divided; leaving us nowhere to go; no homes we might return to."

"We united our people once, we can do it again," objected Darian. "All is not lost; it is simply the way of things presently."

"With life comes struggle," muttered Alde Baran.

"Aye, the gods are cruel; with life comes struggle. It is Haeryn's way, the way of all things that draw breath." His friend agreed, before reclaiming the fork the moment Baran's eyes turned away.

"What do you mean, because of your failure Harbinger is divided?" Petra asked cautiously. "I don't understand."

"The game has ended," Alde Baran uttered meekly.

"It was long ago, before your time, before the First Great War,"

Darian answered. "Other than Baran, the False Rahs, and I; there are none who know the tale. We do not speak of it. In this at least, Assad was not wrong. We too have oaths. We too have secrets we will either make amends for or take to our graves. There lies no other course. It remains the only road before us."

"I made no such oath," scolded Alde Baran. "Perhaps it is high time to let others know the tale. We're not getting any younger, my friend. I ask you, why should we take it to the grave? Why should we bear the burden of an empire founded solely upon a lie?"

"It was never our lie," reasoned Darian after carefully refilling his cup prior to sneaking a large swig straight from the pitcher. "I did swear an oath– *unto you* if I recall correctly." He offered some to me and I did not refuse him; and neither did Petra or Alde Baran for that matter. All the while, as they chattered back and forth, I quashed an incredible urge to beat something until it could move no more. *Kill him. Kill him. Kill him.* My thoughts rang in anguish.

"What does it matter now whose lie it was? Should we have our tongues nailed to our headstones, engraved with the words *forever did they hold them to the detriment of all*?" Alde Baran took a long swallow of wine. I could not help but imagine my hands about his throat– *slowly choking the life from him.*

"And what would you say? Doesn't matter, does it? No one would believe you anyway," noted Darian, flicking aside his long sweaty hair with a hand. "And why in Haeryn's hells should they– after all this time? Besides, what would it change? Nothing. They would simply profess you a liar; raise the bounty on your head; and continue their rule of oppression. Chitter!" He clicked his tongue twice. The kestrel flew to him, and he rewarded it with a small morsel of meat he'd picked from his teeth.

"Perhaps you are right. Perhaps Harbinger is doomed to such misery. Then it is settled; nothing changes; not ever. We failed the One Rah and now we will spend the rest of our lives in the middle of a desert. So be it. Pass the wine and let us be done with it." Alde Baran sighed. "I suppose we should get the remainder of the proceedings over with, so I may continue doing what I do best."

"You mean hiding in the Heartwood– that being, from your past?" Alde Baran ignored him as he rose and spoke hurriedly aloud.

"Here are today's announcements. As you are no doubt already aware, our last trip to market was far more successful than the last– which is why we had meat in our stew tonight." Cheers erupted, and cups were bashed joyously.

"All of our merry wanderers returned safely; save two, Goren and Davos. Goren stayed behind to visit his mother after discovering she was ill. We wish her well. Know that I will go look for him myself should he not return in short order. Davos, I'm told, chose to stay so he might quench more carnal desires." Alde Baran waited for the laughter to subside before continuing.

"As I've asserted before on many occasions, under my command means under my protection. Anything done to appease your individual needs, whatever that may be, is conducted at your peril."

"Keep your assertions to yourself," boomed a voice from the entrance. "For I have returned. And just in time for dinner I might add." Laughter greeted his words though the scowl on Alde Baran's face was plainly evident even through his headscarf. I deduced his name to be Davos purely by default.

"So, you have," he said coldly. "How fortunate are we."

"Honestly Baran, you fret far too much about my welfare. There is no need. I shall always return so long as desires here remain unquenched; and there are several. Even a new one I notice, sitting at your very table. Tell me, what did I miss? No doubt you have added her to your harem already."

"Though it is none of your affair, she has not joined my harem. Her name is Petra, and this is Assad, her escort. They are my guests, and therefore under my protection."

"Guests? Since when did we entertain guests? Did this stump become a hostel whilst I was gone? So, she's up for grabs then?" Davos grinned maliciously.

I started to rise from my chair, but Darian pulled me back down by my forearm. He shook his head making his blind eye twinkle absurdly in the candlelight.

"Don't even look at her without my permission," replied his commander. He cracked his neck, twisting it sharply from side to side. "They are my guests, and you will treat them as such. Is there anything more you'd like to say on the matter? My cat is hungry."

"Your cat is but a blanket awaiting my horse. What happened to that one's face? He looks near as bad as the whore who tried to cheat me two days past." Uneasy laughter could be heard though it proved itself short-lived. As would this newcomer, should he not alter his present course. I'd met his sort before and dealt with them swiftly.

"There was an unfortunate misunderstanding when they arrived. We've sorted it out– for the most part. When he's well enough they shall depart– *if* it pleases me. Now, if that's all."

"It's nowhere near all, but I'm saving that for later. Do continue; and disregard my discourtesy for cramming my bread hole. I am famished." Sitting down before a large bowl, he began to eat ravenously.

"*Continuing...* I won't go over all that was gained but will state that we will not be dry of wine or ale for quite some time. Not to mention the Red Room will see a healthy expansion. Not to repeat myself endlessly, but for those of you who are illiterate, which is to say *not book savvy*, Greta is still willing to trade kitchen help for reading lessons.

"We're well-stocked with salt which is vital. Our supply of smoked fish and salted pork has dwindled to a month or so at best. The next bazaar is still a full season away. Worse still, those lands are now occupied by the Kedera. Thus, Golan will without question relocate the open market elsewhere... but where?

"The closest alternative would be Gadev which, Darian and I agree, seems extremely unlikely given the circumstances. Harkenspear would appear the most likely choice– were it not for the Kestrel. North of Gadev, South Borough in Nyce is a possibility. Along with West Lair in Satre, though that would be a long journey indeed. Then again, chances are it could be any one of the nearer Spears: Gleamingspear; Brokenspear; Whitespear; or perhaps even Echospear." He scratched his chin.

"Perhaps the writing is on the wall. Perhaps we will find no other alternative but to pick a side in this hellish war; or perish in these sands. Should it come to that, each of you will have to make your own choice. I curse the day should any of you meet in battle. As you're keenly aware, my goal has always been to find a way to unite our homeland. But admittedly, I am increasingly beginning to lose confidence that such a thing remains possible. I fear the walls of hate have grown so thick they will soon touch the surrounding seas. Regardless we need not ponder paths as such right now. Let our cups overflow, drink up, my friends!" He raised a cup.

"Moving on... those of you slated to work in The Burl, being that it is now become the bath; can spend your time stripping bark. Myrna is running low on canvases again. Her latest painting is quite spectacular, I might add. *Sideways Rain*, she calls it."

"And it's been hung sideways too!" Croaked a loud voice, stirring greater gaiety.

"It was I that hung it with no less attention than intention, I might add."

"With the lighthouse lying on its side?" the voice queried.

"'Tis your eyesight that lies if you can't see the rain."

'So, not about the lighthouse, or the dock, or the harbor but solely the rain?" The man wished to clarify.

"Yes. It is our viewpoint that blinds us. Because one day the ground will abandon your feet. Because if not for the rain the light would find darkness." A woman's voice affirmed with conviction.

"And there you have it from the artist herself. Ah, Myrna, you're here. What a pleasant surprise. Please join us!"

"I ran out of paint. I need more orange." she said pleadingly, stepping forward with a look of mixed fear and despair.

"Have you eaten?" Alde Baran asked with palpable concern.

"Without orange the sun never sets." She replied absentmindedly.

"Come with me." Greta replied softly, leading her by the hand. "Find you some orange paint Ora will, fret you not about that."

"To paint the sun," Myrna smiled.

"May it serve as a reminder that darkness is fleeting," sighed Alde Baran watching them slowly depart.

"I lost my son." I heard her say softly just prior to her disappearance. Though we'd never met previously, my heart went out to her. So many sons had been lost over the years. I stared at Alde Baran with hidden disdain. Was I not one of them? A large part of me died that day so very long ago. Did he simply forget, or did I matter so little that he chose never to return?

"Lost a fair bit more than her son, I'll wager," sniggered Davos. Alde Baran glared at him for several seconds before finally choosing to speak once again.

"Sideways rain," he muttered before returning to business. "As far as the war is concerned, though the Kedera insurgents retreated to Verdun; Southward, they've invaded Reylos, stormed Mongos, and executed the Khalifah– which is why Darian and I assume Gadev to be next. I think I've covered everything for the most part. The new duty roster has been posted. Did I miss anything Darian?"

"Just the usual reminders– ale and wine are not permitted in the warrens. The Black Pail need not always be quite so black. For the sake of the Gods and our guests– show some pride!" Whilst Alde Baran waited for the hilarity to subside, Darian could be seen wiping bird crap from his arm again, which Petra referred to as *irony*.

"That's it then; re-fill your mugs and allow me to ask, though I think we all know the answer now that Davos has returned. Are they any grievances to be aired?"

"The cat," yelled a man through cupped hands from a table in the rear.

"What about the cat? Stand up man so we can hear you. Ah, Marco! What about the cat? Might you be more specific, or has it run away with your tongue?"

"It's just that he's wandering further every day; making it harder to entice back into its cage. He will kill one of us sooner or later. It's only a matter of time."

"Show him your arm!" yelled another man.

"No need for that." Baran curtailed him. "We've all had our fair share of scratches. See Greta or Ora if necessary. I am no healer. As noted earlier, we do have meat again, so I foresee the cat being *slightly more agreeable* for the next short while."

"He's going to eat someone sooner or later!" Came the second voice again.

"Though I pray it isn't either of you, should your luck prove less favorable, know that you'll be remembered fondly."

"By the cat." Darian chuckled, causing those nearest to roar.

"Either way, the cat is going nowhere. Now, are there any other *worthier* concerns? Remember, now is the time or forever hold your peace." Alde Baran huffed.

"Where are they staying?" asked Davos rising from his chair and stepping forward into the brighter light. He wore a double baldric slung over one shoulder which was belted at the waist. A saber dangled on his left hip and a short sword on his right. Being that both handles faced outward, I knew him to be right-handed. Not to mention, there was a leather-strapped dagger crossing his chest further justifying my assertion. My sour disposition aside, being that he'd insulted Petra, I did not like the man.

"Where are *who* staying?"

"*They* as in *them two*– your bloody guests! Where are they bunking?"

"They're staying in The Crown. My apologies, I should have mentioned that in the announcements for those of you who were absent. The Crown is off-limits for the time being. That said, should you need a bath and, trust me, you do; you'll find an extra tub in The Burl."

"Why should they hold The Crown? Or are they providing *other favors* we're not privy to?"

"I'd be very careful what you say next, Davos, if I were you."

"Is it not grievance time? Is this not the proper time to state complaints without fear of retribution?"

"You know full well the limits to my patience. You will not insult my guests. They have The Crown because I said so. It seemed prudent given the fact that Harem's Hold is immediately below it and Assad required some care and attention."

"Well, I want The Crown when they're gone— given the fact Harem's Hold is immediately below it. Haeryn knows I could do with some care and attention!" He sneered, fetching a few sniggers from the men. Not surprising, he had more to say.

"We've been living in this god-forsaken stump for near five years now and not once was it ever suggested that The Crown might be used as living quarters. Not until your new friends arrived!"

"It's not up for debate; the matter is settled. Now, is there anything more anyone else wishes to snivel about?" Alde Baran demanded. It was obvious he was finding it increasingly difficult to keep his anger in check.

"It's all fine for you," muttered Davos, pointing a finger. "You don't share a bunk, do you? No, I imagine you are sleeping pretty in that lofty little nest of yours." He spat. "Well, I for one have had my fill of it. The debauchery won't last, Baran. Enjoy it whilst you can." He scowled.

"Are you threatening me?" asked Alde Baran. The room fell silent.

"I do not threaten. I simply speak the truth! I thought you appreciated the truth. Or is that only when it suits you?" Though but a bystander, in my mind, he did make a fair point.

"Hold your tongue, Davos or, mark me; I will feed it to the cat."

"Will you now, old man?" Davos declared, unhitching the keep on his short sword.

"I will indeed," replied Alde Baran. "Clear the tables and chairs!" He ordered.

Well, that changed things rather drastically from my perspective. Feigning to assist with dragging a weighty table aside, I elbowed Davos square in the jaw the moment he came within striking distance. It was an unfair blow for certain. He'd not expected an assault from anyone other than Baran whom his eyes had been wholly fixed upon. Having staggered him soundly, he crumpled to the floor.

I'd seen little alternative but to act immediately. I could not stomach the risk. Alde Baran was mine alone to kill and I wasn't about to let this fool stand in the way of that. Admittedly, I also harbored a mounting desire to beat something senseless. I turned to Alde Baran and the others who stared at me with gaping mouths.

"He is not worth your time, your Grace" I stated, though it pained me greatly to refer to him as such. "I've dealt with his like before; just another fool with a mouth begging for closure."

Davos rose to his feet and spat. It was all I could do to keep from smiling for the blood dribbling from his chin.

"For that will you die!" He sneered. Covering my mouth, I feigned to yawn. I had no fear of him.

He reached for his dagger only to find it in my hand. Knowing he'd pull his short sword next; I stuck his dagger through the hilt causing him to slice his hand as he grabbed for it. Clutching his hand, he swore at me profusely, which I rewarded by hammering the dagger's handle against his ear. Replacing his dagger, slowly and deliberately, I punched him hard in the face. Not surprisingly, the fool reached for his dagger again only to find that I had beaten him to it yet *again*. This time I smashed it upon the very beak of his nose.

He didn't appear to like that much either though neither did he appear to be getting the hint, so I pounded the handle against the same ear twice more with greater ferocity. Buckling over with pain, I felt obligated to bring my knee up under his chin rather firmly. As his head flew up, I caught hold of him by his chest strap just long enough to replace the dagger again. Letting go of him, he collapsed on the ground in a heap.

"I will kill you." He whispered as he fought to keep his eyes open.

"Not today, sunshine." I said quietly. Returning to the table, I took a long swallow of wine regardless of whose cup it might have been previously. Save for Davos' sputtering, the room was silent; and, beneath his headscarf, I knew Alde Baran was smiling. I did not care. As I saw it, his time was also very near to an end. Strutting toward Davos, he stood above him.

"Did I forget to mention he was of the Brotherhood?" He mocked. Davos looked up wrought with rage.

"He caught me unawares!" he hollered, spitting several bloodied teeth. "Twas hardly fair!"

"You're a disgrace, Davos." Responded Alde Baran entirely unmoved.

Staggering to his feet, Davos finally did manage to pull his dagger. Though it had been a short confrontation thus far, still, I found his behavior somewhat tiring. Given his fury I felt compelled, for the sake of those nearest, to smash him with a chair. I needed to put a quick end to it. There were women present after all. The chair was far sturdier than Davos as it turned out for not one of its legs crumbled while I couldn't same the same for him unfortunately. I'm not sure what surprised me more; the fact I hadn't knocked the fight out of him yet; or the fact his eyes remained open. Either way, he began to yell– at Alde Baran oddly. Whether he could endure a solid blow was not up for debate. He could. I only wished his parents had taken more pride in that. Perhaps, then his manners might have been improved.

"I challenge you, Baran!" He hollered, pointing a broken finger at him. "And once you're dead, I'll kill him too." He blathered. I felt a bit relieved. I was fully deserving of a threat or two. I'd done all the work after all.

"Challenge accepted," smiled Baran, rolling up his sleeves. Davos stared back at him with alarm.

"Ah, so you don't mean now," Baran sighed with disappointment prior to laughing aloud. "Very well, you pick the time: I'll pick the place."

"When Goren returns!"

"And what if Goren does not return? What then?"

"He will return; but should he not– the moment I can hold a sword will mark the day you die. One week at best!" he seethed." I felt less certain myself, being that his right hand was bleeding rather keenly. More importantly, I needed to kill Baran. A deadline had been drawn in the sand. It was fate, I suppose. As it turned out I was indeed the assassin after all.

"When Goren returns; or one week's time; whichever comes first. It is settled." agreed Alde Baran. "We will fight outside at first light."

"No! We will fight right here where everyone can watch you bleed out when I stick you in the guts!" Davos replied.

"No! I said you could pick *when* the cat eats not *where*. It is fair. It is just."

"No! 'Tis but another trick! You are up to something! You're planning to blindside me again!"

"There are no tricks. Be assured, one of us will die… and, should it be the will of the Gods, I am not going to spend all eternity stuck inside this frightful tree. Therefore, we will fight outside."

"Then you will die outside! Goren will be my second to ensure there's no cheating this time."

"And Darian mine; providing he's agreeable."

"Agreed." Darian replied to no one's surprise. "I shall ensure the cat is unfed the evening prior."

"Well said, Darian. Now, clean up this mess and get this sorry bastard out of my sight! Let Greta attend to him. Tell her she has my permission to dispatch him should he cause her any grief."

"Darian," spat Davos. "Now it's for certain I'll be blindsided." He scowled. The fact he managed to retain his sense of humor was not wasted on me. Perhaps I was wrong about him. Perhaps, had we met under different circumstances, we might have been friends– *comrades rather*. I had no friends.

Davos was escorted out of The Rookery. The tables and chairs were restored, and we all took our places once again. Renan had awoken. Petra rocked him back and forth gently. An ominous tension prevailed upon the room which Darian took upon himself to dissipate. Standing up and pushing back his chair he placed both hands on the table and proceeded to fart– long, loud, and windily.

"How *ass toot* of you," noted Ruok. Everyone roared.

But I was not about to be bested by yet another eye of his regardless of how *blind* it might be. Pushing myself upward, and my murderous thoughts aside, I assumed the position and mustered my strength. Rumbling on for quite some time, it was an impressive offering. No doubt fueled by my strict diet of pulp, I only wished Greta was still present to witness it.

Applause ensued, Darian bowed, and I turned to Petra expectantly. Unrehearsed events as such typically proceeded in an orderly fashion and she was next in line. Sadly, it proved pointless in the end. Perhaps it was her distraction with Renan. Either way, it appeared she just didn't have it in her in the end. Though her face bunched up with what I assumed to be effort, not the slightest peep came forth. She just stared at me with that scrunched-up face. I shrugged, shaking my head with discomfiture. At least she gave it a go, unlike Baran who shook his head forlornly as though it were beneath him. Of course it was beneath him. He was sitting. Any fool knew one needed to rise if they were to have any measure of success.

Ruok did not let me down however and neither did he need any further urging. Rising and standing atop his chair, he let fly. It was nothing short of glorious and he knew it, pumping both fists enthusiastically upon completion and rightfully so. I found little choice but to sit down. It was obvious I'd been defeated. One after another, men rose to take up the torch only to sit down dejectedly for having failed. It was obviously going to take something *extra special* if it was ever to happen at all.

I was beginning to have my doubts when Lod stood up and the room fell silent with great expectation. Lod was a big man indeed. His girth was so impressive, I was uncertain whether I could reach even halfway around him. That was saying something for me being larger than most in stature. I can't say I wasn't a wee bit jealous. But it was *his time to shine,* and he knew it.

Being a man of little modesty, he began to limber up very slowly and deliberately. He stretched his arms; cracked his back and shoulders, while gently swaying forward and aft. The tension in the room was so dominant, you could not have sawed it asunder had you tried. Grabbing his brimming belly with both hands he pulled it up and let it fall several times. Finally, after taking a long deep breath, he widened his stance considerably. He was ready. It was time.

An eerie wail begat; akin to a lone wolf on a distant hilltop; or the wind when a dire storm approaches. We held our collective breath; our suspense being swiftly trumped by our sincere collective admiration. It carried on, the crescendo ever rising; until it broke within a burst so exuberant even Ruok could not help but applaud. But it wasn't over; far from it. As if a bullfrog had somehow taken refuge within a bugle; or the other way around; it crooned on; magically serenading us until, as quickly as it had begun, it ceased. Or so we thought.

"I am Lod!" He hollered, explaining how I came to know his name. A name which would forever hold a place amongst my fondest memories. Or so I thought.

Slamming our cups hard upon the tables, we could do nothing other than shake our heads and marvel while congratulating him for his prolific exertion. It was then that smugness got the best of him, and he made a terminal mistake. Raising a leg, he gave us one last *salute* which proved fatal. His face turned pale, his eyes ripe with fright and disbelief. The horror of the situation soon became clear as he limped slowly from The Roost. I expect never had a *Groan Throne* felt more distant, while watching him shuffle shamefully away. Though I couldn't help but praise his notable contribution; at the same time, he'd exceeded the limits of what was humanly possible. He'd dug too deep within the proverbial well.

It was then that Petra took her leave. Though entirely unexpected, she did seem quite keen to depart, so I saw no point in trying to restrain her. Then again, I doubted anything could top the evening's entertainment thus far; so, I could not say I blamed her. It had been an eventful night.

My thirst had grown considerably, and I was on the verge of getting drunk when I remembered the steep ladder I'd yet to climb. That curtailed me considerably, perhaps even saved my life for all I knew. Fortunately, the drink had led my thoughts astray. Though still greatly befuddled by the evening's revelations, I'd allowed myself to become distracted by the surrounding jauntiness. It had been a long time since I'd experienced similar camaraderie. As previously noted, most soldiers I knew avoided my company. I can't say I blamed them. I was distrustful, grim, and quick to anger. And they were considered my good qualities by most. As for my lesser qualities, Davos might best be asked.

As far as questions went, Alde Baran did not ask anything more of me, for which I was glad. He and Darian spoke mostly between themselves and, though neither of them mentioned the evening's main attraction— the incident with Davos, not the wind binge— I could tell it had made an impression on them for they nodded and grinned at me often. Without doubt, they would further discuss the matter as soon as I took leave of them.

Unexpectedly, the climb up seemed a lot easier than the descent. Perhaps it was purely due to never having climbed down a ladder before. Point being, upon breaching the walls of a fortress, whether it be days or weeks later, we'd always departed by way of the front gate. Perhaps it was because I was alone and, therefore, had no chance of jeopardizing anyone else due to my own negligence. Not surprising, Petra was waiting for me the moment I stepped into our room. One look at her face made me press a finger to my lips with a pleading look. I felt I'd answered quite enough queries for one night and thought it better to say what I needed to say and be done with it.

"Diwan Ogi, second in command to the One Rah, gave the title Nitesh Alde Baran to my father when I was a small child." My voice was far calmer than I felt. She was smart, I must give her that. She knew what it meant at once. Notwithstanding, she penned this. *She,* as in *the clever one.*

"The Recluse gave that name to your father! And you told me he'd found this place long ago. You think he is your father!" Most unexpectantly, upon her assertion, though it had been I that told her, even so a chill ran through me.

"Quiet," I reprimanded her. "We can't let anyone else know that." *The Recluse* remained a well-known moniker for the reserved

Diwan being that very little was ever really known about him.

"That's why you attacked that man! Isn't it? Your pride wouldn't allow another's revenge ahead of your own. Tell me you're not plotting his death right now! Radesh?"

"Quiet!" I scolded. "The walls have ears! Of course, I'm plotting his death. He stomped my mother to death and left with nary a word. I must avenge her death! It is more than my right; it is my duty— my sole reason for living!" So much for being....

"Quiet," she replied, returning the same reproach. "We will all perish here if you continue down this reckless path. I understand how you feel but there is more stake. Renan and I are at stake. You promised to see us safely to Harkenspear. How can you do that should you be stomped to death and fed to that cat?"

"Have no worries, I have every intention of honoring my commitment; that same task bidden to me by my commander, your husband, Major Bryn. But who's to say I cannot do both. I don't deny it will take considerable planning; but it can be done."

"Major Bryn isn't my husband." She blurted. "He is my brother." She admitted to my utter astonishment. Yet again, she'd lied to my face. Her words struck me not unlike a fist. But if she lied that meant....

"The Major lied! Why would he do that?" I asked gravely perplexed.

"Quiet! He did it because I asked him to; because he is my brother; because he would do anything for me."

"I see. Because you asked him to. But why? What are you not telling me?" Petra burst into tears, and it took considerable attention to make out all that followed.

"Recognize, I am not a girl without dreams. I thought of you so many times; hoping you might return— but you never did. How was I to know you didn't *even remember* that night? As for myself, I relived *that night* a thousand times in my head wondering if I'd wronged you somehow."

"Wronged me?" Once again, I found myself stymied.

"It was the best and worse night of my life. I fell asleep giddy in the arms of *my champion* only to wake up wondering if it hadn't all been a cruel dream. Days dissolved into weeks, weeks dissolved into months; and my dreams dissolved into a horrid new nightmare. Even when it became obvious that I was *with child*, still, I refused to tell anyone about what had happened. What would I say— that my hero saved me from my would-be attackers only to plunder my maidenhead himself?"

"I'm sorry, I d-didn't know." I stammered uncomfortably. "I wish I could somehow alter the past, but I can't. I'm not, and nor have I ever been, the hero of any story. I am what I am; *an ogre*."

"You're not. I'm simply trying to explain how this all came about– so you don't think *me* the ogre."

"Hmmm. You did say it was you who climbed atop of me which strikes me as odd as I ponder it."

"What do you mean?"

"I mean, how is it that you knew whilst never having been plundered prior?"

"Are you questioning my virtue?" she asked, looking as though I'd mortally wounded her.

"Not at all; never. I was just wondering is all." I assured her.

"I read it in a book." She shrugged.

"They write that sort of thing in books?" I queried, utterly amazed. "Is that what was written in *that* love story?" That. That. That. Now she had me doing that… *that thing*.

"I hadn't finished all of it but, yes. I do suppose so. It took me so much by surprise in truth that I had to stop reading– *for a bit*. It was a lot to wrap my head around."

"Legs rather," I quipped. She ignored me fortunately. "Small wonder you got it ass backwards given your purity and all." I grinned.

"That was the following chapter– which I did read twice just to be certain." she added with a flushed face. It was all proving a tad difficult to digest.

"Now you've gone and flustered me," She huffed. "I've forgotten all I intended to say."

"You were explaining how neither of us are ogres," I reminded her, grateful to change the subject.

"Exactly, you see, when my parents disappeared, my brother felt I was in grave danger and feared the worst. He wrote, telling me he was sending an escort to accompany me to Harkenspear. He penned that he was sending you; *you of all people*– as you alluded to yourself– with him not knowing you to be the father of my child." Her green eyes were round with tears.

"Being young and overly optimistic; it did not take much to convince myself that it simply *had to be fate*. In all honesty, I felt as if the universe was giving us a second chance; as though, even amidst this insufferable war, it somehow *willed us* to be together." As naïve as that sounded, I could see in her eyes she meant every word of it.

"It was then I penned a return letter; confiding to him that you were the father. I told him that I lo– *had strong feelings*– for you and that you knew nothing about the baby. I know what that sounds like. Please, don't think unkindly of me. None of that was a lie, Radesh. Not intentionally! Though perhaps I was fooling myself for not knowing how I truly felt about you, I needed to see if you might prove yourself my hero after all. Please don't hate me– and don't blame my brother! He is innocent in this."

"Innocent? I hardly think so. Not to mention, every tale needs an ogre."

"Understand. I begged him, Radesh. I know my brother far better than you. I knew his first course of action would be to dispatch you straight to Haeryn's Wall. It's what *he was* going to do– but I begged him not to. I pleaded, on the life of our baby, that he claim to be my husband though I knew he'd loathe doing so. Still, how could he refuse? I had never entreated anything of him before. Thus, I knew he would do it– *for me* he would do it."

"But why?" I asked. I did not see just cause for bearing such a falsehood.

"Because I barely knew you! Because you were strong and kind and, well, *knightly* was how I saw looked upon you at that time. Because you'd save my life. Because we'd slept together– *once*. I'd never been with anyone before– *or since!*"

Or since. I watched the words melt from her lips like warm salty butter. So, she harbored strong feelings for me. All this time? I swear, not even Haeryn might have guessed such a thing. But *knightly*– me, truly? I very near laughed. Thank Haeryn I didn't. Had I done so, she might have killed me with her hairpin in my sleep. I only wished I still had that fork. It would have evened the odds so to speak.

"But as wonderful as I thought that night to be– *at first*." Apparently, she was still talking. "In the morning you were gone."

Oh, that again. Yes, it's true. I'd left. I'd awoke in a cold sweat not knowing where I was. I'd had too much to drink and, as usual, didn't recollect anything of the evening prior. Then I spied someone's feet poking out of the blanket and made a quick run for it. Why not just behead me and be done with it. I mean, how was I to know the other end would turn out to be so pretty? Haeryn knows I'd encountered more than a few who were quite frightful in the early morning hours. If I am being honest– which I do take pride in.

"I could not risk telling you the truth in case, in case...." She sobbed uncontrollably, unable to complete her thoughts.

"In case?" I encouraged her, albeit rather hesitantly. Truth is, I liked most of what I'd heard up until now and I was unsure whether I'd appreciate what was to follow. My mind began to wander as I recalled an old soldier's joke. *How do ogres do it? With a big fat club.*

"Why are you smiling? What is there to smile about?" she demanded.

Wiping the grin from my face, it was my turn to bite my lip. There was no way I was going to share that with her. It was meant for soldiers' ears, not maidens fair. Truth is, she was making me feel awkward and, if you must know, I sorely regretted never having looked under the north end of that blanket. Then again, it was hardly my fault. If only her feet had been kinder looking. They were rather filthy as I think about it— more callous than you'd imagine had you the pleasure of looking her in the eye. Which I didn't— not that I recalled, anyway.

"I'm sorry. You were about to say… in case I turned out to be *the Butcher* after all," I finished for her. She wiped her eyes with a sleeve. "Just in case I was the man that I am." I continued. My wry smile was gone. Yet another fleeting moment of mirth that suddenly felt centuries old. No one could outrun the past for it never truly left. As much as I despised the man, Baran was right about that.

"You're not a bad person. You're loyal and honest; though perhaps, a bit too truthful at times. I did try to tell you sooner. I did try. You know I tried."

"I know you did," I said, blankly. "Forgive me, I'm unsure what to say. I'm overwhelmed. I'm confused. I feel as though I've been living a lie my entire life. Am I the lone mark? Might there be anyone alive anywhere who's not in on it?"

"I didn't mean to lie! Not to you! I wasn't trying to trap you. Don't you see? I was trying to leave you a way out. That's why I pretended to be wedded. I had to— for both our sakes."

"But your brother? You could have said anyone?"

"Not without complicating things further; not to mention, we do have the same last name."

"I see," I said. It did make sense. She was way too clever for me which needn't be said. *Although no doubt she wrote it.* "That way, if I turned out to be the ogre you could dispatch me to Haeryn's Wall— without me being any the wiser."

"Please! It wasn't like that at all. Far from it, I dreamt of us having a life together and hoped foolishly that it might prove to be so.

It is no easy life being the mother of a fatherless child. My father used to say *fair-minded folk are easier found below ground than above.* I only hoped to find someone to keep Renan and I safe."

"Who better than the father?" I said, stating the obvious.

"No one." She sniffed softly.

No one… just hearing her say the words made the wee hairs on my forearms rise. The words echoed in my thoughts while she stared into my eyes. I felt so many new sensations burgeoning within. I might be the world's biggest dupe, but my life was changing. *For the better*, I hoped. I felt immensely confused. Just what was this peculiar feeling? I'd never loved anyone before– perhaps my mother. Though I wasn't precisely sure what was happening, I was most definitely feeling something. Additionally, there was all this father stuff to contend with. Not just Alde Baran, but Renan too. I'd never been a father before. So very many questions remained unanswered.

"Tell me, if you knew I was coming, why did you act so surprised when I knocked upon your door?"

"I wasn't acting. Well, not as much as you might think. I was angry. I was hurt. You never came back; you just left with nary a word. I think you know how that feels."

"I thought we'd clarified that." *Nary a word?* Who used that tired adage anymore? No one; save for bards and haughty nobles. *I'll wager a proper copper she won't include that tidbit.*

"What d' you mean? Is it not precisely what you said in respect to your father but a moment ago… *left with nary a word?*" Only because I'd heard *her say it…* just to keep the record straight.

"That's different."

"How so?"

"Because, as it turns out, it was *you* who plundered *me*," I shrugged sheepishly. "As far as I recall, not that I do, I was just lying there minding my own business– recovering my strength, following all the heroics and so forth."

"There are times when you are very nearly lovable, Radesh," she laughed. "Some things needn't be read from a book. Some things are too easily taken for granted."

I only wished I knew what it was that I was feeling. I felt absurdly giddy– yet strangely apprehensive. It wasn't right. It wasn't me. On the field, I was the one who charged blindly forward when the others began to falter. *Blindly* being the key word. But this was different. This was unfamiliar ground.

"Tell me what you're thinking, Radesh," she whispered. "Are

you angry with me?"

"No– just, as I said, a tad confused is all. I don't know what I might say. Since the day we first met, my life has been in constant flux." Admittedly, our interpretations of the word *flux* differed greatly. Though I later discovered it inferred feelings of *change* to her, to me it still represented something festering in the pit of my stomach that needed to be expunged. *Tomàtoe, tomato*, I guess. On another note, for all the times I heard it said, I was beginning to hate that saying. Why should potatoes and tomatoes get preferential treatment? Point being, no one said turnip, turnipe; or carrot, carote. I mean, we'd be here all day if they did, wouldn't we?

"And now?" She tapped her chin thoughtfully.

"Prior to that, I found my life held little purpose. I was but a pawn in someone else's war. It was much simpler though." I added.

"You do realize, I felt compelled to do what I did?"

"Yes. But I am not precisely sure what it is that you are asking of me? Are you asking me to acknowledge Renan as my son and provide support– or is it your intention that we be wed?" Petra's face turned crimson. I wasn't sure if that was good or bad. *Bad*, seemed more likely with every moment that passed like an eternity.

"I wasn't proposing marriage," she managed to blurt finally. "I'm not asking you to do anything you don't want to. It's just.–– the more I've gotten to know you, the more I see your worth. I suppose what I'm trying to say is– do you ever think of me *that way?* Have you ever thought of me *that way?*"

"That way, what way?" I blathered, helplessly. *That. That. That.* Would there ever be an end?

"Have you ever thought of sharing time with someone?"

"Sharing time? Do you mean like the two of us, three rather, crossing a desert as opposed to pillaging villages?"

"Yes, I suppose." She sighed aloud. "But I'm not talking about comrades in a damn war! I'm asking whether you have any *family ambitions*? There! I said it." Once again, the wee hairs on my forearms rose as I stared at her dreamily. I could see no way clear other than to offer some sort of answer.

"Truth is, I never considered myself the *husband type*– cannon fodder would be a more accurate depiction. You and I derive from different worlds. There have been precious few fond memories in mine. You are undoubtedly the biggest surprise of my entire existence thus far. I still find it largely unfathomable that you slept with me."

"Even now– after all I've confessed?" Not helping the

awkwardness, we both sighed at that.

"It's just that while you wonder whether I harbor affections, I ponder ever being worthy of you. Do you have any idea how many times I've questioned my own soundness for not remembering *that night*? If for no other reason than… well, let's just say you're quite likely the fairest creature I've ever laid eyes upon." I spat out quickly. It was my turn. So… *there! I said it.*

"Creature? Do you really consider me a creature?"

"Woman!" I blurted too loudly, causing her to blush *again.*

"But are you fond of me, Radesh? Do you harbor feelings for me or am I yet another plundered villager within a long list of yours?"

"Feelings?" I stammered uncomfortably.

"Yes, feelings. Do you love me, Radesh?" She inquired softly yet firmly. "Answer me now and I will never ask nought of you again."

She was plainly flustered. Even I saw the double negative hidden within her words. And there I stood, bare moments after discovering Baran to be my father, trying to decipher how I felt about someone who in all honestly put me to my wits end more times than not. It was only a few sand dunes southward that I felt quite certain I hated her. Or did I? Perhaps I never hated her at all. Perhaps my perceived revulsion was solely due to her making me feel *uncomfortable.* But there was more to it than that. She not only gave me cause to question the world around me but my place in it. She forced me to think for Haeryn's sake. Which wasn't something I was fond of− yet now she had the impudence to inquire whether I might in some way be fond of her. Was that not irony, I wondered.

"Do I love you? But what is this love that you speak of? All my life I've known only pain and suffering. I look around and all I've ever found is loneliness, hate and greed. Even as a child my neighbors threw stones at me. There is no love in this world that I see. Except perhaps, when I look toward you. You changed me. You altered all that I was. You made me see things I never knew existed. I think differently now. Within my bones, the rage refuses to simmer. I am not the man I was. I am not a monster. I am no longer a beast. And for that you have my undying gratitude but is that by itself love?"

"Stars are bred of fire and fire is driven by the wind. But without stars what need is there for a sky? Without air what comfort hath the wind?" She was talking gibberish again. Thus, I decided I best speak my truth swiftly and be done with the painful ordeal.

"I don't know how it happened nor when but, within your

company, I feel as though I matter. Why you suffer my unruly manners will forever be beyond me. Know that nothing I do could ever render me deserving of you. I know that. But I also know little good comes to those too fearful to try."

"So why not reach for the stars? Why not harness the wind?" She pressed.

"Notwithstanding, my tutelage is far from over. So, who am I to deny you that opportunity? Do I love you? Like a sandal with a pebble in its heel. I expect so, the more I ponder it."

"Like a sandal with a pebble in its heel?" She frowned.

"Yes, but in a good way. What I'm trying to say is from the first moment we met you found a way to burrow beneath my skin."

"Burrow beneath your skin? And that's a good thing?"

"It is− because try as I might, I can't stop thinking about you. Not to mention you're clever. I expect you're the wisest of all maidens' fair. So, whether it be love or the deepest admiration, who am I to refute your claim?"

"So, merely the wisest, not the most beautiful." She sulked.

Was there to be no end to this at all, I wondered. What more could I possibly say that I hadn't professed already. I'd confessed her to be *that* pebble in *that* sandal for Haeryn's sake. If that wasn't an admittance of love, then surely no one knew what was.

"Oh, as looks go I suppose you're alright. If you must know I've never really considered it." Ducking in the nick of time I felt her *pebble less* sandal graze my forehead which made me rethink my present course. Was it truly flattery she craved or honesty? I'd already spoken my peace, shared thoughts that made me feel awkward. Honestly, if this was love then perhaps it was never intended for clumsy-handed rogues like me. Save for swords of course. I wasn't clumsy with a sword. Or a dagger though I expect she wasn't interested in that so much.

"That said, as beautiful as you are, you would do well to choose another. Even though I may have *sired the foal*, and I don't see why you would lie; notwithstanding you did lie to me many times prior, albeit with virtuous intent; I very much doubt I am the fathering kind; nor would any woman consider me an admirable suitor. Am I rambling? I think I might be rambling."

"Sired the foal? Do I look like a bloody mare? Perhaps you did mean to say *creature* after all."

"Fathered the child; laid the maid, produced the goose, engendered the vendor−"

"Engendered the vendor? Really?"

"*You know what I mean*. Of all the beautiful women I've known, which isn't many; none were comparable to you— not that I ever looked any of them in the eye, mind you."

"Thank you, I think. But what are you saying? Are you stating you have no interest in me other than my appearance which you find satisfactory? Or are you simply professing yourself to be unfit for the role?" she asked, biting her lip.

"No, what I'm saying is— *are you completely mad woman*? I am Red Radesh, the Golan Butcher— hardly a suitable genitor by anyone's account."

"And why might I not be the judge of that? You think me mad because I envision a measure of nobility within you. Is that so unimaginable to you? Do you think my brother would have sent *his worst man* to protect me? No, he would send me *his best*. Prior to him being privy to any of my scheming— there I said it, I called it scheming— *he chose you*. Has your self-worth truly fallen so low?" Her green eyes implored.

"They are just names, Radesh." She continued softly. "Though they may depict some trifling wrinkle of you— one I have never seen, I might add— they don't offer a fair account from head to tail throughout. When I was round with your unborn son, they whispered harlot. They named me trollop and tramp under their breaths as I passed by. It's been no joyful stroll for me either. Do not imagine for a second that I lived a life of privilege for it isn't true. I have not."

"Who called you such? Tell me their names and I will make them answer for it." I barked angrily.

"Do you never listen? It doesn't matter. *They're just words*. They have no power lest I perceive them true. I seek neither Red Radesh nor the Golan Butcher. I have no interest in either of them. I'm not looking for an imaginary champion splattering blood across the pages of some war-torn book. I'm looking for *my hero*. I only hope he's an actual person. A man that is kind and truthful; witty and protective— the kind that rescues young maidens in distress— whether they be wise or beautiful." She added. I watched a lone tear tumble down her cheek which oddly felt as if it were my own.

"I'm not certain I am who you think me to be, Petra." I sighed. "Still, I'd quite like a home of my own the more I consider it and I'm tired of being alone. I'm tired of the war. I'm tired of fighting. I would settle someplace far from here. With you and Renan, if you're quite certain, you'll have me."

"Ah, so I see; the courtship is over before it ever began. I never said I'd follow you to the ends of the world, Radesh, upon the merest whisper of affection." She scolded. If only there was a pike nearby, I could impale my head upon, I might find a measure of peace.

"What I did say was… I hope to discover whether you might be the same man, I met *that night*. You can't go straight from *stag to suitor* in a copper heartbeat. For all our travels and adventures, we still know very little about one another. You might find you hate me in another moment or two." That made me laugh aloud.

"Hardly; I discovered that in the very instance of our reacquaintance; and several more times crossing the Kestrel; not to mention upon arrival here– now that I think on it." I confessed.

"Whatever do you mean?" she asked, pursing her lips while pressing a finger to them with mock disgust.

"Oh, I don't know; perhaps when you asked them to kill the filthy, lying bastard that raped you; if you care to recall."

"I didn't say filthy."

"You did. You did say filthy– which I was, in truth– to no fault of my own as it couldn't be helped."

"I was only playing my part as your prisoner. But let's not place past grievances ahead of better days to come. How will you entice me to share time with you? That is where you need to focus that spy glass of yours– my spyglass rather, seeing as you stole it. You must woo me to win this lady's favor. You must conquer my heart should you wish me to be yours!"

"Woo you?" I scratched my head. "Know that I've never persuaded anyone to do anything– outside of sacking a village."

"Not to fret, I hear there's nothing to it. You must dote on me. We can start right now."

"Dote on you? Now? I think I liked you better as my prisoner." I grimaced.

"You filthy, lying bastard!" She scowled, punching my ribs.

"Ah, so I've won you over. Thank Haeryn. That was easy."

I then did something I never expected of myself. I pulled her close and kissed her on the lips. I'd never done it before– kissed anyone. I would have remembered that. To my chagrin, she looked more shocked than pleased. Had I done it incorrectly, I wondered.

"You can't just force yourself upon me. You need to proceed slowly as though one misstep might put an end to it. You can't rush headlong into a fire that's not yet been kindled. Recognize, I not yet yours to do with as you please." She replied solemnly.

"Is that the reward… to do with as I please?" I felt a need to clarify. It that how it worked? Had we only been wed first I might have bound and gagged her before dragging her across the desert? Humph, that gave me pause for thought. Perhaps wedlock wasn't so bad after all.

"I'm not some ruddy bar wench, I'll have you know. You'll will have to earn my companionship if that's what you truly want; and work for it you will." she added fervently.

"So, no plundering?" I grimaced.

"Not this night. You might try serenading me. Though softly, Renan is sleeping."

"Serenading you? Like a minstrel? Does that derive from your hefty collection of wanton books?"

"Can you sing?" She asked, ignoring my queries.

"Sing? Are you daft? Do I look like I can sing?"

"What about poetry then?"

"Poetry; you mean words thicker than biscuits drizzled in warm butter?"

"Yes, precisely that. I should like for you to recite some fair verses– words that herald from your heart."

"I don't know any; none that are halfway appropriate at least."

"Make something up; tell me how you feel– *in there*." she said, pressing her hand against my chest.

"Hungry?" I quipped. "Though you can thicken the chicken by fluffing the stuffing it won't whittle the spittle once it does dribble."

It was obvious, she not only failed to see the humor but, worse still, she'd been sincere in her initial request. I decided it was in my best interest to try harder. Though a very steep ladder lay beyond our closed door, I had to suppress a strong urge to ensure no one else might be listening.

"When I look at you, I feel as though I know every thought you're thinking. I am no poet; and certainly, no bard. I don't know what I feel in my heart save for the fact it sings when you look at me. When you look at me *kindly*, that is." I clarified.

"I am a simple man, not a gentle man. But that is not to say I am uncaring. Since meeting you, there've been oft times I try to imagine the world through your eyes; and it scares me. And I'm not easily frightened. Why? Because it does not seem a world that would welcome a man of *my character*. Yet, you give me cause to hope. Not solely for your company but, in hopes, that I may one day become the man you think me to be."

I studied her closely as she gazed at me headily. I figured I was done but I could tell she not only liked it; she wanted more. And, not surprising, she told me so.

"That was wonderful. Can you make it rhyme?"

"Rhyme?"

"Yes, like that chicken only with more affable intent."

Muttering aloud in disbelief, I thought hard for a few moments. I had heard messengers recite poetry on rare occasions. I took a breath, venturing cautiously outward upon a limb less fragile than my pride. Or so I hoped.

"You are a rose petal and I but a stem rigid with hopes of one day plundering again." Her smile broadened so greatly it emboldened me. I thought harder.

"Your light shines right through me, turning rock to porous stone; and my emptiness reaps laughter for the thought of– a warm home." I ended awkwardly.

"That is how you make me feel– warm inside. And now, I feel– *foolish*. Never speak of this for I will deny it happened." I affirmed, feeling quite humiliated.

"Perhaps the courtship has ended," she said, moving closer. "Perhaps I will plunder you after all," she whispered in my ear.

Sliding atop me– *and this time I would remember*– she kissed me, and my entire world dissolved. There was no desert. There was no war. There was no mislaid, lying, murderous father. *Okay, perhaps that last one needed a bit more healing.* Even so, at that moment, there was nothing I ever wanted more in my life, and she knew it. It was impossible to mask my desire. For the first time, my life felt like an open book. My heart was a bottomless well. My mind was a blank page for which she held the quill. I was helpless, but neither did I care. Should she be bent on penning a love story, I could only consider myself blessed for having even the smallest part within it.

Having been *sufficiently pillaged*, I slept like a baby through most of the hot daylight hours. I awoke to find Petra, eyes closed soaking in the bath which only served to delay my start further. Her long, tanned legs were akimbo, feet together, knees aside resting against the peculiarly slanted sides of the wooden tub. Sneaking up on her from behind, I planted my lips upside down upon hers. She awoke with a start, splashing water everywhere to my amusement. She smiled, and I kissed her again, this time running my hands slowly down her torso and giving her hips a meaningful squeeze.

She slid under the water, her long dark hair enveloping her

head like a lioness' mane. Did lionesses even have manes? Humph, I cared not. This one did. She was remarkable. She smiled staring up at me from beneath the water. Emerging, I watched the water cascade down her shoulders and breasts. She stretched her arms before locking her hands behind her head knowing full well, she'd commandeered my complete attention. As I reached for her again, she blocked my arms with her own. Grasping my hands, she pulled her dripping body out of the lapping water.

"Do you want a bath?" She asked. "The water's lukewarm. Unfortunately, there's not room enough for two." She smiled.

Stepping out, I handed her the smaller of the two cloths I saw. *Wisdom.* It did make sense from an entirely selfish perspective. Discarding my djellaba, I hopped sprightly into the bath and slid into the water. It was utterly perfect; not too warm; not too cold. At no time in my life had I ever felt more gratified. There was only one thing I adored more than a good bath. But she'd covered her nakedness– far too quickly, I might add. I found myself content just to watch her squeeze the water from her long hair as she twisted it about.

"How did you sleep," she asked with her head cocked sideways, causing me to slant my own in like fashion.

"Like a tortoise within its shell; no man has ever slept better," I replied candidly.

"I expect not. I awoke with more of your sweat upon me than my own, I think. Which is why I chose to bathe." Her smile made me melt lower into the water to better hide my sudden, rather palpable, desire.

"Where is Renan?" I asked, twisting my head about to distract myself from the urgent need I felt mounting within. It was bad enough that I'd chose to confide in her all that I had. The worst thing I could do now was to let her know just how weak my resolve had become.

"He is with the women; I'm going to collect him shortly. Are you hungry? Would you like something to eat?"

"I am entirely famished; though I'd prefer to savor you." I sighed, eyeing her taut nipples plainly visible through her damp garments. Which is to say, *where else was I supposed to look?* The gods were cruel. She'd broken the stallion.

"Would you now?" She said walking over to me. "There might be time enough for that– after we've spoken." As I reached for her, she placed a handful of red grapes in my beckoning fingers.

"Fair enough," I replied. "But be warned, you have me at a disadvantage. You are very distracting and, as much as I adore watching your lips move; it's your hips that call to me. Which is to confess, I'm not certain I'll hear all that you have to say."

"You will; or you'll find yourself considerably less distracted in the future, if you get my meaning." She answered curtly while pulling invisible hair tangles free with a hand. "What do you plan to do about Alde Baran?"

"You know full well what I mean to do," I stated point blank.

"Yes, but not until *after* we've spoken." She smirked, peering into the tub. I felt my cheeks burn bright until she chose to drop the bowl of grapes onto my lap with a splash.

"Radesh," she whispered seriously. "You do realize, should you avenge your mother's death our dreams of being together will forever end. Is that really what you want? Would you truly sacrifice Renan and I *for him*?"

"I'll not sacrifice anyone," I growled. "But some deeds must be atoned for or what point is there *to anything*? It is no less than I would do for you. I swear, should anything have happened to your parents I will avenge them in like fashion."

"Don't use my parents as an excuse to appease your anger."

"Then answer me this, how might I live with myself if I don't?"

"You will live with yourself knowing you made the wisest choice possible. You will live with yourself by being a better father than he was to you. That is how. That is precisely how," she scolded.

I stared at her knowing full well she was right but, nonetheless, refusing to admit it. As I'd learned throughout my years, there's nothing quite as stubborn as a rooster snubbed. Admittedly, she was a close second though.

"First and foremost, I am a soldier. I do not make the rules," I answered. "I enforce them. It is the way of the land, the way of *our people*. An eye for an eye; justice must be served. I will speak no more of this."

"Then we too are lost," she sobbed. Throwing a shawl about her, she fled the room while still barefoot. Left to my own impiety, I splashed water all about the small room like a petulant child. After chomping several grapes, my rage got the better of me and I smashed the bowl upon the nearest wall. As right as she was; and she was, I dare not let him live. How could I after all he'd done?

It had nothing to do with my own unsolicited injuries, I assured myself while running a hand gingerly across my face. My jaw and cheekbone were still quite sore though the swelling had finally subsided. Plain and simple, it was about avenging my mother. It was inconceivable to me that I should turn a blind eye to such a forceful and unprovoked attack. I remembered that day like one remembers losing a limb or an eye. Even worse I expect while hoping cautiously it would never be put to the test. My mother had done nothing to warrant such a brutal and senseless act of violence.

Then again, I was no angel. A part of me wanted to kill him purely for the joy of it. The first time I crossed the Kestrel, I did so for no other reason than trying to prove myself the better man— or, in the very least, his equal. Though I told myself it was all about my mother— the fact remained, he'd abandoned me. For that fact alone, I hated him.

I waited in the room for a long time, but Petra did not return. Where could she have gone in such haste— not to mention *barely dressed*. I emptied the tub by connecting the drainpipe made from hollow saplings that fed the roots of the giant tree. Everything needs to replenish itself. Why should it be any different? Bizarrely, though it was my third bath since arriving, I could not believe how much sand I found clinging to the bottom. Where was it coming from? Surely, there were no more body crevices where it still might linger. It was absurd. It must be Petra's feet I decided finally. That would explain it.

Having picked up the broken shards, mingled with grapes, I then scrubbed the tub. Still, Petra did not return. Descending to Harem's Hold, I was told she was not there either. I was suspicious however as it took quite some time for the door to come ajar at which point Greta informed me that Petra was *not able to be seen*. A peculiar choice of words. So, it seemed to me— even for Greta's cumbersome dialogue. Though larger than our own, the room's dimensions did not warrant that much time to arrive at the door. Not to mention, the premises housed seven residents— and not even one with a limp. Add that to the fact I'd heard voices speaking in hushed tones. Something was afoot and, if my assumptions were correct, a pair of sandy ones at that.

For the life of me, though unfathomable that anyone could be quite so daft, I could not discern what might have angered her so. Hmmm. Might it possibly be my pigheadedness; the fact I never listened; not to mention that everything I did revolved solely around myself; the way I took her for granted while disrespecting how learned she was for having read so many books even though she might not have been well traveled in comparison to myself who'd been sent all over the realm for no other reason than having followed someone else's orders; whilst possessing the audacity to put vengeance ahead of the wellbeing of my lover and child. *For the record, though I might be stubborn at times, I did not recite any of what you just read.*

I checked the Red Room next; followed by The Rookery; at which point I gave up for having decided my time was likely better spent consuming a hot meal rather than looking for someone who clearly did not wish to be found— in Harem's Hold or anywhere else for that matter. I pulled up a chair beside Darian and his feisty kestrel. Following a large bowl of familiar tasting stew, I shared two pitchers of ale with him. This batch of ale was stronger than before; quite frothy though tepid. I asked Darian where I might find Alde Baran. He informed me Baran was with great certainly holed up within The Heartwood.

"He will come out when he's ready and not a moment before," professed Darian while his falcon stole tiny sips from his foam-soaked mustache.

"Might I knock upon his chamber?" I inquired.

"You may as well beat your skull upon a flat stone." He shook his head negatively. "For all the good it'll do you. He locks himself away countless days at a time. Even if he did answer, he'd be in a right foul state of mind— and quite likely have you buried again. He's a grand host on occasion but a terrible drunk most others. Mark my words; he will drink himself to death soon enough."

"So, he drinks all by his lonesome?" I'd never heard of such a thing. Drink was intended to be shared; unless a leg was being amputated; or a rotten tooth pulled. On such occasions the less fortunate one was always allotted the lion's share. Which isn't to imply the bone sawyer or tooth prier didn't get a sip or two, along with the usual quartet of restrainers, mainly to steady everyone's nerve being that the impending hollers could be quite intense. So, not alone.

"He's far from alone, I fear."

"Ah, I see; his harem." I nodded thoughtfully. *I knew it!*

"Harem? Haeryn no!" Sputtered Darian aggrieved. "It's not like that at all." He whispered, spraying bits of froth from both corners of his mouth in exasperation. "Betwixt the two of us and no one else, the harem is but a ruse. It's solely to curtail the gaze of the other men. Keep them safe if you know what I mean." His good eye darted back and forth, ensuring no other party might be listening even though there was but the two of us present. Then again, I'd heard tell of talking birds from faraway lands. Perhaps, he feared his kestrel might betray us. After studying the creature closely, I decided against it. A brighter bird would have insisted on its own mug.

"He rescued most of them from slave traders. Sad truth is, they've got nowhere else to go."

"Then who in the world is he drinking with?" I scratched my head perplexed.

"His demons, of course," he returned in a low tone. "He carries more demons than a cactus has spines— more than any man I know. More than any other man could, I'll wager."

"What kind of demons?" I asked, quite confident I already knew the answer.

"Oh, you know the kind. The kind of demons that gum the soles of your boots; demons so thick you must wade through them to get anywhere at all. The kind of demons no man can escape. The kind of demons that arise in the night and dissolve into your dreams. Those kinds of demons."

"You mean his past. What of it? What did he do that was so terrible?" I whispered.

"I best not speak of it. I've said too much already." Turning to his kestrel, it nodded in agreement.

"Understood." I sighed refilling his mug to the brim. "If you don't know than you don't know."

"Oh, believe you me, I know." He insisted.

"Because you saw it? Because you were there?" I pressed.

"No, I wasn't there."

"Ah, then you don't know, do you? Say no more."

Though I knew I had him right where I wanted him, at the same time, I felt inwardly enraged. Darian knew nothing. He wasn't there. I was. Still, I wanted to hear him say it aloud— speak the truth no man knew other than the pair of us and the guilt-riddled assailant. Okay, the three of us if you included his nosy kestrel— which I wasn't. *Guilt.* As if feeling remorse somehow made one blameless. *Hardly.*

"The kind of demons that arise from murdering your spouse," He confided in a hushed tone. "I should never have said that. He will throttle us both should he ever catch wind of it."

"He'll hear nothing of the sort." I assured him. I was being honest. If all went to plan, I would kill him in his sleep with nary a word now that I knew he drank excessively and, more importantly, alone.

"But why would he do such a thing? Did he despise her outright or had he truly grown that tired of her?"

"Haeryn, no! It's not like that at all. He loved Audrey with all his heart; that is why it pains him so."

Audrey. Yet another serving of salt to my ever-festering wound. Though I loathed to admit it, I'd forgotten her rightful name for only rarely ever having heard it spoken aloud. She was my mother after all. A poor excuse for certain as it felt unforgivable to me. Though but a child, how could I be so frightfully negligent? It was and would remain to me forever unpardonable.

"So much so that he killed her." I replied, swapping my self-pity for disdain.

"He wasn't himself. If you knew him at all you'd know he could never do such a thing. Though it took many years for him to fully confide in me, she'd awoken him from a terrible dream. He thought he was being attacked and, by the time he realized his mistake, it was too late– far too late. The damage had been done. A bitter pill if ever there was."

"His mistake?" I seethed inwardly, fighting hard to contain my anger. "A mistake is tilling the ground too shallow while planting potatoes. A mistake is neglecting to fasten the cinch on your horse."

"Aye, but you're wrong about that, lad." Darian said evenly. "A mistake is a mistake, only some things can never be undone. You can plow a field anytime. You can double-check that belly strap. But calamity strikes when least expected and, well, you can holler all you like but there's no waking the dead.

I'd said enough and learned all I needed to. I would explain things to Petra when I saw her. Then she would understand that what I was proposing wasn't vengeance. I'd be just putting the witless fool out of his misery; an act of kindness in truth. Not that it changed anything. Not that I saw it that way. I had every reason in the world to kill him and Haeryn himself couldn't change that. At least, that was my plan at the time. As it turned out, what I said to her later was something I might never have presumed.

"He's led a harsh life, Assad." Darian winced. "His past is littered with tragedy and despair. Even so, he remains a great man among men."

"But you said he was broken inside. You said he drinks for days on end– hardly admirable qualities in my experience."

"Aye, 'tis the only way he finds some tincture of sleep."

"And they say there's no rest for the wicked," I mused.

"Aye, but wicked he is not. He is a hard man; and deeply troubled for certain but there is no malice to be found within his bones. Principles, laws, and obedience account for his world. To him, they signify everything of worth. Providing he felt it justified, he would give his life for any one of us here. Perhaps not Davos so much. I am proud to have ridden by his side for so many long years. I've known him longer than any other man here; living or dead. Baran is a man of inordinate morality; the likes of which will never be seen again. I know I won't."

I stared at Darian, wondering how he came to worship him so blindly. He was right about one thing. Baran would never be seen again if I had anything to say about it. I should mention, all this time Darian's bulbous eye was jiggling about like a poached egg which was proving as difficult as ever to ignore.

"Ah, I can tell you harbor doubts about his character. I can't say that I blame you, Assad. I did say he was a hard man. He will do whatever he feels he must to ensure the safety of all those in his command. Admittedly, being on the wrong side of his boot can be a bit jarring. No harm done in hindsight. It's not like he killed you."

Hindsight? *'Tis blind sight you great fool!* I'd witnessed it a hundred times before. A commander commands and you do it without question regardless of anyone's ethics or well-being including your own. It was something I was guilty of myself. But not for long. I was done with following orders– blind or otherwise. I was done with soldiering. I was done with needless killing. Alde Baran's demise on the other hand was the precise opposite of needless. His death was the furthest thing from an indulgence. Ending his life would be a kindness if for no other reason than terminating his ongoing despair. His fanatical tyranny was at an end. Darian would be far better off upon finding he had a mind of his own. I only wished he'd stop ogling me with that slithering, slug of an eye. Thus, I decided it was high time to address the remaining elephant in the room.

"No offense," I said. "But must you always look at me in that fashion? It's akin to when Alde Baran asked you to advise him whether I might be lying." Darian stared blankly at me. "It's unnerving," I continued boldly as he didn't seem to be getting the hint.

"Of course, it's unnerving," Darian laughed wholeheartedly. The man had no shame. As much as I tried, and I did, it was proving impossible not to like him. I could see why he was such a close companion to Alde Baran. You could tell instantly he was a man you could count on. There was no questioning his loyalty for to know him was to have it.

"Ah, and that is exactly why I do not wear an eye patch. I would forfeit that power," he chuckled, giving me the full stare treatment. "Then again, it's not like your face is a bouquet of flowers.

All bruising aside, it looks as though it was dragged through a coral reef. No offense."

"None taken; but at least me eye doesn't jiggle like a jellyfish when I shake my head."

"Jellyfish!" He laughed, before biting his lip contemplatively. "I was in the Brotherhood once," he whispered, looking about him cautiously. To be clear, it was still just the two of us save for his meddling kestrel.

"I had a dagger just like yours. I gave it to Baran. Which is why I snatched this. He owes me." He grinned.

Removing *my fork* from an inner pocket he began combing his mustache with it. *Idiot* was my initial thought– prior to noticing it worked rather admirably. As if the stolen fork wasn't irksome enough; that bit about him being in the BroZil was far from tantalizing. It was the last thing I'd hoped to hear. Being unsure how to respond, I said nothing. Instead, I simply returned his stare, refusing to blink until he did. Which took a fair bit of time let me tell you. At last, as his lid lowered, he broke the silence.

"That's how I met Alde Baran. I was sent to kill him."

I rubbed my ears, scarcely able to believe what I'd heard. He motioned me closer. I took a long sip of beer before doing so. These were not waters I wished to wade into. They were near as fraught with peril as Darian's beard was of ale.

"Obviously, you did not," I said.

"Obviously not," he agreed. "He convinced me to join him instead… and the rest is history." He shrugged merrily.

"I'm quite certain there is far more to the tale than that." I smirked, eyeing him expectantly.

"There is always more to the tale and a wiser man would never have shared it in the first place. I've never claimed to be a wise man however, though my judge of character is seldom wrong. I don't know why but something tells me I can trust you."

"No one leaves the Brotherhood," I stated, quite convinced it was true. It was known– even amongst those things that remained largely unknown.

"So, they say; but there's one thing they forgot. It's hard enough to find a man with no name; let alone a man who looks nothing like his former self. Want to know how I lost my eye?"

Regarding it as a rhetorical question, I remained silent. *Of course, I did. Ever since a young rooster when he professed having lost it hunting unicorns in the land of giants!* One look at that face and any fool's interest would have been piqued. And, let me assure you, I was no ordinary fool. Ask Petra, she'll tell you it's true.

"When I decided to forsake the Brotherhood and join Baran, I knew a high price would have to be paid. I could ill afford to be found. Being completely shorn back then, I ceased shaving my head. My hair grew long; and my beard very thick but I knew it wasn't enough." He paused and then spoke very slowly.

"So, I heated my sword in the hottest coals and waited till it was brightly glowing at the tip. It was so hot the cloth I used to wrap the hilt caught fire. It was so hot I could hear the sweat on my face sizzling as I moved it closer and closer. It was so hot my eye began rattling about— like a boiled egg." His voice dropped to a whisper.

"It was excruciating, and I hadn't even let it touch me yet. But I had to and so I did. Pressing it to my face, I held it there. Well, it got stuck in truth. I had to pry it free with my pretty dagger. That's why I gave it away. I couldn't stand the sight of it. Well, that coupled with the fact you can't rightly claim not to be an assassin while parading about with their prized weapon of choice in hand. The sword was ruined. The tip shattered when I cast it aside. A day or two later, I looked at my reflection in the glass and I was unrecognizable even unto myself. How's that for a story?"

"I've never heard such a thing. Even so, they wouldn't give up; they would hunt you to all ends of the world." Though I held my tongue, the tale seemed suspect to me.

"I'm certain they are— and good luck to them. But what is an assassin without something to hide?" He chorused while gauging my reaction. Though never having played *Blink*, neither was I prone to flinching. A fork in the eye would accomplish it for certain but not words alone.

"Tell me, how did Baran convince you to join him? Since when have assassinations included negotiations or any measure of dialogue for that matter? I'm at your disposal; color me intrigued." I admitted.

"As noted, I was dispatched to end him. He was alone studying a map late at night when I put my dagger to his throat. I can't say why, but I hesitated. Perhaps due to his utter lack of a response.

Whom do you serve? He asked.

The Brotherhood, I answered.

And whom does the Brotherhood serve?

The One Rah, I replied." Darian sighed before continuing to mimic Baran's scratchy voice rather amusingly.

"*If that is true, then you have no other choice but to lay down your knife and serve me,*" he'd stated with great conviction. *They're plotting to kill the One Rah,* he insisted calmly. *You must help me ensure that never happens. It cannot happen. It must not. They intend to ambush him at Standstill Pass– tomorrow.*

Who plans to ambush him, I asked.

The Kedera, using the One Rah's own guards and several others known to be of your sacred Brotherhood. He then tapped his finger on a spot on the map– and that was it. I believed him– even prior to him showing me what proof he had." Darian shrugged.

"Unfortunately, we arrived too late." He lamented, exhaling theatrically.

"You were there?" I inquired incredulously.

"Yes. We failed the One Rah; the only thing that mattered– yet another thing Baran has never forgiven himself for. We managed to kill the assassins, but the soldiers escaped. The remaining question being: who had dispatched me to kill the lone person intent on safeguarding our sovereign? It became clear to me then that the Brotherhood was dishonored." He paused. "Therefore, the way I see it is– 'twas the Brotherhood that deserted me."

"Why tell me this? Are you not afraid I will betray your confidence? I barely know you."

"As noted, I consider myself a fair judge of character and, for some unknown reason, I know you won't betray me." He shrugged confidently. "Not to mention, Chitter would have told me." It seemed clear to me then; the man was plainly mad. Or the kestrel could speak– which I found highly unlikely.

"But why take the chance? Why tell me at all?"

"Because I am old," he laughed. "Because I am a fool, I expect. Though, more truthfully, it is likely because I wanted you to know that there is common ground between us. We suffered the same trials and survived. I suppose I wanted you to know that it is possible to leave. You can get out. I am living proof. If you call *this* living." He laughed, motioning broadly about him, which took his little bird by surprise.

"Forgive me for not plunging a molten sword into my eye. Forgive me if I do not yet share the same confidence in you."

Raising his cup, we tapped them together amicably. I was no fool. I knew I couldn't trust anyone in this place–– other than Petra. The same trials? *Ouch.* Now there was a topic I needed to avoid. Though no doubt a topic never openly discussed, Darian had already rescinded his oath. If all he said was true, he owed them no loyalty.

"Forgiven," he smiled. "As Baran put it, I walked away from a life of senseless killing only to kill more *sensibly*." He chuckled. Oddly, I did like Darian if for no other reason than his *blind* candor.

"And *that* is how he knew you were lying," he added.

"Lying?" I asked, trying to quash the shiver within my spine.

"Yes, lying," he smiled. "The Brotherhood are allotted new titles soon after forsaking those given at birth. Baran knows that. It was I who told him so. Elnath was the name granted to me. I don't care why you are lying. As I've said more than once now, I trust you. Notwithstanding, Baran has lied to me many times. Who can say why we do the things we do? Perhaps we met in a previous life."

Oh, we'd met for certain but, not unlike his own transformation, he was unable to recognize me.

"Perhaps," I chuckled. "It is true. I did lie. That said, outside of the Brotherhood, I do not share my given name. Outside of the Brotherhood, what life remains?" I felt I needed to say something in hopes of justifying the blunder and it was the only thing that came to mind. As my mother often said— and not because I fibbed a lot— *every lie digs a hole lying in wait to claim the whole.* Yeah, I don't know what it means either; though you must admit, it is rather catchy.

"Never confide it to me for I would know if you were lying."

"Ah, but I cannot, can I?" I grimaced. "You no longer side with the BroZil."

"With Chitter as my witness, did you not say no one leaves the Brotherhood?" He felt obliged to remind me.

"It seems I was wrong. It's been happening a lot lately. Ask Petra, she'll tell you it's true."

"We're named after the stars," he added with a wink. "There! Once again, you've found a way to force it from me."

"All save the brightest." I joked in reference to Baran.

"He knows that too." He smirked.

"Of course, he does," I chuckled, feeling the name Dark Star would have been far more fitting as opposed to Nitesh Alde Baran.

After bidding Darian and Chitter good-bye, which only seemed polite, I had a quick stop at the horrid Pail—though not quite quick enough to curtail me from vomiting. Though hard to believe, the place smelled even viler than the last time I'd managed to garner the courage. I hastened my gait for being keen to get back to The Crown without interruption. It was paramount that I convince Petra that killing Alde Baran was not only the proper thing to do, but admirable as well. The man was living a life of unconscionable torment. Poor bloke, it was only right that I set him free.

As fate would have it, it was then that I saw him~~—~~ outside staring up at the stars. The door to the Sand Pit was open and, beyond that, quite close to the well, stood Alde Baran— oblivious to all with eyes turned upward. I could see my dagger glimmering on his hip. I paused watching shimmers of ivory and gold compete for my attention. *Might it be the very same dagger that I was about to kill him with?* It was.

Unless— unless I tossed him down the well instead. I would have to knock him senseless first. A notion that agreed with me greatly. ~~As~~ I couldn't risk anyone hearing him holler~~—~~, I reckoned several good stomps on the back on the head would ~~would~~suffice quite nicely~~, I reckoned~~. Given the softness of the sand, my shadow's footsteps were as quiet as my own. So absorbed was he with the heavens, he did not see me coming. He would never know what hit him for he'd never wake again. It was then I noticed the empty wooden cage and stopped dead in my tracks. Curiously, it wasn't the whereabouts of the Harbinger cat that bothered me. It was my previous thought. The one where Alde Baran dies while *never knowing why.* What point would there be in that? It did present a conundrum for advising him of his impending demise would undoubtably complicate matters somewhat. I heard a loud snarl behind me. Alde Baran spoke.

"I suggest you move closer to me. I feed the cat often— something you'd do well to avoid." He made a fair point. Not to mention, he had my dagger. Admittedly, I began noticing flaws within my hasty plan which had sounded so easy but a moment ago.

"It is a most glorious night," he observed staring upwards. "I can point toward every city and port within Harbinger on a night such as this. The stars are particularly brilliant tonight. Did you know that there are more stars than grains of sand? Even here." he added. My head was far too riddled to contemplate such pointless thoughts. Small wonder, Petra enjoyed his *footle prattle.*

Swirling his head scarf over his forehead and about his cheeks and jaw, he tucked it into his collar. The back of his neck was scarred far worse than I could recall. I hadn't initially noticed that his face had been uncovered. I could feel my heart pounding. I could taste blood in my mouth, something I normally only noticed prior to battle.

"You do not fear the cat?" He asked, turning to look at me for the first time with no hint of surprise that it was I who approached rather than one of his men.

"'Tis the cat that should fear me," I blathered stupidly trying to decide which was better— the dagger or the well. In the end it didn't matter I decided as, either way, I'd hide his body in the well. The cat hissed at me, sounding much closer. Though every hackle on the back of my neck stood strongly opposed, I wasn't about to award it the satisfaction of turning to look at it. A foolhardy stance without doubt but that was me. *More stubborn than hither*, so my mother said.

"The cat guards the well during the day though sometimes I let him out for an evening stroll. His role is crucial, having learned long ago how to survive in this place. Even he understands that nothing can be allowed to spoil the water's purity."

Haeryn help me! I hadn't thought of that. So, I could not simply toss his dead corpse into the well, after all. Whether his body was lifeless or still vaguely twitching was, sadly, no longer even up for debate. Oh, but the gods could be cruel. I couldn't recall the last time I'd felt so unjustly aggrieved. It seemed unimaginable. How might I be given this miraculous opportunity on such a glorious night only to be so callously denied? But there it was. I could not kill him– giving me yet another justification amongst a long list of reasons to hate the man. *Why must he always be such a stick-in-the-mud?* There seemed but one chance left. Petra was clever. Hopefully, she could think of a way to be safely rid of the body. Once she saw the wisdom in it, of course.

"The creature's worth aside, should it creep much closer I may have need of my dagger." I chuckled, trying to make light of the shadowy beast's untimely presence while forcing the latest turn of events from my mind with a weighty sigh.

"Here. Take it. 'Tis yours in fairness." He said, unbuckling its sheath and tossing it to me. In all honesty, I could not have felt more dejected in that moment had the cat bared its fangs and leapt upon me. He, who I longed to kill, was standing right in front of me– unarmed now. I had everything required and yet....

"You trust me?" I asked suspiciously. Pushing every stalled murderous plot aside, it did feel wondrous to have the dagger back in my care. It was only right. I could hardly believe my good fortune– save for the fact I couldn't use it in the same instance. Was that also a form of irony? Because, if so, I despised it.

"Hardly, but you earned it– considering the beating you gave to Davos. That said, if you're thinking of killing me with it– get it over with." he added with a wry smile. That made me scratch my chin and I took a backward step to better study what little I could see of his face.

"I don't fear death." He shrugged. "I welcome it. Haeryn knows I have it coming. Then again, the gods are cruel– which is precisely why they allow us to live."

"I would gladly kill you," I confessed. "If only I could think of a way to get rid of the body. It's not like I could simply toss it down the well." I smirked with an awkward chuckle.

"'Tis a dilemma for certain," he agreed.

"Perhaps, I could feed you to the cat."

"Unfortunately, it would never devour me quick enough— not to mention the bones."

"There is that." I consented.

Yet again I found myself testing waters that might quickly prove perilous. As surreal as the conversation was, I found myself unopposed to pursuing it further. Who can say where ingenuity might come from? Besides, they say one's eccentricity rivals one's shrewdness. Unless that was my mother again. It does sound like something she'd say. Might have said, rather— because the rogue standing before me, alone and in plain sight, had murdered her.

"You could attest it attacked and killed me. Many of them would believe that. They're scared to death of the thing. Alas, but not Darian," he sighed.

"I wouldn't be so certain. Though he can't say why, he does admit to trusting me."

"Not in this case. You'd have to kill him too. He alone knows just how fond the cat is of me. I stole it as a cub from its mother's den. Being that it was a Harbinger cat that took Darian's eye, I'd planned to give it to him to sacrifice— a form of payback if you will."

I stared at him trying to discern the truth, but I was unable to tell he seemed so genuine.

"Darian told me, he took his own eye— said he did it with the tip of a molten sword." I said, judging his reaction critically.

"Did he now?" he laughed. "Well, it would seem one of us is lying." He admitted, turning his attention back to the stars. "But what is truth, I ask you? All things being fleeting, it is no different. Many of the stars you see above no longer exist. Long before Grumble ever took root, this desert was once an inland sea. Now, it is not. Prior to the wall being built there was but one side."

"Because things don't stand forever does not render them untrue. Besides, what difference does it make? Whether here or there, this desert will remain until the end of our days. One day this tree will fall yet before you it does stand." I argued.

"Well said. Ignore my pointless ponderings. Whatever forced you into this desert?" He then asked me, point blank.

"I saw no other choice; the Kedera had us surrounded. Alone, I might have found a way through but not with Petra and her baby."

"So, you chose to try crossing the Kestrel with a mother and infant? Forgive me for saying it but that sounds preposterous to me. Surely, you were aware that no one makes it across the Kestrel alive."

"I did. I crossed it once before. Thus, I thought we could do it again. I was wrong. We would not have survived had we not come across this place— *by accident.*"

"By accident, so you persist— implying that you crossed the Kestrel having no prior knowledge of the well."

"None." I lied. He turned, studying my expression silently.

"Someone came and refilled their water slings three months ago. I saw their tracks. That is why we began leaving the cat out at night— which is why I was initially so suspicious of you."

"It was not I." I said truthfully.

"I don't know why, but I believe you."

"Twice in one day," I laughed. "The Gods must favor me. Darian confessed his trust in me barely a moment ago though he could not provide any rationale— other than us both having been in the Brotherhood. Now, if only Petra would be so obliging."

"He told you about the Brotherhood. I swear that man cultivates impropriety as thickly as his beard. He is a good friend, but far too trusting. I merely admitted an inclination to accept that you'd crossed the Kestrel once before. As hard to swallow as that might be, it isn't as though I'm now going to share my darkest secrets with you. Darian. The man is a complete mystery to me at times. Whatever was he thinking?"

"He wanted me to know that it was possible to leave the BroZil— though the price would be steep should I endeavor to do so."

"In his case, his eye. I surrender; you caught me in a falsehood. Mark my words however, it was far sweeter than his sad tale. As with most lies, there was a measure of truth to it. Darian was mauled by a Harbinger cat long ago outside of a small village near Gadev. I felt somewhat to blame for dismissing his earlier concerns about just such an attack when we'd set camp. Still, he would most certainly have lost that same eye had it not been gone already.

"Then, but three years ago, during a trip to market, I came across a large cat den and from it I stole the same cub silently stalking you now. It is true, I fully intended to offer it as a sacrifice to Darian— an eye for an eye for having been attacked. But, as it turned out, the cat developed an affection for me during our return journey. I suppose, handfeeding it goat's milk thrice a day made it think me its mother."

He laughed, bending low and holding out his fingers.

"Come here, cat. Come." He cooed. The big cat emerged from the shadows and went to him at once, rubbing the full length of is striped body against Alde Baran's haunches so zealously it toppled him into the sand. He sat smiling, alternately his gaze between us.

"No, I suppose it won't eat you." I cursed. "But would not a molten sword have closed his eye completely?"

"Ah, but who am I to question Darian when it comes to his eye?" he snorted. "'Tis his sad tale, not mine."

"What about scorpions? Have you survived their deft prick?" I wasn't giving up that easily. It had worked wonders with the assassin.

"Yet another unlikely path to my demise," he replied. "I been stung at least half a dozen times– four in one go the first time but that was years ago. Long before I knew of the well." Rising to his feet, he continued to scratch the creature's big bristly ears.

"Besides myself, I have not met anyone who crossed the Kestrel without prior knowledge of the well. There was a time when I was quite famous for being the only man able to cross it. Known as Diwan Ogi's messenger, it was, and is, by far the fastest route to Harkenspear."

"Short of leaping the Asunder," I chortled.

"The Diwan was second in command to the One Rah– until the False Rahs murdered him. The One Rah, that is."

"Nitesh Alde Baran!" I blurted. "The brightest star." He laughed to my amazement. "Diwan Ogi gave you that title."

"So, it is said." He sighed. "Yet another missing star."

"What happened to the forgotten one?"

"The recluse?" He laughed. "The hermit is still doing what he's always done best– cowering from his past. Though I find it hard to believe people as young as you profess to know that name. It's been countless years since I've heard it spoken aloud. I did not even know Darian back then. Believe me when I say, that is a long time ago."

"The Brightest Star." I mumbled not without a hint of sarcasm.

"And now, they call me the Sun Rah."

"The One that Speaks as None," I blathered mindlessly. "What does it mean?" I queried.

"Long ago, likely before you were even born; I had in my possession irrefutable proof that the False Rahs had murdered the One Rah. It was my hope to destroy them and end their insurgence before it might take root. Unfortunately, before I could confront them, they declared me a brigand professing I wanted nothing more than to steal the vacated throne for myself.

"Having been deemed a traitor, I was eventually captured. To my horror, the army of men I'd gathered foolishly surrendered themselves. We were to be executed— all one hundred and twenty of us. But we escaped, fleeing into the Kestrel for no other reason than having stumbled upon this place *by accident* long ago. Two-thirds of my men perished that day— most well within sight of Grumble. Though many of us had been tortured, it was dehydration and exhaustion for the most part that claimed their lives. It was a disaster. As for the remainder, we had our lives but little more. It was but a brief time later that I was labeled the Sun Rah. And that is the first time I've spoken of it to anyone since our arrival," he confessed.

I was completely dumbfounded. It hadn't been what I expected at all. On this side of the wall, we spoke of the slain One Rah near as fondly as Haeryn himself. Dead before I even knew his name, he seemed almost mythical to me in truth. Like Haeryn, only far more tangible— akin to a memory you can't quite recall. Near as real as the fingers on your own hand yet strangely imaginary at the same time.

"The Brotherhood gave me a name— one I never share," I fibbed. "I could tell you if you like."

To this day, I have no rationale for having uttered those words. Not the bit involving the name but rather the *sharing* part. Perhaps it was because Darian had admitted Baran knew I'd been lying. I don't think so though. I wasn't thinking at all to be clear. It just flew from my lips like a migrating kestrel.

"On such a night as this, secrets are best kept by the stars. There are rare moments when speculation triumphs knowledge." he smiled, looking upward. "Fawaris, Hamal, Antares perhaps?"

I made no reply. I felt oddly transfixed. All thoughts of how to get rid of his body had evaporated. But a moment ago, I'd wanted to kill him so badly. Though I did not know why, I suddenly felt ashamed and sick to my stomach. It was as though I was a child again fully riveted to one of his many tales of adventure. I felt sad for him and, at the same time, an enormous sense of loss. Though blinded at the time, I'd lost more than my mother that day. I'd lost my hero as well. Dazed, I reached to stroke one of the cat's twitching ears. It hissed at me so vehemently I was immediately shaken from my bout of mindlessness.

"Oh, I wouldn't try that," he counseled. "The cat likes no one save for me. Mark me, it would have killed you already were I not with you." It seemed nothing short of a challenge. He was daring me to do it and I was powerless to stop myself. Kneeling, I held out my hand in the same fashion he had.

"You're playing with fire." He warned. "He will tear you to the bone."

"And how would you dispose of the body?" I asked softly.

"You?" he guffawed. "The sand will see to your body. After which, I might just add your head to my wall."

"Then I shall consider myself honored." I winked.

"Consider yourself foolish for that is what you are."

He reprimanded, moving back a step. Being the wonderful person he was, I expect he assumed increasing the distance between the pair of them would make his fearsome tabby more aggressive. It did not, however, which gave me nerve enough to shuffle closer. Yet again, I felt needlessly compelled to prove myself the better man– or at least his equal. The cat sniffed my outstretched fingers, and I heard Baran gasp as the creature rubbed its wet nose softly against them.

"I would never have believed it had I not just witnessed it," admitted Alde Baran. "Not in a thousand years," he marveled. "As it turns out, the skull wall will remain as is– though, but a second ago, I envisioned but the slenderest of margins to save you. Not that I cared, I only feared telling Petra."

His laughter vanished as the cat chose to drag its slender frame against my arched torso. Though I didn't know how wrong I was at the time, and neither would I have admitted it, I suspected the beast did not attack due to Baran and I sharing the same blood line. As it turned out, in hindsight, Petra's observations regarding our similar temperaments could well have been the reason. Like Baran, I did not fear the beast– though, undoubtedly, a wiser man would have.

"I only wish Darian had been here to see it. His eye would have popped clean out of his head. No doubt, he's still in the Rookery declaring every unscrupulous deed of his sordid past to anyone dim enough to listen." Thinking back, I should have taken offense to that, but my mind had been stretched far beyond my ears. Not to mention how bloody tired I was.

"It is late," I said. "I must go. I need to speak to Petra before sleep finds her. I said something rash earlier that kindled her anger."

I felt overwhelmed by fatigue. My head was so overburdened it felt akin to a smithy's anvil. It was odd, when I'd first arrived my intentions had been crystal clear– but now my mind brimmed with doubt. It was as Petra said. He wasn't the malevolent beast I thought him to be– which made me feel not only uncertain but nauseous. Every fiber of my being craved to loathe him and yet, as Darian attested, I could find no malice within him. Though I alone knew his true character, once again, I was left with more questions than answers. One being far more significant than the others. After all he'd done, *how could I not hate him?*

"It is not yet early," he corrected, "but do as you feel you must. It is all we can ever do, after all."

Petra was lying on her cot, waiting for me when I arrived. Though she stared at me apprehensively, graciously she did not move away when I laid down beside her. I slid my arm around her and stared upward at the endless void— which echoed my mood succinctly.

"I'm n-not sure I can do it," I stammered finally.

"Kill him, you mean?"

"Yes. That."

"Do not," she whispered, turning her face to mine. "His death will afford you no comfort." She insisted.

"I never expected it would," I confided. "It was never about me— but strictly about avenging my mother." I lied, mostly to myself. "My mind is at an impasse for feeling both humbled and ashamed. Still, I remember everything about that day and remain only hesitant for not being able to think of a way to be rid of the body. You're clever; tell me how it can be done. I beg you, please!"

"No, I will not! It is pure foolishness! Have you ever told anyone about that night?"

"No one ever save for yourself."

"Of which the details were sparse. Perhaps it would bring you some peace if you spoke of it aloud. Perhaps you'd be able to make sense of it somehow."

"Sense of it? There is no making sense of it. It was an act of senseless violence the details of which would turn your stomach." I paused for a deep breath, exhaling slowly. She could wait all night. There was no way I was ever going to relive that day. *Voice it aloud?* Preposterous. It would never happen. Not ever. And then my lips started moving of their own accord— as was their custom of late.

"I awoke first that day— to discover my father had returned at some point in the night. He'd fallen asleep in a chair at the kitchen table. I wanted to wake him, but he was making odd grumbling noises which frightened me. He was dreaming for certain. It must have been a cruel dream for his body was shaking and he was soaked with sweat.

"I woke my mother proclaiming his arrival. He remained in a sad state— which, by itself, wasn't that unusual when I think about it. He often returned looking quite worn and disheveled. This was different, however. I'd never seen him thrash about while he slumbered. My mother fetched some damp cloths to place on his forehead, fearing he might have a fever." I paused, exhaling a deep breath, until I felt composed enough to continue– even though, in my heart, I remained adamantly opposed to surrendering the account.

"Mother shook him gently. He grumbled loudly, quivering as though in fear. Flashing a look of mild irritation, she shook him much harder. Then, wide-eyed with teeth bared, he arose. Fully crazed, he flew into a rage the likes of which I'd never witnessed prior. Taken wholly by surprise, he threw her to the ground with irregular strength. He began…" I had to stop. I couldn't get the words out. Closing my eyes which were laden with tears, I took another deep breath.

"And then? Say it fast if you must." She encouraged me.

"He began stomping on the back of her head– over and over. I hollered at him. *Stop! Stop! Stop!!* But he didn't stop, did he? Charging at him, he swatted me across the room as though I was but an irksome bee. I kept hollering whilst he continued to parade upon what little remained of her face." Opening my eyes, I stared at Petra.

"Until there was nothing left– just a thick, red smudge riddled with golden hair." Tears sizzled upon my cheeks. Petra squeezed my hands until they finally unclenched.

"I told you. 'Tis a horrid memory."

"I know. I understand. But what happened next? Tell me Radesh, I feel it is crucial for you to do so."

What happened next? Crucial? As well-meaning as her intentions might be, I did not see how any of this was helpful. Looking back, what happened that day wasn't nearly as painful as opposed to all that I might have done differently. I might never have awoken my mother for starters. If only I'd just let the pair of them sleep. If only I'd minded my own business for once she might very well be alive today. Though Petra's own parents were undoubtedly dead, at least she hadn't witnessed them perish.

"Recognize, none of this was any fault of yours, Radesh. You were only a child."

She was reading my thoughts again. Well, I had no choice in the matter now, did I? We must plow forward because there was no way in Haeryn's Hells I was admitting my darkest secrets to her. There never be an end to it. We'd be rethinking every choice I ever made if we wandered down that dim path. *You can do this. Make an end of it.* I told myself.

"And then he stopped. He just stood there staring downward as though frozen in time. I wanted to scream but I couldn't. All I could do was cry as I stared at him in disbelief. Buckling over upon the table, he pounded his head against it so hard I thought one of the two would break. I yelled for him to stop and this time he did. His face was covered in blood– though unlike my mother, I could still recognize his face without effort. I could still distinguish his features– those piercing eyes, strong chin, and scarred neck."

"Why couldn't he have stopped? Why didn't he stop when I hollered at him?" I mourned sorrowfully. It was plainly rhetorical. I felt out of sorts. Not unlike when the Red Rage relinquished its grip.

"I'm so sorry, Radesh. He was not himself. He was clearly possessed," she sniffed sadly.

"Oh, he knew who was well enough for I could see it in his eyes. He looked straight at me."

"And?"

"Shoving the table away, he fell to his knees. He did not move for what felt like half a day– nor did I for the intense fear that he'd kindled. Without warning, he rose– never once looking toward me. Staggering toward the wall, he removed a large war shield and laid her headless body in it. Dragging her corpse outside, he covered her body with a red cape before placing her in the wagon. He hitched up the horses and left. Without uttering a word– never having glanced in my direction. The bastard didn't even bother to clean the floor! I had to do it– what was left of her head for Haeryn's sake!"

I wished I'd said that last bit quieter. It did not help anything. My throat ached; there was a lump in it the size of a small unnamed village. I was surprised to find more tears burning streams down my cheeks. Embarrassed, I wiped them away staring upward into the awaiting darkness. Petra was silent for a time. And then she spoke– as was her nature.

"What if it was the Red Rage?" She whispered. I couldn't believe my ears. I felt a terrible wrath boiling within me at first for even suggesting such a thing. But, as she took my hand in hers again, it quickly dissipated. Just when I thought I'd tamed the beast lurking within me. How could I turn my anger upon her while she sought nothing other than to console me?

"What if he suffered the soldier's sickness? What if he wasn't truly awake?" She doubled down.

Looking at her, I felt inordinately drained for having shared all that I had. I scratched my head, deeply confounded.

"The Red Rage." I repeated inanely, wiping my nose with a

hand. I was thinking aloud. Though it hadn't been a question, all the same, she answered it– as was her nature.

"Yes. That."

"You think it's the same as the soldier's sickness."

"I do– at least some form of it. You did say it lies dormant within you only to surface should you feel threatened." I took a deep breath after swallowing the mucus that had collected in my throat. I'd learned long ago it was never good to spit anything upwards regardless of how dark it might be.

"Are you suggesting *he infected me?*"

"I hadn't thought about that. It's just that you've both fought many battles and that's bound to take a toll. If you care, and I know you do, how could it not? Scars come in a wide variety of shapes and sizes, Radesh. Some of which remain hidden– until they don't."

"You think we share a similar ailment." Yet again I had to swallow, this time for fearing I might vomit. And now I knew what Darian intended. Twas a bitter pill for certain.

"Do you remember *that night?*" Haeryn hells! Not again– of all times to bring that up.

"What has that to do with anything?' I huffed. "And we've been through this before– you know I don't– which saddens me greatly as has been firmly established many times prior."

"I'm sorry. It's just that before you went to sleep *that night* you told me to be careful how I woke you. Something I never thought about until this very moment." Well, that was disturbing. Largely because I'd never considered it either. Not that I wanted to. Which was why I remained silent for quite some time.

"I often have terrible dreams," I confessed finally, "sometimes responding harshly when startled." It was hard to get the words out for the sting. Could she be right? Well, I for one was in denial.

"We're not the same. We are nothing alike." I grumbled.

"Being different does not propose you have nothing in common." she said softly.

"You think it's like a virus– an infectious disease he imparted to me. Yet another reason to hate him."

"Perhaps, though it might simply be that the two of you share qualities making you more disposed to the disorder."

"Disorder?"

"Condition, rather. I meant to say condition– the circumstances at a given time."

"So, not a plague. I feel so much better." I shook my head

forlornly.

"No, not a plague– more of an illness of the mind."

"Only an illness of the mind, now." I guffawed. "Wonderful. Your gift for words will never cease to amaze me."

"My apologies, but I don't know how to say it any better. I read once that many of our attributes and behaviors are passed onto us from our parents; sometimes grandparents unto grandchildren; or great grandchildren even."

"Everyone knows that. If your parents are farmers, you inherit the pitchfork. If your father's a smithy you inherit the hammer. If your father's a printer, you'll have ink on your hands for life. What of it? Why put that in a bloody book? Unless you're the printer, I suppose. It would explain the epidemic."

"Epidemic?" Petra looked at me quizzically.

"All the books!" I blurted. She could be so clever and yet daft as a casket. Never in my life had I despised books more.

"Ah, the book epidemic, of course. I was merely intending that if one of your parent's legs was a bit shorter it could increase the chances of your leg being a bit shorter too." I felt a need to scratch my knee while mulling that over.

"So, only one of the parents had the short leg?" I felt obliged to clarify.

"It doesn't matter. That's not the point. It could be both parents, I suppose."

"So, is it three good legs and one short one; or two good legs with two shorter halves?"

"The legs are not halved, they're just a wee bit shorter is all."

"I know that but, of the four, how many were cut short?" It was a fair question.

"There were no swords involved. They were never cut by anything. They just grew shorter." She sighed, pulling at her hair. Admittedly, I was feeling a bit frustrated now.

"How could something grow shorter? It either grows or it does not." I glared defiantly.

"Haeryn help me. It's not about the number of legs, Radesh! It's about– forget I said anything." She griped rudely.

"How many children did you say there were?"

"Stop. I surrender." She implored putting a hand over my face. Though I'd obviously won the debate, in all honesty, I still wasn't sure what any of it had to do with anything. Though you'd never have guessed as much, I wasn't very adept with numbers and such. Like litters, flocks, and herds, I found figures that increased, or decreased, a tad perplexing. Thus, I had little choice other than to explain that her proposal seemed suspect given the fact that one of my old neighbors had a wooden leg, yet his sons chased after me just fine. A point she wisely chose not to argue, I might add.

"I think you need to sleep," she conceded. "As do I. It's been a long day."

"Ah, so harem life can be tiring." I smiled. "Good to know."

"I was upset." She retorted. "You upset me."

"I'm sorry. That said, if I close my eyes, I'll be asleep before yester." I yawned.

Though untrue, I drifted off to sleep so fast it felt as though it was. I awoke early the next evening and, in my half-awake state, recalled further specifics regarding Bear Gnarledson, my old neighbor with the wooden appendage. As it happened, knowing me to be rather adept at thievery, a small group of farmers had wagered a silver coin that I could not steal his wooden leg. A bet I took though wary they might not uphold their end of the proposed bargain.

Having a notion how it might be achieved, I began loitering near Bear's homestead. It was unusual not to see his three sons attending their chores. Thus, I assumed they were either hunting or they'd been tasked with an errand of some kind. Just before dusk, the perfect opportunity presented itself when I saw Bear prop his makeshift leg against their outhouse prior to hobbling within its tiny confines. Sadly, there is nothing clever about the misconduct itself for I simply grabbed the wooden stub and ran for the hills.

Come afternoon the following day, I went to see the farmers who'd gathered to gossip as was customary during more pleasant weather. They pointed at me in turn as I walked toward them, brandishing the wooden stump with its flapping leather straps. It was then that they informed me that they had no silver coin for having spoken purely in jest. Knowing it was far from true, I laid an innocent basket of tomatoes to waste with the knotty stump prior to leaving quite disheartened. *Fool me once, shame on anything within reach*, as the old saying went.

Later that same afternoon, having received no compensation, I began to feel exceedingly guilty for having stolen the old farmer's leg in the first place. The more I thought about it, the more convinced I became that it was not a very neighborly thing to do at all. Pondering what he might have thought happened to it only made me feel worse. Whether he might have a spare leg I had no way of knowing though it did not seem likely. Come twilight, I imagined him sitting on his back porch, whittling himself a new peg while wondering if his dog across the yard might be chewing upon the missing limb?

Beset by guilt, I realized there would be no sleep for me any time soon unless I made amends for my unprovoked misdeed. Recognize, Bear Gnarledson was a not a gentle man by any stretch. Point being, it wasn't as if I was about to knock on his door and plead for clemency. No, my plan was to wait until dark; rest the stump against the outhouse; and run for the hills. Which was strangely akin to the first plan– only in reverse. And with no one in the outhouse– just to be safe. That said, sometimes even the simplest of plans find a way to turn against you when you least expect it. The Khalifah call it kismet. In hindsight, I fully deserved what happened next for life has its own way of awarding recompense.

Just when I was on the brow of Bear's farm, for no other reason than to return the senseless leg, I heard a rustling sound. A few shuffles later and Bear's three sons came traipsing from the neighboring woods. Understand, it was not only a full moon, but a harvest moon as well. Which is to assert that visibility was considerably keener than it might have been otherwise.

All three of his sons smelled strongly of ale which is to imply that things took a sour turn the moment they glimpsed me with their father's leg in tow. Moon or no moon, it was precisely then I wished I'd cleaned all the tomato bits off it as it did appear to be covered in blood which, to be clear, did not help the situation. Though I tried to explain it was all an unfortunate misunderstanding, they were not in a mind to listen. In fact, they seemed more intent on delimbing me than conversing. The irony of that moment being, though they were convinced I did not have a leg to stand on– the truth of it was, I had more than my fair share. Not unlike me explaining the part about the stump being covered in tomato guts not Bear guts, they failed to see the humor in it. So, discarding the limb, I ran for the hills a second time. This time to save my hide.

Having heard Renan crying, I awoke from my daydream to fetch him immediately. He felt different to me now. Though he'd been my son all along, he felt as though he was a part of me now. Not like a wooden appendage but a real one. Albeit a much shorter one. Not that I wanted to bring that nonsense up again. Speak of the devil, Petra awoke so I lay back down beside her with Renan on my chest.

"He's getting bigger," I noted.

"Because things grow bigger, not smaller," she winked. "Takes after his father," she yawned sleepily. That gave me pause.

"And that doesn't worry you?"

"Should it?"

"I was just thinking about what you said. I think I understand."

"Haeryn no, it's too early– not the thing about the legs again. Please! Forget I said anything," she pleaded.

"Not that but rather the bit about the farmer's son and such. It's just that I see within him a host of fine qualities inherited from you. But what will he glean from me– the soldier's sickness?"

"No. That's not what I meant. I don't think it works that way."

"I hope not but, short legs and such aside, I don't want him to become a soldier." I clarified.

"Should the gods be in favour, he need not suffer wars and such. Oh, I pray with all my heart that he does not." Though only awake for a moment, already she looked to be on the cusp of tears.

"As do I. I don't want him to inherit a war that has nothing to do with him. For the first time in my life, I am scared, Petra. I fear for him. What if the only thing he contracts from me is the Red Rage? What then?" I asked though fearing the answer.

"Then we shall monitor his behaviour closely." She sighed. "Radesh, not even the Gods can say what he will or will not be. We must all make our own way with what talents and faults we are given. But, even so, it is the choices we make along the way that define us."

"True, but it hurts to imagine that a horrid little beast might lurk somewhere within. I would not wish such a curse upon anyone, not even my own enemy. Especially my own enemy, as I ponder it."

"Just because you have it, doesn't mean he will. He might; but he might just as easily not."

"Have you seen him angered? Does he kick and bite?"

"No. He does get a bit irritable when he's hungry."

"Who doesn't? You mustn't fault him for that, Petra. He's a growing boy. He needs to eat. Not to mention, if he can't yet speak how in Haeryn's sake is he supposed to let you know?"

"You're impossible. I expect he's famished now. Pass him over to me, please."

"Perhaps we should make him wait. See how irritable he becomes– poke him perhaps. Not in the eye or anything but just enough to make him react." I suggested. It did seem a fair test.

"You will do no such thing."

"Now who's impossible?" I inquired. She snatched him from me, swapping my chest for hers. Twas a step up for the lad if I say so myself. As her green eyes met mine, she bit her lip thoughtfully. Uh-oh, I knew that look.

"I was thinking." *Of course, she was.* "I very much doubt the Red Rage is even transmissible," she stated solemnly.

"Trans which able?"

"Able to be spread– passed on like an infection or virus."

"As opposed to a disorder or illness of the mind." It was my turn to wink. "But what about the farmer allotting his son the pitchfork and all? Were you not intending Baran gave it to me?"

"No. I said he appeared to have a similar malaise. It's true. Some traits are inheritable, but it might also be a disorder brought about by severe stress. There are consequences to killing for those that don't end up in unmarked graves. The true casualties of war are not buried, they reside within hearts fighting for breath."

"It's true what you say about war, but I was in my youth when the Rage first took hold." I disparaged. "I was not yet a soldier. As much as I enjoyed a good fight, I didn't even know the war existed."

"Yes, but suffering requires neither soldiers nor war. One must only experience, or witness, something horrific."

"Like my mother's death."

"Precisely; like your mother's death," she repeated, nodding. "A tragedy experienced by your father as well."

"So, there it is," I said. "The fact of it is we shall never truly know. Thus, it seems to me, the wisest course before us is for me to become a farmer– for Renan's sake. But no goats. I hate goats."

"No goats." She laughed.

"Or geese! They're worse."

Or geese; and much worse" she agreed.

I rose, dressing hastily before breaking our fast– cold baobab tea and baobab jam on crusty bread. I was growing fond of it. Being reminiscent of lemon and honey only more akin to a paste while slightly nutty. Following our rustic meal, I applied more ointment to Petra's back and shoulders before putting on my sandals.

"Where are you going?" Petra asked, bouncing Renan up and down upon her hip.

"To see if Greta needs any help in the galley. I need to force my thoughts upon something other than Baran. I thought I might attend one of her reading sessions being that we're here. Besides, it's too early to begin sharing pitchers with Darian in the Rook."

"I can teach you," she smiled.

"To read or share ale?" I winked. "Agreed. You've been

teaching me things quite steadily ever since *that night*."

"Some things just come natural; I suppose." She grinned smugly though I knew better for her cheeks having flushed.

"I'll still speak to Greta. I know how to read; I just need more practice. It's this insufferable idleness. It provides far too much time to think. I fear I shall go mad should I not find something useful to do."

"Perhaps you should visit the Red Room and try starting a book from its beginning for once."

"I might just do that– though afterward."

"Who knows, you might uncover a love story."

I had to force myself to leave after hearing the word *uncover* fall from her lips. I had to admit, the girl had a way with words. Woman rather for she was no longer a girl. And they say wisdom comes with age. I believe maturity springs from adversity, crossing a desert being a prime example. Spend too much time there and you'll be sorely wrinkled before the sun has time enough to set.

As it turned out, Greta had more than enough help on hand as I arrived. Even Darian was there to my great surprise. *Somebody must do the barking* was the sole explanation provided– not that one was needed. The fact of the matter being: there were forty other bored men living within Grumble. As much as Darian thought himself to be in charge, it was the women who really directed the day's activities. The brunt of the chores involved moving water in one fashion or another; whether it be siphoning spirits; filling baths or cooking kettles; washing clothes; dying fabric; or just scrubbing floors and walls.

Having not contributed in any way for such a duration felt nothing short of shameful. Strange as it may sound, in all my life never had I been treated better. Food, ale, wine– and all of it for free. I felt quite special– blessed even, one might say. But it felt wrong. Not to mention, there was a term I had agreed to that I was yet to uphold.

Preferential treatment was for generals, nobles, and mindless geese. Don't get me started on the geese. It's just that they are an entitled bunch if ever there was. Even injured soldiers returned to duty the moment they were back on their feet. Receiving free food and ale without doing anything in return was nothing short of a dishonour. It was unacceptable to the point of being immoral in my opinion. Watching them work was a form of torture to me. Well, not quite. I had been tortured once but it was so long ago I wasn't able to recall all the specifics. Nonetheless, I remain confident it was worse than watching others work. Each time I seized a pail or broom someone pried it from my hands.

"Rest," insisted Darian. "You are a guest; there is no work for you to be found here."

"But the accepted terms insist I do my fair share," I objected. "I must do something!"

"You will, don't you worry about that. But first, you must recover your strength. Besides, does it look like we need any more help? There's far too many of us already." He chuckled. Noticing a bizarre looking tool that looked like a giant curved fork with a wooden handle, I inquired what it might be.

"It's called a rake." Darian replied.

It was then I got one of the worst ideas of my life. It might very well prove to be the worst idea I ever had though I couldn't say for certain as I hadn't done it yet. It was horrifying. Just the thought of it made me nauseated. It was as dreadful as it was despicable and as calamitous as it was corrupt. But I'd made up my mind. I was going to do it even though my personal wellbeing would be critically at risk. Irrespective of the consequences, I would find a way to suffer through it. The things a man will force himself to endure to salvage his honour are implausible at times. This was one of those times. I only hoped it didn't kill me. Why did I do it? Apart from my ethics, it was self-serving as I ponder it due solely to something the Major once said.

If you want men to respect you the first thing you must do is gain their trust. To acquire their trust, you require their attention. To obtain their attention all you need do is something unexpected. Do that and their eyes will follow you wherever you may go. This is the true power of the Red Rage. This why their eyes follow you.

But things were different now, weren't they? I couldn't summon the rage here. Not that I wanted to. I needed to do something else— something no one would ever have imagined.

"Is there any vinegar?" I queried.

"Yes, loads of it; we lost a batch of baobab wine a year ago."

"Good, I will require a minimum of a dozen pails. I shall take one with me now; have some men follow me with the rest."

"Follow you where?" Asked Darian. He did not oppose me oddly. Irony. Was there no end to it?

"You'll see. I will also require that rake, a stout scrub brush, several armloads of rags, and a pail of clean drinking water." I muttered with a grave face.

Having piqued their curiosity, they quickly began gathering all I asked for. I exhaled several times slowly before dipping a rag in the bucket of clean water. Taking yet another deep breath for no other reason than showmanship, I tied the sopping rag about my nose and mouth. Stuffing as many rags as I could under my arms, I picked up the pail of water, and one of vinegar; and headed out the door. At first, I thought, only the men carrying the pails of vinegar were following me. I soon discovered that EVERYONE was following me. That is until I passed right by the Rookery.

"He's doing the Grim March! He's going to scrub the Black Pail!" I heard one of the men cry out in alarm.

"The bloody fool! He can't be serious! We should have tied a rope to him. He's done for." Were but a few of the more memorable pleas thrown after me amid their collective distress. To be clear, though the notion of a pail sounded as though it were something akin to a chamber pot; it was in fact a large barrel– a festering barrel full of rotting shit. But that wasn't the worst of it. The worst of it was the surrounding floor and walls for, it was obvious, that the barrel had been spilled on many an occasion; undoubtedly attributed to unsettled haste during a state of exuberant drunkenness.

Dumping the barrel was a gruesome enough task. Trying to hold one's breath while dumping the barrel was ill-advised. Other ill-advised scenarios included, but were not limited to: putting off dumping it until it overflowed; stepping on something as grisly as it was slippery; trying to pick up the barrel as opposed to sliding it; not enough hands; too many hands; any form of haste (as mentioned earlier); not having relied on liquid courage; succumbing... typically followed by unconsciousness; denial; panic attacks; delirium; dry heaves; catapult vomiting– all while trying to be the hero of a tale no one ever should have written.

Though heroics were not my intention, notwithstanding no one had ever been stupid enough to volunteer before; it did describe my current situation rather adequately. That said, having wrestled the slippery barrel out of its dank pit; I dumped its unholy contents by turning it upside down in the once pure sand of the Kestrel. I let it rest that way for quite some time– until my heaving stopped, dissipated rather. I could still feel my debilitated heartbeat pounding within my ears like a reluctant drum. I took several deep breathes slowly in through my nostrils to regain my nerve which was a grave mistake for the horrid smell made me gag instantly.

I thought I might vomit for a moment but knew I could not as my breakfast had abandoned me at the start of the ill-advised venture. Returning the barrel to its upright position, I dumped an entire pail of vinegar into it before commencing to scrub its deplorable exterior. I wasn't scrubbing its interior. Like me and nobility, that was never part of the plan. With a moon so bright, I was thankful to be in the shadow of the massive tree as it helped camouflage each ensuing layer of infectious filth– for which the rake came in handy.

Once that was accomplished, I emptied it again; dumped another pail of vinegar into it; laid it on its side; and beset to rolling it, back and forth. Following that, I refilled it with a good portion of sand; rolling it in the same manner; prior to dumping it; and repeating the entire process several times. At long last with painstaking effort, it was no longer the fearful Black Pail. It was a kinder pail, a less intimidating, more thought-provoking pail. It wasn't a pail at all really; just an ochre-coloured barrel of no ill intent. Ochre. Who knew?

I won't bore you with the details of scrubbing the hold. Though considerably harder, which was saying something, it was more of the same really; save for having to move the sand much farther; and rake it, rather than roll it about. I will mention one moment of sheer brilliance I wish I'd thought of earlier. I noticed someone high above was draining a tub. Being that the wooden drainpipes were in the same area, I uprooted the flowing pipe to blast water at the foulest areas which really worked wonders.

By the time the desperate chore was fully completed, I was positively dripping with– yah, that. *Negatively dripping* might be more accurate for I felt utterly despondent. What I could never have predicted is returning to a hero's welcome. While my prime motivation had been to garner some attention, it went far beyond anything I expected. No doubt the months on end of boredom had a lot to do with it. As I staggered beyond those previously decomposing walls a mighty cheer erupted, followed by another, and then another. It was so boisterous Grumble's entire torso shook.

"He's survived!" They quipped. "'Tis the miracle of miracles! Whether dharma or kismet the darkness has been defeated!" They declared, raising their mugs high. Apparently, they'd been allowed to leave the Rookery with their ale being that the proximity was so close. Then again, it may well have been that the miraculous achievement– their words, not mine– surpassed the rules.

"Are you certain he's alive?" Queried another. "He reeks of death to me!"

Which was true, I did. A pitcher of ale was passed into my smudgy hands. Flinging my facial covering onto the floor, I half expected it to begin crawling away. I consumed the pitcher in one long swallow, or a series of successive gulps is likely more accurate. Either way, I can assure you it was gone. Those gathered then began taking turns slapping me on the back, causing me to burp very loud which they also found amusing. They did take time to dip their soiled hands in vinegar prior to wiping them dry. And rightfully so.

"Assad! Assad! Assad!" They roared in unison. I grinned broadly never realizing how absurd I looked given the fact my nose and mouth were the only portion of me not slathered in grunge.

"A sad tale it must have been!" Interjected a loud voice further bolstering their entertainment. "Yet we will hear every word for tonight we celebrate the reclaiming of the Pail!" Alde Baran hollered above the din.

"Likely the greatest achievement since Haeryn split the Asunder." Darian gauged it.

Even Davos was applauding with a bandaged hand. "Perhaps, I won't behead you," he cackled. "You may be of use after all." Then again, I deserved to be beheaded for attempting something so foolish.

A group of six men then lifted me up, using rags of course; and carried me to the ladder. After placing me in a well-lined, man-sized basket, they hoisted me up to The Crown. A warm tub was waiting for me as soon as I entered the room. As was Petra– from a safe distance. Not surprising, the water smelled strongly of vinegar.

"Will you be joining me?" I asked, politely.

She did not answer. She just glared at me while holding her nose. She did collect my dirty garments using a long stick. Not surprising, I never saw those clothes again. I was told the soiled rags were burnt as well. As I sunk below the water's depth, a film of debris raced across its glossy surface. I had to scrub and refill the tub three times before I felt even vaguely clean. It was worth the effort for no longer were there any bits of sand leftover. Petra brought me a cup of hot tea. Had I died right then I would have considered my life complete. I'd not just performed my duty admirably; I'd done the impossible. Still, I was overly self-conscious for a fortnight afterward for fearing I might still reek of shit. I hoped I didn't. I did shiver rather terribly anytime the grisly deed was mentioned. Which proved to be rather often, unfortunately.

During that evening's communal dinner, I was treated as though I were a champion pit fighter. Not that I'd ever seen one though I expect it was similar. Being praised recurrently with mugs held high, it proved a drawn-out light-hearted affair. The only things rivalling the replenishment of ale and wine were the relentless jests. Having drank my fill of ale, I opted for the wine which, though white, proved as refreshing as ever albeit a bit light for my taste.

Even Alde Baran took part in the gibes declaring that there'd
be no grievance time allotted for not even Davos could complain about
someone not giving a shit– because now they could and worry free.
Petra bid her good-byes early. I can't say that I blame her for the only
thing worse than our raucousness were the jests themselves. They were
all poor in taste, the foulest of them being utterly revolting while even
the tamest of quips reeked of discourtesy.

The most comical moments occurred whenever someone
returned from having used the facilities as they tried to outwit their
prior returnee. Davos fawned about the experience professing it akin
to witnessing the birth of his firstborn son. If I'm not mistaken, it was
precisely then that Petra took leave of us. Darian labelled it the *Dapper
Crapper* declaring that he'd never have returned at all were it not for
the ale. Another man referred to it as *New Harkenspear*, save for its
defences having proven themselves penetrable. Alde Baran nearly fell
off his chair when I confessed to having wandered outside to relieve
myself for the lingering memories being so raw.

It was then I got my first taste of *Dead Man Quaking*. Which,
as it turned out, was not unlike a game I'd previously seen played
known simply as *Blink*. The rules were humble enough– aside from
the cheating. Guidelines being: one man stands idle while another tries
to make him recoil, baulk, or cringe– without laying a hand upon him.
Hand being the key word as this is where all the deceitfulness began.
Providing the hapless contestant didn't wince, they then became the
intimidator; free to badger whomever they nominated. The winner
being determined by an act of unrivalled daring which, in past times I
was told, often involved the Black Pail in some way. Say no more. I
don't want to know.

Unfortunately, I was disqualified. For the record, it was
entirely unfair– not to mention the first time I recall missing my
dagger throw. *Not missing*, I suppose would be more correct. I would
have been embarrassed had I been slightly less inebriated. Being a bit
more than a scratch, I did apologize. For the record though, the dagger
clipped his pinkie finger by the barest of margins. Being largely
decorative in nature, it's not as though I'd removed a thumb. Though
you might have assumed so for all the fuss.

Darian had quite an aptitude for the competition. Then again,
he did have the only fork– *my fork*. In the end, I told him he could
keep it. It had got rather bloody. At the risk of sounding a poor sport, I
felt his cheating to be a tad excessive at times. His preferred tactic was

to ogle someone with that crazy eyeball of his prior to blindsiding them with a quick fork to the ear. Outside of pointy cutlery, a sharp knee to the groin worked wonders as well. Eye pokes also proved rather popular– though not with Darian as that was deemed to be unfair. Meaningless even, depending on which eye of his you might have chosen.

Without fail, one after another; they always grimaced. That is until Alde Baran put an end to the proceedings when, at the height of our drunken debauchery, Ruok severed yet another man's pinkie finger at the highest knuckle. Unlike myself, he was not even chastised for his indiscretion. Baran simply professed the aggrieved man to be the winner for never having wavered in his resolve. It did seem appropriate– causing me to sneer at my intrant who was still pouting if you could believe it. Had I not provided the coward the very same opportunity? Haeryn knows, had he just knuckled down he might have won the absurd affair acres ago. Being sad on his part, I spared no words berating him.

I was far too drunk to climb the ladder as the dawn arrived. Darian, who could barely walk himself, kindly offered to pull me up with the hoist to which I fool-heartedly agreed. He lost hold of the rope halfway up and I thought for sure I was done for. Oddly, I made no effort to save myself, merely flapping my arms as though a bird in careless flight. I wasn't. Fortunately, Darian managed to step on the rope. Unfortunately, when he bent over to grab it again, he missed– and I hurtled downward again. Luckily, he finally got a forearm wrapped around it. Unluckily, as he stood up, he banged his head upon the exact same basket I was lying in– causing him to lose his grip. Gratefully *for me*, I landed on him instead of the ground.

"I don't fink dis working," he slurred, pulling me up just high enough to stable himself. Obviously, the more he leaned, the more he relied on the basket's ability to hold him upright making it doubly difficult to keep hold of the rope. Up, down, up, down went the basket, swaying this way and that. As I lie there watching Darian struggle to keep himself from tumbling over, I began to feel sick. I was forced to cover my mouth in the end for fearing I might spew.

"Stand up!" I demanded. "Quit pulling the rope! Quit leaning! Quit…." It was then that he handed me the rope.

"Do it yourself." He shrugged. That didn't work either as I ended up sideways with only my feet still in the basket. I lost my grip shortly after that and crashed to the ground. Thankfully, I was only waist high– not to mention far was too inebriated to feel any pain. We both started laughing. Staring down at me, he shrugged dejectedly.

"You look cozy. Sleep d'ere." He mumbled, staggering slowly away. And that is how it came to be that I awoke in that same basket sometime later for feeling a sudden flash of nausea. Opening my eyes cautiously, I saw Petra staring back. She was rocking the basket with her foot while holding Renan high enough to see. I envied him. Not solely for being in her arms for his blue eyes were as wide as his smile.

"Look at the big baby!" She cooed, as she continued jostling the basket from side to side.

"Good morning," I said far more cheerfully than I felt. Renan waved at me while she boasted a look I couldn't quite fathom. It wasn't a smile nor a frown but something in between. I felt uneasy.

"Good night?" I asked. I had no idea how much time had passed. It may have been a fortnight for all I knew though the pounding in my skull suggested a much shorter time frame.

"Please! For the love of Haeryn— stop rocking me." I blathered loudly. That was a mistake for my head pounded even more. Reaching upward gingerly, I was amazed to find it still attached. I was afraid that might be the case. Closing my eyes only served to worsen my condition as the giant tree began spinning about in my mind's eye. Though I wanted to rise, it seemed unwise presently.

"We're going to watch Myrna paint. Renan is wondering whether our pale-looking companion would care to accompany us?" I very nearly vomited right then.

"Never say *that word* again," I squawked.

"Pale as in pasty-looking or pail as in— the Black Pail?" She asked, smiling sweetly.

"That's the one. I never should have done it." I said with a horrendous shiver.

"Trust me, it wasn't the cleaning that's got you out of sorts. But what's done is done. You're a hero now; a champion amongst men— one of which retched all over your accomplishment. You'll be happy to know Darian found the culprit; made him clean it twice."

"Twice?" I asked wondering how Darian might be up and about. The one-eyed rogue was far worse off than me.

"Yes, he became ill again right after mopping it." She chuckled.

"Please! Never speak of it again." I pleaded.

"For all the good it would do; it seems you're all there is to talk about. Nothing else, just you and your ill-advised victory. Wave good-bye Renan. I don't think Papa will be joining us any time soon." She whispered in his ear whilst shaking his wobbly little arm at me. I couldn't believe she'd refer to me as his father especially given my current condition. Which is to imply, I wasn't feeling very fatherly.

"No," I sighed. "Papa needs to go outside and heave his innards. After which I'll slowly crawl up this ladder one rung at a time to die quietly alone."

"Then we'll pass on your regrets to Myrna."

"Myrna makes me uncomfortable. She said she wants to paint me." I shuddered involuntarily.

"And what's wrong with that? You'd make a splendid portrait. Notwithstanding she'd save a lot of paint if she did it today. Your face matches an ashen canvas perfectly."

"The scars alone would absorb all the paint. But, more importantly, I can't risk anyone recognizing me. The Kedera have wanted signs posted in many villages."

"Well, at least *someone* feels wanted," she huffed. *And there it was!* I knew she was hiding something. Luckily, I was feeling far too sick to play along so I wisely ignored it.

"Is the sun up or down?"

"Like you, down for the count. You best hurry if you're headed outside. I hear all the best spots are vanishing fast. Not unlike your book assertion, it's been a proper epidemic thus far."

"I swear, I shall never drink again. Not ever." I vowed, grimacing from the mere suggestion of it. Though my inane assertion didn't take root, for the record, I was very well-meaning at the time.

"Of course, you won't." she cooed while pressing Renan's face against her ear. "And Renan swears it's snowing outside." Shaking her head forlornly, she carried him away. After but a few short steps she turned about to shake Renan's wobbly paw at me again.

"Say buh-bye Ass-dad!" She called out.

I almost laughed. Though humorous, the risk was too great. True to my words, I slunk shamefully outside prior to hobbling up the ladder and falling soundly asleep. I slept like a baby for having finally done it. I'd come up with a way to dispose of Alde Baran's body– though I'd need to act fast. I would wait for him to go outside– cut his throat; then bury his body beneath the Black Pail's former contents. No one would look there. Not ever. His body would rot as deservedly so– in shit. Whether he might be a man of good character did not factor. Whether he'd made amends; pleaded for forgiveness; changed his evil ways did not factor. The only thing that mattered was that he'd been found guilty as charged. Though Darian had failed when bidden the same task, I would not. A crime had been committed. I was the lone witness. I would hold him to account. End of story.

My apologies, I see how that might be confusing. No, the story isn't over. Far from it for I still have much to do. Bury, rather. As you may very well have guessed, I was struggling internally with the whole *kill Baran / don't kill Baran* thing at the time. It was making me insane until realizing if I just did away with him the entire situation would resolve itself. A bit cold-hearted admittedly but that was me.

It was two later that my life would change forever as, about an hour before dawn, envisioning my opportunity I followed him outside. Being unusually dark, I could not see him anywhere. Gratuitously, we were on the north side of grumble opposite to the well– not far from where I cleaned the latrine. I paused to relieve myself so not to appear obvious. I heard his voice. Haeryn forbid, I had walked right past him.

"I see you're wearing your fancy dagger. Any new thoughts on how to dispose of my body?" He called out nonchalantly. Which means *casually* so I was told– to which I replied, *then why not just say that then?* I mean, what point is there in knowing the meaning of a word that's impossible to pronounce?

"Sorry, I've come up with nothing but shit so far." I admitted.

"It'd be all for naught anyway," he sighed.

"How so?" I asked, secretly worried.

"If I went missing my men would blame you straight away. That's a given."

"What about Davos? Would they not blame him? After all, he's threatened you openly several times." I reminded him.

"Ah, but Davos wants to rule the roost. He knows he must defeat me in front of everyone to claim his prize. You on the other hand have no other motive than revenge."

"An eye for an eye," I granted him. "There's nothing more level than a grave."

"True enough; you can never underestimate revenge. It remains and will always be the strongest of motivators."

"The strongest," I agreed. "Tell me, have you ever been wed?" I asked, surprised to hear the words escape my mouth.

"Seven times with little fanfare," he answered. It was a stupid question though I saw little choice but to wade deeper.

"I meant before– before all this." I clarified.

"Never." He attested. *Now who's lying?* I thought to myself.

"No wife– what about children?"

"None."

"But how could you know that for certain? How could any man?"

"Trust me, I know. While hunting as a lad a wild boar skewered my ball sack. I very nearly died. Though my father said I'd been most fortunate, *lucky* was not the word I would have chosen to describe the event. It changed my way of thinking. I was a different person after that. Having no brothers while realizing myself to be the end of my lineage, I was forced to come up with new reasons to live."

"You thought all that as a lad? Haeryn help me, at that age my sole purpose was to hog the potatoes."

"Adversity is ageless." He mused. "You need a cause because, by yourself, your life is worth nothing. Why do you care whether I was married? What difference would it make?"

Why forge such a lie, I wondered. It made no sense.

"I've been thinking about what Darian said. I've been thinking about leaving this life of endless war and settling down." Once again, I found myself sharing more than was wise without cause.

"I had a home once. It didn't work out. Everyone died."

"All of them? How?"

"I do not speak of it; nor will I."

"The gods are cruel." I frowned.

"The gods be damned," he replied. "If there be gods, they don't waste time on us. Why would they? Gods, as we know them, are inventions of men intended to induce a measure of control. Do you know why I remain here in this *god-forsaken place*?"

I held my tongue, knowing yet again I would not kill him on this night. He was right as usual. I would be found to blame. By myself I would not have cared. But I wasn't. There was Petra and Renan to consider. I'd made a promise after all. A promise I had every intention of keeping.

"Because I am tired of fighting over the ownership of apple trees. I am not Kedera. I am not Golan. I am Harbinger and the damn apple trees were intended for us all."

Apple trees? The fool was clearly mad. It reminded me of the sort of gibberish Petra might say— which gave me pause.

"But who decides who gets the apples and what if there isn't enough to go around?" I queried. He was already gone by the time I turned around. Like the ghost from my past he was, he'd completely vanished. As I returned to the Rookery, Davos came running in brandishing his sword. Rising to my feet, I took hold of my chair.

"We are under attack!" He hollered to my surprise. "Amos and

Taggert are dead!"

"Dead! How?" Alde Baran, who I'd not yet noticed, roared in alarm. Unwelcome raiders aside, *how in Haeryn Hells did he get there so fast?* Perhaps there was a secret door I knew nothing about.

"Arrows to the throat while on guard." Davos replied.

"To arms!" Cried Alde Baran at once. "To arms!" He repeated. "Davos take five men and guard the rear entrance."

"Why do I always get the foul end of the stick? Thanks to that fool the sand out back reeks of dung." He grimaced pointing his sword rudely toward me– proving that even the greatest of deeds can be thankless at times.

"Now is not the time, Davos. Darian fetch Agatha and meet me out front. The rest of you… *with me!*"

"We'll cut them into pieces," he winked as he raced past me with his men in tow including myself. *Did he just answer my apple query?* I wondered feeling immensely confused. *He did no such thing!* He was referring to the attackers, my better judgment insisted. Unless he was playing games with me. Why must everyone mess with my mind? I had no time for such nonsensical thoughts.

A sword was thrust into my hands as we passed by the Sand Pit. Having left the safety of Grumble, the first thing we witnessed were the bodies of the two slain men. One lay face up in the sand; the other was still upright; his throat pinned to the Great Tree by a crossbow bolt of unknown origin. His hands dangled limply, whilst his eyes bulged horribly– worse than Darian's monstrosity if you can believe it. Upon seeing the two corpses, the men without shields quickly gave way to those of them that did– save for myself. *Why was I not shield worthy?* Had they forgotten their new hero so swiftly? Either way, it seemed there were few of heart to lead the charge for, shield or no shield, I soon found myself ahead of the pack.

Grey clouds brimmed with wisps of orange as the sun kissed the crests of the highest dunes to the East. The clouds would dissolve shortly, as they always did. It would be light soon; though not soon enough for us perhaps. The bonfire was well-fed and burning brightly which made our surroundings even vaguer. Craning our eyes in vain, it was impossible not to imagine hidden foes within the mottled shadows dancing about us like leaves in the wind– which they very likely were as I consider it now.

"Hold!" Yelled Alde Baran as we neared the well, bringing our entourage to a merciful halt. Our adversaries held the advantage. It was only wise to stop. The circumstances were dire enough without wading forward foolishly. Baran carried nothing other than a small round shield which made me feel a bit better seeing as he wasn't even allotted a weapon. I was unsure which one of the two I would've chosen had I been given a choice. Which, for the record, I wasn't.

Baran's shield was emblazoned with a figurative tree; undoubtedly one of Myrna's creations. Perhaps, I should have visited her after all. I wasn't opposed to my likeness being painted upon a shield. It'd be akin to holding a sacrificial lamb should her talents from a distance have been up to the test. The Baran thing clearly had me flustered— the *not having yet killed him* thing as opposed to the ownership of apple trees which I cared nothing about. Just so we're clear. If only he'd take an arrow through the throat my spirits would have been raised. I had half a mind to dare them to fire whilst standing behind him but thought better of it. It was a bit cowardly. And what if they hit me? I had an oath to uphold.

Pushing past me, Darian handed Baran the heaviest broad sword I had ever seen. It was so big, the sword I'd been awarded felt like a dagger in comparison— making my dagger akin to a hairpin. A small hairpin that is. Unlike Petra's which was ridiculously large— and scary. The sword was so bulky Baran was forced to strap his shield merely to accept it.

Though undeniably magnificent, the sword seemed most impractical to me. Though a two-handed sword was unquestionably preferable during single combat, as per Petra's assertion regarding the assassin, arrows and crossbow bolts were a different story— especially in the half-light hours. In my mind, he'd have been far better off had he but the shield alone. I would have told him as much had I thought he'd consider lending it to me. If only for a short while which, judging by the fondness in his eyes, there was no chance of whatsoever. To be clear I wasn't jealous, I merely hated him more than I had but a moment or two ago. I should have snatched it from him in hindsight. He had taken my dagger after all. Stupid sword. I had no need of the spectacularly luminous double-edged thing— with a hilt that looked as though it'd fit my hands perfectly. Humph. I only hoped he'd trip over it, severing a leg in the process. At which point I'd claim it, albeit not without a fair bit of reluctance given the size and all.

"Loose the cat!" Baran commanded. The hissing creature was quickly carried warily outside— within its cage, of course— and set free. It crept from its cage most skeptically. If ever there was a time to avoid scratching its ears, it was now. Not that I had a mind to.

"Agatha looks thirsty," Darian noted, his one good eye staring into the darkness not unlike a sloth fox in a hen house. Or so I would imagine as they'd always steered clear of my own. Notwithstanding, only charlatans named their swords. A ridiculous undertaking. Not to mention unfair, I thought to myself, staring down at what could only have been called... *Rusty*.

Alde Baran laid the gleaming blade on his thigh as he crouched low beside his cat. Running his hand through her mottled grey stripes, he gave her rump a soft slap. Shortly thereafter two sounds were heard. *Phhhht,* followed by *flop*. Well, that was anti-climactic. The cat had only wandered about six yards when an arrow impaled its head and it fell sideways in a heap. Its legs twitched several times and then it lay still. Having pierced its eye, the arrowhead protruded from the backside of the creature's furry skull. Alternatively, the whites of the eye were forced outward which oddly, or perhaps not so oddly, reminded me of Darian– furry eyebrows included.

Admittedly, it was a bit unnerving for I could not have placed the arrow any better had I shot it from where I stood. As Alde Baran strode toward his fallen pet a barrage of arrows hit the ground ahead of him to block his path. He was so close to them that he parried the final one using the width of his sword. He was brave, I give him that; brave, but brash. Foolhardy with nary a doubt.

"Show yourselves!" Alde Baran demanded. "Show yourselves!" He hollered again crazed with anger. Darian walked forth to stand beside him. As for myself, I was not so keen; notwithstanding the notion of an arrow similarly piercing Baran's eye did not seem an unfavorable outcome. If only I was so fortunate.

"We are all in their crosshairs," Darian whispered. "We should dispatch archers from the opposite side and flank them." He urged.

"I would not recommend that," came a voice from behind us.

I turned and cringed upon seeing Alde Baran's wives standing ahead of their captors with knives at their throats. Petra and Renan were not amongst them. I was uncertain whether I should be thankful or not about that. Forcing myself to inhale a deep breath, I kept the Rage I felt mounting within me in check. This was no time for recklessness. I tapped my blade against my thigh counting only six of his seven wives present. Myrna was missing, busy painting undoubtedly. With luck, not in her own blood.

"Release them at once!" Alde Baran ordered without effect. His appearance quickly turned to one of utter dismay. "Where is Davos!" He barked aloud.

"Looking for me? I'm flattered," said Davos. "I'll going to

have this bitch first. Or her warm corpse, I'm not fussy that way."

Crushing my hopes, he stepped forward, pushing Petra ahead of him; one hand about her shoulder, the other twisting the long hair braid he'd wrapped around her neck. My hand slid immediately to my gold-handled dagger. Weirdly, my emotions turned to stone. My heart had become frozen in time. I judged him to be twenty paces away.

Nineteen, eighteen, seventeen. He stopped. *Come closer, just a wee bit closer.*

"What is the meaning of this, Davos?" Baran demanded.

"What is the meaning of anything?" Davos laughed. "Unlike you, I require no justification."

"You will die for this! You have my word!" Alde Baran threatened.

My own tongue remained lodged in my throat. Admittedly, a small part of me did fear for her wellbeing. Okay, so I did have strong feelings for her. What of it? I am human. She was beautiful, kind, witty, and generous. Not to mention, I loved the way she smelled and how she looked at me in the morning– night, rather– when it was that we awoke to be clear. Haeryn help me, it was precisely then, of all times, that I knew it to be true. I loved the woman. *There, I said it.* The point being, in times of great peril one needed to remain calm. Thus, if I allowed myself to wallow in such frivolous thoughts she'd undoubtedly be done for. I only wished I'd expressed my feelings more adamantly. Thankfully, I recalled the pebble and sandal thing. Surely, she knew; I did say as much.

"I got a better offer," Davos smiled cruelly. "They've come for you not me. I simply get the spoils."

"I will see you get your spoils. That I assure you, coward!" Baran spat.

"Coward, am I? You've been hiding in a hollow tree for five years– and you call me coward. Fool! I call it justice. And now, all I must do is watch you die. Seems easy enough." Davos countered, pushing himself to the forefront of the throng.

Fourteen, thirteen…

"If you were too terrified to fight me all you need do was say so, and I would have released you from my command," Baran taunted.

"Afraid– of you? You're afraid of your own shadow, Baran. No! You would have never awarded me a fair fight. One of your dogs would have blind-sided me. I'm no fool!" He hollered, twisting Petra's hair tighter about her throat as he took yet another step forward.

I did like it when her hair was down around her shoulders–

though not twisted about her neck so much. It made her look… less haughty. I made a mental note to tell her as much the first chance I had. Regardless, now was not the time, I reminded myself. *Focus you idiot, focus!*

Twelve…

And then it struck me. *Petra's hair!* I saw her hands fumbling at her waist and knew at once what she sought. Clever girl, she'd hidden it.

"You will pay for this! Release the women at once! They play no part in this." Asserted Alde Baran, streaking the air with his over-sized sword. With luck it would be mine once they killed him.

"Drop your weapons," came an unexpected response from the opposite direction causing us to whirl about. This side, that side; it was making me a bit dizzy in truth. Their silhouettes became increasingly discernible being that the dawn had begun to break. There were six of them, all dressed in black with their faces covered– not unlike Baran. All of them were brandishing glistening swords of superior quality– causing me to better assess the one I was carrying for the first time. *Rusty* may have been tarnished but it was sharp. It would kill.

"Come and take it," Alde Baran urged. "It is yours providing you have the courage to claim it." He held it broad-sided with his arm outstretched; the heavy sword's tip lay flat upon his shoulder. One of the men ahead of us laughed aloud. The others made no sound or movement.

"Fool's courage is not a game I play. But I have something else for you– yet another gift," the man said. "Bring him!" The faceless man commanded. One of his men scrambled forth dragging a man backwards by the hair. Though certain I'd seen him before, I couldn't say where.

"Don't you recognize him? My apologies, we did beat him rather severely. I think he said his name was Goran. To his credit, he did not say much else. Would you like him back alive, or should we add him to the pile?" He nodded toward the circular wall of skulls.

"Well, he obviously told you something because he led you straight to us." Alde Baran huffed. The man laughed in return.

"No. He didn't. We simply crossed paths unfortunately for him. Have you not read the sacred teachings of Muneakisa? And you call yourself learned. We've known of this place for centuries. Though we stop by only rarely. Why would we?" He shrugged.

"Who are you and what do you want? If you think we will throw down our swords simply because you cower behind hostages, you are sadly mistaken. We died long ago. We died the moment we chose to reside in such lands."

"You know who we are and why we've come. Don't try my patience. I despise the heat. The sun is rising; your time has run out."

"You're of the Brotherhood." Baran stated the obvious.

"And why have we come?"

"How the hell would I know?" Alde Baran spat in anger. "But enlighten me and perhaps we can end this foolish standoff."

"Standoff?" The man laughed aloud. "Hardly. But I'll play. There are four reasons we've come."

"*Four bounties*, rather." Baran corrected.

"What of it? We would never venture into such desolation for just one. Elsewise, we would have come for Elnath long ago."

"Elnath? It seems you've traveled all this way for naught for there is no one here that goes by that name." Alde Baran replied with cynical sadness.

"You call him, Darian. Darian One-Eye. I heard a giant carved the eye from his head with a spoon and ate it, refilling the vacant hole with a great gob of spit. Either way, if you'd turn your head ever so slightly, you'll notice him standing next to you."

"You will have to go through me to get to him," seethed Alde Baran.

"I have no issue with that," returned the man. "Elnath did not complete his task. The circle is incomplete. A wrong that must be righted. So, you too must die. Simplicity is a good thing."

"Ah, so already the lies begin to flow. But a moment ago you said you wouldn't come for just one and now you profess to knowing that the two of us were here all along."

"Fair enough. It's a very long way and sometimes the pair of you are here and sometimes you are not. As stated, I despise the heat. Be assured, between the two of us, you'll be lying soon enough… face down, buried deep in hot sand."

"Providing you leave everyone else alone, I will surrender myself forthwith," Darian stated.

"If it was only so easy," replied the stranger.

"It is," insisted Darian.

"No, it is not." Alde Baran interrupted. "These men hold no power here– and zero honour. They forsook that when they plotted and murdered the One Rah. You know what I speak is true."

"The One Rah died years ago," replied the man equally. "What's gone is gone. What's done is done. We now have Four Rahs.

Can you not count, Baran? Surely, four is better than one."

"So, you don't deny it?"

"I did not come to discuss history or debate petty grievances. The only thing I'm denying is your existence– along with three of your companions."

"Just take me and be done with it," sneered Darian. "It started with me. Let it end there."

"But it doesn't end there, does it?" sighed the man. "We also seek Petra Bryn. We don't care about the child. As far as the Brotherhood is concerned; children are ghosts yet to be born."

"You can have what's left of her after I'm done with the bitch and not before!" Davos swore. "I've taken a shine to her."

"Shut up Davos! That was not part of our agreement." The man attested. "Once we've collected our bounties, you may do as you wish *with the others*."

"She feels like my mine to me," barked Davos, hauling her forward. "Once my wick has been properly wetted you can have her. Quit squirming girl!" He hollered, shaking her hard. "Don't you worry, there'll be plenty of time for that soon enough." He sneered.

"Leave her be. She is not your property." The man ordered.

Nine paces, eight paces…

Davos was fully enraged. He wanted his prize and was not about to give her up without a fight. I had no problem with that. The fight that is– I'd had more than my fill of him touching Petra.

Eight paces it is.

Looking Petra in the eyes, I gave her the slightest of nods. Immediately she hunched down as low as she was able. Davos turned his head just in time to meet my glorious dagger. Apparently, it wasn't too beautiful to be thrown after all. Having pulled and flung it in a single motion it flew just as I thought it would– straight and true. Perfectly balanced, it sunk deep into the middle of his forehead as though but soft wood. There could be no doubting it. Twas a thing of beauty if ever there was. Not the dagger sticking out of his head, that was gruesome– but rather the ivory on gold sparkling in stark contrast to dark flowing red. So many of us fail to notice the simpler beauties life sometimes affords us. It was rather sad in truth.

Ruining the moment, Petra wriggled free to stab him in his arms and chest several times with her hair pin as he fell. *Pierce, pierce, pierce. Puncture, puncture, puncture.* I would have to have a word with her. What point was there to such needless violence? The man was clearly dead. Walking over, I had to twist my dagger to retrieve it. To send a clear message, I cut open his chest and forcibly ripped out his heart– tossing it into the sand while blood still spurted from it. *Don't touch my girl!* Woman, rather. Don't act surprised. I told you from the very onset of this tale that I was not a good person. Swiping two bloody fingers diagonally across my face, I let them know precisely who they were dealing with. Red Radesh stood before them in the flesh. It all felt so nostalgic I felt a bit teary-eyed in truth. *Emotions and such.* What a strange animal they could be at times.

Tearing a sleeve off his djellaba, I wiped my hands. After cleansing the blade, I sheathed it. It was done. Davos was with the cat now. Wherever that might be. I only hoped it would terrorize him in the afterlife– should there be such a thing. I was not a big believer myself. Either way, it was his fault. Davos, that is. He had it coming. He should never have riled me to such an extent. Clutching Petra's arm, I pulled her behind me.

"So, it is agreed," I said loudly. "Petra's going nowhere. I will cut out every heart that tries." Truth be told, my own heart was pounding rather fiercely. Admittedly, the heart throwing thing was a tad excessive. It was all I could do to keep the Rage at bay. I exhaled slowly, counting my heartbeats purposely in an effort to slow them.

Four, five, six… nine, ten, eleven… fourteen, fifteen… nineteen… breathe. In my defence, they were hard to count while retaining my composure at the same time. I heard clapping and turned to see the faceless man with hands raised high. It seemed he did not have a problem with me killing Davos. Once his theatrics ceased, he called out to me.

"What if you accompany her? You are her escort are you not?" He seemed totally unfazed by the sandy heart ahead of him which I noticed had stopped spurting. Okay, so I may have jumped the dagger a bit in that respect. Either way, *now* Davos was dead– most definitely dead, there was no refuting it. His heart had stopped.

"Or are you still feigning to be one of us– one of the Brotherhood? It was a good ruse. You do seem to have the necessary skill set." He added sardonically.

"I am more than her escort. I am her champion." I added vainly. "I am whatever she needs me to be. And she will most certainly accompany me– though you will not." To my surprise, it felt good to declare my love so openly in front of all those gathered. It was as though a tremendous weight had been lifted from my shoulders. I didn't care who else might know– just as long as she did.

"Ugh," he groaned. "That's not going to work either,

unfortunately. The fact of the matter is, we've come for you too. You killed one of our own– Edasich of North Verdun. That same man who you now pretend to be; and for that you must answer."

Yes, yes, yes; whatever. I barely heard him. What mattered was, Petra now knew how I truly felt about her. For Haeryn's sake, I'd decreed it aloud. As much as I would have liked to turn about and see her look at me all *starry-eyed,* I didn't dare risk it. Not to worry, I was quite certain it would prove to be a moment we'd relive fondly as the years went by– providing we survived. How I'd gone from *maybe she's not all bad* to *hands off she's mine* so quickly, I'll never know. To no fault of my own, undeniably, my focus was still drifting here and there at times. In my defence, I'd never been in love before.

"As for the rest of you," he declared loudly. "We don't care. We have no quarrel with you. Stay here; leave; do as you wish." He shrugged. "Just allow us to collect our bounties and we'll be gone. It's a fair proposition; not to mention the only one by which you remain living. To stand in our way is to die. My archers await my command. It would be unwise to aggravate me further. We will cut every last throat should you even blink with defiance. Now, what will it be? Life? Or death?"

"Death." I hollered distractedly. I felt Petra jab me harshly in the ribs. "Your death," I further explained. She did have a point. There was something to be said for clarity, especially in times like these.

"I will kill you first!" I shouted; just to be sure no one mistook my intentions. Notwithstanding, my ribs were still a bit tender from the continual onslaught of finger pokes. *What?* They add up over time.

"If I didn't know you to be the Golan Butcher I'd be laughing right now. I admit, you've made yourself quite a reputation. But don't expect your antics to make an impression upon us. We earn our living tossing hearts in the sand."

"The Golan Butcher?" Queried Alde Baran, turning his face to mine.

"It's him!" spoke up Goren. I dare say, I'd thought he'd stopped breathing until that moment. Goren that is. Davos was dead.

"Shut up!" Barked one of the assassins pulling him backwards him by the hair and putting a knife to his throat.

"Let him speak," commanded their leader. "It seems he has something to say, after all." His henchman relaxed his grip, spinning his fancy dagger before sheathing it. I had to quash an urge to pull mine and show him how to do it properly. Haeryn knows I could have put mine through his eye had I but the tiniest inkling to do so. Just ask

Davos. *Umm, skip that.* I kept forgetting. You could plainly see his heart had ceased beating. It was lying right there; though rather gooey looking, it lay still as a stone.

"I know him!" Goren spat. "Everyone knows him where I come from. He's the Butcher alright! I recognize her too! Me and another chum... *wanted a word* with her. But he got between us. They say he's killed more men than anyone alive. You saw what he did with that dagger. They call him Red Radesh in Gadev! Does he side with us, Baran? I don't trust him." He spat.

Talk about calling the kettle black. As if trying to buttonhole a young maiden somehow equated to *wanting a word*. Had I but the slightest more space I would have added him to my list. The jig was up; but that didn't matter now. Alde Baran didn't matter. His wives didn't matter. Darian didn't matter. All that mattered was saving Petra and Renan– wherever the little fellow was. *If he was!* I'd completely forgot about him. Some father I was. Apparently, Alde Baran and Darian felt elsewise for they both turned to stare at me. Baran rubbed his forehead deep in thought.

"Radesh? Is it you? No! It can't be! Th-that's impossible." Alde Baran stammered. "It's just not possible. I would have known. You perished in the flames."

Darian's working eye twisted about in circles as he studied me. Twas more than rude. I must say, I had half a mind to cut the pair of them down right then and there. You know... that *pierce, pierce, pierce, puncture, puncture, puncture* thing. Or *pierce, puncture, stab, stab, stab.* I cared not. They were pushing my patience for certain.

"Guilty as charged," I admitted. "I can explain– though, if you haven't noticed, we've more pressing matters at hand."

"I don't know what all the fuss is about," spat the Assassin leader. "It's not like he's Oswald."

"Who in Haeryn's Halls is Oswald?" I asked. Things were getting a tad confusing. I was finding it hard to keep pace with it all. My mind was corrupted by love. I had no time for such pettiness.

"Yet another mad bull I will end," mumbled Baran curtly.

"You've never heard of Oswald? Surely, you jest."

"No disrespect intended. You might ask him to step forth if he's so important." I encouraged. Which fetched me another quick jab in the ribs from *you know who*. Honestly, her fingers were so pointy I thought she might have used her hairpin that time.

"He's not of the Brotherhood," the assassin leader admitted. "He's the rebel dog's champion warrior. I've met him. He's a monster of a man. Be assured, he'd make short work of you."

"Would he now? But he's not here; how bloody convenient." It was my turn to spit. It was customary in such instances after all. In fact, I'd attended negotiations were nothing was said at all. Just spit, spit, spit, spit, spit until everyone's mouth was so parched, they couldn't have squeezed a word out had they tried. Just a circle of crusty beards and wet moustaches making faces at one another– and zero progress.

"It's him!" Darian suddenly declared overzealously. "I cannot believe it, but it is true. I recognize him now. Though he was but a lad at the time, the eyes never lie."

"Him who?" I asked completely dumbfounded. "I confess already, my name is Radesh– Red Radesh, some call me though I'm far from proud of it."

"It is him? I'm certain of it!" Darian's tongue wagged.

"Are you deaf? Did I not just say as much? I am the soldier known as the Golan Butcher. What does it matter now? Look around, there are bigger fish in need of frying. I am not the one holding a knife to anyone's throat. Have no fear, I am on your side." I contended.

"Radesh from a small unnamed village outside of Gadev?" Alde Baran inquired. His voice was near to a whimper. What? Of all times, *now* he remembers.

"Yes, but I ask you again; what does that matter NOW?" I shouted. I was getting angry if you couldn't tell.

"Is this true, Petra?" Alde Baran asked, looking past me as though I suddenly ceased to exist.

"It is as he said," Petra answered, poking out her head from behind me. Instantly, I felt calmed. She was so adorable. It took all my willpower not to smile. Thank Haeryn I didn't though. Having said all I said about her, I felt foolish enough already.

"Though he may not be who he feigned to be, rest assured; he is my escort. Anything he might have done was solely to ensure our wellbeing. Renan!" She hollered, placing a hand to her brow.

"Where is Renan? Radesh!" She pleaded as if I might magically know his whereabouts.

"I will find him." I assurer her, turning to go.

"Halt!" Yelled the assassin chieftain. "One more step and ten arrows will split her heart." I froze while resisting the urge to clarify he intended *exactly ten*, no more no less, not nine or eleven perhaps.

"It was you that I met searching the ashes of your home, wasn't it?" Darian begged of me.

Not this gibberish again! I needed to find Renan– but my hands were tied. *Metaphorically speaking,* of course. My hands were free to do as I pleased– only Petra's life had been threatened so they may as well have been tied, if you get my meaning. Don't feel bad. *Words.* They could be a real den of foxes at times– not a real den of foxes, just hard to decipher is all. It had been my hope that Petra had hidden Renan somewhere. Obviously, she hadn't. She didn't even know where he was. This changed everything. Though not so much for Darian apparently.

"You did not die in that fire. You lied to me when you recited your own name while pointing to those graves. You are *that exact* Radesh. Are you not?" Darian grilled me.

"What of it? You were a stranger, and I was a lad. As Baran said when I first arrived– only a fool would blindly trust a stranger. No offense intended."

"What is this about?" The leader of the Brotherhood demanded impatiently. "If this is some sort of hoax it will mark your end. I detest sand near as much as I detest the heat. I swear, do not test me."

It was then that Alde Baran knelt with head bowed and held out his broad sword in front of me with both hands. Darian and the Brotherhood leader were muttering back and forth though I barely heard them. All I saw was Alde Baran's enormous blade. He was offering it to me freely. Thus, I strode boldly forward and took it. The back of his scarred neck called for me to claim that too. Life is a strange animal. One could never predict the future. There is nothing in this world stranger than truth. How did my mother put it? *An eye full of truth can deafen the ears.* Or something like that.

In any case, my moment of reckoning had arrived in a fashion no one could ever have imagined. All that I longed for was being served to me on a silver platter. Not a real silver platter but– you get it. All I had to do was take it– his head that is. Having every right, I had every intention of doing just that. I took a deep breath. *Whatever you do, do not look at Petra.* I told myself. Then, of course, I turned and looked straight at Petra. Her face was white with terror.

"Don't," she mouthed. *But how could I not?* It was impossible to stifle my flourishing thoughts of revenge.

"Whom do you serve?" Darian repeated to the leader of the Brotherhood. Not that I really heard him the first time. I was too busy salivating.

"Whatever are you on about?" The leader protested. "I swear if this is a trick."

"I assure you this is no trick. This is the Heir of Harbinger! Did you not swear an oath of loyalty to his family crest?" Darian probed dramatically.

"The Heir of Harbinger? There is no heir! Deshu Mogashu died with his parents in Standstill Pass! It is known."

"Why? Were you there? Did you kill him yourself?"

"No, I was not there. But I know he died. We all know he died!" Their leader admonished.

"No, he did not die! Because I was there. *We* were there– Baran and I. We killed those that murdered The One Rah and his wife. But their infant son survived. They'd hidden him in a wooden crate."

"No! I would know that if it were true! The Brotherhood knows all."

"It was the BroZil that killed them, you fool! And you know nothing because we told no one. Audre of Eyre raised him in secret in a small village just outside of Gadev. It was she who'd cleverly named him, Radesh!"

"Though, you didn't even know him until but a moment ago– not until we arrived to collect our bounties. How very convenient is that I ask?"

"We thought he'd perished in a fire at the age of eight. It's only become apparent to us now– at this very moment in time– that he did not in fact die. This is him! With Haeryn as my witness, I swear to you– this is Rah Deshu Mogashu in the flesh!"

"So, the Golan Butcher is the One Rah?" He spat. "And Haeryn is my long lost father." He ridiculed.

"On my life, I swear it to be true."

"On your life will it be for I don't believe you. You think me a fool?" The leader scowled. "I have not the patience for this! Archers! Take aim at the four of them! I've heard enough of this camel dung."

"Think!" Shouted Darian. "Who could devise such a tale? No one!"

"And yet you did." The man spat again.

"Answer me this, then. When has Alde Baran ever stooped to using deception? Never! If you know anything about him, you know this to be true. His pride alone would never allow it. Why do you think we've been holed up here for so long? Because Baran has been torturing himself ever since we thought the boy lost! He blames himself for all of it."

"Enough!" Shouted Alde Baran. "You will have proof enough momentarily." His voice fell soft and as he spoke a chilling silence took hold of all those near enough to hear his words.

"I am sorry, Rah Deshu. I failed you, just as I failed your father before and, in doing so, shamed Harbinger and all her people. I offer no apologies for there is no absolution to be found for such a crime. If you will allow me the courtesy of my own final sentencing– I hereby do pronounce myself guilty of abandonment by reason of negligence– punishable by death. As attested earlier by Darian, Agatha is thirsty. Please, I beg of thee– end my suffering; end my ineptitude. I have failed you for the final time. I have no more to say. Take my head and leave it for the scorpions. It is not worthy of the wall."

"No! You cannot!" Cried Darian. "You devoted your entire life to the glory of Harbinger and the One Rah. None of what's occurred was any fault of yours!"

"Tell that to my mother." I stated calmly. "What you suggest about my past is nothing less than preposterous. Clearly, the sun has fried your brains. But I care not. I accept your pronouncement and will gladly deliver the requested punishment. But not for failing Harbinger or the One Rah. I will take your head purely for stomping my mother to death. For that, and no other reason, shall you die."

It was happening. There was no turning back now.

"I accept your conditions willingly," said Alde Baran. He outstretched his neck without looking up. As I raised the broadsword, Darian threw himself at my feet, tears flowing– even from his bad eye as he pleaded for his companion's life. I was unmoved.

"Do not do this, I beg you," he wept. "I respect you envision Audre of Eyre as your mother, but she was not. It is true that Alde Baran did kill her– but I swear on my life it was an accident. There is no malice in him. He did not mean to do it!"

"You were not there!" I screamed, shaking the hefty sword in his face with both hands. "She was my mother! You have no right to call her else! And it was *no accident!*" I hollered. "How do you accidentally stomp someone? And there is malice in him for I have witnessed it firsthand!"

"Let it be, Darian," Alde Baran whispered gently. "Let it go, my friend. He's right. I did kill her. I deserve to die. I wanted to die for it then."

"Yes, and you were determined to," Darian replied. "You brought the body of King Turin's daughter back to him on her own shield. You begged him to take your life. But he refused you– *her own father refused you.*" Darian implored.

"Knowing the history between the pair of you, he threw you in the Hold until, finally, you confessed what really happened that day. He then sentenced you to seven years of hard labour– releasing you after three. *Why?* For having recognized that it was the warrior's sickness that caused the tragedy. Because he could no longer stomach the look on your face. As he put it, *No one in the Isles can rest while your ceaseless parade of agony persists.*"

"None of it matters now. I have failed. My past has finally caught up to me. No longer can I hide, pretending to be some forgotten recluse. I've no life to return to. I've endured enough shame in this world for ten lifetimes." Alde Baran said, shaking his head sadly.

"Not to forget, I kicked the One Rah in the face whilst buried up to his neck in sand. For that grievance alone should I die a thousand times over."

My hands trembled terribly as I listened to their words, It was all too much. No longer able to bare the weight of the sword, I slammed it down between the pair of them and fell to my knees with head in hands. I knew the warrior's illness only too well. Had it not been for my earlier conversations with Petra I surely would have killed him. I may yet have done so had she not been present. Still, the more I considered things, the more my resolve began to weaken. Why did I despise him so greatly? Was it because of my mother or because he'd left me to the wolves? What difference did it make? I hated him because he reminded me of my past. Perhaps, myself even– the person I'd become devoid of any guidance.

"What? So, there's to be no beheading after all?" the Brotherhood leader inquired dejectedly before continuing.

"Oh well, changes nothing, the four of you are still on my list. Admittedly, this is all very touching but, the sun is bloody rising. We need to sort our differences swiftly." I ignored him completely; as did Baran and Darian.

"I don't understand," I snorted, being as near to crying openly as I ever recall. Still, I needed to hear it from his mouth. I needed to hear him say the words.

"What happened? I saw what you did– but why? Why did you do it?" I croaked hoarsely. "Why? Why? Why?"

"A horrid dream," gasped Alde Baran. "Bad dreams without end. I am tormented by them. I relive them whenever sleeps finds me. It all began, so long ago, while building Haeryn's Wall. All but three of a hundred died that night– attacked while we slept– I was stabbed four times. He tore his djellaba open.

"Here and here and here and here," he pointed to various places on his chest while still averting my eyes. His face and skin depicted a tapestry of pain. I could barely make out the scars for a steady stream of burn marks. They were everywhere. Row upon row of the same brand seemingly without end.

"Though I do not plead for mercy, I dreamt it was happening *that night*. It repeats endlessly in my head and only for your benefit will I recount the tale. I thought I was being stabbed *again and again and again*. I felt blood dripping from my torso just as I had so very long ago. Thinking myself surrounded by the dead and dying, a mindless fury within me erupted. It saved my life the first time. This time, it destroyed all that I loved– the only woman I'd ever cherished. To this day, I don't recall anything about it in truth. I only know what I saw upon opening my eyes. I saw what I'd done and a part of me died. And then I saw you. I'd killed the daughter of the King of the Isles, my closest companion, and the only mother you'd ever known."

"So, it was the Red Rage?" I needed to clarify. How many times had I awoke from battle, blood-soaked, unable to recall anything? I sorely wanted it to be the Red Rage. As horrible as the event remained, I supposed I could come to terms with that– *eventually*. It was akin to being an animal. The beast lurking within was wholly devoid of logic. In this lone instance, the Red Rage made sense if only for its utter senselessness. Like a Harbinger cat incensed with the smell of prey except– upon being loosed, the Rage could never be tamed. It had to run its course, burn itself out, if you will.

"I don't know what that is," he said. "It was a bad dream. They're far worse now and endless. But I make no excuses. It wasn't blood lust if that's what you intend. The sad truth is, I thought I was fighting for my life. I wasn't."

It wasn't the answer I wanted. I understood his point, but he had far more to answer for. A bad dream didn't cut it. Save for Petra, my entire life felt but a tragic dream.

"But then you left with nary a word and never returned!" I blathered aloud.

"I did. I felt you were no longer safe in my company. I wasn't sure anyone was. I sent word to Darian to ensure your wellbeing though the message was delayed. Understand, I had to atone for what I'd done. Albeit harbour no misconceptions for I did not mean to return. I'd killed the only woman who'd ever loved me. You asked me if I'd ever been wed *before*. Audre wanted us to be wed, but I refused. Knowing I could not father children of my own, I wasn't about to take that from her. Moreover, there were several sizable bounties on my head. I was trying to stop civil war from erupting and rarely home. That's not the sort of man you marry. That's the sort you run from."

It was then that Darian rose and hauled me forcibly to my feet.

"Whom do you serve?" He asked in a loud voice waving his hands upward with enthusiasm before kneeling beside Alde Baran.

"The One Rah! Rah Deshu!" The unexpected answer was so loud, I nearly fell over. Wiping a multitude of tears from my eyes, I saw weapons being tossed into the sand everywhere about me. And then everyone began to kneel. Everyone. *Even Petra.* As if I didn't feel uncomfortable enough.

"He's not the One Rah! This is a farce. A farce I will abruptly end!" A voice called out. *Okay, so not quite everyone kneeled.*

Though the few assassins I was able to envision had knelt as well, their leader hadn't. Snatching the crossbow from the back of the hunched form ahead of him, he took aim at me and fired. Stunned by disbelief for all that was happening around me, I found myself unable to move. Alde Baran reacted.

"I will not fail you again!" He shouted.

Throwing his body into mine, he knocked me to the ground. Oddly, though he'd saved my life for certain, all I could think of at the time was how warm the sand felt upon my face. I'd clearly lost my wits. I felt strangely at peace. I could not have summoned the Rage even had I wanted to. Though I knew he'd been gravely hurt, I ignored him. I lay there staring at Davos' heart. We were the same, motionless and still. *They'd bowed down to me.* It was utter madness— as though I'd somehow ventured into another world entirely.

Petra later told me that Darian rushed the Brotherhood leader with Agatha in hand. While the assassin leader hastened to reload his crossbow, the man he'd snatched it from rose to block his path.

"Shoot him!" Their leader commanded. "Kill them all!"

"No!" The man shouted back. "The One Rah has risen!"

"Don't be a fool!!" He bellowed. "We serve the Four! Kill them…"

It was then that Agatha's thirst was quenched as Darian severed his head with a magnificent sweeping blow. I believe she'd referred to it as gruesome in truth. She described how his headscarf twisted as it fled his face, separating itself from the remainder of his torso. I must say, it was those types of small details that I appreciated most. Rolling over, I did see Darian clear the blade's fullers by smacking its flat side against his knee tarnishing the yellow sand before him. It made me smile. Undoubtedly, I did look foolish.

"Are there any others who still wish to follow the Four?" He spat. "Assassins of the Brotherhood!" He hollered. "I command you to uphold the sacred oath of old! Kill any amongst you who refuse to bend the knee! The Gods have not deserted us for the Heir of Harbinger has been reborn!"

A small band broke rank and began backing away with weapons drawn. They did not get far. Two of them being swiftly struck by a flurry of bolts to the chest. A third man's arm was severed prior to his chest being impaled from behind by Goren. A fourth man wisely knelt confirming his allegiance— *to me*. Which is why I still found it hard to move at the time. It was all so preposterous.

Hearing hurried footsteps, I turned to see a man rushing toward me. A thrown sword split his chest from behind and he fell face down upon the sand. Ruok stepped forth. After bowing low, he arose to reclaim it. Oddly, the blade mimicked a quivering cross.

"Don't anybody move, or I'll slit her throat!" Yet another voice called out.

Fearing for Petra's safety awoke me from my daze. Scrambling to my feet, I turned just in time to witness an arrow pierce the man's left eye. I watched Greta fling his limp arm off her neck casually before kicking him in the groin. Pulling the arrow harshly back out of his eye, she then returned it to the quiver hanging at his side. She did not look the least bit perturbed. In fact, after he'd fallen to the ground, she gave him two or three stomps for good measure.

"One Rah! One Rah! One Rah!" The chants erupted all around me now that they could see me standing tall. *Standing tall?* In all honesty, my legs shook terribly.

As implausible as it seemed, it was clear, all those that remained, Brotherhood included, *served me*. Even given my present state of mind, *mindlessness* rather; the decisiveness of their actions did not go unnoticed. Based solely upon a fanciful yarn, they'd not only made a critical choice under extreme duress but suppressed a revolt at the same time. As I was to find out later, they were very adept at that sort of thing. Namely, *killing upon short notice*.

Alde Baran had awoken as well. His hands clawed at his back as he twisted from side to side. The bolt had gone straight through the shield slung over his back. He could not reach it. A stream of foamy-looking blood oozed downward from the shield's midst. Spurting sounds could be heard each time he took a breath. I'd witnessed similar injuries many times prior. All of them had died. But a short while earlier I would have felt myself favoured by the Gods.

Contrarily, it was remorse that took a firm hold of my heart.

"Are you alright?" He gagged. "Are you hurt?" The fool inquired of me with genuine concern.

"Confused as hell but otherwise fine." I confirmed. "Unlike you." Though I didn't want to tell him, he'd been lung shot for certain.

"I had it c-coming," he gurgled. "I deserve it. I only hope it's slow and painful."

"Shut it!" I barked. "You're not getting off that easy. Greta!" I hollered. There was little need for she was already at my side.

"Save this impotent bastard!" I made sure to scowl down at him as I said it. Having been confirmed as his superior I wanted to make damn sure that he knew it.

"I don't want to live," he sputtered.

"You're not going anywhere," I said, bending down and poking him in the forehead harshly. "I didn't just inherit all Harbinger only to watch you die now," I whispered. "No, I have chores for you, my friend; a very long list indeed." Greta knelt beside him and shook her head forlornly.

"Found men with this injury before have I. Healed them, I have not." She acknowledged. Hunching low, I grasped her shoulder firmly.

"Listen to me, Greta. You must save him— whatever it takes."

"The Gods are cruel," she replied, snapping the protruding arrowhead as though a frail twig.

"Not solely the gods," winced Baran. "Perhaps, a bit of warning next time." He shuddered uncomfortably.

"I think not." Greta berated him. *Husband and wife.* It was refreshing to see such an open and honest relationship. Perhaps, there was hope for us yet. Glancing to where I'd last seen Petra, I found she was gone. Reaching into a pocket, Greta retrieved some form of root and put in her mouth. After chewing on it for a while, she packed it around the bolt protruding from his chest.

"Send me to hell where I b-belong," gasped Baran.

"You heard him. You must save him or how else might I put him through hell." Baran laughed so hard he nearly choked. Rolling Baran onto his side, Greta cleared the spittle from his mouth with her chubby fingers.

"That one is my tongue," hissed Baran.

"On your side must you lay," Greta huffed, raising her hand as if she might slap him. Which she did not to my mounting dismay.

"You don't suppose. If you hadn't noticed, there's an arrow sticking out of my chest." He spat again angrily.

All things considered, save for the life and death thing, I found their conversation rather comical. At least he could still spit. That was a good sign. Admittedly, the entire episode had me feeling perplexed. What if he wasn't my father? What if all he attested was true? I had no idea what fuelled their absurd assertions, though I was far from a fool. It did seem in my best interests to play along. Whatever the case may be, as ludicrous as it was, they did seem sincere. *Fools.*

Though I recognized that the truth of things would surface soon enough, I saw little other recourse than to assume command. Given the circumstances, I would continue the farce. *What other choice was there?* As it stood, I envisioned no other way out of our current predicament. The ruse was so outrageous, it defied logic. Conceivably, not unlike cleansing the Pail, that was why it had captured everyone's attention so completely. Though they hardly seemed the type, perhaps that was why Baran, and Darian, had conjured the tale in the first place. Regardless of their rationale, I must admit their acting was nothing short of superb.

As if we didn't have enough on their minds already, it was then that Myrna fled Grumble screaming like the mad woman she was— only more so. Relief washed over me to see Renan held tightly in her arms. I heard Petra scream. Upon looking closer, my heart sank. There was blood all over them both.

"They've lit fire to the Rookery!" She hollered. "The Rookery is ablaze!"

Everything became a blur after that with so many of us shouting and running at once. Not to mention the sun had risen. If not for Grumble's shadow the heat would have been insufferable.

"Renan!" Petra and I howled in unison.

"What happened? How badly is he hurt?" I blathered. Darian and I nearly tripped over one another whilst sprinting toward her. Though Myrna appeared frantic, she did not appear to be suffering. Thus, I feared all the blood to be Renan's. Even considering the heat, my skin suddenly felt numb with cold.

"What? He's not hurt. It's crimson root. 'Tis paint!"

"Thank the heavens," sighed Petra with palpable relief as she took the infant from her.

"He's not hurt in the slightest. Upon seeing the threat, I thought it best we feign to be dead. But they did torch the Rookery. That much is true." she reaffirmed sadly.

"Who did?" Darian barked. I could now see a steady stream of smoke billowing from the Crow's nest.

"I don't know who they were but there were three of them," she answered. "As we snuck out of the Red Room, I saw them refilling their water slings. Then they lit the fire and fled. I flung crimson root on the fire, but it only made it worse. It'll take a miracle to save it!"

"Should the tree burn, the lot of us will perish," I grimaced. I turned to look at Darian for guidance. *Foolishly*, I might have added.

"What? You're the Rah– not me." He shrugged. Undeniably, I did lose my mind at that point. Raising both hands to the sky, I shouted aloud in a crazed state.

"Make it rain!" I thundered aloud idiotically. A couple men looked upward as if it might possibly happen, though most just turned to gawk at me with puzzled looks. Darian took over thankfully.

"You heard him! Form a fire brigade! Fetch buckets! Make a line! Get that fire out and swiftly!" After which men began scrambling back and forth hurriedly.

"Pour whatever you can find on it– just so long as it's wet! I don't care if it's baobab jelly! Put it out!" he bellowed.

"But no crimson root!" Myrna yelled through cupped hands.

"Quite right. No paint! Do not use the paint!" Darian barked, reaffirming her instruction.

"I would appreciate a drink later," I said, tugging Darian's sleeve meaningfully. Petra shook her head sadly in disbelief. Ignoring her slight, I tugged harder twice more before getting his full attention.

"What? Oh, yes of course. No ale or wine either!" He roared. "Not all of it anyway!" He then turned his wandering eye on me.

"Make it rain. You didn't actually think that would work, did you?" He asked, motioning toward the heavens.

"How should I know," I snapped. "I've never been a Rah before."

"They're more akin to Kings than Gods. Did you hear him, Baran? Make it rain," He mumbled whist walking away to better organize the line. Though the men were passing buckets back and forth swiftly, there was far too much spillage. I motioned Myrna closer. Unexpectedly, she brought one of the Brotherhood with her as she did.

"Who's he?" I asked.

"If not for him, Renan and I would be dead," she replied.

"What is your name?" I asked.

"Grus," he answered.

"I swear Grus, I would ordain you the new leader of the Brotherhood were not another more deserving. I have a different task for you however."

"Name it, One Rah. I will see it done." He pounded a fist against his chest. Though I very nearly laughed, I must say I did appreciate his earnestness.

"Your task is unending. Protect Petra and my son, Renan. Pick two of your best and my gratitude will forever be yours."

"Upon my honour, One Rah. On pain of death," he said, bowing low and striding away though he did not get far prior to returning.

"Who is Petra?" He asked hesitantly.

"Over there." I pointed. "Petra!" I called out for noticing her walking away. I waved at her pleadingly. Walking over, she bowed awkwardly. Even amidst the turmoil, I found it hard not to grin– though I didn't dare. She did not look in the mood for any kind of theatrics. In her defence, I expect bowing with an infant in one's arms would be a tad cumbersome.

"Petra, meet Grus. He helped safeguard Renan." Returning my attention to Grus. "Protect them always from this day forth."

"With my life," he bowed low again. I may have got off to a bit of a rough start, but I felt I was getting the knack of this Rah thing now. Petra started to leave but I grabbed her shoulder.

"I have need of you. Baran is badly hurt."

"I must attend to Renan after which I shall return, One Rah." She bowed again while holding Renan aloft. I thought I detected a scowl, but it quickly disappeared– as did she. Something about her last bow seemed even more suspect. I decided to pull Grus aside.

"When you get a moment, you might try teaching her how to bow properly. You're rather adept at it." He looked as though I was serious causing me to shake my head in alarm.

"No. No. No. I was jesting. Don't you dare. It'd be the death of us both." I cautioned him. Perhaps I should have chosen someone else, I mused heading back toward Greta and Baran. So much had happened in such a short span and yet there was Baran still lying in the sand. *Dying in the sand,* more likely. Though I was gone but a moment, he looked much worse than when I'd left him.

"Do everything you can, Greta," I pleaded. "Petra will help; she is clever. Everyone is at your disposal. If there's anything you require all you need do is ask."

"Inside we need to be, some place less hot, less sandy; and lots and lots of water." Her face did not look even vaguely optimistic.

"I'm afraid we're stuck here until the damn fire is out."

"Hell knows n-not time," sputtered Alde Baran. "The f-flames of Haeryn c-call for me."

"I command you not to speak," I stated. "I command you to live." I'd never seen a greyer face. Surprisingly, Darian returned at the same time as Petra. She looked flustered though I had no time for it.

"The fire is nearly out, but the damage is great." Darian sighed. "Both the Rookery and Pail are destroyed. Well, the Pail was destroyed many times prior. That is, until you polished it."

"Well said. I was just about to contest that last bit."

"I do believe you are the first Rah to scrub a dung bowl."

"It remains my single greatest accomplish."

"Forever shall we sing of it." He saluted before banging a fist against his chest.

"Now that my true identity has been revealed, I know where your dagger is."

"My dagger. You mean the one I gave to Baran; the one I was looking for that day when you feigned to have died."

"Like father like son." I quipped. "And all this time I thought you'd been looking for me."

"Well, that too though it's hardly my fault you lied."

"That's where the dagger is. Within the last grave I pointed to."

"Right then, I'm off. I'll just go and fetch that right now then." Shuffling from left to right, he feigned marching away while remaining stationary. I swear, even Haeryn must have laughed at that. Not Petra, she looked as stoic as the sea of sand surrounding us.

"So, how bad is it?" Greta and Darian turned in unison. "I mean Grumble. Haeryn knows, Baran is grumpy at the best of times."

"Half the Galley's been cooked. Grumble's north-eastern hide has been badly scorched. It was a wonder we got the fire out. Thank Haeryn, Myrna came when she did. Had it rose any higher we'd never have stopped it. It does seem habitable for the most part. That said, the Gods are cruel. Here's praying it doesn't fall upon the first fierce wind. Fortunately for us, the Gods and winds have been favourable of late."

"We need Baran inside. Greta needs somewhere clean."

"The south side is still accessible and, for the most part, intact. It's smoky within but clearing quickly. The men are reinforcing the Rook as best they can. I doubt we'll be able to reside here much longer. We've lost a lot of our food stores."

"Food stores can be replenished."

"Aye, but is it worth it?" Darian sighed. "Might it not be better to make a run for it whilst Grumble still stands?"

"We need time. We need a plan. Not to mention, Baran is unfit for travel. Have him moved to Harem's Hold for the time being. Ensure Greta has all she requires. Have the rest of his wives relocate to The Crown or Sand Pit– being that the cat is no more. Petra and I will relocate to the Hold to help care for Baran."

"I cannot stay there," cried Petra unexpectedly. "I cannot stay with you!" She ran off with Grus chasing after her. I turned to Darian expectedly.

"Don't look at me," he said. "I know nothing about women. I haven't spoken to my own wife for years. In fact, it's been so long I'm fearful to return."

"Wait. What? You have a wife?"

"Aye, and four children."

"Four?" I echoed in disbelief.

"Aye, but there not like Renan. They're grown. They're big. Very big. Just ask Baran." I turned my attention to Alde Baran who simply stared at me. Then, I remembered.

"I command you to speak again."

"Big goes without s-saying. Big runs in the f-family." Baran nodded uncomfortably.

Though I could tell there was far more to the story, Petra was my major concern at that moment. I needed her on my side. I needed her beside me like never before. Previously, I'd largely relied on my sword and brute strength as opposed to my cunning.

"You know women. What's troubling Petra?" He motioned that he needed a drink. Fetching a water sling, I held it to his lips.

"Water?" He spat. "Wine!" He insisted turning his face away.

"Drink!" I ordered. He did so, reluctantly.

"You are the One Rah now." He rattled. "She is no fool. Rahs do not c-consort with c-commoners. She feels abandoned. She'll n-not be anyone's m-mistress."

"She feels all of that?" I asked bewildered. I must confess, it was not what I'd expected. At least not so soon. I hadn't even come to terms with my new promotion let alone all it might entail. I didn't even believe it myself. Yet, there she was already out of sorts over it. *Women.* As the old proverb went *you can't live without them knowing where you live.*

"But what do I do? I need her. She's everything to me." Embarrassing as was to admit, I felt stymied as usual.

"T-talk to h-her." He panted.

"And say what exactly?"

"You're the Rah," he gurgled. "Say w-what you like." He

stammered whilst fighting for breath. *Not that again*. I had no time for the riddles of the bedridden.

"Pleeeease." I urged. "What might I say to appease her?"

"Say what you would to any woman you seek something from." I stared at him dumbfounded. As my previous experiences mainly involved bartering, it seemed a very poor idea to me.

"Tell her what she wants to hear." He sighed.

"I need words. Give me words!" I demanded. Hopefully, that clarified things for him.

"It's quite simple. Lie to her. Tell her you are the same person you've always been. Tell her… nothing has changed."

"Nothing has changed." I insisted.

"As you say, so it is so, One Rah." He chortled. I could tell, even in his sorry state, he enjoyed dragging me through the mud.

"So, she feels everything has changed." It was my turn to sigh.

"Tell her the truth. Give her something she can hold on to."

"The truth?" By which he meant *his truth*, not mine.

"Yes, the truth. Tell her you are the One Rah. Tell her the truth is whatever you decide it to be. If you want her, tell her so."

"Just like that?" I had my doubts.

"I did say it was simple."

"For her would I refuse all of this faster than an arrow's flight."

"An arrow's flight– of all the metaphors the world has to offer, you had to choose that one?" He sneered.

"Apologies but I am unfit to lead. I am no more the One Rah than I am the Golan Butcher! I am sick of killing. All I want is to remain Radesh. All I want is Petra."

"But you are not Radesh. Nor were you ever. You are Rah Deshu Mogashu. There is nowhere you can run to now." He gasped.

"He's right," cut in Darian. "You cannot outrun what's done. Whether it be to murder or worship you, they will find you."

"But where does that leave me? As much as I loathe being honest, especially given the situation I presently find myself in– I don't believe either of you. Pushing every benefit of nobility aside, which is far from easy considering I only just got them, I don't believe I'm the One Rah. Think about it. *Me*. The High Chieftain of all things everywhere. *Hardly?* I might lie to you and everyone else but not to her. I mean, had it been any other woman ordinarily I would but, it's just not possible with her. She can tell. She always knows. It's very unsettling, not to mention unfair."

"You could command her," replied Darian, selflessly. "Do this!

Do that! Bring me an ale, woman! That sort of thing."

"I don't think you're seeing things clearly," I huffed.

"Only the wobbly eye, the other sees perfectly." insisted Baran.

"Keep it up and I'll pull that bolt and play *peek or boo* through the hole!" Darian threatened.

"Peek or boo?" I scratched my chin.

"'Tis a game played with small children." He explained.

"At the expense of the misfortunate?" I asked intrigued as it did sound like the sort of game Renan would take a shine to.

"Just fingers usually. I was simply pointing out that I see more with my dead eye than Baran does with two. I'll wager a gold coin we'll be wading more than our fair share of woe from this day forth. That said, I prefer dirtying the hands of other fools prior to my own."

"Good to know," I growled. "Let's put that to the test then. Brotherhood of Zil!" I yelled aloud. "Brethren of the Hood!" I shouted, waiting for those within earshot to gather round.

"Allow me to present your new leader, Elnath. Darian One-Eye, should he choose to accept." I squeezed his shoulder roughly.

"I command you to accept," I whispered, causing Baran to gurgle. Which, if Greta's reaction was any indication, wasn't advisable. Lucky for me, the deconstruction of a perfectly good sentence wasn't something she currently had time for. Thus, nothing backwards did she share. As it stood, she was too busy comparing the crossbow bolt in her hand to the one protruding from Baran. I could only assume she was trying to gauge its degree of penetration prior to removing it…so Darian could peek through the hole. I digress.

"Know this," I continued. "Darian never left you; the Brotherhood left him. And now you've returned. So, what say you, Elnath, Darian-One-Eye? How will you answer?"

"This is where you choose to accept," gurgled Baran.

"Quiet you." Greta mocked stabbing him with the bolt. She then squeezed his lips shut with her pudgy fingers to shush him.

"I accept," said Darian. Though his answer sounded more akin to a question, the Brotherhood responded approvingly, pounding their fists eagerly against their chests.

"Name our task and it shall be done." It seemed Darian had found his footing. Employing a sweeping gesture with his hand, he bowed so low I thought his head might graze the sand beneath his feet. It was by far the best one yet. Perhaps, he should teach Petra.

"Return them to their chores," I whispered, returning to Baran.

"Go back to your duties! Ensure the fire is out!" Darian

affirmed before tugging my sleeve. "What about Amos and Taggart? I think they should be added to the wall. I think they'd like that."

Having never spoken to Amos, I felt bad whereas, having shortened Taggart's pinkie finger at least I wouldn't have that reminder waved in my face any longer. Thank Haeryn my mother wasn't alive to witness my blunder. She could have trimmed his beard with both eyes closed. In my defence, she never touched *the drink,* rendering it an unfair comparison by all accounts. At least mine.

"Make it so. Burn the rest. And fetch ale," I added quietly.

"What about Baran?"

"No ale for him but yeah, have him moved inside. Have Petra meet me in the Hold. Then bring the ale." I ordered. *The skull wall.* There was something about being on watch until the end of time that did not sit well with me. Then again, at least they were with their old comrades. So many things to be decided while never having applied for the job. Twas very similar to being recruited, as I pondered it.

"Wine," rattled Baran.

"Wine," nodded Greta. "For the wound," she clarified.

The audacity. It was a hole for Haeryn's sake. She may as well just pour it on the sand. I only hoped Darian would be about. At least he'd have the presence of mind to hold a cup underneath. I made a mental note to have a word with Greta about ̶.̶.̶her attitude in general. Well, perhaps not me though someone should. *Baran!* Baran would be perfect being her doting husband and all.

"Ale and wine," agreed Darian. I noticed Greta staring at me with earnest. *Had she wanted the Brotherhood job*, I wondered. I don't think she'd have been a good fit. She was too heavy on her heels when she walked. Not good, for an assassin. Darian on the other hand…humph. As I considered it, there was nothing even vaguely covert about the man. Still, it's not like I was going to have him protect Petra. The bloke could barely look after himself. The damage was done as they say. It was too late now.

"Speak freely, Greta. What is it you need?" I asked.

"Many things," she sighed. "Hollow reeds of this same size," she replied, shaking the crossbow bolt she held.

"Clean they must be. Very clean," she continued. "I need boiling water, honey, linen and two baths. One very hot. One very cold. From the bottom of the well must it be." I turned to Darian.

"I will see to it," he replied, swiftly departing. And that my friends, is how it's done. Ruling at its best. *Make Darian do it.*

"I don't need a bath," cackled Baran. "What I need is this damn thing pulled out of my chest." Greta slapped his clawing hands away.

"Not like that. Not yet!" She snapped. "Out now and die you will. This, I do need pulled free," she said, tapping the shield several times with her fat fingers which made Baran cringe with pain.

"Oh, you mean this— this bit, right here." I clarified, rapping the shield with my knuckles just to be sure I understood her.

"Please don't do that," Baran hissed.

"Shush! Cease the talk, far quieter must you be." She scolded.

"Allow me," I smiled. "I command you not to speak. And, have no fear, I'll have that shield torn free before you can say... well, much of anything I suppose being that I bid you not to speak."

"There is more I must confess," Baran argued. Yes, I did say argued— with the One Rah. The Heir of Harbinger. *Such nerve.*

"Don't make me put you in the sand pit," I warned.

"There are things that need be said," he maintained, wiping sweat from his eyes. The sun was rising fast. I stood over him to shield him from the heat. Not that it helped. Not to mention, it should of been him who was shielding me— though I chose to overlook it, this time.

"And I will hear it when you are better." I insisted.

"No," urged Baran. "I must say it now before it is too late; before I pass. There are things I must tell you."

"And, as I just said, if only you'd been listening, I will hear it when you have fully recovered."

"But—"

"But nothing. Rest assured; I will hear every word for much have you to explain. Do not force my hand in this for I know you can write. Agatha is not the only blade with a thirst. Don't force me to cut out your tongue." I whispered, brandishing my fancy gold dagger.

It was then that Darian returned to inform us that all of Greta's requirements had been met. He was quick. Then again, in hindsight, all he ever did was bark. Helms off to him. He was good at barking.

"Good. Now let's free this shield." I wriggled it slightly just to incite a bit of panic with him. "Preferably, without killing him."

After staring at it for a short time, I looked at Darian and shrugged. How hard could it be? Being that I had my dagger in hand, I cut the straps away, causing the protruding bolt to take up the weight, causing Baran to wince again. A win/win, I think they call it.

Though fair to say it wasn't the best of starts, neither was it the worst. He was still breathing after all. *Wheeze, wheeze, wheeze. Sputter, sputter, sputter.* It was all very odd. But a brief time ago, I would have adored watching him in the final throes of agony. And now, though I still found a measure of enjoyment in his suffering, I very much wanted him to live. Twas a strange world for certain.

"Should this go poorly, I'll still need a way to be rid of the body," I joked. Baran did smile at that. Greta less so.

It took a bit of work to pare the vanes from the quarrel. Given the yelps, I don't think Baran appreciated the bolt moving about as much as it did. Once I'd whittled that away, I was able to squeeze my hand beneath the shield and grab hold of the bolt betwixt two fingers. I should have pinched it a bit tighter.

"I have it," I said. "Pull the shield away." Taking hold of the shield, Greta and Darian began to tug– somewhat gently. Being that their fingers were the size of carrots it was the best they could do.

"Slower. Wait! It's following the shield. Okay, now try. There we go. It's slipping through– it's loose." We sighed collectively.

"Looks much better. I mean with the shield removed." I clarified. "The wound looks– ugh. Good Haeryn, have a look. The back side's spitting bubbles as though a babbling brook."

Baran couldn't look. He'd lost consciousness unfortunately. Not that he could have viewed it given the fact it was on the backside of him and all. It was as we feared. The short breaths accompanied by wheezing clearly indicated his lung was unquestionably pierced. The bolt had missed his shoulder blade by a finger width. Well, Greta's finger width. Which was saying something being that it was fair bit thicker than Darian's monstrosities.

Baran's djellaba was soaked with pink foamy blood. Removing his headscarf, Greta secured the bolt with it. Having borrowed my dagger, which I already wanted back, she cut a strip down his pin-striped robes to better examine him. Though I took little notice of it at the time, an old key hung on a chain about his neck. *Dagger please!* I thought wiggling my fingers impatiently.

Baran's face made mine look akin to an angel. Okay, a fallen angel. It was riddled with scars, mostly hideous burn marks. Each of which had a peculiar looking swirl in the middle; as per the others covering his torso. They continued down his neck, lower back, stomach, and front of his thighs. I couldn't distinguish the sunburnt pockmarks and blemishes I recalled him having as a child. There was a definite pattern to them leading me to infer he'd been horribly tortured at some point in his life. Every burn mark pulled at my heart. And that was the end of it. No longer did I harbor any hatred for him. It was the opposite. As was customary in my life of late, everything I thought to be true was naught but another lie.

What if I was the One Rah? What if? I dared to think.

"Who did this to him?" I asked Darian, staring out at the horizon imagining that wherever I looked, in whatever direction; it all belonged to me. It was hardly as awe inspiring as you might have thought. It was just sand after all. *Have I mentioned how much I loathe sand? Don't get me started....*

"I'm not sure. He never spoke of it. One of the False Rahs, I expect. Perhaps all of them given the extent. I don't know."

"Cover him up. Get him to the Hold!" I commanded. Being that Darian knew nothing about it, clearly Baran did not wish anyone to see the burn marks. I was not about to humiliate him further. Well of course I was but that was between us, and I would do so in private— *mostly*. Providing he survived that is. The fact I'd been so close to taking his head stood but a foul memory to me now.

While Darian and Greta saw to Baran, I assessed the full extent of Grumble's wounds. I was qualified. I'd witnessed fortifications suffering from fire damage since the ripe old of eight as Darian could attest to. Sadly, not unlike Baran, the overall wound did appear rather fatal. As described, the Rookery was completely gutted; its tables and chairs had been thrown in a heap and lit aflame. You could shepherd a herd of goats through the wall in one location. Not that I'd ever be disposed to doing so. I hated goats— even lone goats. The men were heaping sand and water atop the ground, which I encouraged them to keep doing as whatever lay beneath was obviously still smouldering. Grumble's humble roots, I expect.

Looking upward, I could see straight through East Warren to gauge what little remained of the Heartwood— Baran's residence. If he survived, he would find no measure of solace there. My, once miraculously clean, Pail was now non-existent. The Galley was little less a disaster. Its bark walls were intact but most of the food appeared to be spoiled. A few wooden kegs had caught fire which likely helped douse some of the flames. Though more of a sooty colour now, the Red Room and its many books appeared to have survived. No doubt the gods found humour in that. As cruel as they were. To say the Great Tree was in a depressing state would be akin to calling the Kestrel an oasis. As per Darian's assessment, it was a complete shamble. Any major wind might very well bring Grumble to his knees.

Upon entering the Hold dejectedly, all eyes immediately turned to me— and then they bowed. If for no other reason than awkwardness, I motioned them up at once. I quite liked the individual bowing thing, but kneeling on mass felt unwarranted, for lack of a better word. At least, at this juncture in time. Then again, we all have our crosses to bear, and I suppose I could get used to it if I tried just a wee bit harder. What point was there to disparaging myself? If they were willing to give me the benefit of the doubt, what right had I to deny them?

Darian passed me a large mug of Ale which I immediately drained. He refilled it and I dragged a chair to the back of the room so I might better view them all. There were two baths in the room. One of which hot rocks must have been thrown into for the ascending steam was very great. Alde Baran was stripped bare save for the key still hanging about his neck that, for some explicable reason, we all chose to ignore. Baran lay face down on a small cot. Greta and Petra were washing him. I watched the quarrel rise and fall in time to his breathing. At least his breaths appeared steady.

"Is he conscious?" I asked.

"No, my Rah," answered Petra. "We were just about to pull the shaft."

"Please everyone, call me Radesh— at least in private. After which you have my permission to call me anything you like when I'm gone. Just don't let me catch you." I added drolly.

"Of course, One Rah Deshu." Petra bowed her head. *More games*, I sighed.

"Sit him up," said Greta.

What I saw next, I never would have believed. Unfortunately for me, with each passing moment, it became increasingly harder to watch. Truth was, I felt as helpless as I did inconsequential. I was of no benefit to anyone in respect to Baran's condition. Previously, had I witnessed a companion lying injured as such, the most the poor sod would have received from me would have been a sad shake of the head prior to moving on. And they bow to me. *Fools.*

Choosing a hollow reed, Greta inserted it over the quarrel, twisting it back and forth while trying to force it through his chest wound. As least that's what it looked like she was attempting to do. Even in his weakened state, Baran grimaced and, though I would have thought it not possible, his face became paler. In hindsight, perhaps it was just me who'd turned paler.

"Might this be of use?" Offered Darian, handing her *my fork*, pointy end first. She wiped its surface clean after running it through the flames of a near-by candle.

"Yes. Of use it is." replied Greta. "Hold the skin up nicely it will."

That did it. I wanted it not. It was Darian's fork now. *Hold the skin up it will*, I shuddered. True to her word, after increasing the bend in the estranged apparatus, she then stabbed Baran near to the wound prior to requesting Darian pry the skin upward by gently pushing down on the tool's handle. Outside of the fork, I felt obliged to give Darian a great deal of credit for not having hesitated in the slightest. Petra and I exchanged quick glances thankful that Greta hadn't asked either one of us to assist with so gruesome a task. Of note, I also found bone sawing to be quite uncomfortable to watch– not that it factored here in any way. At least, I hoped she wasn't about to saw Baran in half to retrieve the quiver. Then again, I wouldn't put it past her. Haeryn knows she wasn't the gentlest of women while prone to being a tad heavy-handed at times. On the bright side, at least it wasn't her constantly jabbing me in the ribs. Haeryn help us, can you imagine? *Intimacy with Greta?* Forgive me for saying but I expect one would be lucky to survive such an encounter.

Graciously, amongst the many expressions etched upon her face, compassion was evident. Though, you could tell by her eyes, persistence was far more dominant. I could detect no sense of compromise within her mindset for which I was glad. Regardless of what unforeseen challenges might lie ahead, her will would not be impeded. Rotating the reed left and right, she pressed down hard, forcing it through the wound. Though I thought she'd stop there she did not. Twisting the reed cautiously around the shaft she kept pushing it deeper and deeper within Baran's chest cavity. It was not a pretty sight. I thought for sure that Petra might vomit– before I did with luck.

"You're going to pin him to the bloody cot if you keep at it like that." I scolded.

"As the quarrel is removed, the hole must you cover." Greta said to Petra, ignoring me completely. "Then into the hot bath will we put him for a time; then into the cold must he go."

"Why?" I asked, it seemed more witchcraft than medicine to me. Greta shook her head not even bothering to look at me. I suppose I could have commanded her to answer for all the good it would have done. Fortunately, Petra was more obliging.

"She isn't able to explain it, my Rah." She answered. "That is how she's seen it done with similar wounds. And, before you ask, the answer is no. None of those injured survived." *Well, isn't that comforting.* I thought to myself.

"She also said if you place boiled baobab fruit in cold water it shrinks. Not that I know how that might be of import." Darian added.

"Then why, may I ask, are we doing it? Hot or cold, what sense is there in moving him from one bath to the next? It's ludicrous."

"No time have we for this," chided Greta. "Though ask I knew you would."

"So, our hopes lie with dead men and shrunken fruit." I stammered, wondering if his ball sack might vanish entirely.

"Save him you said. So, save him I will try." Sighing aloud, Greta sported a look of desperation akin to my own. Shaking her head, she left Baran's side to fetch a small cooking vessel. She filled it with water, prior to capping it tightly with a cork. Using tongs, she held it over the candle flame for quite some time— sighing impatiently all the while. No doubt attempting to make me feel worse than I already did. Which was not possible— or so I thought. Once the water within began to hiss, she plunged it into the cold water and the vessel collapsed inward upon itself and shattered.

"Ah, I see." I lied. "Crumble him we will. And just how is that helpful?" I implored.

"Remove the air from the jar it did," replied Greta staring hard at me while tossing pieces of broken clay out of the tub angrily. "And dirty is the water now."

"My apologies, I understand now." I lied again.

"And warmer now is the water thanks to you," she added, shaking her head in dismay. Obviously, she was a woman of many hidden talents— *scorn* being prevalent amongst them.

"No thanks necessary. You may proceed." I cringed.

"I think I understand now. She's hoping to remove the air trapped outside his lungs." Petra clarified further.

"Let's get on with it then," I urged impatiently. I could see where this was going. Regardless of how the old codger crumbled, I'd no doubt be held to blame for it. Only I couldn't be, could I? I was the One Rah and *they* but my willing servants all. Staring down at him, I couldn't help but feel our efforts were in vain. Facts being facts, it was without doubt the worst plan ever. Not helping matters in any way, with all his pockmarks and scars, Baran looked akin to a decaying corpse already— and we hadn't even started yet. Running a finger across the peculiar-looking burn marks, his skin felt like aged leather.

"Did that he did," Greta said sharply.

"He did that— to himself?" I asked in bewilderment.

"I think, yes. Only where he can reach are they— here and here, but not here. No reach, no mark. No reach, no mark." She repeated, pointing about his body.

Shaking my head in disbelief, I slunk into my chair. It was all too much for one day. Placing hands over ears, my skull began to throb. I wasn't sure what was worse: Alde Baran's condition; his self-inflicted burns; the proposed treatment; or the fact I'd once considered attending one of Greta's reading classes. Okay, so not the last one though I'd thought it all the same. I caressed my temples gingerly, but it was no use. All humor aside, there was no answer to that riddle. Undoubtedly, they were all equally as bad. No offense intended to Greta. I needed her to an extreme unlike ever before. All our faith lay with her– and her magical bath water. It reminded me of our attempt to cross the Kestrel. There'd be no back tracking. No: plan B. No: if at first, she doesn't succeed. Baran would either survive or he wouldn't.

Hearing a strange suckling sound, I looked up to see the crossbow bolt in Greta's fingers just as Petra slapped her thumb over the end of the protruding reed. Using the same tongs she'd destroyed the cooking vessel with, she'd manage to tug the quarrel free. Brimming with apprehension, I rose from my chair at once.

"Now, into the hot bath," ordered Greta. "You mustn't let go! You must keep the reed covered or die he will."

No pressure. Except that it was all about air pressure. Not that I understood it. Once again, I was glad to be watching rather than partaking. I did help carry a leg. It was then I noticed that Greta was right. Every burn mark was somewhere Baran might have reached himself. Who would do such a thing? Yet again, nothing made sense.

Petra had to squirm about to do as she was told. She had one hand on the right side of Baran's chest and one hand around his back covering the reed as we lowered him into the steaming water. The water was so hot it made Petra grimace. Still, she looked no less determined than Greta. Difference between, I loved her for it.

"Yes, like that," nodded Greta. "Mouth and nose out." Quite some time passed and then Petra spoke.

"How long must we hold him?" She asked. "I fear my arms are tiring. I'm losing my grip." *Good gracious, already?* It's not as though Baran was peeing into a bucket after being asleep for days on end.

"Long," said Greta employing her usual high standards for clarity. Knowing Petra to be struggling, I let go of Baran's legs leaving their full weight to Darian. He was floating for the most part. Whereas ensuring the reed remained closed underwater, was proving difficult for Petra. Tracing her arms, I reinforced her grip, so she need not press at all. Greta nodded with approval. *What devilry was this? Had I truly garnered some measure of approval?* I felt so relieved. If only I had a third hand. I would have strangled her with it.

All jesting aside, the four of us held Baran in that same fashion for a long, long time. So long my own arms had begun to tire. Not that I cared. It felt good to feel Petra's fingers in mine again. Admittedly it was not as intimate as I would have liked– what with Baran's unconscious naked body floating betwixt us. As awkward as it was, I did sneak a whiff of Petra's hair which did not go unnoticed.

"Make it rain," she said. "Did you really say that? Oh wait, I was there. Yes, you did." Darian began to snicker which normally would have angered me, but it didn't. Being unsure what to say in my defence, I suppose I did deserve it.

"Are you questioning the power of the One Rah?" I demanded.

"No, my Rah, never. No doubt it's raining outside now."

"The Gods are cruel." I grinned foolishly. "Haeryn knows they'd likely cause it to snow just to mock me. Mark my words, I will make it rain soon enough."

"Ale or wine?" She quipped, reading my thoughts precisely.

"Both." Beamed Darian. It was a satisfactory answer.

"It is time," interrupted Greta. "Hold him tight, then into the chill water must he go."

Releasing Petra's hands, I took hold of Baran's bare legs again. Lifting him in unison, all eyes were immediately drawn to Baran's pecker as it floated briefly on the surface. In my defence, it could not be helped. Why Petra chose to include that bit in the chronicle is beyond me. Not unlike a firm prod in the ribs, it does nothing to further the tale. Speaking of *shrunken fruit,* once clear of the water, his barren ball sack clung to his thigh like an empty sail. Forlorn and forgotten, it could not help but remind us of the suffering he'd endured. I did insist on documenting that part for it attests as to how unsettling the ordeal was whilst confirming earlier declarations made by him to be true.

Petra gasped as we lowered him into the second tub. Admittedly, going from hot to cold so swiftly was a bit of a shock. It made the water feel extremely cold, and I was glad not to have been in Baran's sandals. Though Darian said it best as he addressed the *wrinkled elephant* in the room.

"My own ball sack would have shrivelled no less mightily," he confessed. I let go of Alde Baran's legs again for noticing the pain on Petra's face. No sooner had I placed my hands over her own than Greta offered further instruction.

"That is perfect. Now, very closely must you listen. When I say, and only when I say, slide your hand free of the reed. As this she does Assad, One Rah, you must hug him very hard."

A sad One Rah? Honestly, I think she did that purposely. I oft times think the woman is far smarter than she feigns to be. For Haeryn's sake, though but my first day, we'd not only snuffed a burning tree but stifled an attack as well.

"Hug him? Surely, you jest." I crowed. "Baran, are you awake? Are you in on this?" I shook Baran. Something seemed afoot. Darian was ogling me with his crazy eye. He was never any help when I needed him most. Was I missing something or had the heated cooking vessel not crumpled of its own accord?

"Stop!" Greta hollered. "Squeeze him hard you must– to release the trapped air. Do this now!"

"Squeeze him?" I pleaded. I was near to my wit's end.

"Squeeze the air from his chest, I think she means." Petra spoke up in the nick of time.

"Yes. Like that." Greta confirmed. "Petra, let go! Squeeze now! Squeeze hard!"

Pressing all my weight upon Baran, a herd of bubbles rattled from him; the smell of which could only be described as horrible. That being, very nasty. It smelled like wild cabbages briskly boiled for a very long time indeed. Which smells unpleasant for the record. Gazing up at Greta, she did not look impressed. Sliding my arms about him, I gave him a fierce bear hug. As my head became submerged, time stopped. I felt as though a young boy again– greeting my father following one of his long journeys. It was surreal. I kept squeezing. I didn't want the vision to end. I was bringing my old father back to life. Feeling childlike, unexpectedly I began to cry. Someone was tugging my hair. But I didn't want to breathe. Not without him. Petra's fingers pulled my hands away. My head broke the surface and I gasped for air greedily. A moment later, Petra covered the reed as instructed and we pulled Baran clear of the water. Though still unconscious, he too panted for air.

Life was a bit of a blur after that. Someone handed me a cloth. I wiped my face and hands. I wiped my eyes a second time surprised to find I was still crying. Twice in one day even. Darian handed me a mug of ale– which I would have drained in one go had I the breath for it. I saw Greta plug the end of the reed with melted wax. The bath water was pink in colour. Laying Baran on the cot, Greta begat basting him with warm honey. Outside of Greta, only Haeryn knew why. After wrapping his wound with fresh linen, she covered him with a blanket that looked nowhere near as scratchy as the one I'd originally been allotted. Baran was rolled onto his side with his wound facing down. Greta noted this to rather important. *Why?* Ask Haeryn, I don't know, and neither did she say.

"Should we not tie his hands and feet prior to pumping him full of baobab pulp?" I asked. Once again, Greta ignored me. The time seemed nigh to begin writing my terms. It only seemed fair. Darian kept handing me mugs of ale, followed by wine. I drank all of it eagerly and without question. Other than pestering Greta that is.

"Might we poke him a few times to see if he moves or not?" I shrugged. I was quite serious. Not unlike assessing Renan's anger, from my viewpoint, it be good to know if our efforts had been worthwhile. Though I waited no answer appeared to be forthcoming.

I began to feel dizzy. It seemed my efforts to diffuse the situation with humour were in vain for a strange chill took hold, and then it began. The strain had taken its toll. It was all too much– too much to comprehend; too much to endure. The day's events flashed through my mind like a cyclone. I'd come so very close to killing Baran. My desire to do so had outweighed the idiocy of me having been declared the Heir of Harbinger. I had seized the opportunity solely to justify my murderous agenda. Though blinded by my own hatred, Alde Baran had changed. He was no longer the person I knew before. I could see that now. He was no more my father than the person who'd greeted us at the well. He hadn't lifted a finger to save himself. He'd given up the fight. He'd bowed his head. He was tired– tired of reliving that one tragic moment. He sought an end. He wanted to run away forever. No less than he had the final time I'd seen him as a boy. No less than I wanted to run away with Petra and Renan.

I began to see the truth of things. I felt ashamed. As usual, I'd been wrong about everything. Seeing him in his present state caused my entire world to crash down upon me. I began to shake. Quivering uncontrollably, I hid my face in my hands. No one said anything. What might they say? Petra came to me. I'd never seen her face through such mists. It was radiant, full of hope whereas I felt everything but.

"It's raining," she whispered, before kissing me. "It's raining just as you said it would."

Well, that did it. She'd broken me. And wrapping her arms about me, I wept. She was right. I was right. *It was raining.* I expect the Gods had commanded it. And now I knew just how cruel they could be. Renan crawled over to sit on the floor before us. Being that he kept his distance, I surmised he must not have soiled himself. I envisioned the little man differently now too. After all, it'd been him who'd trained me well enough to conquer the Black Pail.

"Rooster never cried." I sobbed. "Red Radesh never cried. The Golan Butcher never cried. The One Rah does not cry." Who was lying now? I'd been many things in my life before but never a blubbering fool. I felt a sham. A complete failure.

"Then a miracle it is," smiled Greta. Apparently, she could be kind. I felt Darian's hand squeeze my shoulder tightly while he replenished my mug with wine. I did not look him in *the eye*. We were friends now and I knew it. For the first time in my life, *I had friends*.

"Let me hold my son," I blathered.

"Our son," Petra correctly.

"Our son," I nodded, wiping the embarrassment from my cheeks as best I could. I took Renan, giving him a cautious sniff before holding him up proudly.

"You should see him piss, Darian. Trust me, Renan knows how to make it rain."

"Let's give him a wee bit of ale," suggested Darian, running to fetch the pitcher. Petra stood to block his path.

"Perhaps another time," Darian noted.

"Perhaps not ever," scolded Petra, placing her hands on her hips. How quickly she could change.

"I could command it," I dared to venture, crossing Renan's arms across his tiny chest defiantly while shaking him gently so his head wobbled from side to side. The little man always looked rather smug. Especially after dropping weight– causing me to sniff him yet again just to be sure he wasn't packing.

"And how did that work out for you earlier?" Petra asked.

"Fair point," I agreed. "Being as cruel as they are Renan will forgo the ale."

"*As cruel as they are*– has nothing to do with it. I said no." Petra illuminated. Rising, I placed Renan in my chair, and bowed low. Which is to infer a proper bow, unlike Petra's inferior version. We all laughed, even Greta. And for a fleeting moment our hearts were lifted.

Once daily, Greta cut away the wax in the reed. The initial time saw the bubbly mucus flee the wooden pipe without any assistance. After that it was reduced to barely a dribble, so she was forced to put her lips upon the reed to suck out the air. Not to mention, the blood and puss that continued to accumulate within his chest cavity. Respect. I did not envy her for it was a gruesome task though never once did she complain. She'd suck and cover the reed before spitting the putrid, foul-smelling contents into a bowel. Suck, cover, spit; suck, cover, spit over and over; each time pulling the reed out just a tiny bit farther before refilling it with wax and re-bandaging him.

"Is it working?" I asked hopefully. "Will he live?" Her answer was always the same for which I secretly reviled her.

"To tell too early it is," she'd chirp. "Breathing still is he somehow." Thought the farthest thing from a healer even I could tell that much. That bit about the breathing to be clear.

Petra and I stayed with Baran the entire time; only leaving in turn to eat, pee, or squat. Darian kept me informed how Grumble, and our new associates, were faring. As before, Grumble's creaks, moans and groans seemed louder than usual. I couldn't tell if it was due to the giant tree's grievous injuries or simply for us having remained idle for so long. Point being, perhaps it had always been that noisy, but we'd simply never bothered to take notice.

Darian had interviewed each of the Brotherhood one by one; *to put the eye to them* was how he described it. He stated that there had originally been forty of them, of which the remaining thirty-three had not only professed their loyalty to me but begrudged ever having served the Four False Rahs. Speaking of weird-looking eyes, the skull wall was not what I expected upon seeing its new modifications. Having begun a new row, the two heads that had been added looked entirely out of place. From the rear it wasn't so bad but from the front, it looked as though Amos and Taggart were trying to peer over it— which I found a tad unnerving. That said, being that I couldn't conceive of a better alternative, I chose to ignore it in the end.

"When will you know?" I begged Greta impatiently.

"When out the reed is, and coughing blood does he stop."

It took three long days and nights until Alde Baran opened his eyes; and two more yet before he spoke. *Wine* was all he said, which I fetched at once without bothering to ask permission from Greta. On the ninth day following his injury I awoke to find Alde Baran sputtering from the mouth. I hollered at Greta who ran to him at once. We sat him up and she immediately cleared his mouth with her fingers— as chubby as they were.

"Cough!" she commanded. *Ahem*, Baran sneered feebly.

"Cough!" Greta barked again. *Ahem, ahem* was Baran's insufficient response.

"Cough you must!" Greta insisted.

"Wine," hissed Baran. "I can't cough. My chest is aflame. Leave me alone. Let me lie down."

"No more lying down until cough you do. You must! Leave

you alone I will not!" *Ahem, ahem.* Baran strained half-heartedly.

"Cough! Cough! Cough!" Greta scolded. Baran looked at me with such despair that I ran to fetch the wine. Petra awoke and followed me back to his cot.

"No! No wine for him until he coughs!" Insisted Greta. "Suck it from his lips I will." That made me laugh.

"Greta you great hag, remember this I will," mocked Alde Baran with a woeful smile. Taking a deep breath, he forced himself to cough before clutching his chest woefully.

"More!" Greta pestered him. "More cough now!" There were tears in Baran's eyes. I truly felt sorry for him. He shook his head spitefully, but Greta was having none of it— and he knew it. She could be a real bear when she wanted to. And she wanted to.

"Just one," urged Petra softly. "You can do it, one cough."

"No. Uh-oh!" Sang Greta. "Big cough and more! Don't make me fetch the six!" She threatened. "Which will it be? All your wives or just me? Then wine you get. Choose now."

"Baran," I counselled him. "Just get it over with, man."

"Shoot me through the heart next time" he pleaded. "Or take my bloody head." Inhaling a deep breath took Baran so much by surprise he could not help but cough. He continued coughing hoarsely while clutching his side. Tears streamed down his scarred cheeks. He spat up a significant amount of mucus. Falling upon his uninjured side, he bit his lip in agony.

"And now will you live," announced Greta proudly.

"Joy," sighed Baran. "Wine," he begged. I handed him the sling and he took several large swallows.

"Slower!" Greta advised too late. She pulled him back up for he'd begun gagging. Baran was beside himself with pain and disbelief.

"It's good," smiled Greta. "Without pain you cannot heal."

"More joy damn you," groaned Baran. "Damn the lot of you." He took a deep breath in through his nose and held it. He began to laugh then clutched his side grimacing.

"By the barest of margins, I can breathe again," he whispered.

"Thank the heavens," I grinned. "We still hadn't figured how to be rid of the body."

"Don't make me laugh," begged Baran, wiping his eyes. "Where's Darian?" He asked.

"I don't know," I replied. "I only just awoke myself. Why?"

"Because we have plans to make. You didn't think I was sleeping all this time, did you?"

"Out the reed comes now," interrupted Greta. "Sleep soon or wish it were so will you."

"Such a treasure," grinned Baran. "I've slept enough. Fetch Darian. It's high time we leave this place. The One Rah has returned. The people of Harbinger await."

"We have to leave," I mused aloud. "Before Grumble takes a tumble. The assassins set fire to the great tree." I confided.

"So, that is what I smell. I was afraid to ask. I thought it was me. It is a sad day. Wondrous, but sad."

"'Tis a good day," I avowed. "Wondrous for certain." After acquiring fresh linen, Greta approached us with Petra in tow.

"I have much to tell you," Baran smiled. "It's been put off far too...." Taking hold of the reed, Greta pulled it free of his chest, Petra slapped a wax-soaked cloth over his wound causing Baran to cringe.

"A little longer will do little harm now," I whispered.

"A little warning next time, perhaps." He grunted before turning to me. "But now that you know who you are, who I really am, there must be all manner of things you wish to know."

"Well, that's just it; isn't it," I replied. "I don't even know your rightful name. It's not Bright Star; that's for certain."

"Ask me anything but that," sighed Baran. "I promise I will tell you though it is a tale, I'd far sooner forget."

"And so, it begins. It seems you and Petra have more than just books in common." Luckily, I managed to block Petra's jab for once.

"Okay, let's start with something simple then," I laughed. "What was in that old rucksack?"

"What rucksack?"

"The one in the yard. The one in our old wagon. It's just something I've pondered over the years. It was always there."

"Mad bulls," smiled Baran. "Mostly elephants as I recall."

"Elephant bulls, of course. I think someone needs more sleep."

"No, I've more to say," Reaching for my arm, he didn't get far.

"It can wait," I urged.

"Perhaps it can," he agreed huskily before closing his eyes.

"You're not going anywhere," I winked, smacking him gently on the shoulder. To be fair, though I considered poking him in the chest, I declined the urge. *An act of kindness?* Whatever was the world coming to?

"I'm going nowhere," he harmonized. His eyes closed, and he fell asleep. Shortly thereafter, I motioned for Petra and Darian to accompany me outside.

"Where are we going?" Petra asked as we began our descent.

"I want to assess what damage has been done to the Heartwood." Petra stopped climbing.

"Assess the fire damage— or is it rather an excuse to rummage through Alde Baran's belongings?"

"Interesting proposal, now that you've brought it to my attention, I suppose it would be inconsiderate of us not to take stock of his belongings the more I think on it."

"I was not proposing anything," huffed Petra. "I don't think any of us should be poking our noses where they don't belong."

"Which is why Darian is coming along."

"Why am I coming?" Darian wished to clarify.

"Strictly as an observer to attest that whatever we may or may not uncover was a necessity or purely accidental." I lied. I had to wait for them to descend further. I should have gone first.

"Observer? You mean scapegoat." Darian scowled. "But why me?"

"Because Baran trusts you. More than the two of us anyway." Petra replied.

"I thought for certain he'd say, *because I said so*," Darian scoffed.

"That too," She agreed. "He is the One Rah." She flourished broadly with an arm.

"Indeed, he is," Darian confirmed.

"Not to mention, he sees this as his last chance to *accidentally* stumble upon whatever it is he thinks might await." She added dryly.

"Ah, I see," said Darian. "Thus, our presence is merely to lessen any appearance of deliberateness."

"Precisely," said Petra, shaking her head. "He can be quite blatant at times."

"Blatant?"

"Pigheaded; barefaced; unabashed." Petra explained.

"Ah, as in wilful, shameless, obstinate, I see what you're saying." Darian further elaborated.

"I'm right bloody here!" I sang out from above. "I can hear every word you're saying. Me, that being, the One Rah in question."

It seemed the troops were revolting. I can't say I never expected it though I did anticipate it taking a wee bit longer. I hadn't even been in charge for two full weeks yet. Though unverifiable, since my sobbing episode, I felt as though the Rage had abandoned me for good. Key word being *seemed*. I felt different. And why shouldn't I? Many things were different.

It took a bit of work to climb into the Heartwood. We had to bring the Crown's ladder with us being that the other one was too burnt to risk venturing upon. I did suggest Darian try it as I couldn't any the harm in that. He did manage about five rungs before it collapsed. I would have tried to catch him had he been half as *bulky*. I couldn't help wondering whether he'd have caught me had our roles been reversed. I like to think he would have stood fast and held his ground. I was the One Reborn after all. So, they insisted.

As it turned out, Alde Baran did not have a lot of possessions. Or if he did, they were gone now. There were bountiful figures carved into the walls, all of which were burned beyond recognition. Most notable, outside of a few tarnished paintings, were the books. He'd kept a lot of books. It looked as though they may have helped quash the fire when their shelves fell apart. Passing the *survivors* down the ladder, I had them returned to the Red Room.

The frames of the painting were oddly out of proportion. They were far too large for the pictures within. Upon trying to remove one I found it unjustifiably weighty. Thus, we had little choice but to investigate further. Using *my fork*, Darian pulled back a corner on the backside of one to find it had been lined with gold coins, making me immediately think of the ones I'd hidden within the chicken coop as a lad. The paintings not the coins. If you recall, I'd buried the coins. Perhaps, there were more. Coins this time as opposed to the paintings. *What? It isn't that difficult if you'd just pay attention.*

"Clever," nodded Darian. I wasn't so sure. I'd found them in an instant whereas I was quite certain my coins were still safe. The ones I buried that is. Not the ones that might be hidden within the chicken coop paintings. *Do try to keep up!* Then again, was anything truly safe amongst this chaotic world of ours?

Strangely, though unsure of the rationale, I wasn't interested in the gold. I expect, being the One Rah, I'd inherited all manner of riches. Castles even, so I imagined. As for the pouch brimming with gold I'd been promised, I wasn't sure I was entitled to it any longer. The entire thing had been a ruse after all. I'd been their escort then. Now, I wasn't sure what I was. Or worse, how much time I had prior to being exposed as a fraud. If not that then certainly for the beast lurking within me and the many horrible atrocities I'd committed.

It was then that I discovered what I sought most. It was right next to his bunk, though I didn't recognize it at first for not being precisely certain what it was that I'd been looking for. It was a burnt silver mug. The funny thing was the end table it rested upon was not burnt; not even slightly. As I picked it up it jingled. Overturning the mug, a single gold coin fell out. At least I thought it was a gold coin.

"It's a ring," stated Petra. I picked it up. She was right.

"A badly squashed ring," I noted.

"I know what this is," said Darian.

"As do I," I attested. "It was my mother's."

"I was there when Baran gave it to Audre of Eyre." Darian smiled. "She thought he was proposing to her at first– until he told her it was merely so she might better act the part. I'd never seen her so angry, laughed Darian fondly. She reminded me of my own Missus. To be fair, my own would have dislocated my jaw had I done the same. Though she rarely showed it, Audrey was madly in love with him. I thought for certain she'd run him through with that infamous spear of hers. I expect the only reason she didn't was because she'd been holding you at the time."

"Ah, so that's what I need. And just where might I find that infamous spear?" Petra jested.

Though funny, my mood had soured. Taking the ring, I spoke no more of it. I couldn't. I dare not try. My mother always wore that ring. She never took it off. The moment I recognized what it was– I knew. It had the same swirl as Alde Baran's burn marks. But that wasn't what was tormenting me. It was far worse than that.

"I guess that's it," I grimaced.

"Not quite," said Darian. Motioning for us to stand aside, he flipped over the charred bunk to unveil a large hidden chest with two hasps but no lock. Fortunately, the chest was untouched by the flames.

"What's in there?" Petra asked.

"The bloody bank among other things, I expect," chuckled Darian. "Though I don't rightly know for certain."

Petra swung open the chest's lid without further urging. At first, the sole contents appeared to be colourful fabrics; until we dug deeper to uncover a smaller chest. This one was locked. I pulled it free. It was surprisingly heavy. I looked at Darian who smiled back, albeit somewhat guiltily. Petra could barely budge the thing.

"I have a feeling I know what it contains. Not to mention where the key is," I added, jiggling its contents harshly.

"Around Baran's neck," Petra nodded.

"I take it the two of you made more than a few *withdrawals* during your many adventures," I winked at Darian.

"More than a few," Darian admitted. "But only from those who could afford it."

"Or never deserved to have it in the first place." I reckoned.

"That too. Baran always divvied our acquisitions equally amongst us. But he's always been a bit of hoarder. Come to think of it, I'm always the one buying the drinks, so I expect half of whatever's in there rightly belongs to me. The bloke's as stingy as they come. I've never seen the man spend as much as a copper upon himself."

"If this is full of what I think, it's worth a small fortunate."

"It'd buy more than a few rounds of ale that's for certain," Darian surmised.

"Ale? He could buy half a bloody castle with this." I clattered the chest up and down, estimating its weight.

"Good because he owes me a full half. Ha! Baran in a castle! That's a laugh. Knowing him, he'll probably give the lot of it to his wives. Or you, should you ever stop testing his patience. As you've likely figured out by now, he's got none."

"I've a trinket or two tucked away myself," I half-lied. After all, I couldn't say for certain whether my secret buried treasure was even still there. Placing the small chest back inside the larger one, I covered it with the vibrant textiles and closed the lid.

"So, I take it you found what you were after," noted Darian.

"I did and more," I said, turning to go. I needed to get some air. Irony aside, the flattened ring had crushed my spirits.

It was sometime later that Petra found me sitting alone, beyond the charred, gaping hole in the Rookery. Dawn had just begun to break. The anger of the gods had been kindled for the skies appeared to be molten with blood. Sitting alongside me, I didn't acknowledge her. I couldn't take my eyes off the crushed ring which felt akin to my heart. Sadly, it was only upon discovering it that I knew for certain that I'd loved my mother. I didn't care what anyone said. I didn't care if I was the One Rah. Audre of Eyre was my mother. The only mother I'd ever known.

"What is it?" Petra whispered. "What's the meaning of it."

I had no words to offer. There were no words. Notwithstanding, there was no way I could get them out had I found courage enough to try. Even so, Petra was far more than pretty. She was the cleverest girl I'd ever met– cleverest person rather. *I expect you know who added that last bit.*

"Your mother was wearing it that morning, wasn't she?" She gasped. "That's why it's…"

She did not finish her sentence and, for that alone, I loved her. I will always love her for that. Moreover, I knew then I could never stop loving her. I learned a great many things in that moment. Not the least of which was, Petra knew me better than I knew myself. I also finally discerned what love truly was. To me, at least. It intended someone needing someone else in their life. A necessity that would forever remain. Although my mother was gone, I'd always felt need of her.

"Look." She implored softly, pulling me from my dream-like state. Following her gaze, I saw a shiny green shoot jutting out from the char-strewn sand.

"There's more! A whole string of them!" It was a true. Tiny Baobab trees had sprouted. There was an entire row of them; more than twenty plants, spaced about an arm's length apart. Out from the ashes, they'd risen in harmony, each doing their part to complete the enormous tree's fractured circle. I couldn't believe it.

"The ring isn't broken," she said. "It's beginning anew!"

It's beginning anew, I repeated in my thoughts. It was a sign. Though I'd never truly believed in a supreme power, maybe there were Gods after all. Maybe they weren't so cruel– or at least not always. It was magical, not unlike a faery tale. Yet, at the same time, overwhelming– too much to comprehend as usual of late. Just as I began to wonder if I'd ever find words again, I did.

"Surely, it is a sign if ever there was. This ground is sacred. No one must walk here. It must be protected. Big or small, to ensure this place's future, the trees must be safeguarded."

"They say Grumble is lost sadly." Petra sighed.

"We must try. I won't abandon him. I'll command lines be tied to all sides of Grumble to secure him from the winds."

"You make him sound as though he were a person."

"I know. It doesn't make sense, but he can't fall now. He mustn't. It's just that, within my heart I feel, should he fall, we will all fall. Coming here changed me. *This place* changed me."

"But what is there to tie ropes to? There's naught but sand."

"We'll dig trenches; bury whatever we have that we can't take with us… then cover it with sand. We will dismantle the inner walls if that's what it takes. We owe our lives to this blessed tree. Our time may be done here but his is not. Though admittedly distant, the future looks bright." I winked, pointing at the closest green sprout."

"Do you really think twine will hold *that* up?" She asked, looking upwards at the massive tree with great scepticism.

"No, but it might buy him some time." I sighed. "It's no more than any of us have after all."

"Where will we go?"

"Harkenspear, of course, to meet your brother as promised. But I can't say I look forward to it. He is a hard man at the best of times. Worse still, he knows my true nature better than most."

"A hard man but a fair man." Petra stated bluntly.

"Aye, but if I can't win him over, I can't win anyone over; and then we are doomed."

"My brother will hear you. He is a soldier first. Ahead of him, as per their stewardship, the Khalifah will be the first to kneel. It is their sacred vocation. It's all that they've desired for so many long years– a rightful successor. Gain their loyalty and Golan is yours."

"And what would I do with Golan?" I exhaled.

"You're a good man so more than most, I expect." She answered without hesitation.

"I've never owed more than a tent before."

"Aye... a tent that's yet to be paid for," she simpered.

"Do you believe them? Do you believe me to be the true Heir of Harbinger?" I inquired incredulously.

"I do. Every word. And that is what scares me." She whispered before continuing. "But the real question is... do you believe it?"

I searched my own thoughts and feelings. Was I still that frightened lad who survived by fleeing upon the merest hint of trouble? Had I merely exchanged my chicken coop for a hollow tree? Or was I rather the battle-weary soldier hiding behind the Red Rage for fearing to face my fears head on? The answer seemed all too clear. How could I possibly be the One Rah– a man predestined to reunite all Harbinger; a man prophesized to conquer whatever foes might come?

"No one knows me better than you. You know the truth of it. I am but an ogre– a beast when cornered. That is no leader."

"Radesh," she chided taking hold of my hand. "I'm not asking you whether you feel competent in the role. Who could? Since children, our homeland has been torn in two by civil war. I'm not asking whether you're comfortable having people bow at your feet? I'm simply asking if you believe what Alde Baran and Darian attest to be true? This is where you must start. This is what you must answer. For yourself; not anyone else... just you."

She was right; and I knew it. In my mind's depths, it was all I'd been deliberating since the arrival of the Brotherhood. I'd been over it a thousand times. It did make sense– and it wasn't as though I wanted it to. I didn't. But, as I'd learned time and time again in this life, sometimes we don't get a choice. The world was far larger than any man's interpretation of it. That much I knew for certain.

The actions of Baran and Darian backed their words. Darian was of the BroZil. I had buried his dagger myself. I remembered my mother's shield. Her identity could easily be verified. Perhaps that would be my first best course of action. Perhaps I would journey to the Isles of Eyre and speak to her father. But first, I had to answer Petra. No! First, I had to answer myself."

"I do." I admitted finally. "But there are still a great many questions in need of answering." I continued. "Such as why have I no memories of anything prior to Baran and Audrey of Eyre?"

"Because you were an infant. I have read of them."

"Read of who? Baran and Audrey?"

"No. King Turin and Audrey. There was mention of them in one of the Moon Books. The eldest daughter of the King of the Isles, it noted her to be a formidable warrior− and childless."

"And yet she hit me with a stick every other day."

"For all the good it did," smirked Petra.

"If it was included in a book, I expect other records exist."

"Then this is where it all begins. One step at a time. Admittedly, this is where my heart pounds like an unruly bear rummaging within my chest." She confessed.

"As does mine."

"I'm scared, Radesh. I want the world for you but don't wish to be an encumberment. The laws of our lands, the laws of your father, don't allow us to be together. I am no Queen; and neither will I ever be your mistress."

"We don't have Queens," I comforted her in vain. "We have the Grand Mother."

"You know what I mean! Do not toy with me!"

"And what did you only just say? One step at a time."

"While every step pulls you further away." She frowned.

"Do not fret, Petra. With, or without, your brother's blessing− or the blessing of the Khalifah− we shall be married. There is nothing dearer to me in this world than you."

"My brother will do as I say but I suspect the Khalifah will oppose you in this."

"Then I will behead them." I winked.

"Don't jest. I have no stature. My father, should he still be alive, is a glorified shopkeeper. Rah's may rule but it is the Khalifah who pass the laws. I fear for Renan! The bastard son of a King is a death warrant. Within every Book of a Thousand Names is it known."

"And this is why we must marry— so Renan becomes the next heir of Harbinger. The Khalifah will do as I say. Mark my words, whether they choose to bend or break is the only choice before them. I will change the laws and they will pass them."

"And you think it so easy." Petra scorned.

"Trust me. They have other worries. They fear the Kedera. They fear for their safety. They will not obstruct me in this. Upon my living soul do I swear, you will be my Queen by whatever title you find most suiting. Both you and Renan will always be safe and by my side. Above all else, do I promise you that."

"Know that I never wanted anything other than your company. Know that I will not be bowed to. Know that I don't want to be anyone's queen."

"Nor I their One Rah. Yet here we are," I said, shrugging. "If they insist on kneeling, so be it. It's not so bad once you get used it."

"Then what is your command, my Rah?"

"I command you to kiss me." And, after wiping the tears from her eyes, she did just so.

"One step at a time," she smiled. 'That was easy. What's next?"

"I'm not sure. I need to speak to Baran and Darian. *We* need to speak to Baran and Darian. We need a plan."

"Shall I summon them for you, my Rah?"

"Stop calling me that!"

"Rah Deshu." She spoke purposely. "I must admit, I do like it."

"So sayeth the Grand Mother of Harbinger." I chortled.

"Grandmother? Say that again and I'll have your tongue." She scolded, sticking out her own.

"Petra the Beguiler, perhaps. Wondrous Seer of all things able to be seen." I finished awkwardly.

"That's hardly fair. How might I continue calling you Radesh when it was never your real name?'

"Because I like the way you say it. Besides, outside of my many cruel monikers, it's the only name I've ever known."

"Then it is agreed, at least between us. Though all you need do is command it for it to be so."

"So, I can command you to do whatever I like? Do you truly believe—"

"No." She laughed. "Haeryn knows, I can't risk being caught consorting with someone of your magnificence and power. I could summon Baran and Darian easily enough, however."

"Summon, I like it. So final yet formal at the same time. But I need to speak with Baran alone first. Advise Darian of my orders. Ensure the men secure Grumble as best as they are able. Then bring Darian, Grus, and Myrna to the Hold and we will devise a plan."

"Grus is nearer than my shadow. He's always close by." She paused. "Why Myrna? You know how sullen she becomes when her paints are taken away."

"I need banners bearing the sigil of the One Rah." It was my turn to pause. "Don't tell anyone but I can't recall what the sigil looks like. Not to worry, Baran will know. All I need do is think of a way to make *him think* he thought of it first."

"I don't understand."

"So, he doesn't know that *I don't know*."

"It's a bright yellow sun."

"Or I could just ask you, of course." I chuckled.

"There were many such banners hanging within the concert hall when I was young." She obliged.

"A bright yellow sun? That's it? You're quite sure there's not more to it? Small wonder I forgot." I said disenchanted. "I was hoping for dragons, or lions at least. A fist of flames might have been nice."

"Sorry to be the bearer of sad tidings but a single sun symbolizes the One Son of Harbinger. What the False Rahs didn't destroy have the Khalifah hid in fear." She added.

"Well, the sun it is then." I said, pumping my fist with feigned pride. *Pun intended* for having felt a bit crestfallen in truth.

"The return of the son is more than fitting," she smiled, wiping sweat from her brow. "All that said, like a spicy radish, it's far too hot already. High time for the two of us to be on our way."

Within the confines of the Hold, Baran and I spoke of many things; though more on one topic than the rest. Most of what was said, I decline to share out of respect to us both. Though admittedly unfair to the reader, such is life. What I will decree is that no tears were shared by either party– not even one. I am the One Rah after all. Therefore, whatever I say is truth. *Live with it*. That said, I will confess our main dialogue to be chiefly about the flattened ring. No spoken words have ever pained me more. Being all that you've likely surmised anyway, little more will I say about it. In fairness, there are no words that do justice to the pain shared between us. Imagine yourself in the dark with whatever you fear the most. Which turns out to be yourself and all that you've become. Not your past self, but your present self. The worst thing about it being, there's no way to be rid of it because, as someone or other said recently, you can't outrun yourself. Like fingers clawing at your own throat, it resides in you now. You did it to yourself and you hate yourself for it.

As you've no doubt deduced, daily did he burn himself with the ring. Well, *nightly* for the most part though it changes nothing. Initially, he took it to a blacksmith to have it reforged. Which briefly made me think of the great tree trying to rebirth itself. Baran changed his mind at the last moment. He felt the flattened ring a far better reminder kept as it was– for all he'd done to my mother. Irritated for having wasted his time, the blacksmith tossed it to him whilst still aglow. Staring at the smouldering burn mark in his palm, Baran tossed the smithy a gold coin for his trouble and a silver coin for his tongs.

As Baran's nightmares continued, as they always did; he'd awake soaked to the skin with fear and regret. He'd then kindle a fire before branding himself with the flattened ring. This he did strictly to punish himself for the dreadful deed. This he did so he could never forget what he'd done to the love of his life. And now that I've said that which I was never going to say, I will only reiterate that there were no tears involved. Rooster did not cry. Red Radesh never cried. The Golan Butcher never cried. Nitesh Alde Baran, Follower of the Brightest Star, never cried. And, so too, did the eyes of the One Rah remain clear and dry throughout. Thus, have I written. Thus, it is true.

Sometime later after retreating to the hold, Darian arrived, followed by Myrna, followed by Petra– who was, as commanded by me, perpetually followed by Grus. Besides Baran and I, Greta was the only other body present. Albeit, being far taller and broader than the rest of us, she was impossible to miss.

"All those gathered represent my Chief Council. To better know how I esteem you individually, allow me to render the necessary introductions. Petra is my trusted advisor. Darian One-eye, Fetcher of Endless Ales, is the new Leader of the Brotherhood. Grus commands my bodyguard. Greta is my healer and Myrna oversees communal affairs. Leaving Alde Baran who will forever remain my whipping boy." I waited. The room fell awkwardly silent.

"I spoke in jest. Baran commands no less than he did," I seethed. "Must I commission a Fool to advise you when to laugh? Must I point out there were, not one but, two cleverly crafted comments freely allotted you. Laugh! Your Rah commands it."

Everyone laughed. Though half-heartly, I remained unperturbed. Having never been considered witty, it did not bother me in the least. What did bother me was the fact they'd lost all their boisterousness. Where was that bravado now? No opinions, no thoughts, no one telling me what to say or do— just gaping faces uncertain of their future. That being their mindset, I decided I may as well have a go at them. Why not pull their proverbial chains? Let them think they'd created a monster. After all, it wasn't so long ago I felt myself no less.

"Dance! All of you. Well, except Baran of course. Fetch ale! Fetch wine! I prefer to be thick with the drink before discussing what's to become of us. Then we shall plan our attack. We will form an army. We will sack every village we come to, one by one or all at once— until there's no one left to oppose us. Dance! I command it. After which, Grus shall instruct you on the many delicacies involved with bowing. I am the One Rah and, by all the Gods of Haeryn, I want to be treated as such. But for now, I command all of you to… entertain me!"

Petra and Baran just stared at me, shaking their heads in unison— as well they should. Grus turned so pale he looked about to vomit. Greta and Myrna began swaying back and forth spritely, quite good in reflection. Whilst Darian, as shrewd as always, excused himself to fetch the requested beverages. I almost let him go. Truth be told I felt sorely in need of a drink. Unfortunately, there was no way I could keep up the charade for that long.

"My apologies. I spoke in hope of diminishing the sombre mood swallowing the room. Though a day for dancing will come, this is not that day. Greta! Stop you may. No more dancing today."

Reaffirming my viewpoint, she did not look happy. In fact, I'd stabbed people who'd looked less distressed. Rattling my lips together, I waited for her to settle herself. I considered farting but decided to stifle the urge. Not to mention, there was a strong chance I'd need to punctuate something far more deserving later.

"My beloved friends, we gather here today…." I paused. It sounded far too rehearsed. Which it wasn't. It was anything but. Truthfully, I was not precisely sure what we might accomplish. If anything. I decided to start with something honest. With that in mind, after clearing my throat, I began anew.

"All of you are here because I need and trust you more than I've needed and trusted anyone prior. That is no jest. That is the truth."

Had I admitted more than I should have, I wondered. Judging by their facial expressions, I seemed to have struck a mutual chord amongst them. Though Greta appeared to be nodding far more than warranted. If it was honesty they wanted, I had plenty more to give.

"Before all those present, do I now apologize to Alde Baran if for no other reason that harbouring an overwhelming desire to cut off his head. It was wrong of me. Thus, from this day forward, I vow to treat him with the respect and dignity he deserves."

I bowed low which caused a bit of unease. Though inklings of discomfort amongst the troops wasn't a bad thing, I didn't want to overdo it. Notwithstanding, admissions of fault need swiftly be followed by a position of strength. I'd heard Major Bryn say that once.

"Except amongst ourselves," I added. "Or unless of course he angers me in some small way. At which time, I will do as I see fit. I am the One Rah am I not." Actual laughter ensued.

"As stated, within our present company, you will refer to me as Radesh. Unless of course I command you elsewise. Though that should go without saying." I reminded them nonchalantly.

To be fair, I was feeling rather mindless at that moment. Having prepared nothing ahead of time, my lips were moving in time to my thoughts. Which should never be considered a good thing. I took a breath to better calm my nerves. I heard my mother's voice in my head. *Only a fool speaks quicker than time.* While some might rightfully assume the adage might spark greater reluctance, strangely I found it a timely insight. I was a doer not a talker. All I need do is speak from the heart. Remembering that being the harder part of it.

"Know that, amongst ourselves, it is permissible to speak plainly. In fact, I demand it. As you're all too aware, I have never been a Rah before. That said, being wise beyond my years, I recognize that I need you far more than you need me."

It was a good start. I'd meant every word uttered thus far. Now what? Though I thought hard it was to no avail. The expectant looks shimmering in time to the candlelight's flickers advised me it was high time to pass the torch.

"Now that the preliminaries are out of the way; it's time to discuss business. Petra, being that you are my most trusted advisor, please advise us what it is that we should be discussing first?"

"Well, my R-r-radesh," she was "R" rolling again. I took it as a good sign. A tad mischievous, but good overall considering the overabundance of ways she might make paint me the fool.

"Though you noted Nitesh Alde Baran would *do as he did*, you did not define his role. Is it up for discussion or do you have a plan?"

"Back to me, so soon?" I grimaced, rubbing my lower lip with chagrin. "Our Brightest Star will, not follow, but *lead* my armies." I hoped referring to him as such didn't sound cynical. It wasn't meant to be. Unless of course it was. It very well might have been in hindsight though I had little time to debate it... even now. Moving on.

"He's to be my War Counsellor, my Chief Magistrate, my Planner. The tool by which things find shape to be clear. I'm not certain what *official title* might be necessitated." I scratched my head.

"No wait, I have it. He will be the Prime Administrator. Should I not be present, in all matters; he speaks for me. After all, it was he who got me into this mess in the first place thus it is only fitting for him to carry his fair share... and then some." I grinned.

"What's next?" I asked enthused. I felt we'd made substantial progress. Far more than I would have imagined. I was not about to allow any form of procrastination to curtail it. I was thirsty, however.

"Is there any wine?" I inquired meekly. After hollering loudly out the door, Darian nodded to confirm it was on the way.

"What next is entirely up to you," said Baran. "Regardless of what you wish to call any of us you remain the One Rah. Rest assured, Radesh, I will be whatever you need me to be. But it is up to you to command. You have but to plot your course and together shall we endeavour to walk it."

He made it sound so easy though I knew full well it was anything but. Still, his final words had kindled a fire within me. I knew not only what I wanted to do but precisely who I wanted to do it too.

"We will gather an army. We will overthrow the Kedera."

It wasn't a request. It was a command. I said it as such. The immediate silence spoke volumes. In fact, it was deafening.

"What?" I asked bemused. "It should come as no surprise. I despise the Kedera. I will see that the Four False Rahs hang. We've been fighting a losing war against them for years. That will change. The Kedera dogs must die!"

My last words were greeted by more silence. Finally, it was Petra who spoke.

"Radesh," she said softly. "You are *the Kedera*." A chill ran through my bones.

"I am not. Why would you say such a thing?" I gasped trying to regain my composure. I felt enraged to be clear. I swear, had it been anyone else I would have reached for my sword. Not that I had one with me and not that I would have delimbed anyone. It was just so unexpected, not to mention untrue.

"Where's my wine?" I hollered like an insolent child.

"Radesh, don't you see? It's like I told you before when I asked what if you'd been born on the opposing side of Haeryn's wall?."

I stared at her in disbelief not wanting to hear the words I knew to be forthcoming. *How dare she?* Though dare she, she did.

"As it turns out, you *were* born on the *far side*. That being, the northern side. Radesh, your parents, aunts, uncles, and cousins; even your great, great grandparents... were all Kedera born."

Chilled to my core, the fire within had been utterly doused. Gratefully, we were interrupted by a knock on the door. The wine had arrived. And not a moment too soon.

"The meeting is over! Everyone out!" I blathered aloud.

"Motion to overrule," exclaimed Baran. "All in favour raise a hand."

Not surprisingly, all save Grus raised their hands. I suddenly liked Grus better than the other *conspirator*s. He could stay and drink with me. The rest would need to leave. And hastily, if I was them.

"You can't overrule me! I am the One Rah!" I sneered.

"You are the One Rah," echoed Baran. "But you commanded us to speak plainly so speak plainly I will."

"Ah, so that command holds merit while *everyone out* doesn't. How foolish of me. I understand now. Commands are commands only when they suit you!"

"Calm yourself, Radesh. Look at me." He had nerve enough to say. "There will always be unpleasant truths. But that does not render them untrue. Make no mistake, governing a war-torn nation is no easy task. In fact, I expect there will be more bad days than good." He sighed. "I would not wish it upon anyone." Baran, also known as... *one of many who would not be getting any wine*, added.

"Yet you wish it upon me. Elsewise, you would have wisely held your tongue."

"Radesh," interrupted Petra. "If Nitesh Alde Baran speaks for you, if he truly is your Counsellor then, as difficult as the words might be to hear, there are times when you need listen."

I glared at her, knowing she was right. She was always right. Is it possible to love someone yet despise them at the same time. I wonder not. You can trust me, it is.

"Wine! And just me, no one else!" I commanded, holding out my cup. It worked. Apparently, I was still able to summon wine. If nothing else, it was a start.

"Grus! Why did you not raise your hand with the other collaborators? Enlighten me."

"I have no love for the Kedera."

"Precisely how I would have said it. Bring Grus some wine." It was obvious that being the only other person drinking wine made him immensely uncomfortable. I was getting somewhere. More progress.

"I take it you're not from there, Grus. You weren't born on the *offensive side* of Haeryn's Wall?"

"No," he admitted. "Far from it."

"But apparently–" And let me tell you, I had to swallow a significant mouthful of wine just to get the next words out.

"Though I've turned fields red with their blood, I find myself suddenly on trial– accused of being the Kedera. Recognizing your next words will likely determine whether, or not, your mug gets refilled, how do you feel about that Grus?" Placing his mug upon the table, Grus made no reply. His face had turned white again.

"Ah, so the same as me– sick to my stomach! I can't say I blame you for I would not drink with a Kedera dog either."

"I did not say that! That is not what I intended at all." Grus pleaded fretfully.

"No one hates the Kedera more than I. No one has butchered more of them than I!" I shouted. "Yet again, my entire life has been a lie!" I continued to rant shamelessly.

"Not a lie," consoled Baran. "You were just born at a different time. A time when it mattered not what side of the wall you stemmed from. A time when our people were singularly united."

"Prior to that, there was no wall," finished Petra.

"Now, what am I to do?" I pleaded in angst.

"Just as you said," spoke Darian. "We gather an army. We hang the Four False Rahs. One by one; or all at once." I took a long sip of wine. It was only me drinking now. It did seem right.

"So, you're suggesting we kill the Rahs, but not the Kedera so much. Admittedly, it's going to take some time to wrap my head around that." I grimaced. "'Tis a bitter pill for certain. I should have known. Nothing good ever happens without some form of misery lurking within. I am a fool. I am a sham. Nothing in my world has proved itself to be true. Nothing."

"Ant grub! We were all Harbinger once," barked Baran. "Not so very long ago, when your father ruled, Golan and Kedera were merely two of nine territories– nothing more. We were all one people. We were united. The Kedera people were wrongly blamed for the assassination of the One Rah. It was wholly the False Rahs who orchestrated the assassination. I know it to be true."

"Then this is my order then." I hissed. "To hell with Haeryn and his bloody big wall! I want that thing taken down. I want it crumbled to be clear. Does that meet with everyone's approval or am I to be overruled again?"

"That works." Laughed Darian. "We need an army first. A very big army prior to attempting such a thing. 'Tis is a bold move for certain. The wall protects us as much as them." Darian attested.

"Convince the people of Harbinger you're the true heir and flock to you they will," added Greta. *Did I mention how much I adored the woman?* She did have her moments.

"But how does one go about gathering an army... *from both sides?*" Petra finished.

"First and foremost, we need to spread word of your return. It need be known within every corner of Harbinger." Baran stated.

"Ah, and that is why Myrna stands amongst us." I exhaled, feeling a bit brighter about the situation. At least, momentarily.

"I require banners; banners bearing my father's sigil."

"The yellow sun," Myrna nodded. "It shall be done." And there it was, even Myrna knew more than I did. Except, following my earlier conversation with Petra, I had something else in mind.

"A yellow sun over a great tree," I corrected. "I'm making a slight addition. The sun may have risen but without the shade of this great tree not one of us would be here."

"I like that," replied Baran.

"What? You're not going to overrule me? Remember this day; the day the One Rah made a command that stood." I chuckled.

"In what style?" Myrna inquired with keen interest.

"What would you suggest?" I shrugged for having not a clue styles might even be involved.

"Gonfalon." She suggested following a long thoughtful pause.

"That's perfect." I nodded inanely. Admittedly, I dodged an arrow there for having misinterpreted her at first. For my initial thought was *yes, I expect we'll be gone for quite some time.*

"And what colour should the background be?" Myrna inquired with mounting interest.

"Blood red." I stated firmly.

"I'll drink to that," laughed Darian. Noting I did not oppose— or so I'd like to think— more cups were fetched. Petra made a toast.

"To the return of the Son." She decreed favourably and raising our mugs, we drank.

"Haeryn help us." I added. To which we toasted once more.

With the worst of it behind us, we continued our scheming

throughout the night. We would head to Harkenspear together; after which Darian would proceed East with the Brotherhood; whilst the remainder would eventually proceed southward to the Isles of Eyre. Though a modest plan, we embraced it for no other reason than it being more than we had before. Which was nothing if you care to recall.

Why East? And why to the Isles? To spread word of my return chiefly, not to mention Darian had not been home for several years. Though there was far more to the Isles. The Isles were full of fierce fighting men and women known to be neutral though sworn to the One Rah prior to the arrival of the False Rahs. Additionally, having been the eldest daughter of the King, within their circles I could learn more about my mother, Audrey of Eyre. I also sought proof in respect to my lineage as that was where Baran went following the death of my mother. So, surely someone there would know the truth of things.

I'd like to profess the sun being a bit brighter after that, but it wasn't. I was sorely sick from the drink the following morning. Then again, I was no longer just the One Rah. I'd become the Kedera. I hadn't seen that coming. That was going to take some time to adjust to– and a hell of a lot more wine. As soon as I recovered my wits that is being that I couldn't stand the sight of it presently.

It had been decided that the first third of us would depart the following evening. Darian dubbed us the *Mighty Ninety-nine*. Being that there were ninety men, eight women, and one baby totalling as much. The remaining thirds would venture forth upon each of the following nights, leaving no one behind. Darian and the Brotherhood, apart from Grus and his bodyguard, would be the first to depart. They would set camp in a small forest by a lake just south of Harkenspear. Being that they knew this route well, and providing they left during the late afternoon, Darian attested they should be clear of Kestrel only slightly after dawn. Though they'd have to walk beneath the blistering sun for a few stiflingly hours, he felt confident they would survive. I only hoped it was so.

Baran and his wives, save for Myrna, would depart next. They would be accompanied by two dozen men who would take turns dragging Baran on his shield. Being that their progress would be much slower, night two's strategy called for a small group of Darian's men to return with tents and meet them half-way. Not merely to replenish their water but provide them some fresh game with luck.

Although Baran looked decidedly healthier with each passing day, he looked positively miserable whilst being dragged away on his newly painted shield– with his small chest of gold, plus a slightly larger one housing the coins from the painting frames, tucked between his legs. Though entirely unbefitting, dragging him was a necessity. No doubt, his wives walking alongside him was a direct a slap in the face to his ailing ego. Oddly, I had no problem with that.

"Hang on tight, old man," I smiled, slapping him on the back and bidding him farewell. *May your days be long and your nights full of cheer*. Darian, with Chitter clinging tightly to his shoulder, was no less sympathetic. Handing Baran his broad sword, Agatha, Darian then proposed he use it as a rudder to better steady himself throughout his journey. Let just say Baran's retort was more long-winded than cordial. He did mutter something about collecting the gold coins he'd scatter behind him so they might be shoved where the sun never shone which I did find rather humorous.

Petra, Renan, and I would leave last, escorted by Myrna and the remainder of men. I was more worried about Myrna than I was about either Renan or Baran. She simply refused to rest. Since having been asked to paint the banners, she'd not stopped once. She'd created near to a hundred of them at last count. To her credit, they all looked precisely the same, which is to say: remarkable. I only wished they bore something a bit more fearful. Then again, following Petra's reminder that goats and geese were the most fearful things in the world to me, I expect I should count my blessings.

Other than Myrna's gallery of paintings, the Red Room's books, and some fermenting wine and ale; I ordered Grumble be restored as much as possible to its original state. I'm pleased to affirm the work went swiftly. We buried whatever we couldn't take with us. As it turned out, burying our excess accumulations served a dual purpose for providing more places to attach ropes to better support Grumble. Of course, I pretended that had been my full intention all along. I did hear overhear someone praising the One Rah for his *profound ingenuity*. Though Petra knew better she chose to hold her tongue. I could not help but notice her bowing had improved as well. It seemed hope had not abandoned us.

I must confess, it was not without a measure of sadness that I left Grumble. I hated the desert. I hated the heat. I hated the sand. *Don't get me started*. But the great tree had been our saviour. We all knew it. I thought about saying a few words as such, but I could not devise a way to impart my feelings that did not sound overly nostalgic. In the end my final act was to place the Harbinger cat head alongside Amos and Taggart's atop the white skull wall. Baran would have liked that. *Keep an eye out*, I told it. Having done so proved to amuse me later whilst shuffling through the sand. As usual, I found myself unable to curtail my thoughts from wandering off in every direction.

"What are you chuckling about?" asked Petra.

I told her what I'd said to the dead cat's head before leaving. She just stared at me. I was just about to explain when, finally, she began laughing aloud. Without question, had I removed the arrow from the creature's eye it would not have been so humorous. But I hadn't. In hindsight, out of respect to Baran, I should have boiled it first. But I hadn't. I'm not sure why it seemed so comical. It didn't matter. Petra was laughing. That's all that mattered. That and the reunification of Harbinger. A Rah must keep his priorities intact.

"You know what's more amusing?" I asked. She shook her head negatively.

"Don't tell Myrna but, if I was to do it over again, a Harbinger cat head with an arrow sticking out of its eye would be my new sigil." I grinned.

That kept us chuckling over the next few dunes. Except when Petra called out to Myrna feigning to tell her. She'd adored pulling my chain. She found it quite entertaining. Admittedly, she got more dunes out of it than I bargained. Petra was reliable that way. You could always depend on her for input of that sort. My time would come. After all, what went around the sun, came around the sun. I figured we'd travelled only five or six leagues thus far with at least thirty still ahead of us. To arrive in Harkenspear that is, just to be clear. In such dire conditions, even the smallest glint of merriment should never be exploited too hastily. Come dawn, a good laugh would be precious. As it turned out, I never did find my revenge for my mood sullied with each pending step. *Pending?* More like never-ending.

It was a starless night. The demeanour of the Gods being what it was, the moon had chosen to abandon us shortly after our departure. But that shallowed in comparison to the sand. I loathed it. It was everywhere you looked as far as the eye could see. Which, depending where you were on the dune, wasn't always that far. Sand was meant to be near a lake or an ocean. If for no other reason than having the ability to wash the frightful stuff off. It got everywhere. Like a sweat-soaked djellaba, it clung to you. Every step taken caused it to scrape the backs of my knees. I could feel it in my ears. I could hear it grinding. It made my skin crawl each time I tried in vain to clear it with a sandy finger. Its agenda was obvious. It wanted nothing more than to stuff my skull. I was riddled with it. We all were.

Even with our faces completely covered, it found a way to scurry up our noses. Sounds of coughing and hacking and wheezing were no less constant than the dunes that arose to taunt us. It made us despise our necessity for breath. Eventually, you stopped trying to clear your nose because it'd turned so dry. The only moisture remaining were the clumps of blood you had no choice but to snort out as best you could. Sooner than later, your mind began to dissolve, and you gave up the fight. You had to face facts. The endless parade of grit was always going to win.

It was then that you began to question your existence. *Why you were here?* Not why you were on the planet but walking through an endless patchwork of sand. There was no rationale. Like a brow beaten dog, the Kedera dog I'd become, my head fell lower. One's perception in all manner of things became altered. Nothing was safe. Regardless of what you thought of, it turned to sand. And suddenly, the desert seemed no different than all I'd become. Living or dead, it would prove itself the eventual heir to all things— the one true Rah you had no choice other than to bow to. Every inhalation hurt. Such was life providing you could weather its persistent sting, the relentless nagging. What had started as an irritation had now become routine. It was the way things were. *Horrific.*

You could taste it in your mouth; being coarse, gravely, and bland. The merest flicker against your tongue caused it to run the length where it piled itself gleefully in the back of your throat like a plug. Having put yourself through this painstaking exercise of futility before, you knew, should you survive, you'd excrete a blood-streaked trail of grit for days on end.

Sand. It had no business being here. Sand had no business being anywhere devoid of water if for no other reason than being the purest definition of the word *devoid*. The Kestrel was a barren wasteland. As empty as it was deficient, it could never quench its perpetual thirst. That was the one lone constant, wasn't it? Other than to crave, deserts had no agenda. Being comprised wholly of ground stone, nothing could ever be equally as parched.

Deserts were forged of thirst after all. Its persistence undeniable, no rock could withstand the resolve of the Kestrel. Scorched by sun, tattered by wind, trampled by fantasies of rain; ages and ages ago, a gargantuan granite headstone was forced to bow unto the interminable dominance of the elements. Having been found wanting, its pride slowly whittled, the rock began to slump. No longer able to stand tall, its once-sharp shoulders became rounded and stooped. It was the beginning of the end for the obstinacy of rock had been brought into question. Therefore, the Gods felt it only right that its acclaimed stubbornness be put to the test. Being as cruel as it was unrelenting, know that any trial adjudicated by the elements was no less than that of the Gods. And to think we were made of flesh and bone. The chief difference being, the rock could not run, and neither could it hide. It had no choice other than to endure. Days turned into weeks; weeks to months; months to years; and years to centuries; until one day a hairline crack appeared within its hitherto impermeable skin.

And there it was, the day had come, the spirit of the rock had been broken. Once cracked, its fate was sealed. The verdict rendered by those once thought to be its peers was merciless. Doomed to undergo further segregation, the rock was degraded unto boulders; boulders shattered unto stones; the stones were smashed into pebbles; and pebbles ground until naught but fine grains of sand. *Fine* sand– the ultimate paradox– as if ever there was such a thing. Such were my thoughts as I walked. I hated the rock. For had it not gave way there would be no sand– and, above all things else– more than geese, more than goats– I hated sand. That said, what might be blander than a sigil of sand? *Grrr.*

Petra spoke to me; the others spoke to me; yet I made no answer. I just shuffled along mindlessly consumed by own dark thoughts. With each shuffled step, the future moved closer. I was fearful of it. As much as I wanted to be rid of this endless ocean of emptiness, I saw no promise of greener pastures ahead for every unfamiliar territory I envisioned were just more realms of the unknown. Declaring oneself the One Rah in the middle of a desert was one thing; pronouncing yourself the One Rah to the people of Harbinger was quite another– notwithstanding their present rulers. Even if I was truly the Heir of Harbinger, who was I to them really? Rooster? A petty thief. The Golan Butcher? A homicidal soldier. Or Red Radesh? A murderous lunatic.

Shortly before dawn we reached the encampment left for us by Darian's group, a few of which greeted us with replenished supplies. They'd brought salted fish for dinner which was a welcome surprise and my spirits rose slightly. The Kestrel could break me without lifting a finger. Like all things, it was only just a matter of time. I was not made of sand, but neither was I a rock and I knew it. Darian's crew informed us we were still six leagues short of our initial destination. They'd erected a large shelter under which we'd have to wait out the day. It was unbearably hot; there was no Great Tree's shadow to protect us here. Had we journeyed onward, most of us would have arrived safely enough; but most wasn't all. And so, we waited, panting like wretched dogs while reeking of sweat.

We had to keep careful watch for the many sand snakes slithering about. Grus queried whether it was the smell of the fish or us that attracted them in such hordes. To help pass the time, I suggested we put it to the test. Retrieving fish bones from the sand where we'd tossed them, we made a hefty pile at the far end of the shelter. I was planning to have them placed farther away in the sun, but Petra pointed out that the intense heat would give the bones an unfair advantage. Grus concurred, stating while he had no problem being our Snee pig, he was adamant that his stench be given an unbiased opportunity.

In the end, we declared Grus the incontestable winner. Though, it wasn't true for every snake having visited the fish bones prior to wiggling their way toward him, it did make for more mirth. Let's face it, insulting a pile of fish bones was boring in comparison to professing one of your own the most putrid thing alive. From that day forward, we oft times referred to Grus as *the Snake Charmer*. He seemed to like the moniker for, in direct contrast to his normal demeanour, he became quite chatty afterward.

Grus attested the Bro-Zil's former leader had not been lying in stating they'd known of the Great Tree and its hidden well for quite some time. Noting, they avoided the Kestrel– as did everyone– as much as possible confessing it to be as good, if not better, an assassin than they themselves. He acknowledged that the Brotherhood had hidden caches of food and supplies throughout Harbinger. Not enough for an army by any means, though ample enough for a small raiding party.

When asked more specifically about weapons, he told me they had one large reserve southeast of Harkenspear in Snee, another smaller one in West Nyce. They also had a blacksmith forge on the Kaen peninsulas and another in West Foot; adding he expected the West Foot forge would fall to the Kedera, if it hadn't done so already, being that the Brotherhood's new allegiance had no doubt reached the ears of the Four False Rahs by now.

By mid-afternoon, it became so hot we begat soaking our head scarfs in water. It was foolhardy to do so, on the off chance we somehow got stranded, but we did it anyway. Grus took us by surprised when he began digging a shallow pit in the sand within the confines of a surplus canopy. I judged Grus to be about thirty years of age; with hair and eyes blacker than a crow. When asked what he was up to he simply smiled deviously. After drawing eight rows of grid lines across the pit with his sword. He then picked seven players, himself being the Eighth, amongst those, including myself, who'd raised our hands purely out of curiosity. Admittedly, I should have known better for no other reason than the arrow protruding from the Harbinger cat's eye. That said, as tired as we were, it was far too hot to sleep.

"Now we bet," he said. "Silver coins buy first row squares; gold coins may start anywhere within the first four. Place your tokens wisely," he advisedly smugly.

"But what are the rules?" I inquired, tossing my gold dagger into a vacant square in the centre of the Fourth row. I was no fool. A coin might easily be lost in the sand.

"Rules are simple; first one to the other end wins!"

"But what's the catch?" I asked, recalling Bear's wooden leg and the scheming farmers. It wasn't the only time I'd been cheated. Far from it. And there was always a catch.

Suspiciously, Grus waited for the other six players to enter their tokens before answering. Looking about feverishly, having spotted a sand snake, he pinned its head with the hilt of his sword, retrieving it as though he'd done it a hundred times before. I tossed him my gold coin in hopes of rattling him whilst his hands were full. Though it did rattle the snake, that being its tail; it didn't rattle Grus in the least.

I knew right then that my gold coin was as good as lost. No surprise, I'd never been very good at gambling. Holding the snake's head in one hand he snatched the coin out of the air with his other hand, pocketing it casually. As though it had been his from the start. Which it no doubt was now. I imagine he could have broken it into silver coins had I asked without the slightest hesitation.

"If snake touches token nearer to its head, the token moves up two squares," he smiled, shaking the snake's head roughly. "If touched by tail, two squares backward you go," he continued, pointing a finger towards its noisy rattle.

"What if it doesn't touch it at all?" Petra asked. Though she wasn't playing, it was an astute question.

"All tokens spared by the Gods move upward one square."

"What if it touches it in the middle?" She further inquired.

"Then we vote, then argue, followed by more arguing." Grus chuckled.

"How does it end?" I wondered aloud.

"As I said, when the snake reaches any opposite side, the round is over. Then we fetch the snake and begin again."

"*We* fetch it? I think one of the losers should have to fetch it." I contested. I didn't like snakes. For that matter, I didn't like any creature you couldn't steep a decent gravy from.

"I'll fetch it." Grus allowed.

"And how many rounds are there?"

"Until we grow tired of it; run out of coins; or someone dies. Easy, right?" Dropping the snake's head he began rubbing its tail, twisting it swiftly back and forth in his hands.

"What are you doing? You're making it angry. Should Petra be bitten, I'll bury you in that pit."

"The snake must be dizzy, or it won't slither properly."

"You're the dizzy one," Petra noted, shaking her head. "This is madness."

"Just a game," Grus sighed.

"And what do you call this game?" She pressed him, clearly not amused with the proceedings.

"*Snakes* or *Adders*." He shrugged. "It's usually played with black adders. They're smaller, allowing for more squares; more squares mean more coins. Notwithstanding, adders are far more deadly."

"And more deadly means… *more coins!*" We finished together laughing.

Grus released the hissing snake in the top left corner of the pit, that being his right. It slithered back and forth heatedly, missing all tokens except mine— which it touched with its head once, followed by its tail. *What did I say?* While I grimaced, Grus hopped eagerly into the pit to recapture the snake precisely the same way as he had before. Holding the wriggling snake in one hand, he then moved my gold dagger two squares up prior to returning it to the exact same square it had started in. It was then I realized he'd been spending far too much time with Petra of late. I mean, why move it at all save to give my chain an underserving yank?

"Perhaps you could make the necessary calculations in your head next time," I suggested. "I see no reason to gloat about the misfortunes of others." I mocked while Petra clapped merrily. Of course, she did.

"Everyone else, up one square." He smiled. I'd forgotten about that part. *Grrr.*

Round two saw the snake's prejudice tail touch my token yet again, leaving all eight of us in a dead heat being that I'd been the only one foolish enough to risk a gold coin. I didn't mind. It was Grus who'd given me the coin, having taken it from one of the dead assassins. He'd refused to keep it for fearing it would bring him bad luck. Now that it was back in his pocket, I could only cross my fingers with high hopes.

Being ornery creatures at best, it took the lives of three more sand snakes to complete the game. At the risk of doing the tale a disservice, Grus did ultimately win in the end. I did note he'd placed his token on the same side the snakes entered the pit. I'm not suggesting that he was cheating but rather that he knew a lot more about the habits of dizzy serpents than the rest of us. They did appear to slither left more so than right. Like Grus, snakes appeared to be attracted to gold. My dagger was touched eleven out of thirteen tries. In fact, it feigned to be a snake itself for having moved upward as much as down. Following the contest, I made a mental note never to gamble with Grus again for having a strong feeling he'd win regardless of the game.

By sunset, at last count, we'd killed seventeen sand snakes in total. I noticed one man skin a couple of them prior to baking them in the sun. After which he ate them. No thank you. They're bony things at best. Aside from Grus's insistence that their venom be milked, we began tossing their headless bodies as far as we could. Which quickly became an entirely new distraction. Outside of the spin method, which was oft times hazardous, ramming a short sword down their throats and giving it a good flick proved the most successful technique. Rest assured, should the pastime provide half as satisfying as it did us, you will consider it time well spent. In all honesty I ask you, what better way is there to deal with an over-abundance of snakes? In all seriousness, there is none.

In hindsight, I never should have given Renan one of their rattles to play with. Hardly surprising, Petra was not pleased. In my defence, it's not as though he'd put it in his mouth. I never realized just how smelly snakes were until that day. As soon as you touched one, it became impossible to rid your hands of the stench. The odour was nauseating. *Worse than Renan poo* was how Petra put it. Which was near as bad as Grus. That being, only slightly less revolting than fetid fish bones. As dusk approached, having run out of snakes to throw, we soon departed. To my delight, the journey passed swiftly. Which is to say, I was in a far better mood than the previous day. Not to mention the terrain had finally changed. After Haeryn knows how many weeks, we were finally free of the desert. Though still stifling, the heat was almost bearable in the daylight. If for no other reason than there being *no— more— sand.*

Just as I was gauging the notable differences between Baran and Darian's silhouettes, they rose to greet us— only to sit back down. For as soon as I saw the lake, I dropped everything. It was magical. It was wondrous. And it was beckoning. Just the thought of being rid of the sand, not to mention that snake smell, was overpowering. Like a loosed arrow, ignoring my awaiting companions, I headed straight for it. The remainder of our company continued to the camp prior to running into the water. To be clear, it's not that they had greater self-discipline, they were simply far more encumbered than myself. Shedding my djellaba, I waded in waist deep, letting myself fall headlong into its refreshing depths. Nothing ever felt so good. Looking up, I saw Petra rushing toward me with Renan in her arms. Disrobing, she tossed her garments onto the shore, untied her hair braid, and slid gracefully beneath the cool water.

Okay, so I was slightly hasty in respect to that *nothing ever feeling so good* thing. This was it and I knew it. The most perfect moment of my life thus far. She kissed my cheek as I swept my son from her arms. Though the moon had returned it was still quite dark, so she was able to bathe without concern of being seen by anyone other than myself. Not that she would have cared. Though I did very much just to be clear. While Renan clung to my neck, I washed myself as best I could prior to giving the wee fellow a good rinse. As Renan refused to stop splashing, I laid him on my chest. We floated together on our backs; him, watching the stars high above; and me, eyeing Petra's every movement. I had changed. I was no longer the man I used to be. Prior to her, had I seen a naked woman bathing— regardless of beauty for Petra had no rivals— well, it doesn't matter now, does it? Though not an excuse, and nor am I proud of it in any way, I was a different person back then. I was a Rah now— *the Rah* rather. The surrounding trees; the sky above; I expect even the lake we were floating in… belonged to me.

I felt ashamed; not merely for how I'd treated women in the past but more so for being unable to see it until now. Was it love that had enlightened me or rather the expectations demanded of a leader? *Both likely*, as much as I hated to admit it. With leadership came responsibility. If ever I was to win over the people of Harbinger, I would have to act as though I was justifiably deserving of the title. If it was permissible for me to haul a naked woman upon the shore and ravish her soft, drenched skin then it was permissible for any man to do so. That said, I wasn't precisely sure if there was a law against doing so. Undoubtedly, we were fashioned after the Gods for what other reason might there possibly be for us being so cruel and heartless at times?

Knowing my actions influenced the behaviour of all those in my charge, I swore to myself that my own conduct would change from this day forth. No longer would I allow myself to act anything other than that expected of a highly revered dignitary. Not that I knew anything about that sort of thing. Still, as much as it might pain me, I would endeavour to set an example of superior etiquette from this moment forth. Whisking me from my ponderings, Renan laughed as a stream of bubbles broke the water's surface. With great haste, I paddled us clear of the area at once for the air smelling similar to fetid sand snake. Let it be known that I was quite serious in respect to altering my behaviour. It felt only proper to make such a pact. Besides, how hard could it be to display a bit of propriety now and again? No, *all the time and without fail*, I quickly reminded myself. It was not something easily achieved however for, even in that moment, I found myself unable to stifle a strong urge to fart. All in good time, I suppose. After so many days of endless heat and sand, the bubbles did feel quite marvellous. Almost magical in truth.

Though I knew neither the word nor the meaning at the time, I was feeling *philosophical*. Tracing Petra's faultless profile drifting atop the serene water, I found myself envious. It caressed her body without asking. *Why should I refrain?* It embraced her entirety every time she sank below its surface, impressing its agenda upon her without entreating the merest nod of consent. Entangling her long black hair, it massaged her skin, before cuddling her brazenly. *Why shouldn't I?* Enveloping her skin with obvious intent; the water breached her hidden alcoves at will. Thus, yet again I found myself second-guessing my most recent declaration.

Why not me? Because I was the One Rah, I reminded myself. I was alarmed by how swiftly I'd sunk to such depths of depravity. Because my intentions were purely selfish whereas the water held her aloft making her feel as weightless as she did safe. *Could I do the same?* While it nourished her with the utmost fluidity, all I could do was pray I'd be able to protect her from whatever evils lay lurking. It was then I vowed to rename the lake upon my first opportunity. I would name it, Envy Lake.

"I have not been a good man," I said, putting an abrupt end to her tranquillity. "I've been a thief. I've committed heinous war crimes. I've treated women unkindly."

"You've done as you were told and taught. As many of us, you did what you must to survive."

"I can assure you; I've done a great deal more than that. Though it pains me to say it; I bedded many women and never gave it a second thought. I expect Renan is not the only child abandoned by me."

"Do not think for a moment that is not something I haven't considered," she said moving closer. It seemed that the lake wasn't quite done tormenting me. Its slowly advancing waterline teased me with glimpses of desire.

"The question is, who are you now?" As she stared at me, I wished my hands were tracing her own if for no other reason than to free them from her hips.

"A fool who is sorry for his past mistakes. A fool who wishes he could run away with you and hide. The fool who wants to wed you more than all things else." I answered truthfully.

"A fool is not a fool providing he learns from his mistakes. Know that a fool is not someone I would ever run away with; and you are no fool, for I will not marry a fool." She countered evenly.

"Will you marry a Rah? I intend to ask the Major for your hand the moment I see him." I replied, biting my lip just as she did.

"Is that a proposal?" She asked. Oddly, though it was I who'd said it, I had not thought of it as such. Thus, her query took me greatly by surprise.

"I suppose it is," I answered.

"You suppose?" Her tone rising near as high as her eyebrows.

"It is." I attested. "It is most definitely."

"Most definitely... and that's the best you can do?" She smirked, before continuing. "It might be wiser to wait until my brother's better acquainted with the whole *Rah thing* before you ask. He can be pigheaded at times, and it'd be a lot to swallow all at once."

"As you say. I would kneel before a thousand dragons it that's what it took to win you. I would kneel right now save for fear of drowning Renan."

"I don't need you to kneel before any dragons."

"I could slay them if you like. Though contrary to my new position, I'm not beyond begging." She ignored that luckily.

"I've decided to accept your proposal, given the

circumstances," she smiled.

"Given the circumstances?" I wished to clarify. It's not like I'd been holding her head under water for Haeryn's sake. Even I knew that was frowned upon. Though arguably acceptable during some avenues of courtship, my offhand approach had been far more cordial.

"Though not how I'd imagined it in my mind's eye, in all honesty, I never imagined we'd be both naked when you asked. It is quite romantic given the moon and all."

"You did say yes, right? You do know it's me?" I wished to further clarify.

"Yes. I did say, yes. No dragons please, but a thousand times yes." She laughed. Her face lit up brighter than the moon.

"It won't be easy," I confessed. "I fear for your safety. Our enemies will see you as the swiftest path to defeat me."

"Then you will have to protect us." She insisted, taking Renan from me. "Rahs do not kneel, not to dragons and certainly not False Rahs! Give me your word that you will not kneel under any circumstances, and you will have my consent."

"You have my word, my lady. I will not kneel before anyone save you."

"Then kneel!" She joked. I took a quick breath as she pushed my head beneath the water. As I moved toward her, she grabbed me by the hair and hauled me back up.

"Not in front of our son!" She scolded.

"He couldn't see a thing," I laughed.

"Nor will he for a long, long time. And know this, he won't be fathering children in every other village!" She blurted.

"Agreed; every village it is then." I jested, which quickly made my right cheek sting. I did have it coming. Truth was, I deserved a great deal more than that. But I was a changed man now. I was the One Rah, and I was determined to act the part. Unless we were alone that is. Thus, bowing low apologetically, I led her drenched bareness out of the water with a guiding hand. Though it took me quite some time to discern precisely how I felt in that moment it did come to me eventually. Plain and simple, I was happy.

"I once read amongst the nobility the proper response after farting is to beg one's pardon." She smirked at me whilst dressing.

"Oh, you heard that." I shrugged.

"I imagine half of Harkenspear heard that."

"Beg pardon for what?" I wondered aloud.

"I suppose it amounts to merely admitting responsibility,

taking ownership of the foul deed if you will."

"Oh, I have no issue with that." I assured her.

"No, I expect you don't," she laughed. "Hark. Hark."

"Who goes there?" I replied, being the only acceptable response to the childhood jest which I hadn't heard since a young lad.

"Tutor."

"Tutor who?"

"Toot or no toot I smell you." *Silliness*. It was a good thing.

Being notably tired, little words were shared between any of us while devouring a stew consisting of duck, rice, wild mushrooms, and something slimy that gave me pause initially. Eels perhaps. I did not ask for fearing the answer. Whatever the case, no doubt it was better than sand snakes. It seemed the mosquitoes and gnat flies were no less famished for they would not relent regardless of how smoky we tried to make the campfire. Having cursed them aloud several times, Darian informed me that our present location was named Gnat Lake. Which was why he'd chosen the place. The flying pests were so aggressive this time of year, he'd felt quite confident we'd have the place to ourselves. Upon receiving that bit of information, I decided not to have the lake renamed after all. It seemed only right. It did serve as a warning; one I wished I'd received prior to bathing. I'd scratched so feverishly my fingernails were thick with blood. I swear, just one more bite on the back of my neck and my head would be hewn. Perhaps there were worse things than sand after all. That said, as ferocious as they were, a gnat would make a very poor banner sigil.

The night passed near as slowly as Baran's ceaseless whittling. I don't think the insects bothered him the slightest. In hindsight, I expect they couldn't pierce that tough hide of his for all the scars. He sat there carving away while staring into the fire. It's like his fingers moved purely by memory. I wasn't sure what was louder, the crackling fire or the constant buzz in my ears. I was forced to tuck Renan inside my djellaba as I feared for his life. Petra took him from me a short while later, likely due to me having nodded off several times. I dreamt of giant insects picking their teeth with the bones of my fallen comrades. Which is to intend, I slept very little, if at all. Sometime before dawn, Darian clasped a hand over my mouth– a terrible way to be awoken while visualizing a gargantuan bug gnawing at your face. And that is saying something, considering his unkempt greasy hair and that big bug eye of his. *Okay, so I suppose I did fall asleep eventually.*

Darian said nothing, thank the gods; or I likely would have

soiled myself. In my defence, the duck didn't agree with me. Then again, it may have been those weird slimy things. They had one eye too, come to think of it. Ogling me like a crazed fiend, Darian nodded toward the campfire not far from us. What I witnessed, upon rising to my knees, kindled my anger so greatly I knew I could not possibly address it without waking everyone. As much as it was a concern, it did not warrant everyone's scrutiny. I could tell Darian thought similarly for he hunkered off in a different direction straight away. As troubling as it was, I would deal with it in the morning. Providing there was anything left of me. It was strange to try to sleep during the night. Which is likely another reason it did not come easy to me even being as exhausted as I was.

Late the next morning, we had a hasty breakfast of berries and cornbread. I passed on the smoked eel. *Ah, so that's what it was! Eww.* The plan was to proceed directly to Harkenspear. The problem with having *plans* is that regardless of the countless hours spent planning, notwithstanding the contingency planning; it is my contention that, things rarely go according to plan. I know this because I'd followed many a plan, concocted by many a clever man, to the letter I might add; and still encountered endless situations completely divergent to that very same plan.

I thought about this a lot, while trudging countless leagues of sand, which has led me to conclude than a plan is akin to wishful thinking more so than any form of reliable plot. In fact, it's my deduction that the only plans with a workable chance are those stolen from your enemies as, at least then, both parties are aware of the plan. Admittedly, this is a long way of foreshadowing that, on this day; yet again, our plans did not go *according to plan.* Which, if you couldn't tell, was neither to my amusement nor surprise.

Once the camp was dismantled, our group departed for Harkenspear led by Darian except for Baran and myself as I needed to speak to him *alone.* The trail through the woodlands was quite narrow therefore I knew we'd catch up with them in short order. While waiting for the final stragglers to leave, I passed the time by skipping stones across the lake's glassy surface. I enjoyed watching the hordes of bugs scatter as the rocks sliced through the morning mist. From time to time, hungry trout drew circular ripples in the water making me hope I'd intercepted a flight path or two. The backs of my ears were so bulbous and itchy, I had half a mind to borrow Agatha, so I might give the black clouds of bugs a bloody good swat.

Looking back, Alde Baran's face did not look any happier than mine. He'd been carried across the desert but now, being that the path was riddled with rocks and roots, not unlike the rest of us, he'd have to walk. Not that I cared. My patience had worn thin. Outside of whittling, he'd drank most of the night. Though that wasn't what had angered me. I'd had more than my fill of his self-indulgent behaviour. It was high time I put an end to it; and that was precisely what I intended to do. He was of little use to me in his present condition. And I don't mean his physical ailment. It was his mental state that was in sore need of revision. That being his dour mood, his endless state of remorse. The choice was up to him; leave the past behind or stay behind. I for one was done with it and, unlucky for him, I was the Rah. *Okay, so the choice wasn't up to him. What of it?*

Every time I looked at him, he just sat there, staring back at me with a blank expression. It was precisely that expression that I wanted to curb. It made me seethe inwardly, so much so that I was forced to put off our chat a while longer. Being that my ire showed little sign of dwindling, I was forced to relinquish a more tactful approach in the end. If I had to hit him to make my point, so be it. The man not only had it coming; he admitted it often. If that wasn't the definition of arrogance, Haeryn only knows what is.

"There's something you wish to say?" He asked, breaking the silence as I walked toward him at long last.

"I told you there was which is why you are here." Was he trying to goad me into a fight? If so, it was working. He had that irritating way of making statements sound like questions.

"Show me your forearm," I sighed. He began rolling up his left sleeve. "Not that one; the other one."

"Ah, I see. Is that what this is about?" He raised his right sleeve slightly to show a fresh red burn mark.

"I did not return the ring, so you might continue maltreating yourself. I returned it as a keepsake; a reminder; nothing more."

"The ring was never yours to return." Baran said coldly. "I will do with it as I please."

"You swore an oath to serve the One Rah; did you not?"

"I did; but this has nothing to do with that. If I may speak plainly, what I choose to do during my personal time is no concern of yours."

"It is entirely my concern when it affects your ability to uphold your oath."

"As I said, one has nothing to do with the other. My oath is my oath; it is unbreakable."

"And what is that red mark? What is the purpose of that?"

"A reminder." Alde Baran said quietly, looking downward with shame.

"Yes, a reminder of another oath. An oath you did break."

"Yes, you're right!" He hollered, looking up at me. "And I will never forget it! *Why* is what you wish to know? Because I will never allow myself to… forget."

'No, you won't," I concurred. "But, as Haeryn is my witness, you *are* going to forgive yourself."

"F-forgive myself?" He stammered. "How can you even ask such a thing? You… of all people?"

"Because I am the only person with the right to ask. Because I am your Rah. Because I demand it!" I fumed.

"No. I can never forgive myself," He answered, shaking his head. "I cannot. I will not."

"You must!" I seethed. "Don't you see? If we are to have any hope of success– I need all of you; not what's left of you. That's not enough; that just won't do."

"It's all I have to give," he sighed.

"Stop. Enough. Give me the ring." I commanded.

"The ring? What for? It's mine."

"Because of this and this and this and this and this!" I scolded, poking his body in different places harshly with a finger. "As well as right here," I continued, placing my finger in the centre of his forehead.

"Baran," I pleaded. "You're right, it's not like I can snap my fingers and the past goes away. It won't. But everything must start anew at some point. It is time, Baran. It is time to let go. Give me the ring." He stared at me for a time, then reaching into his pocket he held out the ring. His expression turned fearful the moment I took it.

"What are you going to do with it?" He asked.

"What do you think I'm going to do with it? Wear it about my neck as a constant reminder of the worst day of our lives? No. I'm going to heave that horrid memory into the middle of this gnat-infested lake."

"Haeryn's hell you are!" He asserted, rising to his feet. "Give it back to me, now. Right bloody now!" He shouted, snatching a paw at it. Closing it within my fist, I held it behind my back.

"Baran," I spoke softly. "I want to forgive you. But I can't. I wish I could. But I can't. Not until you stop tormenting yourself. Not until you forgive yourself."

Baran's eyes brimmed with tears. I thought I was making some headway. I thought he finally understood. That was before he lunged at me. He was a big man with hands like a bear. But he was hurting. Worse inside than out. Albeit it was hard to tell at that precise moment. Which is why I side stepped his advance. Very spritely, I might add. Prior to putting my knee hard into his groin. Though he fell hard; he looked up smiling. *Oh yeah, the lifeless nut-sack. I'd completely forgotten about that.*

Baran no longer seemed himself. He had a dangerous look upon his face. Strangely, the madder he became; the more my own anger dissipated. It wasn't a fair fight after all. He was far from healed. Still, if it was a beating he was after; what right had I to refuse him?

"I don't want to hurt you," I cautioned. "I merely want you to stop hurting yourself."

He unsheathed Agatha; and, for a moment, I thought the situation irreversible. Until he plunged the cumbersome sword into the ground. It did make sense. Though we were undeniably at odds there was not cause enough to delimb one another. I did feel a huge measure of relief all the same. Seeing no other way out of it, I tossed my dagger in the soft ground alongside Agatha. Sometimes a good fight was the only way to get things sorted. I considering throwing the ring into the lake briefly just to be rid of it; furthering kindling Baran's anger at the same time. Unfortunately, from where I stood, I felt it'd be too easy to find. I needed him to know there was no hope of ever retrieving it.

Each time Baran took a step toward me, I backed up moving closer and closer to the lake. Baran may have been angered, but he was no fool. Knowing exactly what I intended to do, he charged me. Surprised by his speed, he caught me mid-waist and we tumbled to the ground. It was then that I wished I'd thrown the flattened ring. Baran was all too aware it was still in my palm. Having quickly pinned that arm, he clambered atop me using his legs to hold me down. I was not about to lose face again. Thus, I saw but two avenues of escape; knee him in the chest; or bite his forearm. Being that I didn't want to risk puncturing his lung again, I chose the latter. After all, what harm could it do? It was already terribly scarred.

Judging by his howl, Baran didn't appreciate being bitten. Even so, instead of pulling his forearm free he twisted it, shoving his elbow further into my gaping mouth. My jaw quickly began to ache. I was finding it hard to get a breath. I did taste blood so at least some of it had been at his own peril. Thinking back on it as I write this, I should have slammed his ribs as per my initial reflex. *No deed of the*

Gods goes unpunished as they say. Weirdly, never once did the Red Rage threaten to swallow me. Whereas Baran's antics had angered me, I deemed our wrestling match as just plain fun. Well, as soon as I recalled one could breathe through their nose, that is.

Being that he'd very nearly grabbed hold of my wrist, so he might pry open my fingers, I flung the ring as far away as I was able. Pulling his elbow clear of my tonsils, he scrambled off me at once. Luckily, I caught his ankle, causing him to trip. He was smiling now. I recognized that smile. It was the same one he sported when back-handing me as child for speaking out of turn at the dinner table. But it was my turn now. Thus, I grinned right back at him no less eagerly. As my mother would have put it, as far as compromise went, *we were two matching peas within the pod.* Or Greta, as I ponder it.

Lunging at him, I grabbed his legs before he had half a chance to rise. Pushing both my knees into his lower back, I managed to grab his left arm to wrench it backward. I could only imagine how much that must have hurt given his recent injuries.

"And who has the upper hand now?" I grunted prior to gouging an eye before backhanding him across the face several times.

Being that we weren't trying to mortally wound one another, it seemed only right to tug his chainmail every chance I might. Not that he was wearing any. On the off chance there was any doubt, it was I who held the upper hand at that moment, quite literally, his right one. I tried twisting it behind his back, but Baran would have none of it. I pressed my forehead against his shoulder to gain leverage to prevent him from turning. Until, utilizing my momentum, he rolled backwards at which point I found him atop me again. Admittedly, dropping both knees upon my chest did force some of the wind from my sails.

To be *fair*, I was hardly accustomed to *fighting fair*. Point being, as per my new behavioural adjustments, I was being far too kind. Okay, so I did bite him, but it had been the lesser of two evils: thus, sustaining my argument. The object of any fight was to win by any available means. Which is to say, in a perfect world; I would have punched him in the face without warning prior to our fruitless conversation.

Unexpectedly, now having my pride placed in jeopardy, I felt the Rage begin to boil within me. It scared me. Though there was no way I was ever going to concede, should the Red Rage take hold, the likelihood of me killing him would be increased by tenfold. It was at that moment that he looked into my eyes and gave up the fight. It was a though he'd sensed that very predicament somehow. He just stopped, staring at me with a sad expression. Though I loathed stopping while he held me at a disadvantage, I saw little other choice. I didn't know what to say. It didn't matter. I needed to catch my breath first anyway. As it turned out, there was no need.

'I'll throw it," he said. "If I am ever to break the spell; I must be the one to do it." He looked utterly crestfallen. I was about to nod in consent when a low voice spooked both of us.

"Throw what where?"

Five men bearing the insignia of the Forth Rah approached with swords drawn, distancing themselves from one another to surround us. I saw three others tying their horses to trees near the woodland path. I could not help but notice one was a brindle mare with flickering white ears. *I had a keen nose for horses*. It looked an especially fine specimen. Baran rose swiftly, grabbing my hand and pulling me to my feet as he did so.

"Who are you and what do you want?" Baran asked coldly.

"Why is it those without swords always presume the right to ask the questions?" A large man leaned on his longsword as he glared at us. Why some men insisted on planting their swords in the ground was beyond me. He had blonde hair and sharp blue-eyes, a clean-shaven chin beneath a broad moustache; notwithstanding that sort of half-grin that purported oneself to be no stranger to a fight. Even so, he answered Baran's query all the same.

"I am Ser Roust of Tullstone though my friends call me Razor," he reported.

"And what do your enemies call you?" Alde Baran asked.

"His enemies?" Hooted a comrade. "They don't call him anything. They're all dead."

"I am second in commander to His Holiness; on official business of the Forth Rah, Lord Delevan." Ser Roust continued, tapping the emblem adorning his chest plate.

Being that I had heard tales of their many past exploits, I had little doubt Baran had as well. There were very few knights left in Harbinger. Though I couldn't speak for Baran, I'd never met one in person before. Bound by lapsed traditions and customs, such as *Seratego,* most of the Grand Houses abandoned the practice of knighthood at the start of the First Great War. It was commanders, generals, and thousands of expendable foot soldiers that were needed, as opposed to haughty cavaliers.

"Far be it for us to distract from official business," smiled Baran. "You'd best be on your way then; no need to risk disappointing

His Holiness on our account."

"Have no fear, we never disappoint. But please refresh my memory, who did you say you were again?" The knight requested politely.

"Farmhands," attested Baran; at precisely the same time I declared us to be *woodcutters*.

"Which is it then?" Ser Roust smirked. "Woodcutters or farmhands?" Baran turned to look at me so we wouldn't confuse our stories a second time.

"Both," I shrugged. "On this day, we are farmhands tasked with collecting firewood."

"And where exactly is your collection of firewood?" He asked; his gold locks flew as he twisted his head about in a mock search.

"We were just about to get started," I lied.

One of the men previously tending the horses advanced. Having retrieved our weapons, he tossed my gold-handled dagger, along with Agatha, harshly on the ground beyond easy reach. I felt the intention was to tempt us into doing something foolish. As if Baran and I needed any temptation. If our recent interactions were any indication, when it came to single-handed combat, wisdom was no talent of ours. Having been utterly consumed by our own affairs, the men had taken us completely by surprise.

"Why do I get the feeling you are lying to me?" He sighed. "Not that I profess to be any kind of weapons expert but, they don't look much like wood axes to me. Now, who are you really?"

"He's my prisoner," I asserted, changing our story on the fly. "I am Eryk; a soldier of the Kedera and those are *my weapons*. I am taking him to Verdun to stand trial for horse thievery."

"Horse thievery? Really? Whose horse did he steal?" He asked giving his moustache a firm tug.

"Mine," I grimaced, trying to feign embarrassment.

"Your horse." Ser Roust laughed aloud. "But why take him to stand trial? You have weapons at the ready do you not? Why not forgo the three weeks of walking; all the red tapestry involved with organizing a trial; followed by yet another day just to build the gallows. Would it not be more apropos to simply kill the crook where he stands?"

"Surely, every man is entitled to a fair trial."

"But you saw him do it, did you not? It was your horse that he stole was it not? Being that you're planning to take him all the way to Verdun I can only assume you're quite convinced that it was he who did it."

"Yes, but I'm a soldier not a judge," I shrugged.

'Well, this is your lucky day then," grinned the blue-eyed knight. "I am a judge."

"You're a judge?" I simpered. I suddenly had a very bad feeling about this.

"With the Razor's Edge as my witness, I am just so." He professed cheerfully, raising his sword, and holding it before him proudly.

"You there, remove your headscarf," Ser Roust ordered Baran. Baran did so, causing the knight's comrades to gasp.

"Whoa, I did not expect that." He scowled, looking away. "You might have warned me first." He decreed shaking his head with disgust.

"Honestly, with a head like that I find it hard to believe there'd be even the slightest hesitancy in taking it. You'd be doing him a favour. No offense; though all of us in fact."

"Still," he continued. "Though you look far too ugly to be innocent− for the sake of a fair trial, I ask you plainly: did you steal this man's horse."

"Do you see me holding a horse?" Asked Baran, looking about him in the same manner the knight had but a moment ago.

The knight giggled at that. Yes, I did say *giggled*. That made me rethink things a bit. Was it that there were very few knights− or was it rather that there were very few *giggling knights* kicking about anymore? I would have to get back to that one later.

"He does raise a fair point," He confessed smirking. "Just where is said horse that you profess him to have stolen?"

"It ran away," I shrugged. I mean, what in Haeryn's hell was I supposed to say?

"Okay, this is taking far too long. We need to hasten the pace. Judgment must be swift if it is to be feared. We will begin again. Being that you declared yourself a soldier, I will accept you at your word. Are you positive that it was *this man*, the one standing before you, that stole your *missing* horse?"

"I never forget a face." I attested, not knowing what else to say.

"That's good enough for me. I don't expect I'll be forgetting it anytime soon either. I shall very likely see it in my dreams tonight. And with that, I shall now pronounce sentence. You there, with the frightful face… what is your name, so I might condemn you appropriately in good conscience."

"Nitesh Alde Baran," Baran stated. Yeah, that took me by surprise. And I was just beginning to enjoy my new role, as preposterous as that might seem.

"Nitesh Alde Baran" repeated Ser Roust loudly. His men had a good laugh at that.

"Nitesh Alde Baran is either a myth or a ghost," he continued. "Either way, I'm quite certain he died long ago in some Kedera dungeon."

"I assure you he is neither myth nor ghost for the legend himself stands at my side." I replied, gesturing grandly with an arm. Admittedly, should our story evolve any more I'd need both maps and charts to keep abreast of it. Judging by their laughter, it seemed clear they thought I was merely furthering the jest.

"Then I suppose history will be rewritten," said Ser Roust undaunted. "So, you're not going to tell me your name. That's not very fair, is it?"

"For Haeryn's sake!" Spat Baran. "You're right; this is taking far too long. I've stolen many horses! Now, hurry up and behead me already." I nearly hurled my breakfast at that point.

"So, now you readily admit to stealing the horse?" The knight queried incredulously.

"Well, not his horse in particular," clarified Alde Baran. The knight then shook his head sideways. Not unlike a horse, as I ponder it.

"But I am a horse thief," Baran continued. "And that is what horse thieves do. They steal horses. Have no misconception, should you not depart henceforth, I will steal all your horses."

"Isn't that par for the path?" Ser Roust asked his men. "Just when you're beginning to take a shine to someone; you end up having to kill them." He sighed with profound exaggeration.

"Oh well, it's a living as they say." Ser Roust conceded, rolling his blue eyes. "So, it's to be a beheading." He shrugged. "I must say it's a commendable choice, given the circumstances. Don't think for a minute we don't appreciate it. Ugh, can you imagine *that head* hanging by a rope– bulging eyeballs, veins popping out, those crusted scars about to burst. No, I expect you've done us a real service there."

"I will do it," I said. "He is my prisoner, after all."

"Makes perfect sense; notwithstanding you do have the only broadsword."

"You have a talent for observation," I smiled. "It was my horse, it's only right that I be the one to end his miserable existence." I added glumly.

"Miserable existence?" questioned Baran forlornly.

"Admittedly, it was a bit harsh." The knight interjected. "There are worse crimes. That said, being devoid of a horse walking can be quite miserable at times." Ser Roust sympathized whilst tugging at his moustache.

"My sincere apologies, Baran." I lamented. "How better might I say it? Render you folklore? Make myth of you? Lead you to the Land of Legends? Send you to the Gods of Song perhaps? Might one of those be more to your liking?" The knight paused to scratch invisible hairs on his chin.

"Strange. Correct me if I'm wrong but, didn't he say it was only right that he be the one to throw *something or other somewhere* when we first arrived."

"He is apt to running his mouth," I nodded, fetching the broad sword without any of them showing the slightest interest. *Mindless fools!*

"Not for long," Ser Roust noted.

"Not for long," I concurred. Swinging the sword's blade round swiftly, I pressed it to the neck of the man standing nearest to me. Taken wholly by surprise, his arms dangled limply at his sides. Disarming him, I pressed his own sword to his throat and tossed Agatha to Baran. It was a wise exchange for my part. Agatha was far too cumbersome to hold lengthwise for any duration. Baran accepted the broadsword gratefully, spinning it nimbly betwixt his fingers to great effect. I can't say I wasn't impressed. I'd spend weeks in my younger days perfecting the art of spinning a dagger whereas Agatha was something else entirely.

"Well, that certainly changes things," Ser Roust declared taking a backward step. "Swords up lads, look lively. I expect it'll be us who'll be performing the beheading after all."

"Potatoe. Potato." I replied unimpressed.

"Don't kill me!" Wailed the young voice immediately ahead of me trembling with fear.

"Stay still and no harm will come to you," I whispered. I only hoped it would prove true.

"I don't want to die!" He hollered.

"Nor do I so quit squirming." I ordered. "Now, I believe you owe Alde Baran an apology. Numerous apologies, in fact."

"And if he's Baran, you're the Golan Butcher!"

"Guilty as charged," I laughed aloud. It was quite a coincidence as Petra described it later. That said, since having been pronounced the One Rah, my old monikers rolled off my tongue with little effort these days. Not that it was I who'd said it.

"He does not jest. Outside of horse thieves, farmhands, and wood cutters— we are precisely who we claim to be." Baran attested firmly. That slowed his step a bit. I could see the wheels turning now as I forced my prisoner forward.

"I must warn you, on the off chance you harm him you will be hunted for life. Standing before is the true Heir of Harbinger. His real name is Deshu Mogashu, son of Lauryn Bryn Mogashu. He is the One Rah reborn." Alde Baran politely informed them. "But I shouldn't let that trouble you. *Headless men fret naught* as they say." Baran added.

"More lies," Ser Roust grunted angrily. "Headless men wander aimlessly and endlessly in the afterlife. It's common knowledge. Unable to discern pathways ahead, what else could they do?"

"I have no quarrel with you and your men, Ser Roust," I stated, lessening the pressure of my sword against the lad's throat ever so slightly.

"No quarrel?" Ser Roust jeered. "You're threatening the life of one of my newest recruits." His blue eyes had turned cold; their previous twinkle having vanished entirely.

"I have no wish to kill him. Know that what next you do will determine his fate."

"Please don't kill me!" Begged the youth.

"Quiet!" I barked shaking him harshly from behind. "We were unarmed and outnumbered. I reacted instinctively and for the inconvenience do I now apologize."

"Inconvenience? A sword at one's throat is far more than that." The lad wished to clarify.

"Apologize?" Ser Roust scoffed. "You're still outnumbered— and now you've provoked us without cause."

"Without cause? You did threaten to take our heads." I reminded him.

"Just the ugly one if you care to recall. Nonetheless, you will pay for this with your lives."

"I doubt that. These lads are greener than basil in spring." Countered Baran. "You should never have brought them. I can see it in their eyes. They are afraid; as well they should be."

"You do realize, the enslaved lad is their dear friend. Do you feel the youth of today to be immune to reprisal? Though far from complete, I trained each of them myself. They will do what is asked of them without hesitation. They will do as I or Rah Delevan commands."

"You have been misled by the False Rahs," Baran argued. "Renounce them, bend the knee, swear allegiance to the One Rah and he will grant you positions worthy of your talents. We have need of a knight and a judge. Especially, once the usurpers are brought to justice. No harm will come to your recruits. Notwithstanding, you may continue their training."

"So, let me see if I understand this correctly. You expect us to ignore our helpless comrade and bend the knee to a stranger feigning to be the long son of our long dead rightful ruler?" Ser Roust queried, tugging at his broad moustache thoughtfully. "Is that it?"

"I do actually," interjected Baran.

"Is it just me or does that seem a tad indulgent?" Ser Roust mused. "I mean, he could be anyone really; could he not?"

"It was no different when we first met, "Baran confessed. "We did not get off to the best of starts either. Hasn't changed much to be truthful the more I ponder it. He always been a stubborn at best."

"Pardon me if I speak out of turn but do you really think that's somehow helpful?" I turned to ask Baran. "I should have kneed you in the bloody ribs whilst I had the chance." I was quite serious. I had half a mind to have another go at him the instant this present predicament resolved itself.

"It would seem we've reached an impasse," Ser Roust shrugged. "Except...."

"Except?" I quizzed him, feeling quite certain I'd be unamused by what I was about to hear.

"There's been strange reports of late, I was dispatched to ascertain the whereabouts of some insurgents." Ser Roust admitted.

His teeth were perfect; something you did not see very often except for the rare woman or child. As per mine own, I noted proudly. He appeared to have gotten over his comrade's predicament momentarily for his arrogance had clearly resurfaced. His green recruits backtracked hastily each time I pushed their chum forward. For all his pomp and ceremony, Ser Roust seemed to be in no hurry. I did make a mental note not to get my feet entangled with my prisoners. The lad's gangling feet did pose a distinct tripping hazard. Falling during battle often marked one's demise. It was known.

"Ah, so that's where the rogue assassins fled." I acknowledged, peeking toward Baran. "The remainder of the Brotherhood serve me. All five hundred of them." It seemed only prudent to try to bolster our numbers. Notwithstanding, it seemed highly unlikely that anyone might have an exact count of the BroZil membership.

"I said nothing of the Brotherhood. Do not put words in my mouth." Ser Roust pouted.

"Who did they propose you to be looking for?" I further inquired.

"An infidel. They said his name was of no import."

"Did they not claim to have lit fire to a great tree in the middle of the Kestrel? A tree hosting an army led by Alde Baran?"

"Do you ever listen to yourselves? A tree in the middle of the great desert boasting an army. Have you been foraging witless mushrooms?" He chortled. "And I suppose there are winged camels prancing about nearby with golden-tipped hoofs."

"We walked in fact," I cringed. "And you were right about that. Walking that is. It was more than miserable. Though surely, they said something more about us."

"So, no horses to no one's surprise. Sorry to disappoint but I was told it was an insurgency. I only hope that's not too big a blow to your egos. I was told to find proof of an uprising and report back. Though now, I dare say, I see an opportunity to overachieve."

"The knights of old swore allegiance to the One Rah," Alde Baran kindly reminded him— myself included.

"The Four False Rahs assassinated Rah Lauryn." He continued unabashed. "I was there. It is the truth. I envision great benefits in forming a kinship. We can compensate you. With Rah Deshu's permission, I suggest you return to the imposters' fold. Keep us apprised of their plans. Tell them you found no proof of an uprising. You would be most useful to our cause, and we would reward you handsomely. I have plenty f gold."

"Plenty of gold— you don't even have a horse man. Not even a stolen one! You wish me to lie? You forget, I am a knight. I am the last of the Roust Host. All that remains is my honour. That's all I have left. Unfortunately for you, I don't believe a single word you say." Outstretching his arms, he raised his hands in jest.

"I give you Nitesh Alde Baran and the One Rah in the flesh," he mocked, stroking his moustache with his thumb and index finger.

"Then speak your intentions." I demanded.

"Given the circumstances, I suppose I'll have to expand my orders. A knight's salary isn't what it used to be."

"But what about me? Please Ser, I beg thee, do not provoke them further. I am far more than an unfortunate circumstance. It is my very breath they hold at stake." The youth ahead of me lamented.

"Hold still, boy." I warned him again. "I'd hate to slip. A credit to you, this sword of yours looks very sharp." Having had a sword held against my neck before, I can't say I blamed him. Not unlike being buried up to your neck in sand, it was uncomfortable. A distinct feeling of desertion accompanied it.

"Ah, so you are mercenaries," Baran noted. "Disappointing, but not surprising."

"No, merely opportunists. Not that I see many alternatives all things considered. I can't very well return and declare having discovered the pair of you we decided to turn a blind eye and flee."

"If only Darian was here," I muttered under my breath.

"Haeryn knows the Four Rahs are an ambitious lot. Unforgiving at times. Most times. Times like these to be clear. I suppose what I'm trying to portray is, they're not the merciful sort." He said, cocking his head and raising his eyebrows. I'd never met someone quite so cynical. Petra would like him, I decided. *Of course, she would.*

"I do hope there's no hard feelings," he grimaced. "But what's a knight to do?" He stuck his sword in the ground before him and turning his palms upward he shrugged theatrically.

It was then the lad, whose life I'd intended to barter, foolishly tried to break free. As he twisted suddenly to the left, my sword arm closed upon him instinctively. Blood wet my face and lips. Having been an all or nothing plan, it was over before it began. His movement had been so determined his neck ran the length of my sword. *His sword rather–* prior to his head rolling free. Letting go of his hauberk, I watched his body crumple to the ground. Side-stepping his head, I could not help but gaze upon the lifeless face staring back at me.

He was just a boy, about the same age as myself when I'd first been inducted into a military life. His eyes were stuck wide. There could be no debate. I'd slaughtered him. His warm blood still dripped from my fingers. For all my foolhardy declarations in respect to starting anew, it seemed I remained the bloody Butcher after all. I felt sick inside. I'd reacted on impulse and without mercy. For all my fighting days, I'd never blindsided anyone so abruptly. Okay, I'd crushed the false salesman's hands in that chest, but it was Petra who killed him if you recall. My emotions were getting the better of me. I was reeling with sensations of guilt and self-doubt. This wasn't soldiering. It was murder.

"Well, you've done it now haven't you? You shall pay for that with your lives, Butcher." Ser Roust seethed. Unlike myself, he was surprisingly calm all things considered.

"H-he, he...." I stammered but there were no suitable words to account for the tragedy.

"Twas plainly an accident." Baran avowed loudly.

"Squires! Avenge your comrade!" Ser Roust commanded. His young men began to advance at once, three towards me with the remaining half eyeing up Baran.

"Yield and no harm will come to you," Baran ordered to no avail.

"Yield and I'll behead the lot of you myself," countered Ser Roust. "As far as justice is concerned, I have every faith in their abilities. As you'll soon find out." Reaching into his pocket, he pulled out a red apple, shining it on a sleeve. Which is to imply, he was an odd man for certain.

"Well, what in Haeryn's hells are you waiting for? There's but two of them and six of you. Get on with it! Chop, chop, chop. Off with their heads!" Sliding the apple through the sword pressed into the ground, he slid a piece of it into his mouth. Again, I ask, was it not a peculiar time to eat?

"Stay behind me, Baran." I ordered for having sensed him stalking forward. "You're in no condition to fight. I need you alive." I hissed.

"Well done," Baran snapped. "Might there be any other disadvantages we might alert them to? Not that it's best to keep that sort of thing to ourselves."

"'Tis the right shoulder that's ailing," Ser Roust advised between chews. "He can barely lift that absurdly heavy sword. Attack him from the left. As for the other– swords high, spread out and advance from all sides."

I had to protect Baran. I began to feel *apprehensive* for lack of a better word. The back of my neck was hot and prickly. My breaths were barely audible. My fingers were sticky with blood. With my adrenalin having peaked, I felt the Rage rising like an interminable tide. I could not help myself. My vision grew blurry, heightening my feelings of unease. There was naught I could do to curtail it and the animal lurking within me knew it. It could smell blood in the air. It could taste blood. Being no foreigner to emptiness, it saw everything at once. Three shadowlike forms approached for being as near to death as anything might be. The heart of the beast beat so loud all things else were drowned. Inhaling through flared nostrils, it expelled steam through bared teeth like the monster it was. *Like the monster I was.*

I felt like screaming and perhaps I did. It was impossible to know. Existing within another world entirely, the creature's mandate was clear. Simplistic in nature, our immoral ordinance never wavered. *All things living need be consumed.* It was an insatiable craving for the unliving lands were forever famished. Any resistance would be welcomed most gratefully for all those opposed were powerless against *our will*. We foresaw every step they took whereas our own hoof-like feet moved with ghostly cunning. Every gleaming weapon arose but another claw at our disposal. The dance had begun. The ballet of death awaited. The epitome of apathy, the growing darkness only intensified our appetite for devastation. All I was before became a thing of fiction. Was I even still breathing? For no longer could I tell.

Within my emotionless state, time lost all meaning. The creature owned the gloom, and it was waiting. And there it was— the opening it so desperately sought. Parrying the paltry strike as though but the wing of a tiny bird, a grotesque forearm slammed an ashen face like a mallet loosed upon hollow bone. Removing its adversary's dagger, in the precise same motion did it slice. The shadow's midriff erupted. Our sword swung round. His helm departed its perch. Our lethal talons became stickier. One down, seven to go.

Whoosh! Splat! The dagger sank to its hilt within the next sinister throat. Falling to his knees, I watched his shadow flee his body just prior to his head. The next one stumbled, cowering backward in fear. But there was nowhere he might run for there remained but one path before him— *that of darkness*. His mouth opened though no sound came forth discernible to bestial ears for it could hear none other than the rage within— *the pounding of blood*. Kneeling and bowing his head, with arms outstretched, he gifted the beast his sword and was swiftly slain. There was no reluctance. All things living need die.

Each newly loosed shadow only heightened the gloom. The surrounding world had become so dark the beast was unable to identify its enemies. Recognizing but the slightest glimmer of my former self, my heart felt as black as coal. Near as dark as the beast, I'd become. No longer could we distinguish friend from foe. If ever we could. It didn't matter. The beast cared not. They were as we were, one and the same. Only by the sword might anything be parted. Feasting upon their mounting dread, the beast became intoxicated by their terror. One by one, they sought to hide. Like worms poking up from black dirt, they trembled upon our approach. There was no escape. Our world grew darker with every feared step. Their end would be swift.

Except… I felt myself falling. The sword within our clutches grew increasingly weighty. As the path ahead of us began to dissolve, our steps became confused. Cumbersome even. A new realism arose. A truth neither man nor beast would ever have presumed. *We were not invincible.* There was no way forward. My thoughts swirled as my head began to pound. What we thought to be our lone ally, the darkness, was consuming us. Though I'd thought it not possible, I'd been deceived. Thus, face forward did we fall into the abyss which, not unlike a headless mouth, arose to swallow us whole. Absorbed and dragged through a lattice of endless gnashing teeth, I became parted from the beast. I thought of black water on a moonless night. I thought of Petra. And finally… I thought nothing.

"Radesh! Radesh! Are you awake?" I heard the words but knew not what they meant.

"Radesh! Wake up, Radesh!" I felt cool water being poured over my head. My eyes began to clear.

"Wh-what happened?" I stammered. My skull was pounding like a drum. I was sitting down, propped against a tree. Everything about me was a blur.

"What happened? What happened?" The voice repeated incredulously. "What in Haeryn's hells was that?"

I remembered him. It was Alde Baran. Having no idea what he was talking about, I made no answer. As water met my lips, I drank gratefully. I could not help but notice it was being fed to me within a badly dented helm. My garments were soaked. I knew the feeling all too well. It was blood and, not unlike sand, I loathed it.

"My head is throbbing. Was I wearing that thing by chance?" I asked demurely.

"No. You did that. I had to line it with leaves just to make it hold water. Do you not remember anything?"

"About what? I don't understand," I confessed. Admittedly, I had a very bad feeling that I'd been through this before. In truth, he need not answer for I knew full well what must have occurred.

"You went berserk! You were utterly mad! Tell me, is it truly you or that crazed lunatic? Do you remember your name? Tell me your name?" Alde Baran demanded.

"Radesh." I answered. As always, I could not remember the details. Only this time, far more so than usual, I felt ashamed. Previously, following similar episodes of unnatural strength, I felt largely disorientated. This was different. Never had I awoken to an interrogation. Okay, so it was Baran, but he was still asking questions impossible to answer. My fellow soldiers had always *wisely* kept their distance. Though common in cause, I had no real bond with them. I could say no much than the little I knew.

"I was not myself. It was not me," I lied. "It was the Rage. It was Red Radesh. I have no control over it and when it overtakes me, I never remember anything." I felt little more than a mindless beast. Even an ogre would have been a huge step up. Save for Petra, I'd never discussed it in depth with anyone before. Following the onslaught, I always reacted the only way I felt able. Namely, to deny it ever happened. At least to myself– which wasn't that hard being that I recalled nothing of it.

"I've never seen anything like it," Baran blurted. "I feared you'd slaughter us all. You were wholly possessed. Is that really what you spoke of before? The Red Rage? At the time, I thought you were referring to blood lust."

"I don't know what it is. It just takes over and I cease to exist."

"Twas sheer madness! I've never seen the like of it. It's not possible to move that fast and yet you did. The lads didn't stand a chance! No man would. One moment you were as still as a statue; and the next– blood flew everywhere. Two of them dead in less than a blink. Though they'd yielded their swords. Even then you wouldn't stop. I had no choice. I had to put you down. Or I doubt any of us would remain to speak of it."

"You did this?" I asked incredulously, cradling my aching head in my outstretched hands. "Again?" I wanted to clarify.

"Yes, and I'll repeat the process lest you're quite certain it's you."

"Oh, it's me alright," I grimaced.

"It took several blows to put you down. That skull of yours is thick."

"Thanks," I muttered. "So I've been told; though I can't remember by whom."

"It wasn't a compliment. I might have very well have killed you." Baran scolded.

"Then the world would be forever in your debt." I smirked. "No one's stopped me prior. They just hide until the bodies run out. So I'm told."

"It was madness! There's something wrong with you for certain. As cruel as they come. Had you been raised by wolves you would have been considered kind in comparison." A strange voice insulted me.

"Who in Haeryn hells is that?" I inquired.

"You really don't remember." Baran was kind enough to observe.

"Must I take an oath? I told you I don't." I barked which proved a painful miscalculation.

"Who yielded?" I asked. "I don't understand. You said someone yielded."

"Not that it made a damn bit of difference." The voice cut in.

"Two of the four dead. His young squires." Alde Baran answered.

"Three by my count though it hadn't even started yet!" Corrected the voice.

"Three of four yielded." Baran nodded sadly. "It was a nasty affair not that my eyes could keep pace. You took all their heads– two in one motion prior to cleaving the final man's helm."

"Whilst he knelt before you on bended knee," added the voice angrily.

"I'm sorry." I offered inanely feeling sick to my stomach.

"Though hardly as sorry as me," the voice chided.

"I don't know what else to say. I don't recall anything. I have no control when the Rage takes hold."

"Takes hold?" scoffed the man. "A choke hold, more like– upon anything within reach."

"Where's Petra?" I asked as my mind began to clear.

"On the woodland path heading toward Harkenspear." Baran replied.

"Harkenspear." I mumbled. It was only then I recalled being the One Rah which made me feel incredibly worse in respect to all I'd just done. Not that I had any inkling what that truly entailed.

"I told you I'm unfit to rule. Do you believe me now?" I asked. "I've been beset by this curse ever since *that day*. At least that is what Petra feels to be the cause of it."

"Ever since what day?" The voice called out rudely.

"Come forth man." I barked haughtily. "Do I know you?" A large shadow limped forward boasting an absurdly large moustache.

"I am Ser Roust," he sneered. "Thank you for not butchering the lot of us," he added sardonically.

"My apologies, Ser Roust. Have we met?" I inquired. "Admittedly, my mind remains a bit foggy."

"Foggy. If this is foggy then I for one would hate to see dark and dreary. I'm not sure our world would survive it."

"Have I wronged you, Ser Roust?" I felt quite certain I had.

"I've been trying to sort that out with your friend here. Had he not thrown his body over yours I surely would have slain you."

"You seek vengeance?"

"Yes, vengeance for having but three of the seven squires I departed with should that be any indication of the massacre inflicted upon us. That aside, which isn't easy mind you, Baran has convinced me you are yet who you claimed yourselves to be. Thus, upon my honour, do I hold myself in account for much of what occurred. Though far from all of it for even having witnessed it, I still can't wrap my head around everything that happened. Not than any man could. What were you saying in respect to a day that beset this wicked scourge upon you?" Ser Roust urged.

"We don't speak of it," I stated flatly. It was then that I remembered the incident between Baran and I involving the ring. "Baran, did you dispose of it?"

"Yes, it's gone for good. It's at the bottom of the lake." He answered.

"And I can trust you?" I asked, staring hard into his eyes.

"More than most," he smiled. It was not the answer I sought.

"Do you toy with me?" I asked again.

"I can vouch for him." Ser Roust spoke up. "The ring is gone."

"Are you whole again, Baran?"

"Are you whole again?" He stammered returning the same question with a wistful glare.

"As much as I am able," I replied candidly. "But I was asking you. I must know the truth of it. Do I have all of you or merely what remains?"

"You have all of me. Twice as much as I am able though quite likely less than half as much as will appease you." He added cheekily.

"Then consider yourself forgiven." I said, rubbing my skull. It was broken. I was certain of it. "All you need do now is forgive yourself. Can you do that for me?" I pleaded.

I never heard his reply for having drifted out of consciousness. I did dream of it, however. *As much as I am able* being his answer.

Perhaps, I wasn't dreaming. Either way, the response was acceptable. It did sound like something he'd say. Notwithstanding, he'd said it twice before. I lay there uncertain if I'd ever wake again. Even in my dreams, my head hurt ferociously. I didn't care. I felt so tired. And then I remembered Renan. My eyes opened, and I saw the stars above and somehow, I knew he was watching them too. I awoke to water being splashed on my face again. The difference being this time I wasn't dreaming. My eyes were in fact open. Strangely, Darian stood before me. I spat following a long swallow of water.

"What are you doing here?" I asked. I had to close my eyes briefly for initially seeing a pair of kestrels atop his shoulder.

"Petra sent us to ensure you and Baran hadn't killed one another. She was fretting terribly." I recognized two members of the Brotherhood standing behind him. Apart from the period where the Rage had taken over, I remembered everything now. Or at least I thought so.

"Killed one another, Baran and I? Hardly. We're the best of friends. Closer than father and son." I lied, causing Ser Roust to cough with contempt. I'd remembered the knight's name. Things were looking up. Well, I was at least– at everyone.

"As you say but is that not blood all over you?' Darian queried. I saw little point in replying. It was.

"Help me to my feet, Darian." I ordered.

"So, you're still in one piece then? Right as rain?" He asked.

"Rain. What is this devilry you speak of?" I winked. "But yeah, I think I've regained my wits for the most part."

"Baran tells me you've made new acquaintances whilst we were gone."

"At great cost, for which I am sorry. It could have been different. It should have been different, much different."

"As noted, I am as much to blame as you," Ser Roust admitted. "Having had more than enough time to think on the matter; we held you at a great disadvantage. A bleak position to be clear. I've had my back against a wall a few times myself and reacted no less terminally. Though I lost four good lads, I gained the one true Rah. Though hard to believe, I expect it could have been worse, much worse."

"I will see to their graves myself," I stated glumly. "If it is I who is to blame it's only right."

"They're already in the ground," replied Baran, pointing toward four mounds a short distance away above which four swords served as crosses, one of which was shorter for having been broken. As I slowly made my way to the lake to cleanse myself, I knew it wasn't possible. The blood might wash away but never the guilt. Returning to the others shortly thereafter, I only wished there was some way by which I might make amends.

"Allow me to offer words; providing it does not offend." I added, turning to Ser Roust and his remaining young squires. Darian had to steady me for my legs were not yet stable.

"As you wish," answered Ser Roust, striding swiftly toward the graves. Having forsaken his former attire bearing the insignia of Rah Delevan; he now wore a black, knee-length cloak which bore the sigil of a wolf. *So, his family crest was a wolf; how bloody unfair.* Gazing upward at the bright yellow sun, I secretly cursed it under my breath. At least I'd added a tree, I reminded myself. What's a wolf without a tree? It'd have nowhere to piss.

I stood silently for a time staring at each of their newly dug graves in turn. Though I'd put plenty of men into the ground, I couldn't recall ever having spoken any words before. But I was the Rah now. I'd wronged them and needed to account for it somehow. If I was ever to become a Maker of Laws, it was paramount we all be made to answer equally. No one was above the law; not anymore. I'd acted recklessly. I'd allowed myself to succumb. Not to the Red Rage, but fear and foolish pride. Had I chosen a path of common parlance as opposed to violence his young squires might have been standing beside us now. In my thinking, the Rage was not unlike a curtain behind which I hid. It was a foolproof excuse I could no longer afford. I had to find a way to contain it. I had to build a wall around it. Or my new world would swiftly come tumbling down.

"Tell me their names, Ser Roust, so I might commit them to memory."

"Ser Eon Sturdy; Ser Clem; Ser Harper, and Ser Yaris," he replied.

"I thought they were your squires?"

"Yes, but they were good squires; thus, I knighted them posthumously."

"You can do that?" I asked.

"What's done is done." He shrugged.

"We're good squires," one of his remaining three comrades called out.

"Aye, but you've got a lot more learning to do yet. Such as knowing when to hold your tongue." Ser Roust scolded. "I can't very well teach them anything now, can I? They're the headless dead."

"I would have liked to have seen that. I've never seen anyone knighted before," noted Darian. "Let alone headless men."

"It was a bit tricky," Ser Roust admitted. Being that this new revelation further dampened my loss for words, I elected to stall the proceedings a bit further.

"Is there a tale you can share so we might esteem them more fittingly."

"Of those chosen, Ser Yaris was the last to commence squiredom." Ser Roust began. Placing both hands behind his back, he widened his stance, implying the narrative to be a much lengthier affair than I'd originally assumed.

"In the evenings, following dinner, as they'd completed their chores; having retired earlier, I'd lie awake listening to their endless prattle for no other reason than not being able to ignore it. Each night the conversations between them never wavered from the same three topics: ale, maidens, knighthood. After a month or more of these repetitive occurrences, I took it upon myself to cure them as it had become painfully obvious that their first two obsessions were curtailing them from concentrating on the sole one of import: that being the third– knighthood. Thus, the following morning we journeyed to the Widow's Spine. The Widow's Spine is…"

"We know it," Darian and I chorused together; causing Ser Roust and Baran to belly laugh aloud.

"I drank alongside them for most of the afternoon and, prior to retiring to my chambers, I allotted each of them enough coin to rid them of their foolish distractions once and for all. I must say my plan did work as it was a full year before any of them spoke of either drinking or women. Two nights later, six of the seven had, for the most part, recovered their wits though the scratching and hollers while peeing continued for another fortnight. Ser Yaris however remained in a sorrowful state.

Am I going to die? He'd asked mournfully.

Most definitely, I answered him. Let me remind you, this was two full days later.

How much time do you think I've left? He then inquired with despair.

Only Haeryn can say, I shrugged.

You need not place a marker on my grave. I was never anything but ordinary. He added, cringing with palpable regret.

Anything but ordinary, I returned. After which I threatened to drag him behind my horse if he did not get on with it. Ser Roust concluded his tale by tugging both ends of his moustache followed by a weighty sigh.

Though far from what I'd expected, it was precisely what I'd needed to hear for I now knew what needed to be said. Thus, I wasted no time in saying it for fearing my thoughts might escape no less quickly than they'd arrived.

"With great reluctance do we bequeath these four unto the

ground. They died needlessly and for that I am both saddened and aggrieved. They deserved better for which I hold myself accountable to Haeryn himself. If Harbinger is to succeed; we must do better. I must be better. No longer can we afford to kill one another blindly. The Kedera are no more to blame than the people of Golan. It is fear and mistrust that remain our true enemy. It is our own arrogance, more so than any sword that dampens the path ahead with the blood of those born innocent. For this I do atone. Let the circle be complete. Let their untimely endings forge beginnings anew."

"Let the circle be complete. Let their untimely endings forge beginnings anew." They chorused with agreement.

"Remember this day," I added. "For with this day so too comes change."

"They were anything but ordinary," Ser Roust finished. For which I was glad for I felt it appropriate for him to have the final word.

"What now?" Inquired Alde Baran after the obligatory moment of silence had been satisfied.

"Onward to Harkenspear, of course. Where else would we go?" I snapped. My mood had quickly become foul, partly because my head was still pounding though more so due to the grievous act I'd committed. Crime rather. For that is how I accounted it. Though Ser Roust and Baran declared it an act of unconscionable misfortune, I held myself fully to blame. Unlike Baran, I need not scar myself physically to reaffirm my feelings of contrition. My scars were profound running far deeper than skin.

"I was referring to Ser Roust and his squires," Alde Baran replied, entirely unperturbed. "Should he not return from whence he came to avoid suspicion and act as our spy?"

"I have not yet decided. Thus, he will accompany us until a time as such arrives."

"Understood," Baran nodded.

I could tell he disagreed with my decision though I cared not. Without further detail, let me just say that the walk to Harkenspear was tedious being strewn with loose rocks and shale and leave it at that. It was early afternoon of that same day when I first glimpsed the North 4th army encampment. Though the flags were still too distant to envision clearly, I knew it at once. I recognized the makeshift horse stalls; the green latrine tents; the blue mess pavilions; the infantry men's sleeping quarters. Notwithstanding Major Bryn's red rotunda which gave me cause to cringe.

Though I did not pause to assess their wares, several merchants had set up tents just beyond the path. I did see Darian exit one wearing strange woollen things upon each of his arms. They looked ridiculous to me being akin to thick sleeves that stopped at the elbow. Their oddest attribute being that they completely covered his hands. His fingers had been rendered useless. It was rather humorous for he could barely keep hold of the reigns of his horse.

"Socks!" He called out to all who'd listen. "They call them socks!" He beamed proudly. Well, that settled it. I was not about to stop now. With Haeryn as my witness, I was quite certain I had no pressing need for socks.

In the backdrop, the stone fortress walls of Harkenspear rose above the farcical bouquet of colour despoiling its foreground fields amid the lavender and golden rod. Beyond that, a Palace of gold and white marble twisted its spires toward the heavens as if in competition with the gods themselves. Twas the home of *Haeryn's Halls.* I'd never seen anything so grandiose and illogical. To think there were people who lived in such haughty heights made me feel inexplicably sad. Having been born a commoner such lavishness was unfathomable to me. Which is likely why I'd enjoyed sacking castles as much as I did.

Suddenly, my whole life seemed but a fantastical dream gone sorely awry. Except for the fact that it was entirely real. All I need do now was convince the resident Khalifah, and my former commanding officer, that I was the One Rah. That being: the true Heir of Harbinger. Prior to requesting his sister's hand in marriage for being the father of her child. That same child he'd feigned to be his own. Which had initiated this whole turn of events in the first place. Now that I'd had a moment to rethink things, a fist to the face seemed far more deserving.

Upon seeing Petra waiting for me at the very first tent I became completely overwhelmed. Having ran to her, we hugged one another until, feeling a bit too obvious, I picked her up and carried her inside so we needn't make a spectacle of ourselves. Flinging our bodies onto the first cot we happened upon, I kissed her repeatedly. I blurted how much I missed her; followed by how much I loved her. I covered her mouth when she tried to speak for feeling compelled to tell her just how much I relied on her courage and wisdom. Or I would have rather had I not been so busy unlacing her garments. The robes she'd wore previously had been far easier to disentangle. Comparatively speaking, her new attire was much more fanciful. Not to mention complicated. It was then that things took an unexpected turn. For better or for worse, only time would tell.

"So, I assume you must be Radesh, the new One Rah we've

heard so much about." Said a woman's voice.

Twisting about abruptly, I saw an older woman rocking back and forth in a chair with Renan perched upon her lap. An even older gentleman stood behind her and beside him, Manu− Petra's man servant whom we'd dispatched so long ago in a desperate attempt to find her parents. I suddenly had a very bad feeling in respect to my present company. It was only then I knew the true meaning of unease. Can you even imagine such a thing? But there they were before me in the flesh− those I thought most certainly to have perished by the sword. Which is to say... *not dead*.

"Radesh, allow me to introduce my mother and father of Studayo House. And you remember Manu, I expect." Petra cooed, smiling up at me. Rising hastily, I brushed off my dusty clothes, pushing my hair out of my face. Cleanliness being of great import to me, I felt my face redden. Not to mention, it then became apparent to me just how much I stunk.

"My Lady, My Lord," I replied sheepishly with an awkward bow. "It's good to see you again, Manu." It seemed bowing was harder than it looked though. All the same, I decided to bow twice more just for good measure.

"I-ah, I-ah," I stammered for having been taken wholly by surprise. "No doubt your journey proved no less tedious than our own. I am so pleased to find the pair of you unharmed. And you too of course, Manu. I would not wish any harm to befall you either." I added ineptly.

"As are we," smiled Petra's mother. "I expect you'd like to hold your son," she said rising from her chair.

"I would, My Lady." I replied, taking Renan from her. I rocked him back and forth hoping to Haeryn Hells he would not wake and begin to cry upon witnessing my dishevelled appearance. No doubt, he would enjoy the smell though. He was very reliable that way.

"Humph. You're a bit scruffier than I might have imagined," she noted, studying me up and down.

"Mother! Did I not tell you in advance he'd be a bit scruffy?" Petra said in my defence. "He just crossed the Kestrel. *We* just crossed the Kestrel." She corrected herself.

"Ah, yes so you said− with Renan. Because all newborns need cross a desert prior to their first trip around the sun. Good thinking, well planned." beamed her mother.

"I saw little choice," I began.

"Of course, you didn't. How might you?" She cut in "My

apologies, it seems my manners aren't quite what they used to be."
Pressing a long-crooked finger against her lips, she continued. *Of course, she did.* She was Petra's mother after all.

"All comings and goings aside, how might I best refer to you? The One Rah, the Golan Butcher, or simply the Heir to all Harbinger? It does seem popular of late."

"Please, call me Radesh," I urged her— not liking where this appeared to be going at all.

"Ah, as in Red Radesh?" She smiled.

"Mother! You promised!" Petra scolded her. "Father, please! Make her stop."

"That's quite enough, Taryn. You will refer to him in the proper manner," chided Petra's father. "My apologies Your Holiness, she intends no ill will. Please call me Alistaire; my wife is Taryn— and we were never Lord nor Lady; merely stewards of a largely forgotten house that burned to the ground so very long ago." He sighed sadly.

"You shall always be a Lord to me, Ser. In fact, I will make it so. Unless of course you prefer to be knighted? I could make that happen should you find it more befitting. As for myself, there is no need of formalities; Radesh, *all by itself,* is fine. Whatever the case, *please,* I urge you to speak plainly."

"Do not award her any encouragement," fumed Petra.

"Your mother has every right." I sighed, turning round to face my future wife. Unless of course her mother had paid someone in advance to have me killed, that is. Which I could neither put past her nor blame her for.

"I am all those people and more." I confessed, turning about again. "*Things* is likely more befitting for some having proven themselves more animalistic in nature. I don't hide who I am. I've made many mistakes."

"Mistakes and choices are two different things," the abrupt woman countered.

"Taryn, that's enough." Her husband admonished.

"No, it isn't," I insisted, though undoubtedly to my own demise. "Know that I didn't ask for this life, though neither will I run from it."

"And where does that leave our daughter— with you or without?" It was irrefutable. She could be no other than Petra's mother. I had to give her credit. The woman did not mince words. And therefore, nor would I.

"I love your daughter more than life itself. I would forsake all I have for her in a heartbeat, but there is nowhere we can run to now. The time for running has ended." Passing Renan to Petra, I got down on one knee.

"My Lord, My Lady," I began; before pausing, unsure of what next to say. "I do now ask for your daughter's hand in marriage whilst knowing full well it is not an easy thing that I beg of you. Know that she is all I want in this world. And Renan too, of course."

"And Renan too! Well, that is comforting. Good to know." She noted dryly. "Do go on."

"I will cherish her; and protect her; love her; and respect her. Know that I will do right by them every forthcoming day of my life."

"And just how many days might we expect?" Asked her mother sharply. "Are we talking a fortnight or, now that you've arisen from the dead for all to see, do you propose the Four imposters will come forth willingly and submit?"

"Taryn!" Lord Bryn shouted angrily. Being that things hadn't progressed quite as planned; I rose to my feet again. Not surprising, it was going to take a tad more persuasion. Okay, a *lot more*.

"Tis a fair question, Alistaire," she insisted, sticking out her chin defiantly. "Are the rumours unjust? Are you not planning to depose the Four False Rahs? Tell me, how do you plan on keeping my daughter and grandchild safe while reuniting two very different sects intend on civil war? Do not think for a moment they won't come for them first. That is the frail link so that is where they'll strike."

"I assure you their safety shall always be my chief concern— along with your own."

"Yes, quite right. You did send Manu." She huffed.

"Already have I assigned guards to ensure their on-going protection. I will move them where I must. Admittedly, the Four False Rahs must go. As I said, I did not ask for this task and neither did I seek it. But we don't always get to choose our paths; do we? The Gods are cruel. So, I ask you now plainly; what other choice is there other than to do what one must? And Petra is no different for neither can I help who I love? The entirety of it is beyond me— all of it. The only thing I can do is what I'm bloody well attempting to do at this very moment— which is to request your blessing. And not as any form of obligation, mind you; but simply because it's the right thing to do."

"The right thing to do?" Droned the crusty old woman. I'd never met anyone so quick to distrust; not to mention, antagonistic and audaciously forthright. Then again, had I stood in her sandals the dagger would have been plunged the moment I'd fallen upon the cot.

All things considered; I supposed I should count myself lucky. If ever there was such a thing.

"And what will be the right thing to do when other sons and daughters scuttle forth from dovetail joineries you feign long forgotten?" I stared into her hard eyes, refusing to blink while searching my mind for an answer.

"She means when other children of yours crawl out of the woodwork," Petra clarified, appearing no less keen on hearing the answer. If the anxiety in her father's eyes was any indication, I was in over my head for certain.

"I know what she means," I blurted. Just because she knew me to be the ogre didn't entail me the dullest axe in the armoury.

"I was no one then." I admitted earnestly.

"I'd hardly say no one," her mother laughed. Yes, I did say laughed. Quite frankly, I didn't know what to make of that.

"Well, no one that matters. Not even to me!" I bellowed unexpectedly. *Yes, I yelled at her… Petra's mother.*

I took a breath. It wasn't going at all well. Still, I was done hiding. I was who I was. Though not proud of it, putting my best foot forward from this moment on seemed the lone course before me. Unfortunately for me, being the Rah didn't include waving an enchanted sceptre to magically alter the past. At least not to my knowledge. I would have to check on that later. Though never having made their acquaintance personally, I did hear tell of mages and such. Then again, as I looked into her mother's glaring eyes, any form of outside redemption instantly felt a faery tale.

"My apologies, My Lady. Having made amends, I'm no longer the same person. Though no excuse, I was suffering from an illness that I still oft times struggle to control. So, to answer your question, past or present, whether good or bad; do I hold myself accountable for all my deeds which I will deal with in turn as best I see fit. If truth be known, 'tis your daughter that's changed me. Know that it is only since confessing my feelings for her that my true birthright became apparent. And not before."

A long silence ensued which I gratefully accepted— initially. Admittedly, there came a time when I was about to inform them that I would wed Petra regardless of their consent when….

"Let it be common knowledge that the pants in this family are mine to wear and mine alone." Lord Bryn suddenly blurted. "I am done with this inquisition. You have my blessing. You have our permission," He grinned widely. Sighing with relief, I turned skeptically toward his wife.

"You heard him," she winked proudly. "What? Did you think I'd just give her up without the slightest contest? I loved her long before you, you know." she added, nodding her head toward Renan.

"And you thought the gods were cruel," muttered her husband in a hushed tone.

"I appreciate your candour." I laughed clumsily.

"No, we most certainly do not." Petra corrected me.

"Expect more where that came from," whispered Lord Bryn leaning over to give my arm a firm squeeze. "I dare say, a lot more," he added with a wry chuckle.

"What was that?" Snapped his wife.

"I said, I expect he'll make a great son-in-law," He grinned.

"That or die trying," his wife agreed.

"That or die trying," I conceded feeling most grateful to be done with it. She did have a way with words, causing me to envision Petra in a slightly different light. Then again, it was easy for me having never known my own rightful parents.

The following day was a piece of cake, comparatively speaking. Admittedly, there were a few awkward moments between the Major and I initially. Fortunately, I let Darian and Baran do most of the talking. It did seem *the Rah* thing to do. In as far as other new acquaintances went, I did my utmost to appear as though I might chop off a few heads upon the merest provocation. In that vein, Ser Roust's constant accounting of our initial meeting proved handy.

We (that being Petra, Major Bryn, Alde Baran, Darian, Ser Roust, Grus, Commander Finn of the Palace Guard whom I'd only just met, and myself) were seated around a massive table the likes of which I'd never witnessed before. No less than two dozen foot soldiers had been necessitated just to carry it. The ornate thing made the Major's pavilion seem tiny, which it wasn't. Upon asking, the Major informed me that the Khalifah, who couldn't be bothered to attend, had insisted we borrow it from the War Room of the Palace. Beside carved miniatures of ships, horses, archers, and infantry men; it boasted a very intricate carving of Harbinger from end to end. It was nothing sort of a marvel and by far the most amazing creation I'd ever seen.

As noted, the Khalifah of Harkenspear did not show but instead sent one of his many overseers. Being that he wasn't the resident Khalifah, I told the man he could join us providing he sit still and remain silent. I didn't bother to ask his name. I had no intention of listening to anything he may or may not have to say for something about the man made me feel uneasy. He was barefoot, his robes were grungy, his back stooped, and he wore a long shroud which covered his face. Though I could not see them properly, there was something peculiar about his eyes. They were dim, almost non-existent. Except when the lantern light struck them, at which point they flashed like clear blue skies. Judging by the pace of his shuffle I expect he was very old. He had a wee dog with him that appeared to nudge him along. Thank Haeryn for that or we would have waited all night for him to be seated. At least the mangy-looking thing didn't bark.

In truth, I was glad the Khalifah hadn't come for having grown tired of the constant pandering. *One Rah this, One Rah that*; their predictable banter had grown irksome. Major Bryn, *my brother-in-law in waiting*, appeared greatly perturbed for the Khalifah having declined our invitation. Meanwhile, Alde Baran had an unyielding compulsion to tell everyone who'd listen what a tremendous spy Ser Roust would make. Having tried the wine, Darian wondered how the ale might fare in comparison. As it turned out, the local inhabitants referred to it as *beer* which was why he'd thus far failed to discover any. It was then that I finally decided I'd heard quite enough.

"How do you propose we assemble an army to depose the Four False Rahs?" I asked loudly.

All parties ceased talking immediately and the room fell silent while they stared at the map as though it might miraculously provide the answer I sought. I waited impatiently. Petra, who was sitting beside me reached for my hand, though I stood before she might take hold of it. Though I felt bad, it was paramount that I appear formidable and demanding as opposed to *mollycoddled*.

"Must I repeat the question?" I asked with exaggerated annoyance. "Is it just me or has the lot of you become mute for once?" I stared at them. In my mind, things were proving far harder than warranted.

"Was it not a simple question." I sighed. "Baran, you may begin."

"Allot me a thousand soldiers and I will defeat them." He stated matter-of-factly to which the Major vehemently disagreed.

"A thousand men? I have nearly five thousand men here now and we can barely protect our bordering lands. Harkenspear is safe enough but, travel in any direction for a time and that fails to be the case. One of our generals is beset in the north and yet another to the south. There are rumours they will soon attack our eastern shores. Their forces grow by the day. By himself, the Forth Rah has twice the men we have here!" He informed us hotly.

"That is not what I asked," I barked pounding my fist upon the table. "I asked…"

"I know what you asked; and I answered it," Alde Baran spoke bluntly.

"A thousand men." Major Bryn laughed. "While I appreciate your enthusiasm Baran, you've been gone far too long. It is just not possible."

"Recognize, we need not best the entirety of their forces to defeat them. We need only depose the Four. Give me one thousand good men— not boys, and not farm hands with pick forks or orchard pickers with scythes— but real fighting men and I will destroy them." Picking up a small wooden infantry man, he shook it as though doing so might somehow further his point. It didn't.

"And just how do you propose doing that?" inquired the Major. "It will take every man here just to push them back to Verdun. So, what will it be? Will you whittle them yourself or conjure them from a caldron?" Baran ignored his jibes. *Whittle them!* I very nearly fell off my chair. I didn't realize until that moment how much I'd missed the Major. He'd always been very direct. I found the conversation to be improving… thanks to my guidance.

"We will bait them." Baran offered.

"Bait them? They are hardly fish, Baran. The Four are no fools; they will not put themselves at risk.

"They will providing right bait is triggered."

"And what, or *who rather*, do you propose as bait? Me, my child, or my future husband?" Asked Petra, rising from her chair to stand beside me. *Whoa.* She'd commanded their full attention. I can't say I wasn't impressed. Not to mention proud. My girl, woman rather, had done that… *whilst secretly praying she wasn't about to reach for my hand again and ruin the moment.*

"I expect it will take all three," Alde Baran admitted timidly.

"Of course, it will," skulked Petra, sitting down and folding her arms crossly. *Phew!* The arrow had been successfully dodged. Judging by the look on her face, it was safe to say there'd be no hand holding any time soon.

"Utter foolishness," chimed the Major. "I'll see you hanged on a hook before utilizing my sister as bait."

"Agreed, we will not," attested Baran. "We need only make it appear so. But answer me this, do we have a common agenda amongst us or do tug upon separate strings?"

"Our agenda remains clear. It never wavers. Depose the Four. Defeat the Kedera."

"Ah, and this is where we differ for the goal as I know it is to reunite Harbinger."

"Eliminate the Kedera and Harbinger is ours." Sighed the Major with mounting aggravation. "I harbor no love for the Kedera," spat the Major. "They have but two choices, bend the knee or perish."

"I am the Kedera!" I shouted so loudly I surprised myself. The room fell awkwardly silent again. I was still standing. Feeling Petra's hand brush against my knee, I managed to unclench my fists.

"My apologies but it was not so long ago that I felt the same as you. But I was wrong." Plucking the tiny infantry man from Baran's fingers, I placed him atop the wall dividing our lands.

"It's not about what side of Haeryn's Wall we were born on." I continued softly. "We were all Harbinger once. We still are. Alde Baran is right in this. Our goal is the reunification of Harbinger. But achieving such a thing will take far more than a thousand men. We need capable fighting men, not enlisted peasants. He is right about that. Above all else, we need to know what the Four are planning."

"Ser Roust," I resumed. "What can you tell us of the Forth Rah?"

"Very little," he confessed. "As much as I hate admitting it, you were right. I was hired as a mercenary. I was hired to train their soldiers. Sadly, they did not trust me well enough to include me in their traitorous schemes."

"That being the case, I see little point in sending you back. You will remain with our forces."

"But he might learn something of…"

"Enough. I have made my decision. Ser Roust will remain."

"If I may be so bold."

"Of course, Ser Roust; you may all speak openly here… providing it doesn't upset Petra or we'll be here all night." I joked, causing all to laugh. Save for herself.

"Horn's Keep is home to a lot of good fighting men. If it's an army you want; you might consider starting with them.

"Apologies in advance but our chances of enlisting Kedera guards seems few and far between to me." The major cut in. "Notwithstanding, if they're as capable as you say, why are they not at the front lines? No, I expect they're either aging or debilitated in some fashion or other."

"Not the guards but the prisoners within." Ser Roust clarified.

"They were knights once; they're adept at training men to fight. Having refused to align themselves with the False Rahs, they were imprisoned. If I could find a way to free them, they would fight for you. I'm certain of it."

"Horn's Keep, northwest of Verdun?" I asked.

"The same," clarified Ser Roust.

"That's farther within Kedera lands than anyone's been since Haeryn knows when." I grimaced.

Ser Roust removed the infantry man from the wall, placing it at a spot farther north than I ever would have guessed.

"It's not merely the wall; you'd have to pass the Monkey House; Barrenlance; followed by Nate's Gash," Darian added. "I would not envy anyone tasked with such a perilous journey."

"Quite right," I echoed. "Even in my father's time they were known to be hazardous lands. Only the worst kind of rogues reside there." I noted skeptically.

Barrenlance was formerly known as Barrenspear. The Kedera had changed all their spears to lances long ago. Purely out of spite, of course. Though I'd never been there, I was told there wasn't much to it. Hence the name, I suppose. I had been to the Monkey House. It's not something one forgets. Short of desperation, no self-respecting Golanite travelled that trail. *Not ever.* Which I expect is why the establishment's owner decided upon it in the first place. That and the fact there was nowhere else by which to replenish supplies for a hundred leagues or more. Though I'd never been anywhere near Nate's Gash, it had a reputation entirely its own. That being, nothing good. Save for being controlled by rogues and thieves, it was said to be akin to Standstill Pass. Though few could say for certain, in my thinking, it was likely more of a hideout than anything truly of use.

"Though some time has passed, I've been there before." Insisted Ser Roust. "Besides, without risk little is the reward."

"About these *so-called* rewards; no offense, but I can't help feeling we're wading into the lands of the faery folk. Tales of knights and such are near as old as Haeryn himself."

"Put swords in their hands and triumphant news shall shortly follow." Ser Roust assured me.

"How many are incarcerated? And for how long? Which is to say: how old are they?" Baran inquired astutely.

"I don't know how many. A decade or so ago, thirty-seven warrants were posted; therefore, most would be close to sixty by now. Though I can't say for certain how they may or may not have fared, knights age well. It is known."

"Do they now?" I winked. "Darian, it seems we have need of that *all-seeing* eye of yours. Tell me, how old is Ser Roust?"

Baran couldn't help chuckling while Darian ogled the knight up and down, not to mention giving his long moustache a couple of firm tugs after standing him up and turning him about.

"It was winter. It was cold," said Darian, scratching at his own bearded chin. "He was born in the early morning light; very near to here on the Eastern Snee Coast. A child of the Black Moon– I reckon he's forty-four years, six months, seven and a half days old being that evening hours approach."

"You're certain you can't be more precise?" I laughed. "I was going to guess forty-five years. So, it seems we agree."

"You'd be out by a full half-year," Darian protested.

"A full half-year?" I countered. "Is that akin to filling a mug entirely to the middle? Something you've never done, I might add."

"One hundred and eighty-eight days rather," Darian scowled. "I could row a boat across the Kestrel in less." I had to wait for the laughter to subside, including my own.

"Ser Roust?"

"I'm afraid you've missed the mark. I am fifty plus four. My mother did confess I was born on the Black Moon, however. I can only commend you for that."

"I beg protest; 'twas an unfair contest. It was those enormous whiskers that threw me off. I mean, how might I wager a proper guess while barely able to decipher his face?"

"Well noted, Darian," I smiled, returning my attention to Ser Roust. "And these knights you spoke of; you know them well?"

"Too well, perhaps. They abhor me."

"Abhor you? That's a strong word." I said with surprise. The word struck a chord with me for having overheard Petra's mother use it in a conversation but the evening prior. And no, she wasn't talking about me. At least, I don't think so. We'd sorted our differences, after all. Not to mention the person she 'd referred was named High Lord Uppity. Someone I was in no hurry to meet, I might add, lest he prove at some point to be a neighbouring resident.

"Why do they hate you, Ser Roust? What did you do?"

"Bending the knee to the Kedera Rahs is what prompted their ire. Becoming a mercenary, I expect, did little to dissuade the matter."

"And what impelled you to follow such a path?" Baran asked.

"As it is, I differ from the other knights in a very distinct way.

I have a family; a wife and six children. Truth is, I saw little choice. I wasn't about to let them starve. Unlike the others, I don't concern myself with affairs of the state. As I saw it or *chose* to see it, we'd sworn allegiance to the Rah. In my thinking, it was not my place to question their right to sovereignty."

"So, you did it strictly for the coin," Baran interrupted.

"Admittedly, the fact there were now four of them afforded greater opportunity. I had a family to feed; which of you would have done different?" Baran was about to inform him precisely who would have done different when I waved him off with a hand.

"What's done is done. Mistakes have been made on both sides of the wall." I sighed. "Yet, you think these knights would hear you out as opposed to cutting out your tongue. You feel certain they would join us?"

"I do." He replied solemnly.

"Well, I think for one they might be just as apt to take your head given the opportunity." Spoke the Major.

"It would be at my peril. But what isn't these days?"

"And what pray tell do you require of me?" I asked.

"Little more than your blessing; though I would ask that my squires be allowed to accompany me should that be agreeable."

"And why not? After all, misery loves company," Darian felt obliged to add.

"Forgive me for saying so, Ser Roust, but that does make me a tad wary. We have battle-hardened men here at your disposal; why not request some of them?"

"I fear they'd draw far too attention. Though they might not look like much, I've trained my young squires well."

"And how do we know you won't sell us out for coin?" The Major glared.

"Because I am a knight. Because I was wrong. Because, just like you, I know the truth of things now. But mainly, because our Houses swore oaths of servitude to the One Rah long ago."

"An oath you were all too quick to pass unto the Four," seethed Baran.

"That is unfair. I knew nothing of the guilt dripping from their fingers. I only just found about it— losing four lads in the process."

"I must say, I am uncomfortable sending your squires." I conceded. "It's a perilous undertaking being yet so green."

"That's precisely why. I owe them. Their training is not yet finished. Because no one would suspect them as opposed to battle-hardened warriors. And, from a selfish point of view, I think it might buy some good faith with the other knights, if you know what I mean."

"And what would you teach them that they could not learn here?" Baran inquired.

"That amends can be made. That our shortcomings and failures do not define us. That it's never too late to realize the error of your ways and choose a better course."

"And I expect that's the first time anyone used *choose a better course* having Nate's Gash in mind." Chortled Darian which brought some much-needed mirth.

I was not amused, however. Ser Roust last words had struck a chord for feeling as though he'd spoken directly to me. It was mere days ago when I thought the same thing. My shortcomings and failures need not define me. I hoped to make amends whilst chartering a better course. He had me wrapped around his finger and I expect he knew it. Did I not say Petra would like him? Not unlike Baran, the phrasing the three of them employed was entirely unsporting at times. A disadvantage I hoped to correct at some point. Not that I envisioned it happening anytime soon.

"Well said, Ser Roust. And just how do you plan on freeing these *ageless knights* of yours?" I asked.

"At the risk of not sounding very knightly, *bribery* for the most part. It is known that new lands are built upon the backs of the common folk. Thus, the saying: *the memories of working folk stretch farther than their feet*. Being that the nearby residents are often employed in the construction of fortresses and prisons; I would start there. Once I know the layout of the establishment, rest assured, I will find a way within."

"And you're quite certain I can trust you, Ser Roust?"

"On my word as a knight," he answered without hesitation.

"I believe you," I replied. "Ser Roust, the fate of, not only your young squires, but all knights rest upon your shoulders. Succeed and I shall ensure that the Age of the Knights is fully restored. Fail and, like the footprints of the working folk, you'll be sadly forgotten."

"I find your terms acceptable, and I shall not fail either of us."

"I believe you won't. I have learned much from you during our short time together; and far more about myself."

"I don't—" Baran tried.

"It isn't up to you!" I fumed. Exhaling slowly through pursed lips, I turned my attention to the rest of those gathered.

"Ser Roust has stood tall and answered my call. Ser Roust

understands what it is that I long to achieve. Now, who else will stand and answer?' I demanded hotly. The room was sullen and silent.

"Must I truly repeat myself? How do you propose I assemble an army to depose the Four Rahs?" I glared, daring them to test my patience further.

"I will speak to the Four that Speak as One," said Major Bryn, rising from his chair. "I will convince the Khalifah that you are the true heir. I will force them to back you if I must."

Obvious in his agitation, he turned to glare at the resident Khalifah's overseer who sat quietly petting his dog. The man seemed oblivious to all that was going on.

"Yes, brother!" I smiled. "Though already very much indebted, for this doubly shall I owe you. Who else?" I demanded.

Darian stood. Picking up the closest toy soldier, he placed it on the mountains of the southern Snee peninsula. Yet another place, no one had ventured since Haeryn knows when– regardless of bloodlines.

"For your sake and no one other will I return to Haeryn's Hills," declared Darian through gritted teeth.

"I will fetch fighting men bigger than yeti-bears and stronger than barge oxen." He assured me. I was less confident.

"Have you been drinking?" I felt obliged to ask. To my knowledge, no one had visited *the Hills* for a hundred years or more for the simple reason, the big folk dwelt there. Having been *largely* forgotten, pun intended; it was rare to hear anyone speak of them. It was known. Aside from being skewered on a stick and slowly basted over a fire, they did not take well to visitors. The big folk were most obstinate in preserving their solitude. They preferred to keep to themselves. *Thank Haeryn.*

"Of course, I've been drinking... save for the ale which appears to be in short supply."

"I'm not sure I understand. You did say Haeryn's Hills did you not?"

"Yes. Let us just say there are things about my past that no men know." Darian returned my stare, albeit in singular fashion.

"Ahem," coughed Baran.

"Few men know!" Darian conceded loudly. "I was born in those Hills. Know that being the runt of the litter is not something one brags about. That aside, let's just say I did some things for which favors are owed. All things being equal, which they clearly are not– have you ever seen one? Let me assure you as big goes, they're bigger. Far bigger. There's a reason they don't climb trees. Speaking of trees, which we weren't, I once knew one so big–"

"You were saying something about *owed favors*?" I reminded him.

"Yes, and all things, regardless of being equal, or not; what I mean to say is... it's high time to collect. The owed favors, that is to be clear. Which I expect I wasn't so much. Until now."

"Well, *that is* unexpected. And you're positive it's not the drink?" I felt compelled to clarify.

"No, 'tis the absolute truth. Though, seeing as it was you who broached the subject, did you know they serve ale in mugs the size of wash basins? In the Hills, that is. Not that I know what size they might serve them in here being that I haven't found any. Not that I think it'd be anyway near as big. There's always hope, mind you. In respect to the mug size, I mean... just so as we're clear."

"Just don't ask him what he did," Baran nodded negatively. "The secret remains with Agatha."

"With Agatha," shivered Darian, turning a shade paler.

"I swear, you two have more secrets than Harmony's Mantle has stars." It was a fact. The pair of them were schemers to the core.

"And what about you, Baran? What does my War Counsellor and Chief Magistrate bring to the table? What do you propose outside of dangling what little remains of my family upon a hook?"

Baran stood and walked the length of the table, stopping behind Ser Roust briefly. Snatching up the infantry man Ser Roust had placed in the northeastern side of the table, he took his time returning to the opposite corner. He could be quite theatrical when he wanted. I could not help but feel envious. He was good at it. Being a born leader, he commanded attention as though it was his to begin with. The man was made for it if ever anyone was.

"As you know, being that they are no longer in need of my protection; I annulled six of my seven marriages upon our arrival. Myrna would not hear of it; bless her heart. Then again, I think she envisions me as some sort of canvas badly in need of repainting. Though I fear she'll be disappointed," he sighed.

If you don't make your bloody point sometime soon, disappointment will reign over us all, I seethed inwardly. Should I have neglected to say so prior, patience was the same as kindness to me for, as far as those two attributes went, I had neither.

"Having allotted each of them a small portion of gold, I now bequeath the remainder to you. It is a tidy sum; more than enough to commence funding our forthcoming endeavors."

"Thank you, Baran. It is exceedingly generous; yet something tells me you have more to say." He did, thank Haeryn. Then again, the One Rah is never wrong even if he is. It was akin to Standstill Pass still being deemed as impregnable if you know what I mean.

"I will bring you the Isles of Eyre," he said, pounding the wee soldier on the largest island in Hangnail Pass so hard the long table rattled from end to end— causing age old memories to stir. *Perhaps that's why we had so many cracked dishes in our home as a child.* It did make sense.

"I will bring you She-wolves and Salt-warriors from the Land Unconquered." He boasted brazenly.

The Land Unconquered. I very much doubted the Isles had been referred to as such since the start of the Great Wars. It was all a bit too obvious, Baran was not about to be outdone. A contest of irrational desperation had not been my intention, however. The implausible had barreled straight into the impossible. Whereas the preceding proposals had been merely reckless; this was a death sentence in comparison.

"You've both been drinking, haven't you? Should he ever lay eyes upon you again, King Turin has sworn to kill you; has he not?"

"Yes, but I refuse to be out-periled by boyish-looking knights or a one-eyed runt. With Audrey of Eyre having been his eldest daughter, King Turin's always known of your true birthright. Therefore, should you truly wish me whole again, I see no other path before me."

"Aye but there's only one way by which that will happen. I will accompany you," I informed him.

"No, you will not." Baran stated, coldly.

"I beg your pardon?" I asked, incredulously. "Precisely what just fled your lips to foul the air around us?"

"Forgive me, Your Holiness. What I intended to convey was that you belong here with your family. You need be protected. You, above all others, must be kept safe."

"Unfortunately for you, I am the Rah." I stared at him in silence for a time, daring him to protest. Wisely, he did not.

"Audre of Eyre was the only mother I ever knew," I sighed at last. "And I'm not about to let her father take you from me too." That took him by surprise.

"In truth, there are answers to be found in the Isles. Thus, I was planning to venture there anyway. The Major will see to my family's safety," I said, holding up a hand to quash Petra's rebuke. "You know it to be true. There is no place safer than Harkenspear. It is known." It was crucial that I added that final notation. Declaring things to be *known* made them hard to argue but, should a One Rah say as much, the debate was ended entirely. That said, if Petra's face bore any indication, not everyone felt similarly.

"Then I will gladly accompany the both of you," beamed Darian, tracing a path across the map with his fat fingers.

"If you travel by way of Haeryn's Hills, you can cross over to East Foot from the south peninsula and likely not encounter a single Kedera on route to the Isles. Their soldiers are either in Verdun or the Disputed Lands. It is known." He finished proudly.

I could not help but laugh. Apparently, I wasn't the only one privy to the ruse. Though hardly convinced his idea was of *sound mind*; neither was Darian. Still, he was a stalwart companion. Notwithstanding that there'd be ample time to ditch him should I so decide. Commander Finn of the Palace Guard rose and spoke.

"Will you require the guard, One Rah?" He asked. "It is our sworn duty to protect the Rah and his family wherever they go."

"No, not this time. Harkenspear must be protected at all costs— my wife and child are here."

"Understood," he saluted, prior to setting a new bar for bowing low. It must be said, the Guard Commander had made a very fine impression upon me thus far. There was nothing extravagant about him. He was all business with no added embellishments. Not to mention he not only knew when to hold his tongue but could do so for a very long time. I only hoped he might rub off on Baran who stood to learn a thing or two when it came to *speaking out of turn*.

"Then it's decided. My quest remains answered more fully than I would ever have expected and for that I thank you all. Darian, I do believe it's time to trial the wine."

"At once," beamed Darian fetching a large pitcher and passing along some ornate silver tankards.

"There," I announced raising my stein. "We have our tasks. Let no wall divide us nor any man remain idle. To Harbinger!" I decreed.

"To Harbinger!" They chanted raucously.

"That's it? That's all?" Petra frowned, impetuously. "Are you not forgetting something? Or are you planning to be on your merry way with a belly full of wine and nary another word?"

"My apologies, I forgot. Oh, and you're all invited to our wedding ceremony tomorrow" I added sheepishly. "Try not to arrive drunk. They'll be plenty of time for that afterward!" I chuckled— until

I saw Petra's face. Taking hold of her hand, I raised it to great cheers.

"Oh, and be sure to speak kindly of me to her mother as met." Which made me think twice. "But say nothing about the war. Or fighting for that matter. On second thought− avoid her at all costs. That is an order." I could feel my right cheek getting warmer by the second and rightfully so. Petra was staring at me rather sternly.

"Lovely woman as I've come to know her more. Fair warning though, she is a bit of a charmer." I added, hiding my face in my cup. *Snake charmer* more like for I expect even Grus would have wagered poorly against her in my stead.

"To my new brother!" Raved the Major to more cheers. "You've changed," he added more soberly. "You're no longer the man I'd grown to fear." Though I granted him the benefit of the doubt, I wasn't precisely sure it was a compliment. You can't pick your family after all. His own mother being a prime example.

"No, I am not." I concurred. "For having finally discovered that my worst enemy lies within." Cocking their heads quizzically, they pondered what I intended. It appeared the merriment had ceased nearly as quickly as it'd begun. Well, save for the Khalifah's overseer, who was still petting his dog as though it was the only thing that had ever mattered in the world. *Witless fool!*

"What do you mean by *the enemy within*?" Prompted Darian.

"Not what most would think, I expect." I replied. "I'm not speaking of the Rage. I refer to other monsters. Monsters I am yet to become familiar with. Yet, monsters all the same."

"Forgive my insolence, but I don't understand." He persisted.

"The monsters that too often accompany power. Pride. Greed. Distrust. Envy. Contentment, even. Those are the enemies I fear most. Only a fool would think himself immune. It is they that lurk within us. Have no misconception, though our pursuit may be for the glory of all; good men will die. What separates us from the Four Rahs is that we will not burn forests, nor orchards, nor farmland. We will not burn churches, nor homes, nor villages. We will not burn people at the stake simply for being divergent to ourselves." I attested firmly.

"Providing you know who you are and remember where you came from, you'll be fine." Insisted Baran.

"I am the Kedera," I winked, rolling my eyes. "But, let it be known in every corner of our lands until the Four False Rahs shiver with fear whilst they sleep… the Harbinger awaits!"

"The Harbinger!" They echoed. "The Harbinger!"

"I apologize," called out the Khalifah's overseer as soon as the din died down.

"I spoke a half truth." He confessed, rising from his chair for the first time. I waited as he pulled back his shroud to reveal himself.

"Khalifah." Spoke the Major and Guard Commander in unison prior to bowing their heads in mutual respect.

The man was more than old for he was clearly blind. Gems of topaz blue had been placed in each of his eye sockets. *If that isn't blind, I don't know what is.* I'd thought at the time. As I was to find out very shortly, never had I been more mistaken.

"I am Diwan Mirant, formerly the resident Khalifah. I offer my services to wed you unless you've made other arrangements. I will ensure the bells ring and the Gates of Harkenspear open at first light. I suggest the Palace steps as a suitable place to proclaim your vows. A new era arises. The people will want to bear witness. The people have waited a long, long time to witness such a thing."

"The Diwans were abolished," I said, hesitantly. "I don't understand. Why appear in such fashion? Why hide your identity?"

"Alas, I am not the only Diwan withholding their identity."

"What are you suggesting?" I asked.

"I may be blind, but I am not deaf for very little do voices change over time."

"Speak plainly." I demanded, albeit rather rudely.

"Simply that it has always been a dangerous title to hold. As you know, the Khalifah were to act as stewards until a suitable successor was found. Being that the search is over, there is no longer a need for such stewards. Thus, as I see it, my title reverts to the Diwan of old. Besides, what may I ask might they do to me now? My toes stub upon my headstone with every shuffling step taken. I am as they whisper. *Beyond useful* is what they say."

"Diwan of old," murmured Darian. "I reckon, he's stubbed more than toes on that headstone. By the looks of him, he's ankle deep if not under to the knees."

Darian shrugged Petra's scowl casually aside as if to imply he'd said nothing inaccurate. All inappropriateness aside, Darian was not wrong. We'd passed skeletons in the Kestrel that looked sprier.

"Most humbly and graciously do we accept your offer," said Petra. "My heart warms to know you'll preside over the ceremony."

"It is I who is humbled," replied Diwan Mirant. "For I'd given up the notion of ever living long enough to see such a day ages ago."

"And them some," muttered Darian. As much as I wanted to ask just how long ago that might have been, if for no other reason than

Darian having piqued my curiosity, I refrained.

"Then it is agreed," I stated. "At midday, we will pass through the gates and proceed toward the Palace. We will climb the Palace steps but proceed no further. Do I make myself clear?"

I was not fond of surprises and still felt unclear why he, and Commander Finn for that matter, chose to withhold his identity until now. And what about the Major? Did they truly not recognize him? Was I being adjudicated; were they merely being overly cautious— or was there more to it?

"As clear as topaz, One Rah." Diwan Mirant bowed. "I don't mean to offend, One Rah, but a great feast will be prepared. They've been slaving on it since the very first word of your arrival. It will be expected for you to venture within the palace. Haeryn's Halls are quite spectacular, I might add. They will expect you to sit at the head of the table and preside over the evening's events. In the very least, they will be adamant you visit Harkenspear Wall and put your mark upon it."

"Then they will be disappointed," I said flatly.

"I assure you the magnificence of the wall is only surpassed by their desire to meet you in person. They will bring gifts; many gifts."

"I have little doubt as to the extravagance of the wall. But it is not my wall. Harbor no misconceptions, I am here to tear down walls, not gawk at overindulgences. Tell them, unless they can deliver the Four False Rahs, they possess nothing I value. We will have a banquet— at the base of the stairs for peasants and dignitaries alike— to which *they will contribute* as much food and wine as necessary."

"And ale," cut in Darian. "I'd very much like to try the ale."

"Am I to understand you do not wish to tally the coffers?"

"The coffers?"

"Our reserves; your reserves rather."

"Reserves?" I queried again.

"Gold, silver, copper; all manner of coin. Our monetary assets. Though far from what it used to be, it remains a tidy sum."

"No, we will survive on what little we have. 'Tis the people's money, not mine."

"Know that I will pass along your wishes though I fear they will be far from pleased," sighed the aged Diwan. "Though they would never say as much aloud, I expect a great many will take offense."

"Understood. It won't be the first time," I smiled. "If you would be kind enough to advise them, whoever *they* are, should they wish to speak more on the matter, they are welcome to join us on the route to Haeryn's Hills. Let it be known, I will not set foot inside any

Palace or Castle not yet earned. Tell them, when I return with my army, having deposed the False Rahs; there'll be ample time to discuss their many accomplishments achieved during my absence. I will expect a full account of our coffers at that time. I will want to know how each hard-earned penny was employed for the betterment of Harkenspear– that of its people. A nation is only as strong as its denizens. A wall has no strength without its foundation."

"Well said, well said," the aged Diwan applauded. "Undoubtedly, that will give them much to ponder," the old man chuckled. "I fear, I must warn you though. The other Khalifah have grown exceedingly comfortable amidst their extended stewardship. They are not like me. They believe only that which they see with their own eyes. No longer do they walk barefoot. They trample pathways previously never intended to be tread. Their memories have grown short. They've forgotten what it means to be… *Khalifah*."

"*Those that go without*," I nodded. "In that vein, to be once again clear, I have no intention of going without. As stated, but a moment ago, I simply want to earn what is mine before deciding what to do with it. I did not come to claim a palace. I did not come for Harkenspear; nor the Khalifah; nor even Golan. I have come for Harbinger."

"So, not for the apples?" He smiled broadly. *Not this again.*

"If I may be so bold, what is this strange infatuation with apples?"

"You're telling me you've never heard of the *War of the Apples*. It's how it all started between the north and south. It was a fight over a vast orchard. Not surprisingly, the Kedera burned it in the end." He sighed. "Do you know the origin of the word Harbinger?" he asked.

"No," I admitted, leaning forward. "In my defense, my bride-to-be has barely begun my tutelage." I whispered.

"Nor mine," he chuckled. Now that was unexpected. "She's younger than me," he continued. "I expect she'll glimpse ninety and four come fall… providing all goes well."

"Providing all goes well," I laughed. "I'd be honored if you'd sit at our table tomorrow. With this unruly lot," I added, nodding my head toward Darian. "If you think your wife can stomach it. I'll sit the pair of you between Petra and I if that helps sway you in any way."

"You honor me, One Rah," he smiled. "I shall count it amongst my greatest days. Did you know, I sat beside your father on more than one occasion? He was as jovial as he was fair. Though less jocund, I believe you have inherited his gift for impartiality."

"I'll take fair over mirth." I laughed. "Now, how do you propose we best go about prodding the memories of the other Khalifah?" I queried.

"With a big stick," he stated bluntly. "If up to me, I would depose them all. They began acting in their own interests before your father's body lay cold in the ground. Not unlike yourself, I have no patience for self-indulgence. I am a firm believer in second chances. Though that is not to imply that you need not earn it."

"Well said," I returned prior to turning my attention to the others. "Everyone, if you would indulge me a final time. I'm afraid there's a few proclamations I neglected to mention earlier." I waited for the room to quiet.

"Major Bryn, forthwith are you promoted to General." Walking over to him we crossed forearms and clenched our fists to honour traditions of old that had been neglected far too long.

"Seratego," I whispered waiting for the applause to end.

"Following our betrothal, Petra will rule on my behalf in all matters. Her word is as mine. Notwithstanding, she's smarter. From this day forth, Petra's parents are the Lord Allistaire and the Lady Taryn. It is known. Petra and her parents will reside within Harkenspear wherever they so choose. Diwan Mirant will be her chief advisor, second in command to us both on all matters of state."

Bowing low, the Diwan lost his balance momentarily and I had to reach out and steady him. As solid as he appeared intellectually, he seemed quite frail outwardly.

"I look forward to being less of an eye sore," noted the Diwan with a wink. *Who knew?* Apparently, it was possible to wink whilst having gems in one's eyes.

"My apologies One Rah but, with your permission, I think it best if turn in for the night."

"Of course, it's been a long day for us all. Please ensure the Diwan is escorted safely back to his residence. No, not you Darian. By the looks of it, I expect you'll require an escort as well." I laughed.

"That's it, farewell. I bid you all good night."

Having said those words, I grabbed Petra by the hand, and we fled. Running as fast as we were able whilst holding hands, which isn't very fast mind you, nor easy to do, we discovered a place beneath the stars far from everyone and everything where no living soul might find us. We talked sporadically throughout the night; or at least when we weren't panting to regain our breath that is. As much as I'd like to say the following day was magical, or somehow dreamlike; it wasn't. Not for me anyway. I'd always hated being the center of attention. As it turned out, my expectations of the whole ordeal had been drastically underestimated. Which is to confirm the event was far worse than I ever might have imagined.

I detested fanfare. Previously, I'd always ridiculed every notion pertaining to such selfish events. I had little choice in the matter now. Not to mention, should I refuse I'd likely perish in my sleep for finding Lady Taryn's fingers about my throat. Not very lady-like of her in my, albeit imaginary, estimation. All I wanted to do was spend every forthcoming moment with Petra and Renan. All I wanted to do was hide beneath the stars. As it turned out, Harmony's Mantle had been corrupted. To my chagrin, as the celebration finally concluded and I sought some measure of solitude, the stars directly above me were spinning rather horrifically. So much so, I had to close my eyes; or risk losing my dinner– a terrifying thought for having eaten far more than my fair share. As I lay there trying, unsuccessfully, to explain to Petra that apparently even celestial bodies were not immune to the drink– while avoiding staring upward– I found myself recounting the day's events if for no other reason than to distract from my self-inflicted debauchery. Darian would have been proud. Providing he'd survived the ordeal.

As planned, we were married on the Palace's grand sandstone stairway. I felt exceedingly uncomfortable in my new pale blue djellaba. Renan wore an identical garment; only smaller. I suppose I need not have mentioned that. Being nowhere near the same size as me, *but of course, it was smaller.* Yes, I did say *pale blue.* Petra had insisted I wear it, *we* wear it rather, the moment she laid eyes on the fabric. *Absolutely not!* I'd implored. For all the good it did. Typical of the tiny traitor he was growing up to be, Renan looked delighted; making me question whether he might really be my son after all. Though it goes without saying, my so-called companions were of no help whatsoever. Baran sputtered and covered his mouth with a hand upon seeing me so dressed, while Darian simply grinned while pointing upward at the sky. Which was no less blue than I felt in that moment.

Petra's gown, on the other hand, was nothing short of miraculous. Appearing as a goddess sent straight from the heavens, I gasped ineptly as she strode gracefully toward me. To say I was taken aback was an understatement. To my dismay, I'd never thought of her as being elegant before. Twin long dark braids cascaded to the waist of her rose-colored dress stopping just short of where my imagination ran wild. Her breasts peaked from her delicate bodice like freshly laid eggs. Not chicken eggs, and certainly not goose eggs but more akin to an emu's if you know what I mean– delicate yet firm, round and full. Having never seen them contained in such fashion, I couldn't help but stare. Until she swatted my cheek, that is. Forcing my chin upwards so I might better gaze into her face, she looked amazingly beautiful. She'd done something to her eyes and lips that made my heart pound like a stallion's prancing hoofs. Having heard braying sounds, I shook my head absentmindedly. Though worried for a moment, it had nothing to do with me, thankfully.

I'd forgotten about the horses. The steps were so wide, ornately decorated horses had been staggered across them from top to bottom. If their incessant prancing was any indication, they appeared no less enthralled than the crowd for the forthcoming proceedings. I, on the other hand, harbored thoughts of leaping onto the back of one and fleeing until my world turned drab again. Snapping me from my stupor, a volley of blaring horns ignited the event. Darian would have quite likely toppled the full length of the stairs had Baran not grabbed him. I'm not sure *volley* is the right word but there were a lot of them. I think they call them trumpets. They weren't bugles. I'd seen those before. These were different; not to mention unimaginably loud– given the fact some were but an arm's distance away. I expect it will be quite some time before my ears are fully recovered. Though you'd think he would have been startled to tears, not unlike his swaddling messes, Renan adored the unwelcome surprise.

As per my forthright direction, the vows themselves were to be very short. I did think that part through and, as much as Petra and her mother wanted to expand the ceremony until the moon waxed full again, I refused their wishes. I couldn't help but wonder what my marriage might have been like had I not been *the One Rah*. We'd still be at it, I expect– with less trumpets and horses but a lot more pledges and heartfelt assurances. Given a choice, I'll choose deafening noise over weighty declarations without pause any day. The ringing in my ears did stop eventually. Speaking of which….

"Rah Deshu Mogashu, will you take Lady Petra Bryn as your wife?"

And vice versa. The reason I wanted the ceremony to be as concise as possible was to ensure there were no *hiccups*. It didn't work. And not just hiccups for I farted as well. The timing couldn't have been more perfect for it happened as soon as the Diwan signaled everyone to be silent. Though admittedly, I did at first consider trying to cast blame upon the Diwan, given the fact that such outbursts were rather common amongst people his age, as per my earlier conversation with Petra at the lake, I did take ownership for the foul deed in the end. *Out of the end*, rather. However, you say it. Haeryn help me!

"Tooter!" I politely acknowledged, raising my hand for all to bear witness. Noticing several confused glances, including Darian, I thought it best to provide some further clarity.

"Amongst the nobility, it's only proper to take ownership," I kindly explained. Hearing murmurs break out amongst the crowd, I thought I'd spoken out of turn at first. Until I noticed other hands being raised followed quickly by the word *tooter*. Had the event been less formal, I might have taken the time to applaud their honesty.

In hindsight, I should have asked more questions; especially considering I'd never attended a wedding previously. Point being, who in their right mind would invite the Golan Butcher to an affair of the heart? Thus, I had no bloody idea I was supposed to give her a ring. *Idiot*. There were so many people watching; my heart began racing the moment the question was put to me. It seemed such a simple request.

"Rah Deshu, the ring if you please?" Diwan Mirant smiled politely, whilst turning my world completely upside down.

Ring? What ring? Lady Taryn's face nearly fell into her lap. Everyone was staring at me. I didn't know what to do. Being that it was the lone object I had on my person, I instinctively unsheathed my gold-handled dagger. *For what?* I stared at it blankly for a few moments, but it quickly became clear it was not about to magically reform itself into a ring. I considered slicing my own throat with it briefly. *Why? Why? Why?* I was so tired of looking like a fool. I looked up to see Petra's sparkling green eyes. Though murmurs and mumblings were breaking out amongst the crowd, her faultless face was completely calm. She trusted me. She loved me. And apparently, on this day, I could do nothing wrong. That small gesture of reassurance gave me the strength I needed. Correction, as always, *she* gave me the strength I needed.

Releasing her hand from my own sweaty palm, I stepped backward to stand directly in front of her. Bowing and bending low, I put the tip of my dagger into the sandstone's smooth face. Very slowly and deliberately, I drew a large circle about the two of us, rising to face her again upon its completion. Let me tell you, regardless of being a Rah, it's hard to appear even vaguely refined while hobbling about on one's haunches. Drawing, *no pun intended*, as much strength as I could from Petra's eyes, I descended the stairs to fetch Renan from my mother-in-law. I must say, it felt good to snatch him from the disapproving crone's arms. If there was one thing I'd learned in respect to parenthood, it was that babies were hugely distracting. Even Baran acted differently around him. If was as if they were somehow blind to the constant splatter dribbling down his cheek; as though they were completely unable to smell the swaddled lump nestled between his fat, sticky thighs.

"Will you be performing afterward as well?" The old bat had nerve enough to inquire while passing me my son.

"You didn't get a ring, did you?" She murmured. I saw little alternative other than to grin, nodding courteously as though she'd said something vastly supportive. *Hardly*.

Returning to Petra, I stepped into the ring I'd scribed and hurriedly wrapped my arm about her waist. But it was Diwan Mirant who truly saved the day. Admittedly, the ceremony did get a bit longer at that point, but it could not have gone better especially considering my grievous blunder.

"I recognize, there are those among you who are feeling a bit confused," beamed the Diwan. "Please, allow an old blind man to enlighten you. The One Rah is flattered neither by fanfare nor possessions. So much so, that he refuses to set foot inside this palace until he's won the hearts and minds of his people." He nodded admiringly.

"Know that a ring is a modest thing. It is perfect as is. It needs neither gems nor gold simply because, like love; it is as unconditional as it is interminable. For in its purest form, devoid of all extravagance, does a circle by its lonesome signify the unbreakable bond."

He paused to let his words sink in before continuing. I was beside myself with gratitude while watching Petra wipe tears from the corner of her eyes. I only hoped the *old battle axe* was sniffling too; or at least rethinking her prior disposition. As much as that seemed unlikely, it didn't matter. The faces around me said it all. They wanted to believe my actions had unfolded *precisely as planned*.

"It is at this time that the One Rah requested I recite words bequeathed us by the Prophet Raeben," he continued with a wistful smile followed by a brief pause. The Prophet Raeben. *Yes, of course I did.* Whoever he might have been for I knew not.

"If I drew a thick-lined circle, would you step inside with me? Could we orbit there forever, or would you need to be set free? If I gave my final breath, and you held it as your own; would I suffocate of angels? Might this soul fall free of bone?"

"Now, hold her hand above her head and spin her about," Diwan Mirant whispered. Though a bit awkward for having Renan, I did as commanded. The man was my savior. *For this will I declare you a saint*, every thought within me whispered.

"By the powers proclaimed by Haeryn himself, do I now pronounce you man and wife. Good people of Harkenspear, I present to you His Holiness, the Heir of Harbinger, the One Rah reborn, Rah Deshu Mogashu and his beautiful bride... daughter of Lord Allistaire and Lady Taryn; brother of our own General Bryn to whom we owe so much, Her Imperial Highness, the Empress Petrella Ursula Mogashu."

Intense cheering erupted at that juncture, and we were forced to remain at the forefront for quite some time. Although quite different circumstances entirely, I could not help but be reminded of the cleansing of the Black Pail. Renan began to squirm, and I put him down absently mindedly. He immediately let go of my hand and began stumbling toward the horses. I had to run and snatch the little man by the back of his blue djellaba to the great amusement of all. I turned to Petra sporting a look of awe– mixed with equal parts of flourishing ineptitude. Which is to say, I felt oddly giddy.

"Oh, and there's that," Petra said through flushed cheeks that were positively bursting so bright was her smile. I'd known Renan could stand and stagger a clumsy step or two, but this was something new. The little man was walking– very near to running in fact. We both started laughing. It was all we could do really. Petra appeared to be crying at the same time. Though I prayed my days of sniveling were behind me, I couldn't say that I blamed her.

Petra later told me it was by far the best moment of her entire life. Was it the best time of my life? Without a doubt, putting an end to the daunting formality ranked exceedingly high. Petra was mine now. It was all I wanted– outside of an end to the prolonged festivities. I would never host a bigger affair; that seemed certain. There was more entertainment than I ever might have imagined: musicians and minstrels; jugglers and jesters; dancers and acrobats; even fire-eaters and conjurers. The latter two capturing my attention far more than the others. Though no one could say for certain, largely due to clattering mugs; there was likely more wine being spilled than Darian had previously consumed in his lifetime. That said, awarding proper accreditation as merited, on this night he did seem intent on setting a new standard for drunkenness.

Then there was the food. It was seemingly endless being that a plethora of decorative platters just kept coming. There were iron pots boasting ham and leek soup; pork pies; salvers brimming with pickled eggs and wedges of cheese. There were figs, sugared almonds, candied fruit, and crispy, fried oranges. There was all manner of jellies, troves of butter and fresh-baked breads and cakes. But that wasn't all– not by a long shot. Next came the roasts of wild boar and lamb which had been turned upon the spit until crisp. You could smell it everywhere. Darian was falling-down flighty by this point. There was stuffed chicken, partridges, pheasants, and woodcocks. I was told nearly five hundred fowl had been plucked for that one night alone.

And I haven't yet made mention of the fishmonger's wares. *Haeryn help us!* There was roast mallard, brook trout, broths churning with eel and salted carp. I dare say, I did wave the braised seal away. It seemed to me it would have been better served with the jams and jellies; with no need of any butter; though a great deal of bread. I'd never seen such a hapless looking creature. Diwan Mirant kindly explained they moved more aptly through the seas than over land. I'd only witnessed the seas from great distance myself– typically whilst forcing the Kedera from high cliffs and so forth.

For dessert, Petra and I were served an enormous cake shaped like a castle with giant pastry-filled towers surrounded by a blueberry moat. Everyone else got tarts. Prone to bouts of sugar jealousy since a lad, it was not long before I experienced a terrible yearning for not having been offered one of the dainty-looking tarts. Given the huge cake before us, Petra expressed skepticism regarding the true urgency of my appeal. So, I tried a new tactic. I told her the castle cake was a scheme concocted by the nobility to test my resolve. Thus, I had little choice but to refuse it for not having earned it. It must be trial by tart I insisted. It was then she relocated an entire tower within my bursting cheeks. It was only then I discovered them to be full of pastry which melted upon one's tongue not unlike a honey wafer. Which is to admit, shortly thereafter, three more towers found themselves breached; to say nothing of the walls and moat I spooned into my face in droves.

"How are our plans coming along?" I asked the Diwan, nodding my head toward Ser Roust while licking icing from my hands and fingertips.

"Precisely as planned. You'll be pleased to know the commissioned monument is finished. It is to be erected at the lake by mid-day tomorrow." He smiled.

Though I had anticipated as much, the Diwan also informed me the yellow eye opals he wore were in our honor. *Two suns outshine the one*, I'd replied ineptly, having drank a lot of wine. He laughed at that. Purely out of politeness, I expect.

"Long ago, your father noted my eyes to be as keen as those of a Harbinger cat," he smiled. "Perhaps, at long last, I've proven myself worthy of his assertion."

I felt obliged to raise my cup toward him at the point as, from that day forward, his words made me consider my House sigil secretly akin to a one-eyed Harbinger cat. I must tell Darian I thought looking about. I finally found him dancing with what looked to be the hind leg of an ox. Chitter was flying in erratic circles above him hoping for a chance to land on his shoulder.

"They call it beeeer!" I heard him yell whilst pulling up the socks on his arms which had slid to his wrists. "Beeeer!!!" He hollered again. *On second thought not*. It seemed best to leave him be.

"Poor fellow has had a hard lot. I suppose you can't blame him for overindulging now and again." Noted the Diwan.

"Now and again?" I guffawed rhetorically. Because that's a thing. *Rhetorical guffawing*. Perhaps not. In my defense, I was far from sober.

"Which isn't to intend him blameless." The Diwan continued. "It's only that Darian confided earlier how he came to lose his eye in his youth whilst attempting to charm a snake."

"Did he now?" I replied with heightened curiosity.

"I can only imagine the pain." The Diwan cringed openly.

"Nor more than he recalls," I added dryly.

"Lessons of life can be excruciatingly cruel." The Diwan observed, removing his yellow opal eyes and setting them upon the table ahead of him. It was obviously something he did routinely.

"The gods are cruel," I agreed, while wondering just how many tales Darin had fabricated about losing that eye of his. Which wasn't truly gone mind you. Proving my previous assertion to be true.

"Though there are few who know it, I can still see out of both my eyes— dim shadows and shapes mostly." He confessed, wiping them in turn with a sleeve before continuing.

"Being that it's a sad inevitability, I thought I may as well get used to it. Blindness, that is." he added, gently tapping one of the opals in front of him with a crooked finger to further his point.

"Your father wore a single citrine gem upon a gold band. And your mother, a flawless pendant with matching earrings of yellow sapphire," Diwan Mirant continued with a sigh.

"I buried them in my youth." I confessed.

"What?" The Diwan queried, moving closer still.

"I buried them," I hollered above the ruckus.

"Buried who?" He looked at me quizzically. It's hard to explain, but there's something unnatural about a puzzled look on a blind man's face. Though I can't say why, I was reminded of a three-legged dog I once saw barking at a squirrel. *Good luck with that.* I'd thought at the time. Fortunately for the Diwan, I finally recognized the origin of his confusion.

"Not my parents; the jewelry." I explained. "I never met my parents." Once again, he cocked his head quizzically.

"I don't remember them, rather," I clarified. "'Tis a sad tale but, when our home burned to the ground, I found the jewelry in the ashes and buried it. I was but a lad at the time."

"Buried treasure; how wondrous. I do hope you remember where it is," he laughed.

"Providing I live long enough," I smirked.

"Then I suppose my chances of discovering how the tale turns out are drastically thin," he sighed. He was right; with my luck some two-legged dog ran off with it long ago, I mused prior to chastising myself for continuing to refer to the Kedera as such. Still, change didn't happen overnight. It would take time for wounds as such to heal. I very much doubted they ever would entirely.

"I could not help but notice you seemed rather upset for having discovered yourself to be Kedera born." The Diwan appeared to be reading my thoughts. *Well, let's get right to it then.* He wasn't one for bush beating, I give him that.

"Yes. It wasn't easy to stomach at first but I'm working on it. Truth be told, I've spent my entire life hating them. That said, in my defense, they were charging me with spears, axes, swords, and such."

"Do you know what diversity is?" He asked unexpectedly.

"A medley of sorts. If you're speaking of people, I think it refers to the many differences between us." Undoubtedly, had it not been for Petra I would never have known.

"And therein lies the rub, as they say. For the more things are different the more they have in common."

"I don't understand." I confessed.

"It's an age-old problem with our thinking patterns. Even before languages were invented, we found ways to name all that we encountered. And by *all* I entail not only plants and animals, the surrounding hills and the weather, but invisible things like feelings and such. For this are we blameless though it did not come without a toll."

"How so?" Admittedly, he had me intrigued if for no other reason than having not a clue as to what he intended thus far.

"Simply put, the more we attached names to things the more they lost their uniqueness. That was the sacrifice we made in doing so. It is our nature to box and sort everything. Hiding behind placards touting our so-called similarities, we formed cliques, clans, and churches so we need not have to think. Now, as a result, when we see zebras, we can't see past their stripes."

"My apologies but what have zebras to do it?"

"Everything and nothing." He winked. Upturning his palms, he held them aloft. "Did you know that no two person's fingerprints are the same?"

"I did not." I shrugged, feeling even more confused. Perhaps his mind was failing him. He was very old after all.

"Being entirely unique unto themselves, zebra stripes are no different. I smell oranges." He smiled.

I felt for him. He was clearly losing his focus. Then again, considering how poor his eyesight was, notwithstanding the oranges had only been placed upon the table a moment ago, at least his nose was still in ship shape. Thank Haeryn Lod wasn't sitting with us, or his nose might have had more than it could handle. Feeling for the bowl with outstretched hands, he placed it ahead of me.

"What do you see?" He inquired after a moment or two.

"Oranges." I sighed. "But you know that already." Was it a game we were playing– some odd form of test, perhaps?

"Anything else?" He asked patiently.

"Round oranges. There is nothing else. It's a bowl of round oranges."

"Look deeper," He encouraged me.

"Did I mention they were orange in color?" I blurted. Causing him to chuckle.

"Ah, you've given up. My apologies, I was only trying to better make my point."

"Which is?"

"That we see purely what we wish to see– that being, what we expect to see rather than that which truly exists." Picking oranges from the bowl he began to assess them carefully within his frail fingers.

"This one is bruised having thicker skin. This one is scarred yet tender. This one has a stem while the previous one did not. And this one… is sticky. And the one thing impossible to tell," he paused, tearing away its waxy skin, "is what they might be like inside.

Regardless of our beliefs, where we were born, or the color of our skin, people are no different. If we refilled the bowl with all manner of fruits, would you still choose your favorite or try something new?"

"I see what you're saying." I nodded. "Diversity is a gift." Tearing the orange, he gave one half to me.

"Exactly. One should never be in a hurry to die for their beliefs. Embracing our differences allows us to change. Though far from simple, it remains a choice. Not to mention, sticky fingers should always be shared." Which made me laugh aloud, though he'd given me far more than that to ponder.

"So, aside from the War of the Apples, Harbinger is naught but a big bowl of oranges." I sighed.

"And a sticky situation for certain," he smiled. "See past its colorful façade and, regardless of which side of the wall you peer from, there's still plenty of good in the world to be found. Now what if I was to tell you, diversity is a myth. It doesn't exist."

"I would say, you've lost me again."

"What if you commanded all men to come forth and not just from Harbinger but the entire world; and not just the men but all the women and children as well."

"I would say we're going to need a lot more oranges." I quipped.

"And, after checking all of their fingerprints, and finding them all to be different, in your great wisdom, you declared them all the same."

Admittedly, even with my great wisdom, I didn't know what to say to that at first.

"Because if everyone is different, in that they are the same."

"More than that, it wasn't merely their fingerprints that differed but their fingers themselves; and not just their fingers but their toes too; and not just their fingers and toes but their lips, and skin, and hair, and eyebrows, teeth, nails, ears, noses, cheeks, frowns, smiles, breaths, sighs and laughter were found to be different as well. Yes, even their laughter for, though they were prone to mimicking one another, no two voices were identical. Some men found themselves hitched to a plow while others inherited a castle. And it didn't stop there for, within their mind's eye, they viewed things differently. Therefore, they had different attractions and different dislikes. Wherefore, their minds considered things adversely under different lights even though they all stood beneath the same sun ...which was different from every other star in the universe, though to us they all looked the same."

"So, you're asking... if everything differs does it differ at all?" Petra cut in.

"Exactly. But not just humanity. I intend everything we've ever encountered. Diversity is everywhere in all things and, if so, then it is it truly even a thing? I mean, if everything is different, as the One Rah said earlier, is it not all the same? Just the way things are. The way everything is... ever-changing and unique. The key is to celebrate this diversity for being a common thread. They need be appreciated, rather than compared. The most common element being *we too shall pass*."

I ran a finger along one of my many facial scars deep in thought which caused the aged Diwan to chuckle.

"Don't celebrate those so much. We did that to ourselves. Our scars serve as reminders. Learn from those. It is the differences that make us feel uncomfortable that we need celebrate most for it is the insecurities hiding within us that hold the most potential. Recognize, we are copiers by nature for that is how we learn... to hide from ourselves and one another. We do so largely out of jealousy and fear sadly. In that, we are not diverse. In that, what should have remained a myth, all too easily found shape." He sighed.

"What did you mean when you claimed not to be the only Diwan withholding his identity?" It was my turn to be nosey.

"In my old age, I've found that some things you learn are not yours to give. Not to mention, I've grown no less possessive than crotchety. Thus, I beg you to permit me to withhold the odd secret now and again. I believe some refer to it as *poking the bear*. The truth of it is, it is not for me to say. That said, the truth can never be stalled indefinitely. Have patience and it will reveal itself in good time. That said, you will come to learn the truth is little more than a convenience at the best of times."

I pondered his words in sullen silence. Haeryn knows I was not a man of patience. And to think a bit earlier I'd considered sharing one of my castle towers with him. *The crotchety old prude!* Keep your damn secrets. I'd even considered offering him a chance to lap up the blueberry moat remains. I can assure you that ship had sailed. It had been quite delicious in fact.

Petra inquired what I liked best about the day's events. *Proclaiming our vows before all.* I'd lied. She seemed satisfied with that answer. Much later that night, I opened an eye to see if Petra was asleep. She was– providing me an opportunity to rethink her query more fully. Outside of the vows? As I considered it, punching one of the overseers did feel rather gratifying. The fool grabbed the sleeve of my new robe insisting I walk through the palace with him. Though I declined his offer very politely, his insistence persisted. That was ill-advised. Which is why I struck him.

"What did you do that for?" He'd stammered with a glazed look on his pouty face.

"Because I can. Because I'm the One Rah. I am not led; I lead." I advised him clearly.

Watching Darian drink ale and wine at the same time with both hands was entertaining. Until it wasn't— being that he eventually collapsed in a heap. Conversing with Petra's mother proved as soothing as ever; like trying to kindle a fire in a hailstorm. Which is to say: *pointless*. I wasn't convinced the woman liked me at all. And to think I'd made her a Lady.

Alde Baran's toast was enlightening. *Change is coming*, he proclaimed unabashedly. *With every new dawn comes a new sun; a sun that sets upon tight-fisted, covetous, penny-pinching swine.* That made me laugh until Petra advised otherwise. The table next to us full of Overseers had the nerve to wave him off as though he was but a pretentious fool— until he unsheathed Agatha and waved it toward them. At which point they turned very white. Especially the one I'd punched. Though perhaps a bit early to judge, I believe it's called *progress*. With all that in mind, I still think my fondest moment was when Diwan Mirant leaned over to quietly whisper in my ear.

"Forerunner," was all he said. Admittedly, it took me quite some time to figure out what he meant.

"Ah, the origin of Harbinger," I whispered back finally.

"Quite right," He nodded. "Last night, I dreamt a murder of crows flew down from the heavens and pecked out my eyes. Not a very good portent," he said.

"Crows are luckless creatures," I attested. "As dark outside as in they say. I saw three dead crows upon first setting out upon this journey. Not a good omen either, I expect."

"It might herald a new beginning. Without darkness what need is there for light?" He asked softly while placing the glowing opals carefully back into his eye sockets after moistening them in his mouth.

Smiling amiably toward me, he looked more at peace in that moment that any man I'd ever met. More eerily, he also looked strangely akin to a lot of dead men I'd seen— save for having had coppers placed over their eyes. I never forgot those words for they became my saving grace. They hardened my resolve; affording me the necessary strength to arise each time I fell. If there was but one thing

I'd learned thus far, it was that I fell no less hard than I did often. It was my way. Adversity did seem the sole path awaiting me.

Petra woke me later that night. It might have been early morning. Either way, I was relieved to find the world had ceased spinning at which point I resolved never to drink again.

"When will you depart?" she asked solemnly.

"Soon," I answered sadly. "Too soon; in three days at most. As much as I hate to go, we need to end this." As it turned out, being that the wedding lasted three full days and nights, we departed on the morning of the Fourth day. I must confess, my resolve proved weaker than my desire for camaraderie for I witnessed a good deal more spinning over the course of the following two days.

"It's not fair," she cried, burying her face in my chest.

"No, it's not," I agreed. I felt sick in the pit of my stomach— and not purely from the drink.

"Return as soon as you are able," she sobbed. She'd undone her hair braids which fell in dark, wavy curls not unlike my own.

"Where will you stay? Within the palace?"

"Of course, within the palace. It is the safest place; not to mention its beauty is beyond words."

"Your beauty is beyond words," I told her.

"Don't pillage my words for lack of your own." She sniffed. "If it was truly so you wouldn't be departing in such haste."

"I do only what I must. Be careful, the palace worries me. It's too much; no one deserves such lavishness. It changes a person; it corrupts men leading them to believe they are something they are not."

"It need not. Magnificence by itself holds no power. It is a testament declaring what we can achieve at our best. Am I nothing other to you than a similar predicament? You claim that I have changed you. You call me beautiful and yet… you're leaving."

It seemed we'd reverted to talking in circles again. I'd explained the situation many times over. The last thing I wanted to do was leave. But sometimes difficult choices were the only ones available. As hard as it was, I saw no other path that did not hold us apart.

"Because I must; not because I want to. It's true, you have changed me. Last time, when the Red Rage took hold, I saw a shadow flee only to die ahead of its master. I've never remembered anything of that nature before. I feel as though the day is not far off where I can control it. I believe a time will come where it never seizes hold of me again. Had I not met you, that would not be possible. You've changed me far more than you know."

"And what will happen then? What will happen when the Rage no longer protects you? You do realize it's as much a blessing as it is a curse? They say Red Radesh cannot be killed. They say many battles would have been lost were it not for the Golan Butcher."

"They say a lot of things absent of truth. They say the same about someone named Oswald."

"Oswald? Who's Oswald?" She queried with a look of concern.

"Never mind; no one of import. I'll be back soon enough after which you can protect me with that sturdy hairpin of yours." She finally smiled, which made me feel glad.

"It'll be fine. You'll see, it will all work out in the end," I said.

"It always does," she agreed. "One way or the other. I pray it is above ground rather than below."

On the morning of our departure, I was surprised to find Manu sleeping outside our tent. He informed me he wished to accompany me on my travels. I felt torn. Though I respected Manu greatly, he had saved my new mother-in-law condemning me to a life of endless scrutiny. In the end, I felt compelled to tell him that the best place for him was precisely where he stood now. Fact was, where we were going was no place for an old man. That made him angry; which woke Petra; which, of course, changed everything– as was her nature. *Like mother, like daughter*. A thought that pained me regularly of late.

"Old? Feel these arms!" He demanded hotly. "There's no fat on these bones! I'm no less agile than the day I leapt from my mother's womb! I'll have you know I once swam Hang Nail Pass all the way from East Foot to Broken Toe. And largely against the tide, I might add."

"I did not mean to insult you," I stammered. "I simply intended you might be of better use here."

What need have *they* of yet another servant?" he crowed. "The palace is ripe with groomsmen, and I am no man's stable boy. Please, One Rah, I beg this of you. All I want to do *is matter*."

"Matter?" He touched a chord within me. Wasn't it all anyone ever wanted? That is, to be somehow relevant.

"I don't want to die nameless," he clarified, "an old man without purpose. Don't let me wither like a weary crow."

"Manu is the wisest person I ever met," attested Petra. I sighed unintentionally as I mulled that over. If Petra said the man was wise, only a fool wouldn't accept his services. It was settled. Once again, it seemed I had little choice in the matter.

"Pack your things," I urged him. "We will depart the moment our fast is broken."

"I am packed." He smiled, puffing out his chest. "No disrespect, One Rah, but I was never not going."

The other men were already at the stables as we arrived. Darian was bent over and looking pasty green. No surprise, it was morning after all. His kestrel sat on a fence post eyeing him forlornly. There were twenty-six of us in total, including Manu and myself. Not counting Ser Roust and his three squires, that is, who were just about to depart in the opposite direction. They were dressed in the black garb of the Kedera. I nearly failed to recognize Ser Roust for his huge mustache having been completely shaven. Alde Baran was already bidding him farewell.

"Take care, my friend," said Baran as he climbed atop his own mount. "You would have made a bloody good spy," He smiled. He just couldn't let it go, *could he?*

"We will meet back here to drink and share tales," Baran told him. "As soon as our errands are complete." He added. It seemed unlikely to me at the time. There was no way by which to approximate how long our differing paths might take. A messenger rode up and handed Alde Baran a note. Baran read it, pocketing it quickly.

"Tell her, she has my word," he said to the messenger. "Tell her, on my life will I make it so."

Though none of my business, I felt obliged to ask ifif the note had been from his wife.

"No, yours." He replied. "No doubt mine is busy painting; she's always painting."

"May I ask what she wanted?"

"No, you may not."

"I am the Rah after all." I urged.

"You want to know the contents of the note she clearly sent privately to me whilst knowing full well you'd be here?" He felt it necessary to clarify.

"Yes, that note. I am her husband after all."

"It says, don't bring him back…"

"On a slab," I finished, with a grimace. I felt tears welling in my eyes. It was hard enough to promote a positive disposition without such adverse forebodings.

"I hear congratulations are in order," Darian called out.

"He doesn't know," snapped Alde Baran, raising a finger hotly.

"How can he not know?" Darian smirked with disbelief.

"I don't know but I think it best he be kept in the dark." Though you might think me naïve, at the time, I had assumed they were referring to the surprise I had in store for Ser Roust. They weren't. As it turned out, they knew nary a whisper about that. *Bloody fools!* By which I intended *the lot of us.*

I sighed watching Petra strolling toward a hilltop with Renan in hand to better view our departure. The little man was leading the way, pulling her along hurriedly. It made me proud. I could see Grus watching them from a distance. He'd also be keeping a careful eye on the fortress. It was his job to hold it in my absence. He was a good man; I could count on him. Without question, he would die prior to letting any harm befall them.

I saw Petra hunch over, clutching her stomach as she heaved her morning pudding and biscuits. I can't say I was surprised. She'd been similarly ill each of the last few mornings. Our forthcoming separation had taken its toll, the poor girl was sick with grief. Having said our good-byes, I told her it was preferable for her to wave from afar. I knew she'd start crying and it was hard enough to leave without any added theatrics. She'd cut her hair shortly thereafter. I reckon she did it purely out of spite though she swore it was to make her appear *statelier*. It did make her look less of a girl and more of a woman if that's what she meant. It did me no good at all. She looked completely transformed. I couldn't take my eyes off her. And now I had to leave.

Making life no less arduous, she'd informed me that it was Renan's *name day* which took me entirely by surprise– not a dagger to the ribs but a solid kick for certain. Though the timing seemed suspect, I saw little choice but to accept her claim. I mean why would she lie– apart from all the other times she'd done so? Her mother made a right spectacle of it, of course. Having already decided to depart the following day made the celebration increasingly awkward. The fact that I'd been wholly ignorant of his birth in the first place only added to the festering pit within my stomach.

"Are there many books within the castle?" I'd asked her casually while munching bread wafers drizzled with warm butter and honey. I was hoping to trot off with more cordial memories in mind. Ones that might make me feel a little less *ogre-like*.

"Many," she confirmed.

"Then I expect I'll be back before you realize I'm gone," I smiled.

"Just come back to me Rah Deshu," she replied.

"Remember *that night*?" I asked. "*That night* when you said I spoke both gentle and kind. Know that men speak *gentle and kind* when they want something," I confided– providing her fair warning what she need be mindful of during my absence.

"Are you speaking gentle and kind now?" She asked.

"No, I speak plainly."

"You will," she winked. "You will when you return."

"All the hounds of Haeryn could not stop me," I assured her. It was true. Not that I was certain he had any hounds but, if he did, I'd send them to live with the angels if that's what it took just to hold her in my arms again.

"I read that the women are different on the Isles; not unlike warriors, so they say. It's said they are neither gentle nor kind but *far more forward* if you get my meaning."

"I'll be sure and keep a wary eye out for that." I nodded with feigned eagerness. Though I'd never visited the isles I heard similar tales myself many times. Tales with a great deal more detail which I wasn't about to confess anytime soon to her. Though popular amongst the soldiers, they were largely inappropriate in fact. At least, from a *trying to put his best foot forward* One Rah point of view.

"Falter but once and I'll take that wary eye of yours," she scolded. "Make no mistake, alongside you Darian would look like a god. Know that just because I cut my hair isn't to in any way imply that I've retired the pin."

"You do realize I find you adorable even when you're not threatening me?" I grinned. "Say goodbye to your mother for me. That's odd. I wonder what made me think of her?" I quipped.

"She foretold me of your return. She said I would see it from afar for the trail of wee ones scuttling along behind you."

"Did she now?" I laughed.

"She swore the trail would be longer than the eye can see."

"I will miss her sorely," I said, feigning to look aghast.

"It would be in your best interests to prove her *mistaken*. I told her as much without mincing words. Don't play me for the fool." She cautioned. "Know that you are mine and not something I will ever share willingly."

"I'm wed not dead," I sniggered.

"Rest assured, you'll find them one and the same should you stray from your course even slightly."

"Have no fear, there is no one else for me. You are my sole path." I meant every word. All I need do now was live up to them.

"How did you sleep?" She inquired, changing the subject abruptly.

I confessed to having the same reoccurring dream. Not the sweaty one where my enemies were trying to skewer me with all manner of weapons but the one with the ripe orchards, peaceful meadows, and babbling brook. Petra called it my *Oasis*. The smell of lavender had been so intense it had caused me to sneeze in fact. As always, it was the first thing I noticed though a few things had been different this time round. The brook was teeming with crayfish and trout. The groves were thick with pecans and oranges. But all signs of wild game had vanished. Why? I don't know. It didn't matter. It was just the kind of talk one made to avoid discussing unfolding events beyond our control. Notwithstanding, 'twas a dream.

"Perhaps it implies you'd make a better farmer than butcher." She sighed. Which made me snort aloud.

"Rahs do not farm," I corrected her.

"But there are other ways by which to cultivate."

"But I thought you said that was forbidden whilst I am away." I jested. She ignored that thankfully.

"Nothing grows faster than a whispered secret." She smiled. At least I had something to ponder on my journey for I hadn't the slightest idea what she'd intended by that.

"Do not return to me on a slab, Rah Deshu Mogashu. You are no good to me on a slab."

"No slab," I agreed wholeheartedly. It felt good to finally agree on something. I swear, I felt so sick to my stomach I could have *hewn my leg with a wooden spoon* as my mother, Audrey of Eyre, used to say. I was quite serious. I'd sooner cut my bloody leg off than be parted from her. And, for all my days to come those feelings prevailed.

"May your days be long," hollered Darian, shattering my stupor.

He was trying to pull himself onto his horse. Outside of his significant belly, his saddle bags were so full he was finding it nearly impossible to swing a leg over them. Farting successively, perhaps to better propel himself, he kept tugging the animal in circles upon each ensuing failed attempt. In the end, Alde Baran had to dismount, grab hold of the creature's bridle, and let Darian stand on his knee. The man did not know the meaning of shame. Which is largely why I adored him so.

"And your nights full of beer," he finally finished with a triumphant grin.

"And where's your precious socks?" I called out.

"Stolen, I expect. Either way, I've lost them." Clacking his tongue, Chitter flew to perch on his shoulder. I shook my head sadly before leaping spritely atop my own steed. Diwan Mirant had told us to take whatever we desired. I was not the least bit shy when it came to the horses. For myself, I chose a magnificent stallion. Being the color of smoke, it had been aptly named *Smolder*. I nudged the beast closer to Ser Roust who was riding *Nutmeg*, his white-eared brindle mare of equal size and girth.

"If that's ale within his sling, I'll bridle him before day's end," I half-joked to Ser Roust.

"He'll only deny it. He'll claim it's *beeeer*." We both laughed.

"Has he ever told you how he came to lose his eye?" I asked curiously.

"Told me a kestrel plucked it for having stolen a fledgling from its nest; then said it was jackals whilst he slept... the following night."

"Of course, he did." I grinned. "Baran told me Darian found the bird within the great tree Grumble."

"One of them is lying."

"Both likely. All I know is he's been telling tales about that pouched egg since we first met. And that was some time ago." I huffed, slapping my thigh.

"Be well," said Ser Roust. "With luck, I'll see you back here before the next harvest. The Diwan might consider planting an extra crop of barley just in case Darian does make it back with big folks in tow." We had another good chuckle at that.

"Would you do me one last courtesy?" I asked him.

"Name it," he replied without hesitation.

"There is more I wish to say prior to departing our separate ways. Would you accompany us as far as the lake, so we might speak at greater length?"

"Gladly," he bowed. "I'll have my squires ride ahead to ensure the gnats are well fed before our arrival." Whistling through his teeth, he motioned for his squires to swing about as they'd already trotted off in what was now the wrong direction.

"Take this," I said, tossing him a pouch of gold coins from the many bequeathed to me by Baran.

"I'll be sure and put it to good use," he said, pulling on his reins to turn his own horse around. I took one final look at Petra and Renan before cantering off. They both waved before covering an eye with their hands. She was funny. At least I think she was joking. Either way, I'd miss them both terribly.

"Send some coins to your family," I suggested. "And, whatever you do; don't drink anything the Monkey Man isn't drinking himself," I forewarned.

"Did you say the Monkey Man?" Interrupted Ruok, swinging his horse about to face us. A twisted look invaded his face.

"Of the trading post known as the Monkey House south of Barrenlance. Yes, one and the same. I met him long ago. A debt that remains unsettled due to the unfortunate encounter." I admitted.

"Allow me to collect it for you," Ser Roust kindly offered.

"I'd steer clear of him," Ruok cautioned. "My brother isn't right in the head."

"Your brother? I thought you said your family was dead."

"They are. Thanks to him, I expect. He's dead to me and certainly not family." Opening his djellaba, both sides of his torso were heavily scarred.

"Most of these are from him on the same fateful day."

"You're lucky to be alive." I noted.

"Lucky isn't the word I'd use. I was only a lad at the time. He kept asking if I was alright; and then he'd stab me again and laugh. *Are you okay?* He kept asking prior to stabbing again and again. His real name's Will. My father called him Ill-Will," he sneered.

"And he runs the Monkey House?"

"Right into the ground, they say. I ain't seen him since that day. Pa took me to an orphanage. Said I'd be a whole lot safer there. Heard my folks died shortly thereafter. I was born in the Monkey House. It was called Ore Knott Manor back then; named after my Pa. I will kill him one day should our paths ever cross." he added whilst retying his robes.

"I'm surprised you ain't done it yet," I confessed.

"I'm just biding my time. You can only kill a man once. I reckon, I'll draw it out in my mind a few more times yet. Besides, he ain't going nowhere. Never has."

"So, his weapon of choice is the short sword?" Ser Roust wished to clarify.

"Unless things have changed, which I very much doubt. I heard tell he keeps a dagger up both sleeves and another in his left boot. He's right-handed. If you see him cross his left leg over his right; he's very likely reaching for it."

"I will keep that in mind," nodded Ser Roust.

"Should you require him to be gone for a spell, give him this.

Tell him, I'm waiting." Rummaging in a pocket, he retrieved a split gold coin and tossed it to Ser Roust.

"And he'll up and leave just like that?" Ser Roust queried, whilst pocketing the coin.

"He will. He'll be gone for three days at the least; a week at best. Be sure to be gone when he returns. When he doesn't find me waiting, he'll be in a right foul mood." Swinging his horse about, Ruok trotted off ahead.

"And you thought the Monkey Man owed *you* a debt," sighed Ser Roust.

"He does. I was bushwacked in the dead of night. They stole my horse and all my belongings. Being badly hurt at the time I hobbled away as best I could. Elsewise, I wouldn't be here to tell the tale. I'd steer clear of him if possible. Like Ruok said, he ain't right in the head." I counseled.

"Fair warning," Ser Roust replied. "May I offer you a similar caution?"

"*Please*," I encouraged him.

"Should you hear of a Kedera rebel named Oswald, I would strongly suggest you avoid the encounter. He's a brute of a man with a penchant for mindless slaughter. Nothing good will come of it."

"I heard tell of him once before. The Bro-Zil leader mentioned him just prior to losing his head." I smiled coldly.

"He is the Kedera version of you only larger. Much larger! If you're the Golan Butcher, he's the Kedera Butcher for certain. He enjoys killing. They call him *Oswald Who Ends*."

"Oswald Who Ends," I repeated.

"Yes, and for good reason. He does it well." He scowled.

Time having passed amicably between us, we quickly found ourselves at the lake. Having previously advised them to do so, Baran, along with Darian and the others, proceeded through the forest without stopping. It had little to do with them. It was a private matter in my mind concerning only Ser Roust, his squires, and myself.

"Shall we pay our respects?" I asked, motioning in the direction of his fallen comrades' graves. Looking in that direction, he immediately took notice of the white marble shrine. Snapping his reins, he brought Nutmeg to a short gallop. I watched as he trotted his mare around it several times. I could tell he was pleased. His squires joined us and were quickly moved to tears.

"Don't spend all of it drinking," I said, tossing each of his squires a gold coin. They assured me they had no plans to return to the

Widow's Spine anytime soon. I laughed at that and bid them well. Taking the hint without further urging, they turned and left at once.

"So, it meets your approval?" I queried Ser Roust.

"It does. It is more than I ever could have hoped– or afforded. *Anything but ordinary*," he read aloud. "You even had their proper titles engraved." He grinned.

"They were knights after all. I take it you noticed our own farewell gracing the opposing side."

"Yes, I saw it. It's perfect. I won't fail you," He pledged.

"I know you won't." I motioned for him to come closer.

"Seratego," I whispered. We crossed forearms and clenched our fists tight. I could tell I'd surprised him for his voice quaked while echoing my sentiments. It felt good to witness someone else looking out of sorts for a change. He turned the tables quickly, however, by leaning over and whispering something that very nearly caused me to fall off my horse.

"And you're certain?" I asked.

"You're speaking to a man with a wife and six children."

Nothing grows faster than a whispered secret. I exhaled slowly, fighting an intense urge to return with haste to my new bride. As hard as it was there was no point. Returning to her now would only make things worse. There was no plan B; no if at first you don't succeed sort of thing. And roosters never cry. Ser Roust spoke aloud the words I'd had engraved on the rearward side of the stone. Though some things need not be said, it did seem an appropriate conclusion.

"May your days be long–"

"And your *knights* never-ending." We finished together.

"Do you ever feel as though you've been somewhere before?"

"What do you mean?" See Roust tugged an invisible moustache before scratching at his chin. "I've been plenty of places before." Which sounded oddly like something I might have said.

"I mean what if we're doomed to repeat every mistake of old over and over again? What if stabbing one another remains our sole answer to everything we deem to be amiss?"

"Then I suppose our entire world will walk with a limp by the time we next meet." He chuckled.

We turned our horses away from one another trotting in opposite directions. It was hard to see him go. Not unlike the final line of that book that haunted me… I need not let it define me.

And when every wound crusts hard with salt how then shall we turn the page?

* * * * *

To be continued.

About the Author

The characters clamored.
With hopes, the reader would be likewise enamored.
Pages were turned, unbounded by time,
With more than a few sporting axes to grind.

About the author,
Some pleaded for peace.
So fearful were they of provoking the beast.
Most others sat idle knowing not what to do.
Like stringless puppets, they hadn't a clue.

About the author
They made quite a mess
Where the popcorn ended up was anyone's guess.
Childlike in nature, carefree as a curse,
Their behavior was lacking though hardly their worst.

About the author
They pleaded to shine.
"Just give *us* the chapter and *shove* all your rhymes!"
They were hardly polite though no less to blame.
For craving attention doesn't guarantee fame.

About the author
Arose a mind of their own
I couldn't curtail it; they wouldn't leave me alone.
"In the least, let us edit the bits about us!"
They hollered aloud with mixed angst and distrust.

About the author
Swarmed a riotous crew,
Demanding their freedom and page numbers too!
But I hadn't the patience, so I crinkled them all.

Missing the wastebasket with that last crumpled ball.

Manufactured by Amazon.ca
Bolton, ON

41415043R00231